He's Dead—She's Dead:
DETAILS AT ELEVEN

He's Dead—She's Dead:
DETAILS AT ELEVEN

John
Bartholomew
Tucker

St. Martin's Press
New York

MAI 263 4949

Design by Amelia R. Mayone

Library of Congress Cataloging-in-Publication Data

Tucker, John Bartholomew.
       He's dead—she's dead: details at eleven.
         p. cm.
       "A Thomas Dunne book."
       ISBN 0-312-04325-2
       I. Title.
   PS3570.U33H4 1990 813'.54—dc20 89-77997

First Edition
10 9 8 7 6 5 4 3 2 1

*To my oldest and best friend—Jim Bashline,
And to the memory of Jim Tucker—my Dad.*

He's Dead—She's Dead:
DETAILS AT ELEVEN

Chapter 1

"She was a Phantom of delight
When first she gleamed upon my sight;
A lovely Apparition, sent
To be a moment's ornament. . . ."
      WORDSWORTH, *Poems of the Imagination*, "VIII"

Actually, it had been much more than a moment. Actually, it had been all the way from Los Angeles International Airport to our landing at JFK.

But she'd slept the entire way, the only person I'd ever known who could do that. I'd awakened her when the seat belt sign came on, and we started to make our approach.

She was instantly alert, and smiling. A dazzling smile. With deep blue eyes that suggested all kinds of wonderful things.

"Thank you," she said.

She was the most beautiful woman I had ever met in my life.

"You're very welcome," I said, wishing that I could have thought of something just slightly more fascinating to say.

"You're James Sasser, aren't you?"

"Yes—" I was very pleased.

"The mustache threw me for just a second, but I recognized you when I first got on."

"Oh—?"

"But I didn't want to bother you."

"No bother—" So far, my part of the dialogue was decidedly dull.

"I've read all of your books," she said. "Delightful."

(My God, but she had a glorious smile.)

I kept up the high level of eloquence, which I had set, by saying, "Well, thank you."

"I must say, though, that I've missed your television commentaries—"

"But you're much too young to have remembered any of those." She was probably thirty.

"I was in college." She smiled again and her eyes, I thought, really *were* like limpid pools. Fortunately, I didn't verbalize that last bit of brilliance. She said, "I think all of us had a sort of crush on you." At that point I would, indeed, have followed her anywhere.

I had a feeling of enormous well-being. Never, ever, had a landing at JFK, while sitting in the first-class section of a 747, been more pleasurable.

"And you're Dr. Antonia Hastings." She raised an eyebrow. "I read the name on your attaché case."

"Oh—" She grinned. "That's official. I prefer Toni with my friends." She reached over and touched my arm in a casual, but subtly intimate way. "Please call me Toni."

"And I prefer Jim. With friends."

Ah—but life could indeed be sweet.

We landed.

It was inevitable. We shared a cab into Manhattan, and I invited her to cocktails and an early dinner at Il Gattopardo on Fifty-Sixth Street.

By the time we got there, I knew a lot more about her. She was a Harvard graduate, and her Ph.D. from Columbia was in mathematics. She worked at my old stomping grounds—*RBS*—the Republic Broadcasting System to its friends and stockholders—as a specialist in statistical research.

"The ratings," I said.

She grinned. "Well, if you want to make my position less grandiose sounding, yes."

I amended myself. "*Statistical research*—to show what the ratings mean."

"Uh, uh." She waggled her head. "To show how the ratings reflect well for—*us*."

I raised my glass. "To absolutely the most beautiful specialist in statistical research I've ever met." I meant it.

"No intelligence involved—?"

"That's implicit in the title."

We dined well. One always does at Il Gattopardo. Manicotti, *vitello tonnato,* salad, *tiramisu,* and cappucino. Two bottles of Gavi di Gavi and, afterward, port. We talked about everything.

At one point, she stood, to view more closely a contemporary painting on the wall, and to make a phone call. She was wearing a classic kerchief at her neck and a well-tailored tweed jacket that was cut just short enough to reveal everything about her body that was revealed by her tight, gray slacks. I studied her with all the ardor of a dedicated Swedish masseur.

When she returned from the phone call and sat down again, she reached across the table and clutched my hand. "Thank you," she said. "It's been a lovely dinner."

"Thank *you*. It certainly has."

Her hand tightened slightly on mine. "And I feel that I've known you for so much longer." She smiled. Her blue eyes were hypnotic. "But then, in a way, I have. Since college. My television crush . . ."

At that point, at about twice the speed of light, she determined that since the apartment I would be subletting was on *West* Sixty-Ninth Street and since her apartment was on *East* Sixty-Fifth, we would go to hers, which was closer.

I'm a youthful forty-seven, but the difference in our ages suddenly seemed enormous.

"You're leaving me breathless," I said, and knew that I sounded silly.

"I feel like kicking off my shoes," she said. "I just spent a whole week, at an affiliates convention, trying to statistically justify a second-place finish."

"And I'm coming back to New York after seven years—and after eight weeks of working on my first and *last* screenplay." I had told her about my zany experiences over dinner.

"Well then—" she smiled—My God, but those eyes—"you could stand a little kicking off of the shoes, yourself."

As I had thought earlier, I would, indeed, have looked into those eyes and followed her anywhere, so following her to East Sixty-Fifth seemed entirely in order.

Sixty-Fifth is tree lined, with town houses, some of which have been renovated into apartments. Hers was a duplex. Very modern. Very comfortable.

"Will you still respect me in the morning?" I said as she handed me a brandy.

She frowned.

"I'm so very tired all of a sudden," she said. Her back was toward me. "The plane ride, I suppose."

"You slept the whole way."

"Fitfully," she said.

The evening was beginning to disintegrate. Ah well, my conversation had not been up to its usual level, however good that might be.

We talked about people I knew who were still at RBS. But the talk was suddenly desultory and without sparkle.

I finished my brandy and stood as if to leave.

"We just got here," she said.

"I know, but—"

"Have one more. A nightcap."

"No thanks."

"I insist. You're making me feel as if I'm throwing you out."

She was.

"I'll just pour us each one more," she said. "A small one."

I nodded. She smiled and turned to her sideboard.

I looked at some sketches on the wall and wondered why the evening had so suddenly turned sour. That stupid remark of mine was probably it.

"Here you are. One for the road."

We talked about the prints on the wall, and her various objets d'art without her once acting as if anything had changed.

She glanced surreptitiously at her watch, something she had

done several times before when she had, apparently, wanted me to leave.

"Okay—" I said. I was tired of whatever game we were playing.

"What—?"

"I'll be on my way. It's been a very pleasant evening."

She frowned.

"Thanks for the drink," I said.

She put both her hands on my shoulders and looked me straight in the eye. "Don't go," she said. "Please."

I shook my head.

"I'll just be a minute," she said. She headed for the bedroom.

I allowed five minutes to go by while I finished my brandy. I went to the bedroom door and knocked. No answer. I knocked again.

"You okay?"

No answer.

I opened the door and went in.

She was standing by the bed, holding a telephone to her ear.

I said: "I just wanted to say good night and thank you for the drink."

"Stay a minute."

"I'm tired, too." I was exasperated. "And I *didn't* sleep on the plane."

At the door, with my back to her, she said: "I've got a gun pointed at you."

I turned. She did. And she gave one the feeling that she damn well knew how to use it.

"Okay—I'll stay a minute," I said.

Chapter 2

Big Bill Braddock, who always signed his letters *Shoulder to shoulder with you,* President of the Republic Broadcasting System, bully speaker of a constant stream of hogwash, a man who gave all the fine graduates of Dale Carnegie courses a bad name, came around from behind his desk, pausing for a dramatic split second as he glanced at the picture of two adorable children (they were actually his second cousin Kate's kids, but they gave the desired effect), made sure his hand brushed past the Bible, which was prominently displayed, and slapped me on the back with one hand, while he grabbed my arm in comradely embrace with the other.

"Jimbo—it's *good* to see you. Thanks for dropping by. *Loved* your last book. And the new mustache . . . well . . . interesting. *Very* interesting."

I said: "I can't stand to be called *Jimbo.*"

He guffawed and I paid the price for my remark by getting another whack on the back. "True—true. Good to see you're the same old, salty Jimbo." He guffawed again and gave me another back slap. "Sorry. That one just slipped out."

"And I didn't just drop by," I said.

He looked questioningly at me.

"Ms. Mata Hari and her magic pistol."

"What do you mean?"

"Dr. Antonia Hastings."

"Oh—" He slapped my back again. "She's *something,* isn't she? Beautiful woman. Beautiful and bright as a button."

I extricated myself and put five feet between us before I spoke again. "I resent it," I said.

"Resent?"

"Yes."

"Resent what?"

"Being set up like a schoolboy and then brought here at gunpoint."

"Gunpoint?"

"You could have picked up the phone and given me a call."

"I did."

"Sure—"

"I did. I called your lawyer—Alan Siegel. He said you were probably on the plane, coming in from L.A. He said he'd give you my message tomorrow."

"Sure—"

"You'll see. Wait till tomorrow."

"Then why the seductress and the Walther PPK?"

"I don't know what you're talking about, Jimbo."

I told him.

When I finished, Braddock said: "My God almighty, Jimbo, no wonder you're pissed. I'd be, too." Then he started to laugh. "But you're a lucky man, too, you know. A lot of people at RBS would give a month's salary for dinner with her."

"And for being threatened with a pistol."

"Well, yeah, yeah—I know what you mean." He got serious then. He regretted that the whole incident had ever happened. He apologized for it. But he had known nothing. He had thought the whole thing had been pure serendipity and nothing more. He had wanted to talk to me. My lawyer had said that I was traveling. "And then—out of the blue, Toni—Dr. Hastings—called to say that she was having dinner with you."

Big Bill Braddock spread out both hands in a gesture of extreme innocence. "All I said was—'I'll meet you at your apartment. Don't let Jimbo leave till I get there.'"

"Jim—"

"Right. But I actually said *Jimbo*. Oh . . . Sorry."

"Her reaction was rather extreme."

"How do you mean?"

"Her method of not-letting-me-leave-until-you-got-there. Rather extreme."

"Well—" Braddock smiled abashedly. "To tell you the truth,

I don't recall *exactly* what I said. You know—*you* remember—sometimes I kinda holler at people. Sometimes my bark sounds a little worse than my bite. It intimidates some people." With the alacrity of a leopard, he was suddenly close enough to me to give me another of his comradely whacks on the back. "Never you, Jimbo. Never you. But I guess there are quite a few people around RBS who kind of squat when I yell."

"And," I said it slowly, hoping he heard the irony in my voice, "Toni—ah, Dr. Hastings—is one of them?"

He shrugged. "Guess so. I . . . well, I probably said enough to . . . intimidate her. And then, too—she's only been with us for about a year. She probably doesn't know the real me." If true—lucky woman, I thought. "She probably felt that . . . well, her job is already on the line as it is. Everybody's is, of course."

"You're saying that the whole incident was an act of desperation by a woman worried about her job?"

"Well . . . what else could it be? I mean, God knows, I didn't tell her to pull a *gun* on you." The image amused him and he guffawed again and slapped at my back.

I sidestepped. "I don't believe it," I said.

Braddock frowned. "You *gotta* believe it." His normal shout rose a few decibels. "I'm tellin' you that *I didn't tell her to pull a gun on you to keep you there, for Christ's sake.*"

I held up both hands to quiet him. "I mean, I can't believe that an intelligent woman would lure a guy to her apartment, and point a pistol at him, just because she was worried about losing her job."

"Why else then?"

"I don't know."

"Anyway," Braddock smiled, "you're here." He reached for the cigar box on his desk. "Cigar?"

"No thanks. I've got this." I indicated my pipe.

"I know it's late, I know you just flew in from L.A.—but can you give me twenty minutes?"

I said: "Sure."

"Good."

We busied ourselves with pipe filling, and cigar clipping, and lighting them.

"A drink maybe?" Braddock asked.

"Always."

We fixed ourselves drinks. Braddock didn't speak, which was so unusual, that I found myself—someone who had been anxious to leave moments before—now anxious to know what was on his mind.

Braddock raised his glass: "Here's mud in your eye—"

"Mud—" I said.

He took a swallow from his glass, smacked his lips, pulled on his cigar and blew out a plume of smoke. He didn't look at me. "You know about the Northern takeover?"

"Of course."

"Yeah, of course. Who doesn't? But how much do you know about what's been going on since they bought *RBS?*"

"Only what I read in the papers."

"It's all true." Braddock sighed. "But it's worse. It's a lot worse. Every day it gets worse."

"I thought they'd stopped the firings."

"No—afraid not. But I'm not talking about that. I'm talkin' about—well, give Terry credit, it was his idea—I'm talkin' about why Terry and I decided we'd ask you to help us out."

I felt myself starting to smile. "Terry Jones? Is he around tonight?"

Braddock shook his head. "No—I'm only here this late on a fluke. We both thought we wouldn't be in contact with you until tomorrow." An exonerating thought occurred to him. "See— you'll see tomorrow. You'll get a message from your lawyer that I called."

I said, "Okay, I believe you. But it's all still kind of crazy."

"The whole thing is." Braddock sighed a second time. "It's been crazy from the first hint that Northern Industries was considering a run at a takeover. I mean, my God—*taking over* the Republic Broadcasting System, for God's sake."

"Well, in the end, they didn't."

Braddock snorted. "Yeah, in the end, they didn't. In the end, they just plain bought us outright."

I tried to look properly sympathetic.

"And, Jimbo—*Jim*—they're not broadcasters. They don't give a tinker's damn about broadcasting. They're a lot of Harvard Business School graduates, and corporation lawyers, and—" he sneered—"*manufacturers*. All they do is look at the bottom line. They don't see any of the excitement, the romance in our business." From William Big Bill Braddock, the last sentence was as poetic and passionate as he would ever get.

Braddock stood. "We could be makin' refrigerators and washing machines for all they care."

"That's the way of the world now, apparently."

"Yeah—even their Goddamn motto"—he pointed to a brass paperweight on his desk—"*Pinched Pennies Produce Profits*— D'you believe that—?"

I let him talk. He was seemingly compelled to talk about his life as a broadcaster—*not* manufacturer: ". . . and then WUTJ in Utica, we put that baby on the air . . . sold the most time in the history of Triangle in Altoona, got a bonus trip to Bermuda . . . Buffalo, my first shot as head of sales . . . Pittsburgh, number one in every book, and I was the assistant G.M. . . ."

Braddock held up both hands. ". . . and then, Philadelphia—and there it was for the first time: *Vice-President and General Manager,* right on the door. I still get kinda choked up when someone says Philadelphia. . . ."

And so it went, right on through his time at *RBS*.

He had just drained his second drink when he said: "And now that I made network president, I'm worried about even hanging onto a job."

We sat silently for a minute or two; I relit my pipe. "I sympathize," I said. "I've thought a lot about everyone here, a lot of good friends. So many let go."

Braddock stared at the wall. "And so many still here, who really aren't. Like me." He looked at me. "Northern Industries didn't take away my title, but they might as well have. I'm still around—for now—because I know everyone on the affiliate level and can keep everybody happy enough during the changes. And I'm the one who signs his name above the word *President* whenever someone gets the axe. But how long this will go on—who knows." Braddock looked as forlorn as anyone I'd ever seen. Almost against my will, I felt genuine sympathy.

I said: "I'm sorry. I didn't know it was this bad."

"Worse."

"But where do I fit in? Certainly, you don't want me back to do cheerful commentaries. Not that I'd even consider the news department again."

Braddock shook his head. "No, we knew you wouldn't. But there's something else. I said *worse,* and I meant it. Northern has given me an ultimatum. And if I don't cover this, I really am out."

"But where do I—"

"Frankly, I wanted to go in another direction, but Terry came up with you and talked me into it." Braddock scowled at his faux pas. "I should've said: And I agree with Terry a hundred percent."

I smiled. "I have a feeling that you and I are somewhere in the middle of *Alice in Wonderland.* What the hell are we talking about?"

Braddock stood abruptly. "We're talking about everything that's been going on *besides* the corporate bloodletting. Everything that—so far—we've been able to keep out of the papers. But it's getting worse. Terry will fill in the details, but what I'm leading up to—"

His phone rang. Braddock automatically glanced at his watch. "Excuse me."

He picked up the phone. "Braddock here . . . yeah . . . *what?* . . . you're sure? . . . have you called for an ambulance? . . . the police . . . yeah . . . I'll be right down. . . ."

He replaced the receiver and stood still, almost catatonically. Perspiration had sprung out on his forehead.

He turned to me. His eyes were strange. "This is what I was leading up to." He seemed to groan. "Only this is even worse."

She was quite dead. A young woman who appeared to have been in her late twenties. Probably attractive. Her clothes were. It was difficult to look at what had once been her face.

The ambulance attendants did their job. The police officers did theirs.

Four uniformed Republic Broadcasting System guards stood near us.

One said: "She was okay a half hour ago, Mr. Braddock. The doors to the street were unlocked. But then they always are on nights when they're taping *News Night* in Studio Eleven."

"Thank you," Braddock said. "Have the police spoken to you yet?"

"No, sir."

"I'm sure they'll want to." Braddock's voice was full. "Be sure to tell them that she was a fine employee and . . ." He paused. "Tell them . . . whatever they need to know."

"Yes, sir."

"Ah—" Braddock glanced at the nameplate above the guard's breast pocket—"Burke. Don't blame yourself. You can't be everywhere at once."

"No, sir—" The guard looked troubled, as if, until Braddock's comment, it had never occurred to him to blame himself.

Braddock stared at me. His voice was suddenly lacking in any energy. He said: "I said before that things were worse than bad. And now this. Things . . . are . . . getting . . . even . . . worse than *worse*."

Chapter 3

I woke up the next morning feeling wonderful. I was in New York and out of Los Angeles.

I showered and shaved, enjoying a further delight, listening to Mozart on WNCN-FM. After that, I explored my subleased apartment and found it entirely to my liking.

As I was dressing, the music still filling the room, I was

ecstatically aware of yet another delight of being back East. It was October, brisk, bright and crisp, and I could wear my favorite tweed jacket with a *tie,* and with a *sweater.*

And I could *walk* to breakfast. I had barely walked anywhere in two months, except for a brief sojourn down Santa Monica one early evening, only to be stopped by an LAPD patrol car for appearing, I suppose, to be doing something of a suspicious nature.

Yes, this morning, once again, I could *walk* to breakfast.

I was about to leave when the phone rang. It was even pleasing to hear that the telephone in my newly acquired, and temporary, apartment had a quaint and lovely ring to it.

It was a newspaper gossip columnist, prodded by my publisher's public-relations department, who was calling for material for her column.

She was pleasant enough, asked me all the right questions, both for my ends, and for her column, and it was easy.

"Yes, I'm standing in it now, my first morning . . . wonderful . . . no (a laugh), none of his girl friends has surfaced so far . . . yes . . . yes, other than a few quick ins and outs, it's my first time back in New York in years . . . yes, here for a book . . . no, not another thriller . . . something different this time . . . a sort of Studs Terkel thing, interviews with famous and potentially famous people . . . ah, yes (modestly), a pretty fair advance, I'd say . . . no, not all five novels were best-sellers, my first couple certainly weren't . . . just now?—Los Angeles . . . yes, a screenplay . . . no, not much fun . . . what? . . . ah, let's see . . . seven years since I was on the air . . . no, don't miss it . . . except for the friends, of course . . . yes . . . yes . . . no . . . no . . . yes, no"— and the interview was over.

My good spirits returned, I sauntered down Broadway, past the cluster of ABC studios. Peter Jennings waved from the other side of Broadway; I waved back. Whistling now, I marched along to the ASCAP Building and went into one of my favorite coffee shops.

I had slept late, and, with the thought of lunch with Terry Jones in a couple of hours, I ordered only juice, tea and a muffin.

Feeling very good about things in general, I opened the *Times*.

There is was on the front page:

RECEPTIONIST AT RBS BROADCAST CENTER BLUDGEONED

I had completely forgotten.

I read the story. There was nothing there that I didn't know except that the young woman had just received her college degree after seven long years of part-time classes at NYU, and that she was engaged to be married in a month.

Unconsciously, I kept reading that paragraph over and over again.

"Hello, Jamie. I thought it was you."

It was Marilyn Friedman, a director at ABC.

"Hello, Marilyn."

Her face bore an amused expression.

I tried to smile. "I was reading about last night's killing up at RBS."

Marilyn sat down with me. "That place is almost like a corporation run by Job. We've been getting three rumors a day from RBS for three months. The worst of it is, most of them are true. And now this."

We chatted about the RBS situation. It seemed that everybody in broadcasting knew that things were awful. I thought of Big Bill Braddock—*Shoulder to shoulder with you*—despite his best efforts to quash the fact, everyone assumed that many people were still nervously dangling in the wind, even after the huge initial layoffs of the Northern take-over.

"Remember the old saying, Marilyn: 'When times are *good*, they're *bad* at RBS. And when times are *bad*—'"

Marilyn finished—"they're even *worse* at RBS."

"Amen—"

Marilyn ordered some coffee, and I asked for another pot of tea, and we chatted about other things, her children, my children, the show she was directing for ABC, my sojourn in Los Angeles, the Mets. . . ."

I paid the check.

"You always were a big spender, Jamie."

"I can't help myself. It's in my blood."

Marilyn gave me a quick kiss on the cheek. "It's good to see you."

"Same here. Give Stan my best."

"Two bits says Stanley is on the phone tonight, trying to arrange a golf date."

"I hope you're right."

Suddenly, she started to laugh; at first, it was just a giggle, but it ended up as a classic side splitter.

"Oh, Jamie—I'm sorry."

"For what?"

"Wait'll Stanley sees you. The *mustache*."

I smiled. I knew her too well to be offended.

"I kind of like it," I said.

"Oh—" she covered her mouth with her hand, and swallowed, and tried to stop the laughter—"it's very handsome. Sort of operatic."

"Really? I thought it was more British-military. Thin Red Line and all that, you know."

She nodded, still smiling. "How long have you had it?"

"About three months. I kind of like it," I said again, defiantly.

"I'll warn Stanley."

"And he'll have a hundred one-liners ready for the golf course."

"Probably—"

Laughter burst out of Marilyn again, and she blushed and blew me a kiss as we waved and headed in opposite directions on Broadway. She was off to work, but I now had the luxury of strolling around Manhattan for a few hours.

I arrived at the Broadcast Center ten minutes early for my one o'clock luncheon meeting with Terry Jones. The reception area was as neat as an operating theater, with not a sign of the awfulness that had occurred the night before.

A pleasant-looking gray-haired woman greeted me from behind the reception desk. I wondered what she was thinking about, sitting exactly where it all had happened the night before.

"May I help you?" She smiled.

"I have a luncheon engagement with Mr. Terry Jones," I said. "—Jim Sasser."

"Of course, Mr. Sasser. I recognized you when you came in. Agnes Sevinsky. I used to work in the News Wing when you were here."

"Of course—how are you?" I'd remembered her, but not her name. "How's your little boy?"

She smiled proudly. "In college now. Bucknell."

"Time flies—"

"Yes—"

She rang Terry Jones's office and was told to ring Mr. Fulton's office. She spoke briefly to the secretary there before hanging up.

"She asked if you'd come up to Mr. Fulton's office. Apparently, he'd like to say hello. It's the third floor."

"I remember," I said. "Good to see you again—ah—Agnes."

"You too, Mr. Sasser."

R. Randolph Fulton was Vice President in charge of Programming for the Republic Broadcasting System. He had decided, long ago, that his logo would be a bow tie, which he always wore. He was forty. He looked to be thirty. And he often acted like twenty.

Randy Fulton was sometimes maddening and foolish, but he had more energy and more boyish charm than almost any man I had ever known.

He was waiting for me outside his office, sitting at his secretary's desk, while she stood behind and massaged his shoulders.

"Jimmy Sasser—" he leaped up when he saw me "—good to see you. Hey—new mustache and everything."

He introduced me to his secretary, another in the line of blonde Viking goddesses that he always seemed to favor. "Jim, this is Helga Berger. Helga—James Sasser, best selling American, nay, international author—*and*—a man who had the brains, and the guts, and the ability, to escape from this zoo we work in."

Fulton opened his office door. "Come on in. Drink—?"

I went into the office. "No, thanks, I'm having lunch with Terry." I had expected Terry to be in Fulton's office and was surprised not to see him. "I'll wait until then."

"Wrong—" Fulton said behind me. "You're having lunch with me." I turned. He was smiling. "My good luck. Terry can't make it. Asked me if I'd pinch hit—I said you're damned right, I'd love to."

I covered my disappointment. Besides the obvious curiosity—since the previous night's murder anyway—of what Terry was going to propose to me, Terry was one of my favorites. I'd really been looking forward to the luncheon.

"My good fortune, too," I said and smiled. What the hell; R. Randolph Fulton was a good egg. Lunch would be fun, at least.

"Great. I had Helga make a reservation at Des Artistes, if that's okay."

"That's perfect."

"We'll see a lot of ABC types there, and we can start another rumor when they see me talking to you." He gave me a rueful expression and shrugged his shoulders. "At least everybody's *talking* about us." He scowled. "And not a day goes by that they don't have something to talk about."

"So I've heard."

He suddenly smiled. "What the hell—let's go have lunch. It's great to see you."

As we stepped out of the elevator into the reception area, Fulton stiffened. "Oh my God, I'd forgotten—" Sotto voce, he said: "Back me up. Just nod and agree—"

R. Randolph Fulton was still the same old R. Randolph

Fulton I had known in the past. The brilliance of his tactics in battle would have caused even a Casanova to gasp with wonder.

As we crossed the lobby, a tall, lithe and lovely red-haired beauty stood to greet us, an enchanting smile on her face that was zeroed straight in on Randy.

"Hi—I'm here," she said.

"Wonderful. Perfect timing—just perfect." Randy Fulton was very fast on his feet in situations of this sort. He had had an enormous amount of practice. "Cynthia—this is the *distinguished* American author, Mr. James Sasser. Mister Sasser—this is Cynthia Kranepool."

"Kranepuss—"

She continued to smile for Randy alone.

"Yes—of course." Randy turned to me. "This is the young woman I was telling you about, Mister Sasser. We're trying to find a property that's worthy of her obviously enormous talents."

She continued to smile.

"It's not easy," continued Randy. "She's so—ah, so—*unique*."

"Yes, I see," I said.

Randy gave me a pleading look.

"Yes—so you were telling me in your office."

Randy smiled.

Hearing my remark, with all the instincts of a female praying mantis, the young woman quickly included me in, at least, the penumbra of her smile.

Randy was rolling now. "Cynthia—Miss Kranepool—"

"Krane*puss*—"

(Randy was *extremely* fast on his feet.) "Oh, no longer. I've given hours of time to the decision—from now on you're Cynthia Kranepool."

"Really—?"

"I—ah—I—even had the Research Department do a printout on it." Fulton made it sound as if he had really said something.

He turned to me and spoke ponderously. "Do you see what we see in her, Mister Sasser?"

"Oh, yes, indeed."

"Your—ah—property seems to be just the thing we've been looking for, one that's truly worthy of her obviously enormous—ah—talents."

"Yes, indeed."

"So—" Randy segued to his salesman's voice—"I'm going to take you to lunch and try to convince you—even though you say you won't—convince you to sell us that perfect property for Miss—ah—Kranepool."

The young actress—or whatever she was—looked suddenly disappointed.

Fulton said to me, "Excuse me for just a moment, Mister Sasser," and pulled the young woman quickly to one side, where he began talking to her quickly and continuously in a low voice. I don't read lips, but I knew that he was saying something to the effect of how completely disappointed—devastated, in fact—he was at not being able to take her to lunch, but that duty called, and, after all, if he succeeded, it would all accrue to her.

It all took slightly over three minutes and Cynthia Kranepool née Kranepuss had bravely, smilingly, said good-bye to the two of us and waved gallantly from her departing taxi.

R. Randolph Fulton pretended to wipe his brow. "I've got to remember to explain to her why I couldn't get you to sell. But that's for another day."

I laughed. "I don't know if it's good or bad, Randy, but you're a master at it."

"Thank you, *Mister* Sasser." Fulton smiled.

Lunch was fun. Wine and laughter and plenty of stories. But, then, Randy spotted two men at the Des Artistes bar. One I recognized; one I didn't.

"Both let go just ten days ago," Randy said. "Christ—we're now the home of *Pinched Pennies Produce Profits*—have you heard that one—?"

I nodded.

The conversation got serious then. The details, the examples, I heard were different, but the theme was the same as what I'd heard from Braddock: a state of emotional chaos existed at RBS. Every day it seemed that Northern Industries tightened the screw a bit more. Randy concluded the same way that Big Bill Braddock had: "And I don't even know if I'm going to last here myself past Christmas. . . ."

He stared morbidly into his glass.

"Why so glum, *Mister* Fulton—?" She was almost six-feet tall and everything she wore could be described as delightfully too tight for her.

Randy brightened instantly. "Susan—meet Jim Sasser. Jim—Susan Mazur." Randy got her a chair, asked for an extra glass, and ordered another bottle of wine.

It seemed that Randy was also considering Susan for an as yet undiscovered project. He pulled excitedly at his bow tie. "Something *mucho biggo* he explained to me. Something . . ." he pretended to be searching for the right phrase—"something . . . worthy of her—ah—obviously *enormous* talents."

I silently agreed that, yes, Susan Mazur's talents were even more enormous than the redhead's.

But she was fun. She was bright and witty and delightful—and I enjoyed myself.

When I thanked Randy for lunch, I really meant it. "Tell Terry I'm glad he couldn't make it. By the way, what happened?"

"His back—*boing*." Randy made a face.

"I didn't know he had a bad back."

"Neither did Terry, I guess. He sounds as if he's in a helluva lot of pain."

"I'll give him a call—see if I can do anything. Run an errand or something."

"He'd like to hear from you, anyway."

As we got up to leave, I saw Dr. Antonia Hastings settle in at the bar. She was looking our way.

I said: "Thanks again, Randy. Susan—you're lovely and charming, and it's been a pleasure to meet you."

"Same here—" She gave me a kiss on the cheek.

To Randy, I said: "I'm going to have one more drink. I just spotted someone at the bar."

Randy glanced in that direction. "Dr. Hastings?"

"Uh-huh."

Randy made a face. "Potential *mucho troubleo* there."

"Really—?"

"Well . . . that's probably unfair. But . . . well . . . she's a loner. She's"—he shrugged—"personally, I could never get a real fix on her, that's all."

"I'll watch myself," I said. We shook hands. "Thanks again. Lunch was delightful—especially our companion, Ms. Mazur."

They left.

As I turned and headed for the bar, I decided that R. Randolph Fulton was probably right about Dr. Antonia Hastings.

I kept on toward the bar anyway.

Chapter 4

My God, but she's even more beautiful than I'd remembered, I thought. Because of what she was wearing, her eyes were an even deeper blue, cobalt, and today they were flecked with green and gold.

Her first words were: "It worked."

"What did—?"

"I willed you to come over here." She smiled. "There *is* power in positive thinking."

"Lured would be more like it."

"How so?"

"You looked in my direction."

"That's not luring. To look is not the same as to lure."

"It depends on who's looking—" I stopped myself short and laughed self-consciously. "When I'm with you I say the damndest things."

"Yes—" She looked amused.

"May I join you?"

"Please. That was the whole idea. I was lunching over

there"—she indicated with her head—"and didn't see you until we got up to leave. So I decided to sit at the bar."

I smiled. "Yes, indeed—it worked."

Her lips moved slightly, "Yes—"

By the time I'd ordered, we were the only two at our end of the bar.

"Cheers," I said.

"Cheers—"

We looked at each other. "I don't understand," I said.

"Understand what?"

"Your attitude now."

"What do you mean?"

I said: "Last night you pulled a gun on me. Today you're acting as if we're old college chums."

She made no response for a moment. Finally, she said: "That's why I was hoping you'd come to the bar."

"So you can pull a gun on me again?"

She looked around. There was no one within ten feet of us, but still she lowered her voice. "I'm sorry—" frown lines appeared between her eyes—"I'm ashamed."

"You should be. I don't appreciate being threatened."

"That's not what I'm like—the woman you saw last night."

I thought of the delightful time we'd had at dinner. She must have had the same thought.

She said: "Oh, at dinner . . . that was . . . well, natural. I meant . . . afterward." The frown lines deepened. "If only I hadn't called my boss. But then you wouldn't understand. You'd have to know him."

"Is Big Bill Braddock the man you called at dinner?"

"Yes."

"I know him," I said. "I know what he's like."

That seemed to encourage her. "He took an earlier flight back. Right after we ended the affiliates meeting. I stayed behind for a final session with just the Nielsen people. He told me to call when I got in to let him know what had happened. So I did. And I just happened to mention you."

"And he said—take him to your apartment and pull a gun on him."

She blushed. "No—but, well, he's always been a bit of a bully—"

"You're being generous."

She smiled again, encouraged. "But he's worse, much worse, around a woman. Add to that his increasingly erratic behavior since the Northern takeover, and—" She stopped.

"And you"—I said it as gently as I could—"like everyone else at RBS—are worried about your job."

She nodded, almost apologetically. "He shouted at me on the phone. He told me to take you to my apartment, and he'd meet us there. His language was awful. He said . . . vulgar things. I'm sorry I didn't tell you."

"It's okay—"

"When we first got to the apartment . . . you said . . . well you made some remark . . . and I realized. . . . This is very difficult," she said. "I didn't want you to think . . . well, that I was a one-night stand. I'm not. . . ." She looked away. "At dinner I . . . really liked you."

"And then because of your retort to my wise-guy remark, you thought I was going to leave, so—"

"Yes—"

I exhaled loudly.

Her eyes were very close to mine. "I . . . well, I . . . considered . . . seducing you . . . trying to. But that would have been . . . you see, I liked you and . . . I didn't want . . ." Her voice trailed off.

"I understand," I said.

She tried to laugh, still very inhibited. "Oh, God, but this is embarrassing. I feel like a schoolgirl. What you must think—"

"I think you're beautiful," I said.

Her eyes widened. "Oh—"

"I do. Very."

She looked at me for a long moment. The gold flecks danced in her eyes.

I said: "I still resent the gun, though."

"My father bought it for me years ago. For protection."

"But you know how to handle it."

"I've always gone shooting with my father. Since I was a little girl."

"Would you have used it?"

"Of *course* not." She frowned. "But when I called Braddock again to say that you were leaving, he said that his limousine would be at my apartment in three minutes to bring you to his office. And that you'd better damn well be there. If you weren't, he said, he'd fire me on the spot. I was desperate—"

I nodded. "If I were you, I'd be looking for someone else to work for."

"Yes—"

Her eyes were very large and very close and her lips were moist. I leaned closer and kissed her, very lightly.

She reached out and touched my hand. "Then can we . . ."

"What?"

"Can we . . . start again?"

"What a good idea."

She smiled. I raised my glass and touched hers. We drank.

Her eyes were very close. "But I should warn you to be wary of me."

"Oh, I will. I am."

"No, I'm serious," she said.

"So am I."

"No—" she held my hand with both of hers and then impetuously kissed the back of it—"No, I'm very serious. I think—" her half-smile was shy and self-conscious—"I think I'm someone a person ought to stay away from."

I thought immediately of R. Randolph Fulton's advice.

I said: "What do you mean by that?"

"I don't know."

"Then, why—?"

"Someone is following me," she said. "It started three weeks ago. At least, that's when I first noticed it."

"Are you sure?" I considered for a moment that she was a

whacko, but rejected the thought. "Can you think of any reason why anyone would want to have you followed?"

"No—well, of course, we've all had little things in our lives—but, no." She squeezed my hand. "There, I'm glad that's out."

I looked into those blue eyes and thought, Here I am; I've just met the most beautiful woman in the world, and there is a distinct possibility that she is—in the wise words of the poet-philosopher R. Randolph Fulton—"*Mucho troubleo.*"

Chapter 5

Everyone commented on my new mustache, and everyone seemed to feel, somehow, duty bound to say something funny; but there was dinner with Stephanie, lunch with Harvey, and drinks with Roger. And the next day Clare. And cocktails at the Readings. And three days went swimmingly by before Terry Jones's back was again in shape and he called me.

"Why wouldn't you let me do anything for you?" I asked on the phone.

"I told you, I didn't need to have anything done. Now I do."

"Name it," I said.

"Have lunch with me. Nicola Paone's, on Thirty-Fourth Street. Tomorrow at one?"

"You're on." I hung up and smiled. Terry Jones was always someone I looked forward to seeing.

I arrived at Paone's a few minutes early, but Terry was already there. He stood and saluted as I was brought to the table.

"Good afternoon, Sergeant Sasser—"

"Good afternoon, Corporal Jones—"

I returned the salute. Terry grinned. "I remembered the table. Old number six," he said. "As I recall, it was always a favorite of yours with—was it Leslie?"

I nodded and grinned myself. "Your memory, sir, is most remarkable. I haven't been here since those happy days of long ago."

"A broken heart?"

"She married a gastro-enterologist from Hempstead."

"Same thing." He smiled. "You're looking great. How long have you been doing impressions of Tom Selleck's upper lip?"

"You've got to do better than that. I've heard that one at least three times now."

Terry laughed.

"Besides, I kind of like it," I said, giving my mustache a brush or two.

We each ordered a bottle of Beck's.

I looked around Nicola Paone's. "I'm glad you did this. But why a place so far downtown?"

"First of all, the food is great." I nodded. "But mostly, I didn't want any broadcast types seeing us together, and—very important—the tables are situated so far apart that no one can hear our conversation."

"You seem very mysterious and serious."

"I am." Terry frowned. "*Very* serious."

"Then—?"

He quickly smiled. "Plenty of time. Let's order."

We each ordered pasta, a salad and veal. Terry asked for a bottle of Brunnelo di Montellcino.

We chatted about everything from sports, to music, to the movies, to books, to women.

"Ah . . . anybody . . . new?" Terry asked. He was one of only two or three people who could ask me that question, and even he was tentative. Of course, everyone who knew me knew of Nancy's death. It had been seven years now. But only Terry, and maybe two others, were close enough to talk about it with me.

I smiled. "No, Terry. But thanks for asking." He started to apologize. "And . . . thanks for caring."

"I'm afraid I've never been very subtle—"

"You've always been just fine."

We looked at each other.

Terry raised his glass to mine, and said, "*Salute.*"

"*Salute.*"

I said: "And now—what about the venerable and much beloved Republic Broadcasting System? I've already heard that *Pinched Pennies Produce Profits.*"

The bantering note dropped from Terry's voice and his expression was suddenly serious. "We're in deep trouble, Jim."

"I've heard it all from Randy Fulton and Big Bill himself."

"No—" Terry frowned—"No, you haven't heard the half of it."

For the next ten minutes, Terry talked and I listened. His voice was emotional, agitated, his knuckles white as he clutched at his wine glass. Terry had always operated on a high level of energy, but now, he seemed almost ready to shatter apart. He smoked three cigarettes in a row, lighting one from the other.

It seemed that the new company, now known as Northern Industries/Republic Broadcasting System, was being systematically terrorized. Threats were a daily occurrence, both on the corporate and on the personal level. "I've had letters myself, Jim. We all have. Bomb threats that turn out to be hoaxes. Death threats. We've had some minor incidents of arson. It's frightening. Even Whitehead—"

I stopped him. "Who's Whitehead?"

"Our new leader, M. Seabury Whitehead, President and Chief Executive Officer of Northern Industries. The son of a bitch," Terry added in a gratuitous mutter.

"He's had threats, too."

"Like everyone else. Suffice to say, *everyone* has had threats made."

"But not the company as a whole? Only individuals."

"No—*Especially* the company. And word is seeping out into the press, day by day, and the stock is sliding down a little at a time, and if we don't—can't—stop it—" Terry's expression was grim. "It's awful," he said again.

"And now—a murder."

"Yes. And now that."

He drained his glass, poured another, and drank half of that in one swallow.

He talked some more, and I listened. Finally, he leaned closer across the table, and his eyes were pleading. "This is why we called you, Jim. We need your help. We're desperate."

I had no idea what he was talking about. "I'll always listen, Terry. Anytime." I smiled. "To you, anyway. With Big Bill Braddock, maybe one conversation a month is about all I can stand."

Terry's arm waved the air in frustration. "You don't understand, Jim. We want you to help us."

"How?"

"Conduct an investigation."

I was dumbfounded. "Terry—you're right. I don't understand."

"We want you to find out who's behind it. Why?" His voice rose. "Why—for God's sake? We've *got to know*."

"Terry, I'm—"

"Whatever the cost. Carte blanche—whatever—"

"*Terry*—" My voice was just slightly too loud for a restaurant, and it stopped him. A few heads turned our way. I waited to make sure that he wasn't going to prattle on before I spoke again in a normal voice. "Terry, you're right, I don't know the half of what's going on at RBS. And I can see that it's serious. In fact, I can see that it's so serious that I have one very simple, *serious* question to ask you. If you and Big Bill Braddock agree that the situation is this bad, then why the hell are you fooling around with the likes of me?"

"You're perfect for the job."

"Perfect? For what? I wouldn't know how to investigate a car theft, for God's sake. And you expect me to come in and do what professional investigators have failed at so far—"

Terry said, "There haven't *been* any professional investigators."

My mouth must have opened. I said nothing.

"We were trying to keep it *quiet,* Jim. But the situation keeps getting worse." He downed more wine. "And now that reception-ist the other night—"

"Yes, and that's exactly why you should go to the phone right now and call—whoever the hell one calls for something like this."

Terry shook his head. "Nope. Bill and I were ordered by Whitehead to stop this. But discreetly. We gave it a lot of thought, considered a lot of options." He waved his hand. "We laid them all at the feet of M. Seabury Whitehead. And he agreed with our choice. *You.*"

I sipped some wine. "Well, Terry, first of all—just to be fair to you, I'll say, right up front, that my answer is no. But secondly, I'm doing you a favor."

Terry shook his head. "No, Jim. First of all, you understand the business of broadcasting. All the subtleties. The half business, half *show* business aspect of it. An outsider might not grasp those subtleties."

I shook my head, but Terry went on. "*And*—you know this company. You worked here. You understand every ego that wanders around those halls."

"Terry—"

But he was undaunted. "You know the business, you know the company, you're well respected as a broadcaster—"

"Former—"

"—former broadcaster. You're a famous and serious novelist—"

"—I write thrillers—"

"—Thrillers—what the hell—you've had three best-sellers in seven years."

"Actually four," I said modestly.

Terry's face broke into a grin, the first change in his tense expression in several minutes. "Excuse me, *four* best sellers—and I tried to talk you out of leaving RBS that day."

We laughed. And then Terry was quickly back on the attack.

"Jim, you're the perfect man for the job."

"Terry—you're crazy."

"Come on, Jim, it's right here." Terry rummaged in his briefcase and pulled out a paperback. It was a copy of one of my books. He held it up, somewhat apologetically. "I—ah—missed the hardcover. All sold out."

I feigned a petulant voice. "At least the sales don't depend on my friends."

Terry opened the back of the book to the page where the author's biography is always printed and started to read: " 'For years, James Sasser was known as the cheerful, peripatetic commentator on *The RBS Evening News*. So it was a surprise to the entire industry when Sasser left television and turned his energies to writing thrillers. His last four have all been best-sellers, translated into several languages, and his latest, *A Man Named Martin,* is the third to be made into a major motion picture.' "

"They always say *major* motion picture," I said. "About everything."

Undaunted, Terry read on: " 'He is the proud father of four children, his hobbies are riding and golf, his favorite author is, not surprisingly, Eric Ambler, and he is also a partner in—' "

Terry looked up at me and emphasized each word. " '—a partner in *Maloney, O'Neil and Sasser*—a private investigating firm located in New York City.' "

He playfully slammed the book on the table. "Ha—"

I looked at him. "Terry—"

"I repeat, *Ha.*"

"Let's order a cognac."

"Are you going to reply to my *Ha*?"

"Over a cognac."

"Okay. But you're playing for time. Probably an old trick used by wily private investigators." He got the captain's attention and ordered. "Now you'll have had time to think up a suitably devious explanation."

"I'll tell you right now. Yes, I'm a partner in Maloney, O'Neil and Sasser. And yes, we're located in New York City."

"So—"

"But I'm not a private investigator."

"Aw, come on, Jim—"

"No, I'm not. Maloney—is Joe Maloney. A great guy and an old army buddy."

"Like me."

"Yeah. But he never saved—"

"Aw, shit, Jim," Terry said.

"Okay."

"Anyway—I'm an old army buddy, too. How come I never knew him?"

"He came in after you got your ass blown off and were shipped out of Nam."

"I never met him in New York, either."

"Neither did I. I ran into him at the Whitehall Hotel in Chicago a couple of years ago. And the timing was perfect. I was thinking of starting a thriller, with a detective as the protagonist. There was only one problem. I didn't know anything about private detectives. Well, of all things, that's what Joe Maloney does for a living."

We accepted our cognacs from the waiter and clinked glasses. Terry lit another cigarette.

"Anyway, Joe was a big help while I was writing the book. And I kept wondering how the hell I could ever repay him. Over lunch one day, my editor solved the problem: Let me become Joe's partner. We'd put it on the jacket of the book. It just might give my credentials a bit of weight—but it sure as hell would give Joe some publicity. Joe agreed. We did it. And it worked."

Terry squinted at me over his brandy glass. "Hogwash," he said.

"The truth."

He thought a moment. "It's *still* good. It'll give you weight during the investigation."

"Please, Terry, be realistic."

"Aw, hell, Jim. You're intelligent. Your mind is logical, conceptual. I've read your books—"

I laughed. "That's fiction, Terry."

"And you'd also have the services of Joe Maloney."

"Joe's a great guy. But he handles industrial theft, surveillance, that sort of thing."

Terry looked at me pleadingly. "Jim. For old times' sake. At least meet Whitehead. A favor. For me."

He was very serious. I looked at him. "How do you stand with Northern? Are you in trouble, too?"

He grinned ruefully. "That's just the point. If I can solve this psychological terrorism against the company, I'll be fine. For some reason, they like me. I'm the *only* RBS executive who got a promotion."

I reached across the table and shook his hand. "Hey—congratulations."

"I feel so damned bad for everybody else, though. I look around and feel kind of guilty for being saved. You know?"

"Yeah—"

"But their first week here, they moved me up from Assistant Vice President of Sports under Sam—to Vice President of the network."

"Right under Big Bill himself."

"Yep."

"I guess they do like you all right."

Terry looked into his brandy snifter. "But M. Seabury Whitehead has given Big Bill and me the job of solving these threats. The *or else*, is sort of implicit."

Terry made a face. "So you see, Jim. Unless I'm successful—there's a good chance that I'll be moving out along with everybody else."

I looked at Terry. "Hell, you'd do it for me. Why am I giving you such a hard time?"

"Damned if I know."

"Okay. I'll say I'm *considering*. Because of you."

"You will?"

"Sure."

Terry looked hard at me. He took a deep breath and exhaled. "Oh, man . . . thanks, Jim. Thanks."

He was instantly smiling.

"You know when I got the idea, Jim?"

"For what?"

"To ask you to do the investigation. I read that you were going to come to New York for a few months. At first, I just thought—great. A chance to see a lot of each other. Then it hit me. Wham. I'd ask *you* to do the job for us."

"By the way—when I told you I'd drop by RBS when I got to New York, I didn't say that Bill Braddock could have someone bring me in with a gun."

"You mean Dr. Hastings?"

"Yes."

"Aw, Jim. That was a mess. I'm sorry."

"Of course, I did get to see another side of Dr. Antonia Hastings. Maybe I should thank Big Bill. Dr. Hastings is *something*."

Terry let out a long and passionate sigh of yearning, and we both laughed.

"But, Terry—remember. I left Chicago to do a book—not to become James Sasser, Private Investigator."

"I know. But you *will* meet Whitehead?"

"For you—anything."

Terry smiled. "Great. What's the new book, Jim?"

"A series of essays, and a series of interviews, with famous, almost famous, and potentially famous people. It's my first shot at something besides a thriller."

"Sounds like fun."

"I'm really excited."

"So will M. Seabury Whitehead be when he meets you tomorrow."

I had to laugh. "*Tomorrow*. When you bite into something, you don't let go, do you?"

He grinned. "Tenacity is my middle name. I'll buy a couple copies of your latest—"

"—hardcover, please."

"—hardcover. You can autograph one for him and one for his wife, talk a bit, and, at least, say you're *considering* it."

"Okay. Tomorrow. But hardcovers."

Terry was all smiles. "Maybe I'll buy three."

"A gentleman, indeed."

Terry smiled sheepishly. "I checked Whitehead's schedule

before I came here today. How about around four in the after-noon?"

I had to laugh. "Okay. In that case, I'll take someone pleasant to lunch. But someone even prettier than you."

"Have anybody in mind?"

"Let's see . . . ah, I just met her the other day at Des Artistes. Very bright, witty, beautiful. Tall . . . Susan some-body."

"Susan Mazur?"

"That's it."

"She's A.D. on one of our sports shows." Terry consulted his RBS book and gave me her number. "I don't know her too well. But she looks like a great partner for lunch."

The captain brought the check, along with a complimentary cognac for each of us.

Terry got very serious. He raised his glass. "As I said, Jim—we're in deep trouble. Thanks for helping out."

"I'll try, Terry," I said.

Chapter 6

Susan Mazur's voice on the phone was as delightful sounding as I had remembered it. And she was pleasantly lacking in coyness. Yes, she said, the next was an off day for her, she would love to have lunch, and when I suggested Des Artistes, again her reaction was a simple, "What time?"

We agreed to meet at twelve-thirty.

But when she appeared, time seemed to stop for several seconds, and not just for me alone, but for most of the men in the restaurant, and even a few of the women.

The nearly six feet of her entered rather quietly, but never-theless, there was a figurative bang. As she was greeted at the front desk, she casually removed her jacket, revealing a mind-rattling silken blouse, and, as she walked back to the table at which I was standing, a few other men, unconsciously, stood up, too, in a kind of tacit respect for what they saw.

She was wearing leather slacks whose sole mission seemed to be an attempt to crush her pelvis.

I looked forward to a wonderful lunch.

Susan Mazur liked to drink. "Bloody Mary. Lots of vodka," she told the waiter.

I ordered a beer.

Susan Mazur liked to talk. She quickly rattled off three of the latest New York jokes, none of which I had heard.

Susan Mazur liked being sensual. "What do you think of this blouse? It's silk. My mother sent it to me, but actually, I think it's quite attractive, don't you?"

She knew it was. Underneath it, her body seemed to be in constant motion.

Susan Mazur liked to dine well. "If I order caviar, will you? And then we can have some champagne."

Susan Mazur was fun to be with. It was that simple. She was attractive and she didn't pretend that she was unaware of it. She was witty, and, best of all, she was relaxed.

I was having a great time.

Susan Mazur liked to be frank. "I'm glad you asked me out to lunch. When we met the other day, I suspected that you were my kind of guy."

"What kind is that?"

"Oh—intelligent, not too serious." Her hand squeezed my thigh. "You know—civilized."

"And that's exactly why I called you for lunch."

"Good." She drained her glass. "We could use some more champagne."

Susan Mazur liked to know her luncheon partners. "Are you married?"

"No—"

"Divorced?"

"My wife died. Seven years ago."

"Oh—I'm sorry. I suspect that sometimes I'm too direct."

"No. Nowadays it clears the air."

She squeezed my thigh again and smiled. "Yes, it does."

Our waiter was coming our way. "Shall we order?" I asked, "Or would you—?"

"You read my mind. Let's have some more caviar and champagne. This is too much fun."

She was right. We drank. We talked. We laughed. Susan Mazur was the perfect person for someone like me to meet, someone who had just spent fifty-six consecutive days of frustration in Los Angeles, trying to fashion a movie script, with two guys named Charlie and Barry.

Susan Mazur was also no fool at protecting her front, rear, and both flanks, when it came to holding onto a job in television.

"At lunch the other day, you and Randy Fulton seemed to be the best of friends?"

"We are."

"But I hear that your *best* friend at RBS is Terry Jones."

"Yes, that's right."

And I knew, instantly, why Susan Mazur found me so attractive—or, at least, pretended that she did. Oh, she liked me, yes; but, then, she probably liked strawberries and cream and chocolate mousse; but I offered something that they didn't—because of the people I knew, I could, perhaps, help her to keep her job at RBS.

"Somebody said that you were in Big Bill's office the other night. Are you thinking of coming back to RBS?"

"What'd you do—run me through a computer?"

"Whoa—" She grinned. "There I go again." It's my inquisitive nature. Sometimes it doesn't come out just right."

"No, no—" I poured us each more champagne. "Anything else you'd like to know? The rack won't be necessary."

She squeezed my thigh again and allowed her body to undulate just a bit more. "I'll back up and start again if you'll let me," she said. "We met the other day. I was hoping to see you again. You called and invited me to lunch. I was delighted that you did. I'm here. You're here—" She raised her glass and her smile was lovely. "Thanks for asking."

"Thanks for accepting."

We never quite got around to ordering anything else at lunch, but I did ask the waiter for more caviar and champagne an astonishing number of times.

By three-thirty, Susan Mazur had one leg crossed over mine, was rubbing the hair on the back of my neck, and telling me this was almost her idea of a perfect time.

"Almost—?"

"No, no. Don't take it wrong. I meant—well, first of all, I like good companionship. Male. You're male, and you're a great companion."

"Thanks."

"I love to talk about everything under the sun—which we've been doing—and with lots of laughs thrown in—which we've had. While eating caviar and drinking champagne—which we're doing. But as for the almost—"

She let it dangle in the air.

Oh, yes, indeed, I thought; this woman was some piece of work. To William Makepeace Thackeray, she would have been called a *coquette;* to F. Scott Fitzgerald, a *flirt;* and to Elmo Leonard a . . . *teaser*.

She was a teaser, indeed, a compulsive tease. But so what, I thought, as I sipped my champagne—*so what*. This was fun.

She tickled my ear. "Anyway—here's what I was thinking."

"—Hello."

It was Dr. Antonia Hastings.

I was instantly very aware, and very conscious, of my somewhat less than dignified posture.

"Uh—hello—" I tried to stand, but with my legs entwined as they were with Susan Mazur's, such a move was impossible.

Dr. Hastings continued to smile.

I tried to introduce the two of them in my most dignified manner, but the culmination of all the champagne somewhat dulled my usual savoir faire.

"Dr. Antonia Hastings—Ms. Susan"—what the hell was her name—"ah—Mazur."

They exchanged greetings. Susan kept her leg draped over mine.

"You both work at RBS," I added.

Each explained where.

I said: "How about joining us for a drink?"

As her gaze touched on the bottle of champagne, and as she said "No, thank you, I'm meeting someone from my department"—I had the feeling that she was seeing all the other bottles that had been on the table, and had been emptied during the course of the afternoon, and that my condition must sadly reflect the results.

Her smile was distant, "I'm surprised to see you here."

"Used to be one of my favorite spots."

"No, I mean, I just left the tail end of a meeting at Mr. Whitehead's. It was my understanding that you were going to meet him."

"Oh, my God." I motioned for the check. "So I am. The afternoon just got away from me."

"Yes. So I see." She was still smiling.

She deliberately waited as Susan and I tried to extricate ourselves from each other.

"Enjoy your . . . meeting," I said lamely.

Still smiling, she said: "Yours, too."

Out on Columbus Avenue as we headed up to RBS, Susan said: "She likes you."

"Umm—"

"Why are you shaking your head so much?"

"I'm trying to clear it."

"Is this meeting so important?"

"It is to a friend of mine."

I spotted a deerstalker hat in the window of a shop titled *Hats 'N' Things* and was inspired.

"This is my first time," I said.

Her arm had been around my waist. She let it fall lower. "Really?" Her voice was breathy. "My *God*—"

"No, Susan. I mean to go into any store marked *'N' Things*."

"Oh—" She laughed.

She came into the shop while I bought the deerstalker.

"I meant to tell you—" she said.

"Yes—"

"Your mustache—I've never seen one quite like it."

"Thanks," I said. "—I think."

"No—it's cute." I donned my deerstalker. "And now you look like Sherlock Holmes," she giggled.

"Elementary—"

We caught separate cabs.

I have never quite determined what exactly happens in my brain when I drink champagne in large amounts, but it always seems to snap a few circuits that deal with my synaptic appraisal of the world. Everything seems much less serious. Pomposity in particular seems silly. And even dullness becomes amusing.

Thus, when Terry Jones introduced me to M. Seabury Whitehead, Chief Executive Officer of Northern Industries/Republic Broadcasting System, a man of enormous pomposity and infinite dullness, I was greatly amused.

I was also just a bit drunk.

M. Seabury Whitehead shook my hand with great solemnity and told me, in a voice that was pitched loud enough to speak to a ballroom filled with a gaggle of other Chief Executive Officers, that it was a great pleasure to meet me, an honor indeed. *That* caused the champagne to bubble in my brain, and the effervescence had its usual effect.

"Charmed," I said.

He smiled.

Terry produced three copies of my latest novel, which I dutifully autographed, while Whitehead went on and on about my writing, and the movies made from my writings, and, in particular, about Sarah Carpenter, who had played the lead in two of them.

I wrote a nice inscription in the book to his daughter, a bit of verse that my own daughters have always liked; I inscribed Whitehead's own copy in what I thought was a suitable manner, trying to write in a style somewhere between William F. Buckley and George Will (I even found a way of working in the word *xylography*), and for Whitehead's wife, I wrote: *I'll never forget that evening at the Great Northern Hotel.*

He smiled as he read his daughter's inscription, was greatly moved as he read his own, and was nonplussed upon reading his wife's.

"I've been told that Mrs. Whitehead has a great sense of humor," I said.

Terry Jones was staring at me with eyes that were saying, "What the hell did you write?"

Big Bill Braddock was frowning.

Both were greatly relieved when Whitehead broke into a broad grin and laughed.

"My God, it's perfect. Perfect. Nell is going to love this. Love it."

He shook my hand a second time. "Thank you. Thank you very much."

M. Seabury Whitehead felt honor bound to say that the sun had crossed the yardarm before he offered drinks.

Both Terry and Braddock ordered Perrier. Whitehead followed suit.

I asked for champagne.

Terry glared at me.

M. Seabury Whitehead said: "By God, I should have been an author. It's obviously a lot more carefree than the business world."

I said: "Maybe you should try it."

"Oh, one of these days I will. I've got a lot of good ideas. Why the stories I could tell you—my life alone. We'll talk about it one of these days."

With an air of great joviality, he ordered our drinks from a secretary, who looked as if she spent her weekends training pit bulls, and even called after her, "And bring an extra champagne glass"—He winked at me—"If I'm going to consider writing one of these days, I'd better start to learn the life, uh?"

I smiled and decided to put my deerstalker hat back on my head.

For the next twenty minutes, M. Seabury Whitehead summed up the situation, most of which I had heard from Big Bill and Terry.

His view of the situation was somewhat different from theirs, of course. He was the top man. So one enormous element in his appraisal of the situation—fear of his own position—was missing.

"Twenty-one percent of the stock," he said at one point.

"But"—he stopped pacing—"I don't want any damned golden"—he chortled—"in my case—*platinum*—parachute anymore than anyone else here does." By anyone else, it was quite clear that two of them, Big Bill Braddock and Terry Jones, were in the room.

Whitehead had thought the first threats to be those of a prankster. He now knew that they were very serious. No one had the foggiest idea where they were coming from.

"It's damned frightening—*damned* frightening."

He was standing in front of me. "We need to find out who's behind all of this. Because it seems God-damned clear to me that someone's trying to wreck Northern Industries' acquisition of the Republic Broadcasting System."

And then, remembering Braddock and Terry, he added, "—and RBS, itself, of course."

He stepped closer. "Mr. Sasser—"

"Jim—"

"Jim—" He paused and smiled. "Jim, I know this proposal, this . . . request we've made is . . . something that you . . . I mean, a best-selling author and all"—he patted one of my books—"well . . . you need this like a hole in the head, but—"

"Exactly my thoughts," I said.

Whitehead frowned.

And then, remembering Terry, I said, "But because Terry asked me to consider—"

Whitehead was smiling again. "—Well, *yes,* just the point. Terry asked you, I know. So I'll just simply say—will you take the job?"

I looked at Terry, who was watching me intently, his face strained.

"Well . . ."

"Yes?"

"I . . . may I . . . have some more champagne?"

"Of course." He poured it himself.

I took a sip. My question was genuine: "What in hell makes you think that someone like me is, in any way, suitable for a job like this?"

Whitehead nodded vigorously. "Exactly. Good question. Exactly the first thing I asked when Terry proposed you. I wanted a large, completely professional organization."

"Well then—"

"But they thoroughly convinced me that you are precisely the man."

"But—"

He waved his hand. "The most important word is discretion. So a big outfit is out. And you know this company. You know a lot of the personnel. You'll be respected, and they'll talk to you. And you'll be able to employ"—he glanced at Terry—"what was the name—?"

"Maloney, O'Neil and Sasser."

"Yes. Your own agency, as well. In short, you're perfect." He reached for the champagne. "Here—" He filled my glass as well as his own. By now, the two of us were well into the bottle. "Do you agree?"

I didn't want the job. As Whitehead had already ventured, I needed something like this like a hole in the head. I looked across the room at Terry. We're friends, I thought, but this is going too far to prove friendship.

I downed my glass of champagne in one swallow, turned to say no, when M. Seabury Whitehead said, "My God."

"Excuse me?"

Whitehead was smiling broadly. "My God, you even *look* like a detective."

By now I was feeling very giddy. "It's elementary, my dear Whitehead. I am wearing a deerstalker hat. Sherlock Holmes often affected a deerstalker hat. Sherlock Holmes was a detective, albeit fictional. Ergo, I look like a detective."

I bowed with a flourish. "Also—I assure you, sir, fictional."

"Amazing." Whitehead was a bit giddy himself.

"Elementary," I repeated. I could see now why Sherlock Holmes had used the word so often. It gave one a warm, cozy feeling, like sitting in front of a friendly fireplace, to murmur *elementary* at fairly regular intervals in a conversation.

I eyed Whitehead, pulling my deerstalker a bit lower on my forehead, and beginning to really relish my role. "And as for you, my dear sir"—he was emptying the last of the champagne into his glass—"I'm afraid that I must question the *M.*"

"I beg your pardon?"

"As in *M.* Seabury Whitehead."

"Oh—"

"I suspect, quite strongly, that the *M.* stands for a name that you would rather ignore. Perhaps, Martin—no, that's a very pleasant name—or, perhaps, Manley—no, with that name you could run for senator . . . ah . . . perhaps . . . *Marion*?"

"My God." Whitehead wiped his brow.

"Elementary, my dear Whitehead. Elementary."

"Absolutely remarkable."

"And as for Whitehead—"

His eyebrows shot up.

"Could it have been—at sometime or another—originally the German—*Weiskopf*?"

"I didn't know myself until a few years ago. My great-grandfather changed it when they first landed here. Amazing."

"Elementary, elementary, *elementary*." I had a mad desire to pull out a magnifying glass and examine a portion of the carpet.

I pointed at his desk. "Now I notice that—"

"*Jim*—" It was Terry.

"Yeah, Jimbo." Big Bill did his best to chuckle. "I think we—ah—get the idea."

I stopped. Terry was my friend. Enough.

M. Seabury Whitehead née Marion Seabury Weiskopf looked at me eagerly. "Then you'll accept the offer?"

I started to make a hasty exit before the giddiness turned to dizziness. As I reached the door, he called, "Carte blanche."

I turned, a stunning Basil Rathbone-like turn. "Carte blanche, my dear Whitehead is—*elementary*."

Chapter 7

It was nine in the morning, and I was sitting in my favorite Greek diner on upper Broadway, enjoying my monthly eggs and bacon for breakfast, and reading the sports section of *The Times*.

I felt splendid, barely a trace of a hangover. But, then, I had slept for nearly ten straight hours.

Outside, it was raining lightly, and I watched a woman dash across Broadway, leaping a few puddles on the way. She saw me through the window and waved. It was Libby Nolan.

She came into the diner, ordered coffee and toast at the counter, and sat down across from me in the booth.

"You're alive, anyway," she said.

"What did you expect?"

"When I got your message on my machine last night, I had serious doubts that I'd ever see you again."

"I called you last night—?"

"In a manner of speaking."

Libby took off her raincoat and Boston Red Sox cap and shook off some of the rain. She always dressed the same: penny loafers, navy blue slacks, navy blue sweater, red shirt and a Red Sox cap.

"How many navy blue sweaters do you own?"

"I don't know. A lot."

"Don't you ever consider any other color? Yellow? Orange?"

"I don't like yellow or orange. Why should I buy a sweater in a color I don't like?"

"Always navy blue?"

Libby thought. "I bought a dark green one a few years ago. I wore it a few times. I didn't like it." She took a bite of her toast and stared at me.

"Okay," I said. "I can stand it no longer. What did I say when I called you last night?"

"Not much." She sipped some coffee. "Not much that was discernible, at any rate."

"How much did you discern?"

"I discerned, most of all, that you'd been drinking far beyond your capacity. Other than that—besides your endless chortling over what was, apparently, a ribald story, but which I couldn't make head nor tails of—you seemed to be saying that you *had* a case, we're *on* a case, I *wanted* a case, or we *are* a case—that you wanted to see me here this morning—which I now realize you completely forgot about—and then I heard deerstalker a few times. Quite a few times, actually."

She sipped some coffee. "It was actually sort of poignant sounding when you said it—*deerstalker*—sort of like *Rosebud*. It didn't hit me until I was jogging this morning that it probably had something to do with the new book." She patted a hip pocket where she always kept a supply of three-by-five cards. "So I added it to the notes."

I said: "Aren't you getting just a bit too elderly for jogging?"

Libby eyed me for a moment. "My dear fellow, I'm seventy-four years old."

"Isn't that just a bit too elderly?"

"Hell, no."

"I only said for jogging—"

"Stop trying to change the subject. What happened to you yesterday?"

I held up a last piece of bacon. "Bite?" Libby shook her head. "It's nice and crisp—"

"What happened?"

"Well—as you discerned with your amazing perspicacity— I was just a bit over my limit for drinking. And it was champagne—"

"Oh my God. No wonder."

"But you did pretty well on getting the highlights of what I was trying to communicate. I can't remember the story or I'd—"

"Just as well," Libby said.

"But deerstalker refers to my latest chapeau, which I purchased only yesterday." I pulled it from a hook on the booth's coatrack and popped it onto my head. "Voila."

Libby made a face.

"And as for the rest—"

Libby started to laugh. "Take it off. I can't listen to you and take anything seriously when you're wearing that."

"Very well. Break my heart." I removed the hat.

Libby blessed herself and looked heavenward to give thanks.

"Okay, you've made your point—"

"It's bad enough with the mustache—"

"You promised—"

She started to laugh again.

"You *promised*—"

Libby held her breath and nodded. "Sorry."

I said: "As for the case part—I do, indeed, have a case. I have almost—not quite—agreed to do a kind of intra-industrial investigation for the Republic Broadcasting System. As with everything else, I shall need your invaluable assistance or I shall most certainly fail."

Libby shook her head. "You and I are about to begin your sixth and first *important* book."

"We'll postpone—"

She scowled.

"—For a few weeks. Still making notes. Still thinking, talking."

The scowl deepened.

"We'll be better prepared—"

"We're prepared now."

"We'll be even *better* than better prepared."

"*Mister* Sasser, what in hell are you talking about?"

When Libby called me Sasser and not James that meant that she was a bit riled up. When she called me *Mister Sasser* that meant that she was at her limit.

"Give me five minutes. Just five minutes to explain the whole thing."

She didn't relent in the severity of her mood, but, at least, she let me talk.

I talked very fast for five minutes.

When I had finished, she stood, went to the counter, got a second cup of coffee, and returned. Finally, she said, "I still don't understand exactly why you're considering this—and second, it doesn't sound very much like the lark you're trying to paint it to be."

"It might not be. But in three weeks, a month, fail or succeed, we'll be out of it. And who knows—maybe we'll get an idea for a book."

Libby groaned and looked heavenward again.

"Well, *maybe*—"

After another several minutes of questioning on Libby's part, partial answers and pleading on my part, she agreed.

"You'll really need Joe Maloney," she said.

"Absolutely. And that's something else, too. A job like this—all expenses, et cetera—won't exactly hurt Joe's pocketbook either."

Libby nodded and smiled. She and Joe were as close as the two of us. "And Joe has really good connections with the NYPD—and, of course, we'll need dossiers on everybody at RBS—and we'll need . . . and we'll . . ."

I liked it more and more as I heard Libby's liberal use of the pronoun *we*. There was never any halfway with Libby about anything. And now she was fully committed.

The two of us got lucky and immediately caught a taxi, despite the rain, and were walking into the lobby of Joe Maloney's building on Fifty-Seventh Street across from Carnegie Hall some ten minutes later.

Before we rang the bell, Libby pulled out a handkerchief and polished the brass on the impressive lettering that read: Maloney, O'Neil and Sasser. It had been her Christmas present to Joe the year before.

Maureen answered the door.

"Well, well—" She smiled and embraced Libby. I got a peck on the cheek. "You must've caught the first cab you saw."

Maureen was as Irish as Paddy's pig—black hair, blue eyes, very attractive—and big. Those who read comic strips called her *Wonder Woman*.

"Hey, Joe—the gang's all here." Maureen's limp was almost indiscernible as she moved toward Maloney's office. Four years on the police force had ended abruptly one bad night in Brooklyn— and the doctors had had to fuse her left knee.

"I heard 'em comin' a mile away. A mile." A smiling Joe Maloney emerged from his office and shook my hand, crushing it as he always did.

It had been a while since the four of us had been together, so we chatted away about dozens of things as we sat comfortably in Joe's office drinking coffee and catching up. I looked around at Joe with his red hair, gray now at the temples, at Maureen, at Libby. I said: "My God, I feel as if I'm at a meeting of the Friendly Sons of St. Patrick—Maloney, O'Neil and Nolan."

"Maureen," Joe grinned, "how did this bastard Sasser get in here anyway? Have him thrown out."

"But he brought the coffee."

"In that case, sit, friend, and be welcome."

Later, as we had a second container of coffee, he said, "Okay, Jimmy, what is it? Ever since you called, Maureen and I've been sitting here on tenterhooks." He looked at me quizzically. "Can a person sit on tenterhooks?"

"Uncomfortably, but yes."

"That was us." He squinted. "Well—?"

I told him everything.

Being Joe, he listened intently without interrupting. When I had finished, his questions were cogent and to the point.

"And what about you?" Joe turned to Libby. "You've been uncharacteristically quiet to say the least."

"I was trying not to prejudice the case."

Joe grinned. "So you just sat there, stone faced, scowling, clucking your tongue, and groaning."

"Groaning—?"

"Yeah. You sort of gave me a small hint about the way you felt."

Libby smiled grimly. "I said if he was dead set to do this, I'd help, of course"—she glanced at me and wagged a finger—"for one month—no more—then we start the book."

I nodded in agreement.

"I have just one more question," Joe said. He filled his pipe and tossed me his tobacco pouch. "Just as a friend, Jimmy—why do you want to do this?"

"What do you mean?"

"Just what I said. Why?"

I took my time filling my own pipe and lighting it. "Okay—I'll give you a straight answer." I tossed back the pouch.

Joe caught it and grinned. "Hey, Jimmy—I kind of expected that. A straight answer."

"Well . . ." I had to grin myself. "You know, sometimes you ask the damndest questions."

Joe scratched his cheek. "Yep—"

"I don't know," I finally said.

"Then maybe you oughta forget the whole thing," Joe said. "Because, for one thing, Maureen and I have plenty of work and—"

"Hey, Joe—"

Joe's chin was stuck out an added inch. "Business is good—we don't have to—"

"Joe—Libby and I are here because—if we do this—we're going to need your professional help. Now as for your fee and expenses—what the hell. Why not?"

"But I still say—why?"

"Well . . . just for the hell of it maybe." Libby snorted again. "No—that's a reason. And a good one. Maybe I need an adventure. I just finished two dull months of work in L.A. So maybe this will be a kind of tonic. Just what I need."

"And there's friendship involved," Maureen said, "with this Terry Jones—"

"Yeah—there's that—but maybe my real honest-to-God reason boils down to just what I said: I want to do it—just for the hell of it."

Joe looked at me for a long time. Finally he said, "It's as good a reason as any, Jimmy."

He glanced at Maureen. She nodded.

"Count us in," Joe said.

"Thanks, Joe."

The next hour was spent in drawing up a preliminary plan of battle. Joe, and Libby, and Maureen did most of the planning.

At one point I said, "I feel like just another pretty face."

"Don't flatter yourself," Libby said. But she was smiling now.

At the end of the hour, I called Terry Jones to tell him that Maloney, O'Neil and Sasser would accept the job.

Terry was ecstatic. "Great—wonderful, Jim. I'll tell M.S.W. right away."

"Who—?"

"M. Seabury—"

"Oh, yeah. And tell him"—I glanced down at the figure that Joe had written and tripled it—"plus all expenses."

"You're on."

After a round of handshakes, Joe led the way across Fifty-Seventh Street to the bar at the Parker Meridian. Spirits were high, and all of us were in a just-for-the-hell-of-it mood as we got our drinks.

"Now, Jimmy"—Joe's face was suddenly serious—"this is all fine—and fun—so far. But don't forget one thing—" Joe was extremely serious—"someone's been killed."

"Yeah—" I *had* forgotten.

"Keep it in mind, Jimmy," Joe said. "*All* the time."

Chapter 8

M. Seabury Whitehead was brisk and to the point.

He said: "All department heads have been notified that you are working directly out of my office, with my full authority."

I nodded.

"And"—he smiled and winked conspiratorially—"Just for those who might be ignorant of your past successes in news, I mentioned a few things you did when you were here."

I raised my eyebrows.

"Oh, Terry was very thorough when he sold me on you. Very. You had a most impressive record at RBS."

"I had a lot of help," I said.

"And modest too."

"Never that—"

Whitehead laughed.

"Uh—" Whitehead was hesitant—"some—ah—champagne?"

I said. "Never when I'm working. And never at ten after ten in the morning."

"Ah." Whitehead nodded his head. "I thought, well, you know, being a writer and all . . ."

"It takes a modicum of self-discipline."

"Um—" Whitehead looked thoughtful for a moment. "Yes— yes, I suppose it does."

My initial stop was at the office of the Vice President of Human Resources, a nervous little man with eyes that twitched constantly and seemed to focus on everything except the person he was addressing.

My first attempt at a lighthearted remark fell on barren ground, so our conversation was fairly brief.

But when I left, I had all the vital material I needed, for the moment, on several people still at RBS.

More important, I had the names and dossiers of every person who had been given *early retirement,* or whose job position had been *terminated* or who had been *made redundant* since the Northern Industries take-over. The Vice President of Human Resources, apparently, did not have the word *fired* in his vocabulary.

I made one faux pas. When I left, I said: "Thank you for being so helpful here in the personnel department.

He looked pained. "Human Resources Department—"

"Yes—of course. Human Resources Department. Thank you for your complete cooperation, Mr.—ah—Sparrow."

"You're most welcome." He twitched even more. I had the feeling that Mr. Sparrow worried every hour of every day that he would be the next person to be *terminated* or *made redundant.*

I met Maureen O'Neil in the lobby and gave her my box of stuff.

"My God, what do you have? The complete works of Charles Dickens?"

"Too heavy?"

"Hey—for Wonder Woman? Never."

"That should keep you and Joe busy for a while."

"We'll try to distill things down for you. I'm assuming you want us to begin with all of the ones who've been fired."

"No—*terminated.*"

"Huh—?"

"Yeah. The ones fired," I said.

She motioned through the lobby windows, and pointed to the box. A driver emerged from a long black limousine. "Just one of the pleasures of doing business with an expense account," she said.

Maureen smiled and waved. "See you, Jimmy. Take care."

The News Department was the same as it had always been—quiet chaos with six inches of tension on the floor at all times. It was only midmorning, and probably a half-dozen bottles of Maalox had already been consumed.

I headed straight across the huge main room, where wire machines rattled, desk assistants scurried, and word processors blinked, and made for what had always been the office of the Vice President of News.

The secretary outside the office door was an old friend. "Hello there, Mr. Sasser, do you still recognize an old Nittany Lion?"

"Mary—" She stood and we hugged.

"You're looking great, Jim."

"You, too, Mary."

"And I'm still here." She grinned and crossed her fingers. "One more year and then retirement."

"Early?"

"My choice."

"Good."

Mary picked up her phone. "I'll tell him you're here."

"Is it Johnson or Johnston?"

"John*son* . . . Mr. Johnson . . . Mr. Sasser is here . . . I'll tell him." Mary smiled. "Tom Mix will see you now—" She opened the door and announced me.

I immediately saw Mary's point.

As Johnson rose to greet me, he squinted his eyes, as if looking off into an Arizona sunset, and drawled, "Howdy, partner. Nice to meet ya'. Sit down and take the weight off your feet."

"Thank you."

"Mr. Whitehead called and said you'd be droppin' by." He extended his hand. "Howdy, I'm Billy Bob Johnson."

"How d'you do." I shook his hand and sat in the nearest chair.

Billy Bob smiled and said, "I'm afraid I've never read any of your books."

"You haven't missed much," I said.

He chuckled and waved some papers in my direction. "But I gotta tell you, partner, I'm impressed by what you did as a reporter. Till I got this info, I'd always thought that all you'd ever done in news were those iddy-biddy commentaries."

I said "Thank you," again, despite what I was thinking.

"It's a pleasure to meet a real reporter." He smiled again. "At least, you *were* a reporter. My own thoughts about reporting are . . ."

Billy Bob Johnson had a lot of thoughts about everything. He talked for a long time, and I had more than ample time to decide that I thoroughly disliked him.

Very much like a country-and-western singer from Nashville, he affected garish cowboy gear: high-heeled boots, a tan suit replete with leather on the shoulders, and piping on every seam, and a shirt collar that, instead of a normal necktie, was embellished with a jade bolo.

At one point during his dull harangue, he even donned a cowboy hat. I half expected him to pick up a lariat to twirl, and I was a bit disappointed when he didn't.

I knew from his personnel dossier that William Johnson—now Billy Bob Johnson—hailed from Secaucus, New Jersey.

He was a Northern Industries man, who had been with the company for ten years. He had been news director for the only four television stations Northern owned, before they bought RBS: stations in Altoona, Kalamazoo, Peoria, and Sandusky. And he had been the first man to be moved into RBS after the buy out. Two days after the word had hit Wall Street, Billy Bob Johnson took over as Vice President of News, and Buzz Berman was out on his ear. Or, as the company announcement had said: "Mr. Berman's long desire to pursue independent production can now be realized."

Billy Bob finally stopped talking.

I was momentarily stunned by the sudden silence.

"So what can I do for you, partner?" he asked.

I asked a lot of questions. Billy Bob didn't seem to mind answering any of them, especially when it came to the firings. There, Billy Bob grew animated and excited.

"Oh, shucks, I'm used to takin' over a new operation and spillin' a little blood—you know, just to keep the troops in line and let 'em know you're in town. But this"—Billy Bob slapped his thigh—"this was more like a massacre."

"You do it fast, I suppose. Over lunch or something."

"Frick lunch," Billy Bob said. "Who has time for lunch? I just call 'em in and give 'em the news. Shake hands and holler— *Next*."

"Even Peter Douglas?" I mentioned one of RBS's mainstays in the news.

"Oh, him I took a little longer"—Billy Bob slapped his thigh again and chortled—"With him I spent an extra minute or two."

Billy Bob took special delight in naming, specifically, every prominent, well-known news personality, producer or writer whom he had let go. A lot of them were friends of mine, but I kept my mouth closed.

"And Richard Ainsley—just yesterday."

That name snapped it for me. The last straw. I said: "Dick Ainsley is just about the most respected broadcast journalist in the country."

Billy Bob sneered. "*Was*—" he said.

"And he's a good friend of mine."

"Fortunes of war."

"You seem to take great relish in it."

Billy Bob Johnson shrugged his shoulders. "It's my job," he said.

"Sure—"

His narrow eyes grew colder and meaner. "But him—your friend Ainsley—him I didn't just *relish*. I loved it."

If I'd had a custard pie, I'd have thrown it at Billy Bob Johnson's face.

"Firing him was fun. Do you know what the son of a bitch did to me? I called him in. In *here*." Billy Bob pointed to the floor of his office. "I called him in—and before I could open my mouth, he invited *me* to *lunch*."

I controlled my smile.

"Who the hell does that smart-ass, intellectual, leftist think he is? I'm the boss—hell, I'm vice-president of the whole frickin' news operation—and I'm gonna fire him, and he has the nerve to invite me to lunch."

"Maybe he just likes you."

"Shit—"

"Did you go?"

Billy Bob paused for a moment, leaned back against his desk, and his voice got so low that I could barely hear it. "Yeah, I went. And you'd better tell your friend Ainsley that, for the rest of his life, he'd better never, ever turn his back on me."

I said nothing. I waited.

"Do you know what he did to me? He took me down to the Ginger Man for lunch."

"He always did like that place—"

Billy Bob's eyes were concentrated on the floor. "I ordered a Perrier and he ordered a Bloody Mary. And then your—*friend*—said to me—to me—the vice-president of RBS News, who was about to fire him—he said, 'Now before we get around to talking about why you called me into your office, I'd like to propose a toast.'"

I thought, that sounds exactly like something Dick Ainsley would do.

"And then"—Billy Bob looked at me again—"your *friend* stood up and said—and he said it loud enough so everybody in the whole frickin' place could hear—he said, 'To all the good folks at RBS News, to all the good stories and the good times over the years—'

"And then"—Billy Bob's voice was an angry hiss—"that son of a bitch threw that Bloody Mary right in my face."

There was silence in the office.

Finally, I stood up and started to applaud. Slowly. Rhythmically.

Billy Bob's face was blank.

"Thanks for your cooperation," I said. "I'll probably be dropping by from time to time."

Billy Bob Johnson jammed on his cowboy hat and pointed a finger at me. "You tell him," he said. "You *tell* him."

"I'll tell him."

I ran into Terry Jones in the hall. As usual, he was lighting a cigarette.

"Hey, Jim, I was just thinking about you. Here we are friends—and we've seen each other maybe only three, four times in seven years. Now—for a month anyway—it'll seem like old times."

I said: "Yeah—"

"Hey—what's wrong?"

"Let's go over to McGurk's. I'll buy you a drink."

"It's a little early for me."

"It's eleven-thirty. Come on."

Terry looked concerned. "Sure. Let's go."

We went down the elevator and walked the four blocks to McGurk's in silence.

McGurk's is always filled with people from RBS and Cap Cities/ABC, particularly news crews. We found an empty spot at the far end of the bar.

"Gentlemen—?"

"Hi, Don." Terry shook hands with the bartender. "You remember Jim Sasser."

"Sure do. Hi, Jim."

"Don—" We shook hands.

"I'll have a beer—a Beck's," Terry said.

I said: "No, you won't. Two Bloody Marys, Don, please."

Don looked at Terry who shrugged his shoulders in acquiescence.

"What's up, Jim?"

"I just met Billy Bob Johnson, your cowboy from Secaucus."

"Ah—"

I told Terry about the firing of Dick Ainsley.

Our Bloody Marys came.

Terry clinked his glass on mine.

"To the best—"

I raised my glass: "To Richard Ainsley, a man of infinite grace and infinite style."

We hoisted one to a friend.

Chapter 9

I declined a luncheon invitation from Terry and headed for a little deli I knew near West End Avenue, where the chances would be good that I could find myself a table in the corner and have the peace I needed to draw up a plan of action.

On the way I called Libby Nolan.

"You just caught me at the door," she said. "Maureen dropped by. She's taking me over to Joe's—in a *limo*."

"I was hoping that you'd take a few days off."

"At my age? For what? Have you gone *loco*?"

I had to smile. "Where'd you pick that up?"

"What?"

"*Loco*."

"I'm reading Louis L'Amour."

"That explains it. Anybody call?"

"D'you really want to know?"

"That's why I asked."

"Mona—"

"Oh, God—"

"No, it's good news. At least for today. She said she's really got to talk to you because—"

"That's what she always says—"

"No, wait—because she's finally come to her senses. She's finally realized that it's all over between the two of you."

"Thank God."

"She asked if you'd call her so she could tell you that herself. I said I doubted that you would. She said in that case, to hell with you forever and good-bye."

"Good."

"I give it three days," Libby said.

"My God, but you're a pessimist."

Libby grunted. "No—optimist. If we were betting money, I'd give it two days."

"Anything else?"

"Nothing. I spent the morning"—Libby's delivery was deliberately studied and stilted—"typing up the rest of your notes for—the *book*."

"You've made your point."

"Good. Now I'm off with Maureen to help get this box of stuff catalogued so you can play detective with Joe."

"Come on, Libby—give it a shot."

"I'll give it my *best* shot, baby. I'd like to see you wind up this thing in a week. Believe me—I'm planning to help as much as I can."

"I appreciate it."

"So will your publisher."

"You *made* your point already."

"With you—it never hurts. Now I'm off. I'll tell Joe you plan to call him later. Right?"

"Right."

"Good. Bye, bye, Peaches."

It was comforting to know that Libby was in a good mood and on the job. And Maureen. And Joe. Because, as the four of us knew too well—I didn't exactly know quite what I was doing.

The deli had been a good choice. Three of the six tables were unoccupied. I got myself a pastrami on rye and sat at the table farthest from the door.

While I ate, I went through the latest roster booklet of all the employees of the Republic Broadcasting System and made check marks next to the ones I knew.

Next, I got out my packet of three-by-five cards and spent several minutes remembering and writing down the names of anyone I had known who was not on the roster and, therefore, was presumed dismissed since the Northern takeover.

Then I saw the pay phone and decided to call Joe Maloney.

I got some quarters at the counter. "How long've you had the pay phone, Murray?"

"Oh, about five years." He grinned.

"I've been away longer than I realized, Murray."

"It's good to see you around. Ya gonna be with us for a while?"

"A few months."

"If you drop in again, maybe you could autograph your books for me. I've got every one."

That explains why I always sold at least one copy. It'll be my pleasure to give you an autograph."

"Oh, not to me, Mr. Sasser. To my wife, Edna. She loved 'em."

I laughed. "You just put me in my place, Murray."

"I mean—I'm just not a reader, you know—other than, maybe, *The Daily News*. . . ."

"Murray, you tell Edna that I'm very flattered that she likes my books, and that I'm coming back especially to autograph them for her."

"Hey, thanks." He was relaxed again. "I'll bring 'em all in tomorrow."

The phone call found Joe in a good mood.

"Do you have one of your fabled notebooks with you?" I asked him.

"Of course."

"Write down the name *Buzz Berman,* would you?"

I spelled it out for him.

"Who's Buzz Berman?"

"A saint of a man, and he *was* Vice President of News for RBS—before the arrival of some jackass named Billy Bob Johnson."

"I'll assume that you're making sense."

"I am. Unfortunately."

"Okay. What do I do now?"

"See if you can find him."

"Where do I look?"

"No idea. He had a lot of pride. After Northern canned him, the guys tell me, he didn't hang around. He just walked out with his chin up and hasn't been seen since."

"And you think we should talk to him?"

"Absolutely. Don't you?"

"Absolutely," Joe said. "Even saints can make threats."

That stopped me cold. "I wasn't thinking of it that way, Joe."

"I know you weren't. But it's time you did. You can't go around liking everybody on a thing like this, Jimmy. *Someone's* sending these things. *Someone's* lighting those fires. And *someone* murdered that girl."

"Yeah . . . I see what you mean."

"Anything else?"

I told him how I'd checked off the RBS roster, and I gave him my plan, which was to call, and then meet with, everyone I knew who had been canned.

"Makes sense," Joe said.

"Then I'll meet everybody I know who's still there at RBS."

"Fine."

"I'll start this afternoon then. Oh, Joe—"

"Yeah?"

"Tell Libby that Peaches says hello."

Joe chuckled. "I'll tell her."

I got a coffee from Murray on my way back to the table.

"I did read a couple of chapters of your first one, though, Mr. Sasser. I thought it was terrific."

"Thanks, Murray. May I borrow *The News*?"

"Sure."

I was sipping my coffee and was engrossed in *Doonesbury* when Dr. Antonia Hastings walked in. She seemed out of place in a spot like Murray's Deli, but she was obviously a regular customer.

Murray greeted her with: "How ya' gonna have it today, Doc? With or without a schmear?"

"With, Murray, please. And tea today instead of coffee."

"Straight?"

"Please."

She saw me and smiled. "Hello. May I sit for a minute while I wait for my bagel?"

"Please." I stood up. Once again, her blue eyes seemed to sweep over me.

"My God—"

"Excuse me?"

"Your eyes are very blue," I said.

"Oh—" She blushed—"thank you."

Her blush continued. "I'm afraid that I was rather rude the other day. I'm sorry."

"I honestly don't know what you're talking about," I said, "so you must be wrong."

"The other day at Des Artistes. You were—sitting with another young woman."

"Thanks for the euphemism. But I wasn't exactly sitting with—I was really more entangled with."

Her blush became slightly deeper.

"And I'm sure you weren't rude. And I'm sure that you realize that I was in such a condition that I'd hardly remember if you were."

"Yes. You were very . . . relaxed."

"Yes . . . I was."

We smiled at each other.

Murray shouted, "All set, Doc—"

"Thanks, Murray—"

She looked intently at me. She said, "You're a very—charming man."

Before I could answer, she leaned across the table and kissed me on the lips. It was very erotic. I'd never been kissed by a beautiful woman in a delicatessen before.

She stood. "Just in case I *was* rude," she said.

I sat there, stunned, and watched silently as she paid for her things. Before leaving, she came back to the table.

God, what eyes.

"Yes . . . very charming," she said again. Then she kissed me a second time and left.

I looked over at Murray who was doing his best to pretend that he'd seen nothing.

"Do you know what a coquette is, Murray?" I asked him.

"No. What is it?"

"*It* . . . is a woman who tries—without very much real affection—to gain the amorous attentions of a man."

"Yeah?"

"Um hm. And I think that . . . maybe . . . I've got two of 'em on my case."

"No kiddin'."

"Yeah, Murray. No kiddin'."

Dick Ainsley was my first call, not because of any investigation, but just because he was an old comrade. We had worked together, and we had been friends for a long time.

He had sounded strange when he answered the phone, and I had been momentarily concerned, until it occurred to me that almost anyone would sound just a bit strange the day after he had been sacked from a job he had held with high honor for some twenty years. In fact, it would have been odd if he hadn't sounded strange.

Dick's apartment was on Central Park West, and I cut through Lincoln Center as I walked to it. It was almost three in the afternoon, yet the outdoor cafe in front of Avery Fisher Hall was nearly filled with people enjoying the warmth of the October sun. There was a very European feeling to the whole thing, and, to add to that impression, a tall gentleman, formally dressed, replete with top hat, a cane, and a long red-lined cape, came out from the crowd. Probably some visiting conductor, I surmised.

I found myself whistling "Manhattan" all the way to Dick Ainsley's building.

And—just like that—I changed my mind.

I decided to give up what Libby, Maureen, and Joe Maloney had known from the beginning was an absolutely idiotic scheme.

The meeting with Billy Bob Johnson had been the thing that had begun my change of mind, I realized. If someone were threatening Northern Industries/RBS, he or she probably had a damned good reason. To hell with it. Besides, to be honest about it, I was the least qualified man in the world to investigate *anything*.

Dick Ainsley greeted me at the door of his apartment with a wry grin. He had been drinking. What the hell, I thought, why not?

"Welcome, dear friend, to the humble abode of the late Richard Ainsley."

"Hey, let's have none of that."

He raised his glass. "*D'accord*. That was the beginning and the end of any self-pity for this conversation." Dick coughed. As long as I had known him, Dick had coughed his way through life. He reached out and shook my hand. "I'm glad you called."

"So am I—"

We drank and talked and laughed for nearly two hours.

"—and there you were making some last second changes in your copy during the commercial break and—" Dick paused to break into laughter—"you said to Charlie—'Quick, what's the word for someone who likes horses?' and Charlie said, '*Sodomist*,' and the whole studio broke up, and, about two seconds later the talley light went on, and you had to get through that piece of commentary with a straight face—I still don't know how the hell you did it."

"Neither do I—" We laughed even more.

Both of us were pretty sloshed at this point, but Dick was in high spirits, quite different from the way I had found him.

But all that changed abruptly.

His face darkened suddenly and the flesh seemed to sag. His sparkling eyes were quickly sunken and hollow.

"God . . . that all seems like a long time ago."

I looked at him for a moment. "Well, it *was* about nine or ten years—"

"—No, I don't mean just that. That last story. Or any of the things we've been rambling on about. I mean all of it." He got up. "Another?"

"No, thanks. I'm fine for now."

He made his way to a sideboard and fixed himself another drink. "I mean all of it," he said again. "All of it for you ended when Nancy . . . sorry . . . died. And you hung it up and left and then . . ." He turned back to me and smiled faintly. "You know, I've never said this, but when your first book came out, and it was *good*—I was so proud for you, so happy for you."

"Thanks. Thanks, Dick."

"I remember Charlie Stern coming into the newsroom with your book and shouting, 'Hey, the son of a bitch can really write.' We were all proud of you—happy for you. We all were—"

He started back to his chair, keeping his feet wide apart, weaving slightly. He was coughing again.

"But—all of it for me didn't end seven years ago." He slumped into his chair. "It ended . . . yesterday. And still . . ."

I didn't say anything.

Finally, he said "Funny, isn't it . . . ?"

I nodded my head.

"Do I sound a bit . . . off?"

"No—there's been a shock—"

"I don't feel in shock."

"Well—you probably *are* just a bit. Something that momentous—that sudden—"

"It wasn't sudden, Jim. I knew it was going to happen. I knew for three months. Right after the Northern take-over. I used to work with one of their execs back in Cleveland. He tipped me off."

He laughed bitterly. "Yeah, I knew all right. That's why I was rooting for whoever it was who was doing all the threatening. It even crossed my mind to do a little threatening myself."

What crossed my mind was that I was glad that I had made my decision to give up my mission for Terry Jones, Big Bill Braddock and M. Seabury Whitehead. Otherwise, I would now have to question Dick Ainsley at a time when he was as down-and-out, and as vulnerable, as he would ever be. And I was supposed to be Dick Ainsley's friend.

"Time will heal a lot of this, Dick."

He guffawed. "God, with platitudes like that, I just might pull through."

I smiled apologetically. "I'll try not to be platitudinous. But you're a resilient guy. You're gonna bounce back from this. As soon as you've had a little time. You're not the sort to carry around anger—"

"The *hell I'm not*." He had to struggle to stand up, but he stood now, defiantly. "The hell I'm *not*," he snapped again. "I've carried around a ton of anger for those sons of bitches. Ever since Northern Industries came in and got out the wrecking machines—I've hated every Goddamned one of them. M. Seabury Whitehead, and Roland R. Sparrow, and—maybe most of all— that phony little bastard—Billy Bob Johnson."

"That's natural—he's the one who actually fired you—"

"No—no, not just that. For three months I've watched good guys at RBS get the axe. One after another. And I've seen one bastard—*one*—help get them out—clean the axe, and get ready for another whack. With a *smile* on his face." His scowl deepened. "Billy Bob Johnson."

He glared at me. "I don't think I'll ever get over my feeling of despising him. *Despising* him."

He coughed again. And spit phlegm into a handkerchief.

Chapter 10

I took my time in going to the elevator, descending, crossing the lobby, walking down to the Mayflower Hotel, and ordering a beer at the bar.

I sipped at my beer and pondered what to do. It had been a very lousy couple of hours at Dick Ainsley's apartment.

"Another Beck's, sir?"

"Ah—no, thank you. Check, please."

"Yes, sir."

I sauntered slowly across Columbus Circle, waiting for every light, observing every traffic rule. As I crossed at the corner of Fifty-Ninth and Broadway, the same tall, lanky man I had seen earlier at Lincoln Center, still replete with top hat, white tie, cane, and red-lined cape, crossed from the other direction.

For whatever reason, I stared directly at his eyes. He avoided meeting mine.

He certainly spends a lot of time walking around, I thought.

"Hey—how are ya', how are ya'? What a sight for sore eyes—*ya' know what I mean*?"

I didn't even have to turn around. It could have been no one else but Ziggy Charles.

"Hello, Ziggy. How are you?"

"How am I? I'm great, just great. And *you*—you look great, too."

He pumped my hand with both of his, his face very close to mine.

"Hey, lemme look at ya'." He stepped back and spread his arms wide. "Great—just great. Haven't changed a bit."

Neither had Ziggy. And some might say that that was a shame.

"How about it, Babe?" Ziggy said.

"What—?"

"You know—representation. Dynamic representation. Now ya' need it more than ever."

"I'm with McIntosh and Otis," I said. "I'm happy."

"Sure, sure. Nice guys. But I'm talkin' *dynamic representation*! *Dy-nam-ic*."

"In short—you."

Ziggy laughed, hard, as if he had just heard the wittiest remark ever made.

"Hey, stop it, will ya'? Just *stop* it."

And then, very quickly, a suddenly sober Ziggy Charles, his

face a study in earnest concern, said: "You really need me, Jim. You really do."

"But you represent rock groups and comedians, Ziggy. Why, you have four guys alone with the first name of *Jackie*."

"I can represent *anything* that's good, Babe. And that's you."

"No, Ziggy, I'm—"

"Think about it, will ya'? Just—*think* about it."

"Okay," I said.

"Good." Ziggy slapped me on the back and quickly changed gears. "In from the Windy City to work on your new book?"

I must have looked surprised.

"Hey—what don't I know—*what*? *Hey*—" He snapped his fingers and his eyes brightened—"right there, I could help ya'. Titles. I'm very good with titles. Good—hell, I'm *great*. That's my forte"—he pronounced it for-*tay*—"Now don't get hurt. But this new book you're workin' on . . . it's called . . . what?"

"The working title is *People Who Have Made a Difference (And Some Who Might or Will)*."

"No offense, but it kinda just lays there, don't it? Now how about something like . . . hey, how's this?"

Ziggy stepped back, thought for a second, and proclaimed: "*Some Candy Colored*—with a *K* there—*Some Kandy Kolored, Cellophane-Wrapped, Sugar Sweet, Tell-Tale Tales*."

"It sounds a little familiar," I said.

"Sure it sounds familiar. All great titles sound familiar. That's their appeal."

I smiled.

Ziggy grabbed my arm. "Just . . . *consider* it, Babe. *Consider* it."

"Okay, Ziggy. I certainly will." I started to make my escape.

"Hey . . . *hey* . . . *HEY*."

I had to turn back.

Ziggy had an enormous smile on his face.

"I know what it is now." He cackled. "The mustache. Yeah—the *mustache*. I like it, Babe. I mean . . . I . . . *like* it."

At that moment, descending like an amorphous damp cloud, I felt my first—really—serious—doubts.

"Yeah . . . *I LIKE IT*."

He waved again. "I'll give ya' a call in a couple of days."

I waved back and tried to smile.

At least, he didn't have my phone number.

At least, that.

I took a deep breath and sighed.

I rubbed my fingers over my mustache. So . . . *Ziggy* liked it.

I sighed again.

The beginning of a broken illusion is a difficult thing to bear.

It was nearly four-thirty in the afternoon when I arrived at Maloney, O'Neil and Sasser. Maureen had made tea and there were sandwiches. I poured myself some tea.

Maureen and Libby were busy sorting personnel dossiers in Maureen's office. "Stay away. Don't bother us," Libby snarled.

"I have no intention—"

"Good."

Joe was at his desk, enjoying his own mug of tea.

"How'd it go over at RBS?"

I told him.

"This Billy Bob Johnson sounds like a real charmer," Joe said.

"He made me decide to pull out of the whole thing."

Joe looked at me for a long time, digesting what I had said, then he nodded toward Maureen's office. "Shall I call off the troops?"

"Yes. . . . No. . . . Yes. . . . I don't know. After seeing Dick Ainsley . . . well . . ."

"Yeah—?"

"I don't know."

We sipped our tea for a moment or two.

Joe broke the silence.

"I did a little work myself this afternoon."

"What?"

"Some details about that young woman who was murdered. The receptionist."

"Yeah, poor kid."

"It breaks your heart. She just got her college degree, after seven years of night school. And she was gonna get married next month."

I nodded. "I saw it in the papers."

"The bridegroom tried to kill himself this morning. O.D.'d on sleeping pills. He's okay now."

I groaned.

"They'd just met three months ago, coming out of a Gristedes of all places. The families say it was love at first sight."

I cracked my knuckles.

"His family thought *she* was wonderful—her family thought *he* was wonderful. She has the—" Joe frowned—"*had* the nicest name. Mary Frances Fahey. Pretty, huh?"

"Yeah."

I took a huge swallow of tea and stood up.

Joe stood up with me. "There's something else, too." Joe took a deep breath and swiped at his forehead with the back of his arm.

"Of course, I couldn't get a look at the Medical Examiner's autopsy report, but a buddy tipped me. It seems that the late Mary Frances Fahey used drugs on a pretty regular basis."

I sucked air through my teeth. "Hard stuff? Pot?"

"Don't know. As I say, I can't get any details. My buddy just said—*controlled substances.*"

I took another swallow of tea.

"There's one other thing—"

I turned. Joe was looking strangely at me from behind his desk.

"What's that?"

"She'd been working at RBS for just about a year. It seems that the one who recommended her for the job—and was pretty persistent down at personnel that they hire her—was—you ready?"

"Yes—"

"—Richard Ainsley."

I had nothing to say.

Joe sipped some more tea. "Here's the hardest part. It seems that there is the possibility that they were having an affair. At the very least, they were seen together an awful lot. By everybody."

"Ah, God, Joe—" I sat down.

"I know, Jimmy. I'm sorry."

"What happened after she met this young man at Gristedes?"

"You guessed it. Mary Francis Fahey was never seen once with Richard Ainsley after that."

"She broke it off right away?"

"Seems that way."

We didn't speak for a few minutes. Joe finally sat on the edge of his desk and, not too subtly, cleared his throat.

"What, Joe—?"

"Forgive my thoughts, Jimmy—I know how much you like Dick Ainsley—"

"*What*, Joe—?"

"Well"—Joe eyed me—"he's got one hell of a temper, hasn't he?"

I looked at him. I finally said: "What're you implying?"

Joe said: "What're you inferring?"

"You playing games, Joe?"

"No, Jimmy, I'm not."

I sighed. "I know," I said.

"I wish I hadn't found out. I mean—I wish it weren't true. But there it is."

"Yeah . . ."

Libby called for Joe on the intercom.

Joe shrugged. "Excuse me a second, Jimmy." A minute or two later, he came back, accompanied by Maureen and Libby.

Joe looked at me. "In or out, Jimmy?"

I sighed. "In."

He smiled. "Okay. Maureen and Libby have us pretty well organized. Now, we'd like to draw up a sort of battle plan. It'll probably take a couple of hours."

"Fine," I said.

Joe hesitated. "We thought maybe . . . you'd like to go out to dinner while we do it."

To my surprise, I was a little hurt, but I hid it pretty well. "Sounds fine to me. I'd just be in the way." The last sentence was one of the bravest things I'd ever uttered.

All three smiled self-consciously.

Libby said: "I called the service. Dr. Antonia Hastings, Susan Mazur, and Mona called in. In case you're looking for a dinner companion."

I had to smile. They had obviously decided on their plan before approaching me.

"What does Mona have to say?"

Libby consulted her pad and read the message in an intense, emotional voice, very much like Mona's. "The message just says—'please, *please, please,* call.'"

"What do you think she means by that?"

"It's hard to say."

"Maybe I'll call and find out."

"Good idea."

The three of them were clearly, awkwardly, waiting for me to leave.

"Two hours—?"

"Two hours." Joe smiled. "We'll just lay things out. Then when you come back, we'll take a fresh look at everything through your eyes."

"Fine," I said, feeling grateful to Joe for his thoughtfulness.

I crossed Fifty-Seventh and went into the Parker-Meridian. Just in case she was serious, I called Mona first.

"Hello."

"Hello, Mona. Jim Sasser."

"*Jim* . . . oh . . . you're calling . . .?" Her voice was a combination of Camille and Mimi, in the last act of *La Bohème*.

"Yes—I'm calling. I'm calling because you *asked* me to call."

"Oh, did I?"

"Yes. You did."

"Well, if I did"—her voice weakened dramatically—"then . . . thank you . . . for . . . calling."

"Yes—" I was sorry now that I had.

"I've got to see you. Or . . . I'll . . . just try it again."

It was Mona's way of gaining attention. *It* always involved the top of the Brooklyn Bridge, or the Empire State Building or, on one particularly creative call, a threat to throw herself in front of an elephant during the opening spectacular of the Ringling Brothers and Barnum & Bailey Circus.

"Mona, I'm very busy—"

"Oh, Jimmy, please—"

"I—"

"*Please—*"

Several more *pleases* later, I relented and agreed to meet for a drink.

"The Jockey Club would be fine," she said. "I've just been sitting here praying that you'd call. Just—*all alone by the telephone.* . . ."

Mona had turned the knack of making others feel guilty into something so deft, so subtle, that it was its own art form, as different and removed from other guilt creators as quantum physics is from simple arithmetic.

I was at the Jockey Club within five minutes. Twenty-five minutes later I was still there. Alone.

I went to a phone booth on the second floor and called.

"Hello—"

"Mona, where the hell are you?"

"Who's calling, please?"

"You know damn well who's calling."

There was a pause. "Then you *do* care."

"What—?"

"It's all over, James. Good-bye now. And have a most pleasant evening."

I could see the headlines. Minor novelist found dead. His last, unexplained words were "Mona . . . is a nut."

I fished out the card of phone calls that Libby had given me, selected Dr. Antonia Hastings' number, and gave it a try.

To my surprise a secretary answered. It was her office at RBS.

"Ah, yes, Mr. Sasser. Just give me a second—ah, here it is. If you're interested in dinner, please have her paged at the Algonquin Hotel. She'll be either in the bar, or in the lobby, which is a sort of lounge–"

"—thank you, I know the hotel quite well. What time did she suggest?"

The young man's voice at the other end had a pleasant smile to it. "Right about now would seem just about perfect, Mr. Sasser."

"Thank you very much."

"You're quite welcome, sir."

Dr. Antonia Hastings, Ph.D., Director of Statistical Research at the Republic Broadcasting System, was most warm and receptive on the phone.

She wanted to give me dinner, a kind of repayment for her rudeness of that first evening.

"But I told you before—you really weren't rude."

"In New England, we consider pointing a gun at someone to be just a *little bit* rude."

"Well—perhaps a bit—yes."

"Well, then"—her voice was smiling and light with a hint of laughter—"Yes? I'll make a reservation right now and see you in ten minutes."

I said: "You can be very commanding."

"Only when someone's company is extremely pleasurable. Is your answer yes?"

"Yes—"

"Good."

I was whistling softly as I came down the stairs, thoughts of Dr. Antonia Hastings, Ph.D., dancing in my head.

And I was just retrieving my hat at the door when I saw him peering into the windows.

It was the same tall gentleman, formally dressed, replete with top hat, cane, and the long red-lined cape.

I moved to the door quickly and, outside, I found him

scampering down to the corner of Fifty-Ninth and Sixth. I charged after him, and, just as the light changed, the two of us made it across Fifty-Ninth to the Central Park side. We threaded our way through heavy pedestrian traffic until, halfway down the block, he bolted back across the street and headed for the New York Athletic Club.

At that point, I was puffing and wondering if my friend with the cape was a middle-aged marathon star.

I got to the entrance of the NYAC a good minute after the man had entered.

"Your card, sir?"

"I'm not a member."

"Oh—sorry, sir." He was firm, but very polite.

"Ah—I was wondering if you could tell me the name of the gentleman who just came in ahead of me. Tall. Top hat. Red-lined cape."

"I don't believe I noticed, sir."

I pulled a twenty out of my pocket.

The attendant shook his head. Politely. Firmly. "Sorry, sir—"

Two more protests failed. I gave up. Hell . . . after all, it was only some zanny with a top hat and a cape who was following me.

Yeah . . . sure . . . but why?

Chapter 11

We assembled, as agreed, for the breakfast buffet at the Parker-Meridian the next morning.

Joe and I got there first. As we got our coffee, Joe said: "I was too tired to ask last night—but how was dinner with Dr. Toni Hastings?"

"Very pleasant."

"And—"

"And what?"

"How'd it go?"

I put on my Larchmont lock-jaw voice. "Well, *naturally,* she finds me absolutely *delightful* to be with."

Joe grinned. "Naturally—"

"She's strange, Joe—she's stunningly beautiful—"

"You're telling me—"

"—and obviously very intelligent, sophisticated, et cetera— yet when she talks to me—she's almost like a bashful schoolgirl."

Joe made a face. "I'll bet she doesn't talk that way to other men. My guess is—the lady likes you. Maybe a lot."

"Maybe."

"*That's* why she talks that way—to *you.*"

"Maybe." I poured some milk into my coffee. "I don't know."

Joe had a notebook out. "Did she tell you anything else? I mean—besides the fact that she thinks you're so delightful?"

"No."

"Did you ask her anything?"

"Of course not."

"Why not?"

"Joe—she was taking me to dinner, for God's sake."

He was dogged. "Next time—ask her."

"Why'd you write down her name?"

"*I'm* conducting an investigation."

"Okay." I grinned, and got up to get myself some cantaloupe.

At the buffet, I was joined by Maureen and Libby, who were discussing the latest Woody Allen movie, and—of course—Libby pointed out that probably at the very moment we were talking about his latest effort, Mr. Allen was hard at work, writing his next one.

"We agreed on a month, Libby."

"Why do you think I'm breaking my tail. I'm hoping to clear things up sooner."

Back at the table, Joe had ordered more coffee and was busy with yet another notebook.

But it was he who said, "Okay, everybody, let's enjoy breakfast."

Still, he put away his notebooks reluctantly.

After the table had been cleared, we spent a good half hour dawdling over coffee and reviewing the modus operandi agreed upon the night before.

It still seemed to be a good way to proceed: Joe was going to hire, on a per diem basis, a two-man former F.B.I. computer team to check out anything, and everything, in the dossiers.

I pretended to be a grizzled detective. "Computers. *Hah*. It's not like the old days." I sighed.

Joe grinned. "This can save weeks of work."

While that was going on, Joe—aided by Maureen—would start questioning employees, both fired or still working, at RBS.

I had my short list of current and former RBS people I knew well. When I finished, Joe would hit them again.

Libby would hold down the fort—but not from her study—rather, from Maloney, O'Neil and Sasser on Fifty-Seventh Street.

As we parted in front of the hotel, we had the absurdly merry air of people who were about to take part in some frolicsome scavenger hunt.

The first one on my list was *Investigative Reporter* Rafael Miguel. (I could still remember when reporters would, of course, investigate their stories, but were called, simply, reporters.)

He made his entrance into the RBS lobby exactly on time, for him—which meant, about ten minutes late by everyone else's standards.

Rafael never simply entered a room. He always made an *entrance*. He greeted me now with his man-of-destiny pose—legs wide apart, hands on his hips, head thrown back, teeth flashing, looking for all the world like the second coming of Douglas Fairbanks.

"Sasser—it's you."

I had to smile. "Yes, 'tis I."

"How *good* of you to come."

Again, I had to smile. I had made an appointment to see him, so I had not exactly come at his bidding. But if Rafael chose to see his world through rose-colored mirrors, what the hell.

He reached out suddenly and shook my hand in an extremely firm grasp. I assumed that he lifted weights; it was the latest thing to do. And if there was one trait that characterized Rafael Miguel it was that he did, wore, spoke, danced, ate, or appreciated whatever was au courant.

When I had first met him in the newsroom some twelve years before, I had christened him the a la mode kid.

Then, he had worn very long hair, shoes with soles two inches thick, and everything else that was advertised in the fashion pages and would appeal to readers of *People Magazine*.

And his various female companions of those years would always appear, hopelessly and unfortunately, garbed in whatever Bernadine Morris or Charlotte Curtis were gushing about in the fashion pages of *The New York Times*.

Now—with changing times—Miguel's hair was shorter. He wore a jacket with the obligatory wide, wide, wide shoulders, obligatory suspenders, and the obligatory mustache.

He also sported the new pirate-like boots that had just come into fashion some sixteen days before.

Releasing my hand, he stepped back and appeared to examine me. "You look great, man. Great. Love that mustache."

"Thanks—" Well, I thought, a *mustache* was okay for Raffie, too. It was all the other things, really.

"Come on up to my office—I've got plenty of time for you." He started for the elevator, stopped and turned. "I wanted to greet you myself. No sending down the secretary for best-selling author and former *colleague*"—he also loved that word—"James Sasser."

He continued to prattle as we rode up in the elevator. "Working on something big, man. Very big. A story that's going to break in about two weeks."

When I didn't question him on it, he turned—man-of-destiny pose again—and hissed triumphantly, "*Prostitution In the Cities. And—small towns.*"

"I had no idea," I said.

When we reached Miguel's office, he immediately called to a desk assistant to get us some coffee. I declined, but he ordered some anyway.

When the young woman was out of earshot, he winked and said, "Keep her on her toes."

We then settled back to talk. Talking with Rafael Miguel is very simple. He talks. You listen.

For ten minutes he rambled through a litany of his magnificent achievements during the years since we had worked together at RBS: " . . . I don't know how I got that interview, but I did . . . it was dangerous, sure but . . . imagine me with the Prime Minister of Israel . . . Prince Andrew and I—he's a nice guy, by the way . . . so I said, maybe your wife calls you Senator, but to me . . . I don't really like those White House dinners, but I go . . . I couldn't believe it—me—Rafael Miguel on the arm of Barbra Streisand, but I said . . . do you know that I get more mail than . . ."

As he paused for one split second—at about the ten-minute mark—I leaped in.

"I suppose you got the memo about me from M. Seabury Whitehead."

His eyes widened. "Oh, sure."

"That's why I'm here."

"Sure. I just thought you'd like to hear about some of the things I've been up to."

That was a genuine remark.

"It's been fascinating. But I don't want to take up all of your time."

He beamed. "Not a bit. You're not. So—where was I—oh, yeah—do you know that I get more mail than—"

I leaped in again. I said: "How do you stand with the new management, Raffie?"

He didn't answer immediately. "How do you mean?"

"Well—a lot of people are getting pink slips. It's no secret."

He frowned. "Yeah, true."

"So—has anybody made any noises your way?"

He smiled. "Billy Bob Johnson made a point of taking me to

lunch his first week here. He told me he liked my stuff. To keep it up."

"Good for you."

"Yeah—" Miguel smiled. "I like that Billy Bob. I *like* him—you know what I mean? He even gave me a few special assignments." Raffie put a finger to his lips. "That's strictly confidential. You're the only one I've told. Not even the newsroom knows—"

Raffie smiled smugly and heroically.

I took a wild shot. "That was pretty awful the other night, wasn't it? That receptionist here in the Broadcast Center."

Miguel immediately got his on-camera expression of manly grief and courageous sorrow. "It was—awful," he said. "A waste. Such a beautiful young woman."

I said: "Knowing you, you must have broken her heart a little."

He modestly demurred. "Well—"

"I hear that she and Dick Ainsley were pretty thick. But you must've gotten in there, too."

"Hey—Mary Francis was a nice girl. Really nice."

"You mean to say"—I forced a chuckle—"that a nice girl wouldn't fall for you."

He liked that. "Well—"

"I thought so—"

"Yeah, we rolled in the hay a few times. You know how it is. She was really nice. I liked her."

"A lot—?"

He paused. "Yeah . . . a lot."

"A damned shame. . . ."

"Yeah. . . ."

"You knew she was engaged to be married?"

"Yeah . . . I knew."

We talked for a few more minutes and I left. The second I got out of the newsroom and into the lobby, I pulled an index card out of my pocket and jotted down: *Mary Frances Fahey: Who knew her? Rafael Miguel . . . Dick Ainsley . . . who else?*

I resolved to buy some notebooks at my first opportunity. Joe Maloney had a good system.

On my way to Terry Jones's wing of the Broadcast Center, I passed by R. Randolph Fulton's office.

"Jimmy—say hello for a minute. I want you to meet somebody."

I smiled. There was no way for me to know who the somebody was, but I bet myself a quarter as to her sex.

I nodded to Randy's Viking goddess of a secretary and was pleased with myself that I remembered her name. "Hello, Helga, how are you?"

She smiled.

Randy corrected me. "This is Ingrid, Jimmy. Helga—ah— left last week."

We exchanged pleasantries.

A brunette, for a change, was waiting patiently inside Randy's office. Randy introduced us. Her name was Claudia. She was, of course, beautiful.

Randy was bursting with his usual energy, aided, I knew, by surges of adrenaline because he was in the midst of the hunt—for Claudia.

". . . and here I was just saying to Claudia that it might take a little time until we found the right property—a property that's worthy of her—obviously enormous talents—and you come along, Jimmy."

He then explained me to Claudia, making me sound like Hemingway and Fitzgerald with a dash of James Michener.

"We'll have lunch and talk about it, Jimmy."

I nodded.

"Claudia and I will"—he smiled at her—"really have something to talk about at dinner tonight."

I had no doubt of that.

Randy clasped the young woman's shoulder. "Until we get Claudia started in some series—or special—or whatever—I'm going to recommend her for the receptionist vacancy in the News

Wing. Give her an idea how things work and, of course, a damned nice paycheck."

I was getting better at this, I thought, as I said, "Did you recommend Mary Frances Fahey for the job?"

Randy Fulton pulled at his bow tie and looked surprised. "Why . . . you know . . . I think I did. Why?"

"Just a thought. Everybody tells me she was a special sort of person."

"Yeah—" Randy's face was suddenly sober. "Yes, she was."

Moments later, after another cascade of talk about Claudia's obviously enormous talents, I left—and immediately added V.P. of Programming, R. Randolph Fulton's name to the list on my index cards.

Terry wasn't in.

"Mr. Jones is having an extended meeting with the Engineering Department, Mr. Sasser."

"Thank you, Mrs. Clark."

Mrs. Clark was always formal but extremely cordial. She had been with Terry, through thin, and now thick, for years.

"There must be a lot of new duties now that he's Vice President of the network."

"Oh, there are. But Mr. Jones is handling everything extremely well." She smiled. "He has so much energy."

"Jimbo—"

There was no need to guess. I knew instantly. I turned to find William Big Bill Braddock bearing down on me.

Before I had time to react he had whacked me full force on my right shoulder.

"Jimbo—right on the job, I see."

"One more Jimbo and I'm off."

"Sorry. It slips out."

With his apology came another whack on the back that was too swift for me to parry.

"How are things going?"

"Fine. Just fine."

"Everybody cooperating?"

"One hundred percent."

"That's the ticket. You might mention that when you see M.S.W."

"See who?"

"The Old Man"—Braddock lowered his voice for one of the few times in his life—"You know—Whitehead."

"I'll do that."

"Good. I suppose you're on your way to see him now."

"No—"

"He said he wanted to see you."

"I didn't know."

"There's probably a message at your office." Braddock beamed. "But come on—I'll take you in myself."

I said: "I don't have time."

It took a very long time, perhaps three seconds, for that to sink in. Obviously, no one ever lacked the time when summoned to the presence of M. Seabury Whitehead.

"What'll I tell him?"

"Tell him that I just had a conversation with you—that I said that you've been a big help—given me another lead—and that I'll contact him as soon as possible."

Braddock was pleased. He squeezed me around the shoulders in a bear hug. "That's the ticket. And remember"—it was his favorite anthem—"I'm always standing right here—*Shoulder to shoulder with you.*"

I tried to sound suitably moved. "Thanks," I said.

I turned to leave him. "Good-bye, Mrs. Clark."

"Good-bye, Mr. Sasser." The corners of her eyes were crinkled in a smile she was doing her best to hide.

Chapter 12

I bought three notebooks at a stationery store on the corner, and afterward, I went to a pay phone next to it and called Joe.

Libby answered. Joe wasn't there. And she didn't expect him until the end of the day.

"You just got started a few hours ago, James."

I accepted the reprimand. "The eager amateur, I suppose."

"What a laugh?"

"Anytime."

"Mona called."

I groaned.

"Wait—she just inquired about your mental state now that you know she no longer cares."

"I hope you told her that I'm fine."

"I did. Now she's worried that you're not releasing your sadness. She offered to comfort you whenever you need it."

"Fine—"

"Hey, wait—don't hang up. Joe just popped in."

After a pause, Joe came on the line. "What's up?"

I laughed. "I don't know. I think I just wanted to tell you that I now own three notebooks."

"Good." There was something wrong with Joe's voice.

"But what's up with you, Joe?"

"Well . . . it was the hard stuff."

"I'm not following."

"Mary Frances Fahey. Her controlled-substance abuse."

"Oh . . . hard stuff, huh?"

"Yeah. . . ."

"Too bad."

"Yep . . . too bad."

We didn't talk any more about it, only about other things, until we hung up.

A voice behind me said: "Jim Sasser—how the hell are you?" I turned to find the friendly face of Charlie Bohanan grinning at me. As we shook hands he said: "Got time for a coffee?"

"Anytime with you, Charlie."

The coffee shop was one of the few places on Columbus Avenue that was more than five minutes old, and that didn't have a name like Eggs 'N' Things.

Ed's Place was just what it sounded like, and it had been a hangout for RBS for years. It was crowded, as usual, but Charlie and I found a table by the window. For the first time, looking around, waving to several editors, directors, and technicians, I felt nostalgic about the old milieu.

We each ordered coffee and Charlie asked for steak and eggs. I had to smile. I had forgotten that night or day, morning or evening, he had always ordered the same thing.

Our coffee came. "How's the best sports director in the business?" I asked.

"Out of work—"

That stopped me cold.

Charlie nodded. "Last week. I'm just putting in my time—no assignments—until the first of the month, and then it's good-bye, baby."

Charlie Bohanan was one of the top directors in the business. Football, baseball, ski jumping, Ping-Pong—Charlie did it all, and better than almost anybody.

"My God, Charlie—"

"I know. Twenty-six years."

"Is Sam still V.P. of Sports?" I was referring to Sam Bigelow, another RBS fixture, and the man responsible for the dominance of RBS Sports.

"Yeah. Northern kept him on."

"How the hell could Sam Bigelow fire—?"

Charlie stopped me. "Not his fault, Jim. Blame Northern. Don't blame Sam."

At the end of an hour, eventually sitting at the long common table with eight or nine other men from the sports department, I had the story.

A lot of men in Ed's Place that morning were out of work, in their last few week of work, or wondering, am I next?

No one blamed Sam Bigelow. Most of them had worked for him for years. Or *with* him. In over twenty years, Sam Bigelow had never said that anyone worked *for* him—it was always *with* him, and those who didn't like him a lot loved him.

Charlie Bohanan said: "The first thing Northern said to Sam was—welcome aboard Northern—and we want a twenty percent across-the-board budget cut in the sports department."

Fred Baker, a grizzled A.D. said: "Yeah, I can't blame my pink slip on Sam. It was Northern that made the specific personnel cuts."

"Did *anyone* feel vindictive toward Sam?"

"No one."

"Did anyone feel vindictive toward Northern?"

Charlie said: "I'll sum it up poetically. Yeah. Every damned one of us does."

Half an hour later, walking down Columbus, and thinking that there were a hell of a lot of people who could feel justified in threatening Northern Industries/RBS, I realized that I was one of them.

The bastards.

It was time for lunch. I'm never one who minds dining alone. I bought a copy of *Newsweek* at the newsstand on Fifty-Seventh and Eighth and headed west down the block to Le Biarritz. As usual, the place was packed.

But in the back, in a corner, three arms went up and waved. It was a table for four. Madame smiled and led me to it. Another place was set, and I forgot about my magazine.

The story was the same at lunch as it had been up at Ed's Place.

All three were RBS news correspondents I had worked with. Actually, Frank Carpenter had been London Bureau Chief at the time, so I knew him the least. But Pete D'Amico and Ralph Bates and I had rubbed shoulders nearly every week for years.

The score was: Carpenter, offered a new contract at exactly half the previous one; Pete D'Amico, fired; Ralph Bates, one year to go on his contract and wondering.

Pete D'Amico said: "I think Dick took it the hardest of any of us who was canned."

I said: "Ainsley—?"

"Yeah," Pete said. "He was always a hard drinker, but now . . ."

"He's a bitter man," Carpenter said.

"Hey—" Pete smiled ruefully—"what the hell do you think I am?"

Feeling very much like a Judas goat—I, nevertheless, made a note to add Pete D'Amico's name to my list.

Bates made a face. "The heavy drinking started a long time before he was canned."

"Yeah," Carpenter said.

Pete D'Amico said: "The girl—"

They all nodded.

"What girl—?" I thought I knew the answer.

Carpenter said: "The receptionist who was killed the other night. You hear about it?"

"Yes."

"Mary Frances Fahey. As nice as they come. Bright. Pleasant. Dick was head over heels about her."

"How did she feel about him?"

"Don't know."

"I hear that they were together a lot."

"All the time," Pete said. "But who knows. Personally, I always thought she was just being nice."

Bates said: "She'd do that. As Carp said—she was as nice as they come."

I said: "But Dick Ainsley was crazy for *her*."

Bates nodded. "Everyone knew it. It was written all over him. He acted like a twenty-year-old kid around her."

I asked: "Was it embarrassing?"

Bates hesitated. "No . . . no, I wouldn't say that. . . ."

Carpenter said: "In a way. May-December. It's nice to see, but . . . you know. . . ."

Bates said: "Christ, the minute she met that other guy . . . nice guy, too . . . Dick Ainsley went to hell. In a day . . . two days, maybe. Just like"—he snapped his fingers—"*that.*"

"Hey—" Pete D'Amico broke into a smile—"Jim, these guys were about to buy me lunch, now that I'm gainfully unemployed. I hope they include you in the offer."

Carpenter said: "That's why we waved. You're our guest, Jim."

"Then I'm buying the wine," I said. Madame appeared at my side with dispatch at the sound of the word *wine*. "I just realize that I *do* miss this business after all. I miss sitting with guys like you—having lunch, and talking."

"Hear, hear—"

I ordered a bottle of Pouilly Fuissé and, after thinking a bit more rationally, ordered two.

We talked about a million things that didn't matter. Andy Rooney and Harry Reasoner dropped by to chat a bit before they left. Walter waved from a corner table. We were all in the merriest of moods.

But over brandy I realized that Pete D'Amico was on the edge of being drunk.

His eyes, suddenly dark and angry, met mine. "Screw 'em," he said. "Screw every one of 'em at the Republic Broadcasting System."

Twenty minutes later the luncheon broke up without ever getting back on track, despite valiant efforts by everyone, including D'Amico, himself, to bring back our previous mood.

Out on the street, we all made pledges to keep in touch, and I resolved to really try, especially in the case of Pete D'Amico, who was out of work. And then I felt another pang of guilt as I remembered to write down his name on my list.

I called Libby at the office.

"Where the hell have you been?" was her first cordial remark.

"Having lunch."

"Oh, wonderful."

"It was part of the investigation."

"Okay, Sherlock Holmes, how long will it take you to get here—fast."

"I'm three blocks away."

"Good, Joe wants to talk to you."

"I'll be right over."

"Thank you, Sherlock."

I hung up with a smile.

By dumb luck I spotted the man in the red cape across the street as I passed the Art Student's League and glanced at a display of faculty paintings.

His reflection shown clearly in the window. I would never have noticed anyone else, but the red cape was a beacon. If he really wanted to follow me—and by now it was obvious that he did—why the hell the red cape and the top hat?

Trying to behave the way I imagined Joe Maloney would behave in a similar situation, I continued on down to the corner, crossed Seventh Avenue, pretended to gaze across at Carnegie Hall, then sauntered a bit farther down, and admired the new building next to the Russian Tea Room, all the while giving my man time to cross to my side of Fifty-Seventh Street.

I strolled to the end of the block, stopped in front of Wolf's Deli, then turned quickly and strode back toward him as rapidly as possible.

It caught him by surprise for a second or two. But he recovered and started to run.

Damn. I had forgotten that he was a track star.

But I got a break. Right at 119 West Fifty-Seventh—the building that housed Maloney, O'Neil and Sasser—the man fell down. I came close to catching up with him, but he managed to scramble to his feet and get into the building.

Once in, he started to run like hell again. It was obvious that he was familiar with the building's layout. He headed for the door on the opposite—Fifty-Eighth Street—side.

Again, luck was against him.

Two electricians had a ladder exactly in front of the door and it was blocked. The cape man turned back, saw me coming at him, and desperately tried to hide inside a telephone booth.

It was silly. I ran to the booth and pushed at the door. He tried to resist, but in thirty seconds it was over and I had the door open.

"I have a gun—" His voice was trembling.

"Then keep your hands right where they are, on the door."

"I'm dangerous—" I thought he was going to cry.

"Hey, Manuel—" I called for the elevator starter, a big burly young man in his twenties. "I need help."

"Coming—"

"I'm dangerous—" the man in the red cape hissed again.

Manuel easily subdued him and kept him that way for me all the way up to the fourth floor.

Coming out of the elevator, the man said: "Where are you taking me? This is false arrest."

I said: "I'm not arresting you. So it's not false."

Manuel grinned.

I opened the door to our suite and hollered. "Surprise, everybody—"

"What the hell is that—?" Libby was laughing.

I plucked my deerstalker cap off the hat rack and did a passingly good impression of Basil Rathbone: "I call it *The Case of the Man in the Red Cape.* Now go write it up, Watson, and this time be sure to get a decent publisher."

"Shall I let go of him, Mr. Sasser?" Manuel was smiling.

I glanced at Joe. "What do you think? He says he's dangerous."

Joe looked hard at the man. "You be good now. Okay, Manuel."

Manuel released the man, who brushed at his cape, as if to rid himself of any indignity caused by his temporarily embarrassing situation, drew himself to his full height, and, in as dignified voice as possible, said: "I *am* dangerous. *Very* dangerous." The effect was sadly comic.

"Yes"—Joe eyed him—"I'm sure you are."

"I also have a gun," the man said.

"Well—anybody who's dressed up in a cape with a red lining and a top hat, who's carrying a gun, has got to be considered dangerous, I suppose."

The man in the cape bowed slightly as if acknowledging a compliment.

"Hey"—Maureen called from her office—"What's all the noise—?"

As she opened her door, the man in the cape bolted, ran full force into Maureen, and hurled her back into the office along with himself.

The door had been slammed shut and locked before any of us could move.

"I've got a gun—" the man shouted again.

Joe shouted: "Maureen—"

"He's got a gun all right." Maureen's voice came very calmly from inside her office, but it was serious now.

We were suddenly all serious.

I looked at Joe. He shook his head.

I whispered to Manuel, "You'd better get out of here. I don't want to get you involved in this."

Manuel whispered back, "I'll go next door and call the police."

Libby whispered: "At least *someone* around here can think."

The scuffle started then.

It began with what sounded like a chair being thrown against the wall. Or a body hitting the wall. After that it sounded as if everything in Maureen's office was being smashed.

The whole thing lasted perhaps a minute, before the door opened and Maureen stepped out, blood on her cheek.

"Maureen—" Libby moved toward her.

"I hit my Goddamned face opening the door just now." Maureen wiped at it with a tissue.

I said: "Are you okay?"

She grinned. "Sure"—she gestured toward her office—"and Cape Man promises to be good now."

Cape Man was in the middle of the office, on all fours, blood streaming from his nose. "It's broken," he said to no one in particular. "She broke my nose."

"And here's his gun"—Maureen handed the automatic to Joe—"It looks real, but it's not. I don't know where the hell he got something like that."

Using the desk, the Man in the Red Cape—his raiment now torn and tattered—pulled himself up to his knees. "It's broken," he moaned again. "Six thousand dollars to Dr. Gelfand—and she broke his best job." He looked at me entreatingly. "Dr. Gelfand told me that *himself*. His *best* job."

He was a humbled and totally defeated man.

As Maureen and Joe were starting to pick up the mess, I shook hands with Manuel. "Thanks for your help."

"Anytime, Mr. Sasser."

I walked him to the elevator.

"I'm not going to report this," I said. "Okay?"

"No harm done to anybody."

"None at all."

I folded some bills and put them into his shirt pocket.

He reached for them and tried to hand them back. "Hey, Mr. Sasser, there's no need—"

"I know." I pretended to be angry. "That's the trouble with you, Manuel. You never let anybody say thanks."

He grinned. "Okay. And thanks."

I smiled. Nice young man.

Back in the office, the Man in the Red Cape sat quiet and subdued.

Joe yelled at him, "Take off your cape, your jacket, your vest, your shirt and your trousers."

"But," he protested weakly, "that would be—very . . . undignified."

Joe said: "You should've thought of that before you started waving around phony automatics."

Cape Man began to undress himself.

"Joe Maloney is a very compulsive man."

"I prefer the word meticulous," he said with a smile.

He searched the pockets of one garment at a time and waited until the other three of us had each, separately, gone through the same article of clothing before he moved on. It seemed like a waste of time to Libby and to me; Maureen went along with the procedure.

The cape actually did have two breast pockets inside. Empty.

The vest had several pockets. Nothing.

The cutaway jacket yielded a comb, some Kleenex, a ball-point pen and a wallet.

The wallet contained some fifty-odd dollars, a picture of a Siamese cat, several snapshots of our man, and miscellaneous cards, including a driver's license and an Actors' Equity membership card, both identifying our man as a Mr. Beauregard Jolay.

"A stage name?" I asked him.

He refused to answer.

The trousers yielded the least. Joe pulled out some change, a few more bills, a handkerchief, subway tokens—nothing more.

He handed the trousers to Libby, who dutifully went through the pockets a second time and passed them on to me; I did the search a third time and gave them to Maureen.

It was Maureen who found the little watch pocket, nearly hidden by the fold of a pleat.

There was only one thing in the watch pocket: a small folded piece of paper with, what appeared to be, two telephone numbers written on it.

Joe grinned as he took the paper from Maureen and handed it to me. "Compulsive, huh?" His grin broadened. "Meticulous."

I dialed the first number. A woman's voice answered. "Mr. Jones's office—"

I dialed the second number. A man's voice, on a recording, pleasant and friendly said, "Hello, you've reached 718–8877—"

It was Terry's voice.

I said: "Son of a gun—"

"What is it?" Joe asked.

"I don't know," I said.

Chapter 13

"Cigarette?" Terry held out the box.

"No, thanks."

The buzzer on his intercom sounded. I could hear his secretary's voice. "Mr. Jones—it's Mr. Whitehead on two."

"Excuse me—" Terry reached for his phone.

"Yes, M.S. Sure . . . got the figures right here . . . sure . . . fine. Yes, as a matter of fact, he's here now. Yes, of course . . ." Terry grinned and said to me, "Mr. Whitehead asked me to tell you that his wife loved your inscription in the book."

"Tell him I'm pleased."

Terry said: "He's delighted, M.S." He listened for a long time, scratched a few notes on a pad, and finally concluded with, "You'll have it on your desk in the morning."

I had lit my pipe during the phone conversation.

As Terry hung up, he said, "You always look so professional and serious when you smoke that thing."

"I am—"

Terry grinned. "Which? Professional or serious?"

"Serious."

He saw that I was. "What's up Jim?"

"I don't know."

He frowned.

I looked at him. Terry Jones. Corporal Terence Jones. A man who had once saved my life. I felt, suddenly, very silly.

I said: "I'm sorry, Terry."

He tried to smile. "Hey, Sergeant Sasser—are you okay?"

"I think so."

" 'Cause I don't know what the hell you're talking about."

We smiled at each other.

Terry said: "Come on, it's late. Let's go have a drink."

"First, let me tell you about this crazy bastard I've got back in the office who's been tailing me for the past two days."

I told him about Beauregard Jolay, the man in the red cape. Terry started to laugh.

"Oh, God, Jim, I should've known—let me explain Mr. Beauregard Jolay."

He got his laughter under control. "Well . . . just the way I didn't know your buddy Joe Maloney in Nam—because I got out before he got there—you didn't know Beau. He got out before you and I hooked up." Terry shook his head and grinned. "He's a good guy, Jim. About as nutty as a fruitcake, but a good guy. He works for RBS."

"As what? Resident intellectual?"

"No—as a guard."

"Dressed in a top hat and a red-lined cape."

Terry started to laugh again. "Oh, my God, really? Well, that's just his creative side. Beau's an actor. Sometimes, he works, maybe a dozen times a year, in *Make It Till the Morning*—one of our daytime soaps. The rest of the time, he's a security guard."

Terry was suddenly serious. "It's one cut I refused to make when Northern took over. I owe him."

"But why was he following me—the cape and all?"

"Oh, God, Beau *is* weird, isn't he? It gets boring for him. As you can tell, he's pretty flamboyant. So when you came aboard—"

"Temporarily—"

"—Temporarily. I asked security to assign him—temporarily—to me. I told Beau to keep an eye on you. I confess that, just to make him feel important, I told him it was a very serious matter. And that he was to tell no one. Not even you." Laughter bubbled up again and threatened to choke him. "I should have known that Beau would make it as dramatic as possible." Terry looked at me. "Really? Top hat, white tie—and a *cape*?"

"With a red lining—"

"Oh, God—" Then quickly serious, "Did he hurt anybody?"

"No. And no one hurt him."

Then I remembered his nose. "Well, he was given a very nice bloody nose by Maureen. He thinks it's broken. I doubt it."

"Oh, God. Last year he put every cent he had into plastic surgery for that."

"He'll be okay." I felt so guilty about good old Beau that I silently vowed to pay the, apparently, famous Dr. Gelfand myself for a second job, if it were needed.

"May I use your phone, Terry. Then let's have that drink."

"How about dinner, too?"

"You've got it."

I called Joe, told him to release Beauregard Jolay, and to take him right down to Dr. Sealy's office, and ask him to look at Beau's nose.

"Why so thoughtful?" Joe sighed editorially.

"He's harmless, Joe. I'll explain when I see you in the morning."

"Okay, Jim. You knocking off for the night?"

"Yeah. I'm going to have dinner with Terry."

"I guess we'll knock off, too, then."

"It's been a long day. But don't forget—"

"I know. First I'll take Twinkletoes down to see Dr. Sealy."

Terry and I grabbed a cab for Gallagher's. It was just the night to have a couple of good steaks and some beer.

As we raised our glasses, I said: "Let's not say anything serious for this entire meal."

"*That's* a toast," Terry said.

We were still sitting there nearly four hours later.

As Terry flagged down a cab on Fifty-Second Street, he said, "You're sure you don't want to share this?"

"No, thanks. I've still got a few phone calls to make."

Terry grinned. "You're certainly earning the enormous amount of money we're paying you. I'll be sure to mention your devotion to duty in my report to Mr. M. Seabury Whitehead."

"It's a personal call."

"I'll mention it anyway." He lit a cigarette.

"Thanks for dinner." I gave him a half salute. "I really enjoyed it."

Terry smiled. "Yeah, it was good to just sit and have a few beers, wasn't it."

"It was very good—"

The cab driver leaned on his horn.

Terry waved. "Good night, Sergeant Sasser—"

"Good night Corporal Jones—"

The cab pulled away.

I stood for a minute on the sidewalk, feeling pleasant and warm. Then I turned and went back into Gallagher's.

I got some change from Mike at the bar and went back to the pay phones on the wall by the door.

I called Dr. Antonia Hastings.

As the phone rang, I glanced at my watch. It was only ten-twenty.

"Hello—"

"I hope I didn't wake you up."

"No . . . who is this, please?"

"It's Jim Sasser. Thought you might invite me over for a nightcap."

She paused. "It's . . . a bit late."

I felt very, very boorish—for good reason. "I'm sorry," I said. "I just acted on impulse, and . . . I'm sorry."

"Now you don't have to be *that* contrite."

"Then may I come over? Whoops—there I go again."

She laughed. "You're a most persuasive man. Why don't you come over"—she said it breezily—"come over for *a* nightcap."

"Thank you. I'd bring roses but it's a bit late." God, I thought, I always make such idiotic remarks around her.

I got out at the corner of Sixty-Fifth and Lexington and walked the half block down to her apartment, wondering why I had done something so completely out of character (I fervently hoped) as calling up a woman, late at night, and inviting myself for a drink.

When she opened her apartment door, I didn't care why. She was wearing her hair pulled tightly back, which revealed the fine lines of her face even more than usual. And those *eyes*. Those blue eyes that seemed to fill that face.

I must have stood for rather a long moment without speaking, just gazing at her.

She flushed slightly and said, "—Yes, and good evening to you, too."

"Oh . . . good evening. Thanks for inviting me over. . . . I mean . . . thanks for accepting my invitation to myself to come over."

We both laughed. A bit nervously. But, at least, I stopped staring at her.

She poured us each a brandy. An Armagnac.

"Cheers," she said.

With those blue eyes looking into mine, I almost forgot to drink my brandy. "My God—this is wonderful."

She smiled, pleased. "My father flew in from Boston over the weekend. He always loves to have some little surprise. But this time he outdid himself. It's a 1936."

The aroma had already filled the room.

"It's . . . indescribable."

She smiled. "That's just what my father and I said."

We talked about Armagnac, Cognac, and France in general.

I felt myself teetering very close to the edge of drunkenness. And it wasn't from the drinking. It was those blue eyes.

And everything else about her. She was wearing, not one of the sensuous veils of Salome, but, rather, a simple terry-cloth robe. But still, her whole being was one overwhelming aphrodisiac.

I sighed.

"Yes—?" She looked at me questioningly.

"I was just laughing at myself."

"Why?"

"Because I was suddenly, acutely, aware of what I've been saying and what I've been simultaneously thinking."

"And you find that laughable?"

"Amusing."

"Oh—?"

"I was thinking that you're probably the most beautiful woman I've ever met in my life."

She raised an eyebrow. "And that's amusing?"

"Well, I was thinking that in great anatomical detail."

"Oh—" She blushed again and tried to change the subject. "And what have you been doing this evening that put you in such a wild mood?"

I told her about the dinner at Gallagher's with Terry.

She sipped at her brandy as I talked, her lips full and moist over the rim of the snifter, the blueness of her eyes nearly hypnotizing me.

I remembered how she had leaned over the table at the delicatessen and kissed me. I told her what I was thinking.

And I took her in my arms and kissed her.

For a moment, she returned my passion with her own, then pulled away.

"What—?"

"I didn't know that you and Terry"—she took a deep breath—"were such friends. You see . . . Terry . . ." She looked at me. "I'm very . . . fond . . . of you," she said.

An extraordinarily large bucket of ice water was slowly being poured down my back.

The evening had officially ended.

After enough chitchat to extricate me from the situation on the couch, and get me to the door, she said: "I'm sorry if I embarrassed you. It's just that"—her face flushed again—"Oh, God, Toni, but you do sound silly sometimes."

I shrugged and tried to smile.

We both laughed. Nervously.

I left very shortly after that.

There was an inviting French restaurant a few blocks down Lexington and, through the sidewalk-level windows, I could see what, for a French restaurant, was a fairly long bar.

I asked the owner if he minded if I sat at the bar and ordered only a drink.

"Of course, Monsieur. Please."

I ordered a bottle of French beer and looked around. It was fairly near closing, and most tables were finishing their meals. As a testament to the restaurant, even at such a late hour, it was nearly filled.

I sipped at my beer and wondered what it would feel like to fall in love with Dr. Antonia Hastings.

It didn't faze me at all to find the entrance door unlocked.

"Hello—"

A pleasant voice. A most pleasant voice.

If I'd been completely sober, I would never have entered, but because I wasn't, I merrily called out, "Hello—whoever you are."

"It's me."

It was Susan Mazur.

"Oh—how'd you get in?"

"I picked the lock."

"Really?"

"It was easy."

"What about the doorman?"

"I'm your cousin from Cleveland. And I have my own key."

"He believed you—"

"Of course."

She was wearing her usual impossibly tight, pelvis-crushing leather slacks and—another silk blouse.

The sight of such magnificence, of such sheer, sensual puissance of pulchritude further boggled my already boggled mind.

"What brings . . . ah, you here?" It was the best that I could do.

"I wanted to see you. Remember the other day? I gave you my address. I haven't seen you since." She smiled, a deep, marvellous smile. "And I wanted to tell you about my good luck."

"Good. Good luck is always . . . good." (At least I was making *some* sense.)

She smiled. "It seems that I'm suddenly *rich*."

"You mean *rich? Rich* rich? Or . . . rich?"

She gave out a gurgle of laughter. "I mean *rich* rich."

It was one of those stories that you read about in the papers, usually *USA Today,* or you hear about on television or radio, usually Paul Harvey.

It seems that a half uncle on her mother's side, one she had always befriended as a child, had always been kind to as an adolescent, and, later, had, out of habit, but out of kindness, too, always written letters to, had died a wealthy man.

And he had left every cent of his fortune to the "only Goddamned relative in my family that I've got any use for at all." That relative was Susan Mazur.

"My God—" was all I could say.

"It's something, isn't it. Like one of those stories. Or like a movie with Gregory Peck."

"You don't look the least like Gregory Peck."

"No, I mean—back when they made movies with real dialogue—before special effects—one of those great movies with, say, Gregory Peck—and then the leading lady would suddenly be rich—"

She did a little dance. "Well—that's me. You're the first one I've told. I don't know why, but I wanted you to be first. D'you know what this means?"

"The first thing you're going to do is quit your job."

"Anything *but.* I love my job."

"Good for you—"

"But . . . no pressure. None at all. And taxis everywhere . . . no, better yet . . . limos . . . and all the money in the world to spend. *That's* life."

"That certainly is," I agreed with feeling.

"Look," she said, "I know you're half out on your feet, but just drink some beer with me for a while and let me babble about what's happened. *Please.* I've never been rich before and *this"—* she laughed again—"this is the most fun I've had talking in my whole *life.*"

I started to laugh. Uncontrollably.

"It's got you, too, huh?"

"No," I said. "I was just thinking about Alexander Hamilton."

"Alexander Hamilton—?"

"My old high school. What would they ever have thought in those days, if we could have projected into the future, and seen me being served beer by you, easily the most sensuous woman in the world."

She twirled like a fashion model, holding her arms high above her head. "Oh, you like it, huh?"

"Lovely."

She winked. "I'll get some beer."

We drank beer, and Susan talked, for a very long time. Somehow, my eyes stayed open.

Finally, she was talked out and she leaned over me to turn out the light behind my head. "It's time for you to sleep," she said.

The last thing I remember was her reaching for the lamp, and then I was asleep.

When I awoke in the morning, she was gone.

And I was glad, again, that Susan Mazur had come to visit me. It was a lifesaving tonic, after my dreadful debacle with Dr. Antonia Hastings.

Chapter 14

Joe Maloney looked at me with a very serious expression on his face.

"D'you want my pickle?" he asked.

We were unwrapping our sandwiches from Wolf's Deli.

"No, thanks. A turkey on rye and a pickle don't mix."

Joe grunted. "Maureen—d'you want my pickle?"

"No, thanks—" came from that office.

"Nobody asked me, but I don't either," called Libby.

"I would've asked," Joe hollered back.

He got up to close his office door. "I'm off pickles. No good for you. Too much salt."

We munched away on our sandwiches for a few minutes before Joe said, "I give you credit, Jimmy. You did a helluva lot of legwork and came up with a helluva lot of information."

"But—"

"I didn't say—*but*."

"Sorry."

He took another bite and chewed for a minute. "And here's what I've got to go with it."

He reluctantly put down his sandwich and pulled out a sheaf of papers. "Now, I've been doing a lot of thinking about this maybe-it-was-maybe-it-wasn't affair between Richard Ainsley and the late Mary Frances Fahey. Okay—so he was crazy as hell for her—okay, so he's been drinkin' like a madman since she fell in love with the other guy—and, okay, so he put pressure on personnel to give her the job—we can't overlook any of this—and we won't. But let's not put blinders on ourselves either."

"I'm not following."

"Just this—" Joe took a sip from his coffee container. "Let's not assume that the threats to RBS—and the *murder*—are necessarily related."

"Ah—" I understood.

"Maybe one has nothing to do with the other. On the other hand"—Joe shrugged—"maybe it does. It's just that we have to keep lookin' both ways at the same time."

I nodded in agreement.

"So, while Dick Ainsley is still a suspect in the girl's death—even your buddy R. Randolph Fulton, V.P. of Programming—"

"Ah, come on, Joe—"

"He recommended her for the job, too, didn't he?"

"He's probably recommended a few hundred people for jobs—particularly attractive young women."

"Yeah, but this one was killed."

"Okay—"

"All I'm saying, Jimmy, is that—while we have quite a good-sized list of suspects—we keep in mind, too, that just maybe the girl's death had *nothing* to do with all the trouble at RBS."

Joe did his W. C. Fields impression, something he was very proud of: "*On the other hand*—maybe it did."

"You've really cleared the air," I said.

Joe laughed at himself. "That's me. The original *obfuscator*." He looked at me over his glasses—"I got the word from you—I looked it up."

"What do your friends at NYPD say about it?"

"My friends at NYPD are very overworked friends. Charlie MacBain—you've met him, I think—detective, big guy, red hair—"

"Yeah—"

"He thinks it was some street bums. All her jewelry was missing, her shoulder bag and wallet. And it was so brutal—"

"What'd the police do—spend five minutes on the investigation?"

"Hey, Jimmy, what d'you expect? Ask Maureen what it was like when she was on the force."

"Yeah, I suppose so." I was looking at my notes, and I started to chuckle.

"What—?"

"I told you that Raffie Miguel had the poor kid in the hay a few times—at least, according to him."

"Yeah—?"

"I was just thinking—we *know* that it wasn't Rafael Miguel who did it. Because if he had—he'd be filming his dramatic confession—complete with tears—for the evening news."

Joe's sense of humor had momentarily vanished. "When you told me—I put him on the list of suspects. And he stays there."

Joe finished his coffee. "Now comes the hard part"—he took a last bite of his sandwich and chewed for a minute—"I *think*."

He took a cigar our of his desk humidor and lit a match.

"Oh, God, Joe—"

"Just one a day, Jimmy. One a day."

I countered with my pipe. "What do you mean the hard part—you *think*."

"Well"—Joe blew a plume of smoke into the air—"You kind of see Dr. Antonia Hastings as a combination Maria Von Trapp—as played by Julie Andrews, of course—Mother Theresa, and the girl next door. Am I right?"

"Well, I wouldn't—"

"I'm right," Joe said.

He toyed with his cigar.

"So, Jimmy, that's why this is kind of hard to tell you. You see, Dr. Antonia Hastings has been a very active woman at the Republic Broadcasting System."

I said: "I know that."

Joe talked right over me. "—when she was first hired at RBS, she was a member of the Statistical Research Department. She soon—very soon—came to be *head* of that department."

"She's bright as hell, we all know—"

Joe kept going. "Her rapid rise, I suspect, was greatly aided by the fact that she quickly became Big Bill Braddock's mistress."

"That big, fat jackass—"

"I knew—I knew you cared." Joe sighed. "Then came your friend Terry Jones."

I said: "You're wrong there, Joe."

"She hopped into bed with Terry. After she left Big Bill."

"Terry would've told me. He hardly knows her."

"He *knows* her—very *well*. Believe me. Dr. Hastings made her strategic move right after the Northern take-over. When Terry was the only RBS man to be promoted."

"I'm sorry, Joe, but I just don't believe you've got it right." I thought grudgingly of what she had implied the night before.

"I know, Jimmy. You don't *want* to. But believe me, I've got it right. Right up to her latest move."

"What's that mean?"

"This young woman must read tea leaves or something. Or do statistical research on everybody she goes to bed with. I have a feeling that, despite Terry's promotion, Dr. Hastings now thinks there are better men at RBS to put her money on. Or—her body on."

"Goddamn it, Joe."

Joe held up his hands. His voice was gentle "I'm sorry, Jimmy. I really am. I apologize. No need for that last remark."

"Nevertheless, what were you driving at?"

"Dr. Antonia Hastings—"

"Joe—you don't have to use the full title every time you mention her name, for God's sake."

"Sorry. She's now the afternoon lover of the Vice President of News at the Republic Broadcasting System, that delightful and sophisticated chap—Billy Bob Johnson."

I said nothing. I smoked my pipe. Joe smoked his cigar.

I finally got up and went to the window. I watched the traffic down on Fifty-Seventh Street for a long time.

"You're sure, Joe?"

"Afraid so."

"She seems so . . . well . . . so . . . what I guess she isn't."

"Yeah," Joe said. "She really does, doesn't she."

We smoked in silence for a long time.

Ten minutes must have gone by when Maureen knocked on the door and stuck in her head. "Phone, Jim. It's Sam Bigelow."

"Thanks, Maureen."

"Hey, you elusive bastard" were his first words. "Am I the last person you're going to come around and see?"

I grinned. "How about this afternoon, Sam?"

"How about right now?"

"I've had lunch. But how about around four?"

"Good. We'll sneak out and have an early libation."

"You're on."

Sam feigned petulance. "When I got the memo about your investigation, I thought the old sports department would be first on your list. But, no—you didn't call—you didn't write—"

I laughed. "I saved the best for last."

"Hey—*good*. I always said you should be in sales. God knows you can't write."

"I'll see you around four."

"Great, Jim. See you then."

Libby was making warning gestures and holding her hand over the receiver of another phone.

"It's Mona."

I shook my head.

"She's pretending to cry—"

"Okay." I pressed the proper button and picked up. "Mona—?"

"Jimmy—oh, Jimmy—"

"Yes, Mona—"

"Jimmy, I miss you. My body is aching for you, yearning for you."

That stopped me. For one brief human moment, I pictured Mona's magnificent body—aching and yearning for me.

"Now, Mona. I thought you said you didn't care anymore."

"You must've known I was lying."

"No I didn't, I—"

"And all this time, you didn't call . . . you didn't write—"

I chuckled.

"Why are you laughing at me?"

"I'm not. It's just that a man just said the same thing to me three seconds ago."

I could hear her breathing sharply. "What . . . does . . . that *mean? What?*"

"He was joking."

"Well, I'm not. You've got to see me."

"I can't, Mona. I'm sorry, but I can't."

There was a pause. "*Is that your final offer?*" Somehow I kept from laughing.

"I'm afraid so, Mona. I simply can't see you now."

"Then I'm heading for the Brooklyn Bridge. I'll call you before I jump."

"Mona—you tried that last year, remember? There's no phone on the Brooklyn Bridge."

"Then I'll find a bridge with a phone. *Good-bye.*"

At her end of the line, she did a slam dunk.

As I hung up, Libby said, "She's starting to repeat herself. At least, before, she was always innovative."

I smiled. "Ah, Libby, Libby—what did I do to deserve this?"

"Obviously something very wicked."

Maureen said: "My, but you're popular at this hour. M. Seabury Whitehead's secretary on the line. He'd like to see you. Soon, if possible."

"Say, I'm on my way. Wait—Joe—anything else?"

Joe shrugged. "Nothing interesting. Go on. Have fun with M. Seabury."

Today M. Seabury Whitehead was no foolish buffoon; today he was very much the Chief Executive Officer of Northern Industries/ Republic Broadcasting System.

He shook my hand and said: "Thank you for coming so quickly."

I nodded and accepted the chair he offered.

Whitehead got right to the point. "I've just made a decision about releasing—"

Whitehead's intercom buzzer sounded.

"Excuse me." He picked it up. "Yes? . . . All right, put him on. Yes, Mr. Johnson . . . yes . . . all right, if your story is potentially that big, I'll see you here in . . . five minutes."

He hung up, and buzzed his secretary. "Mr. Johnson will be seeing me in five minutes." He winced. "Yes—*Billy Bob* Johnson. And would you ask Mr. Jones and Mr. Braddock to come over as soon as possible."

Whitehead turned back to me. "Sorry . . . now where was I? Oh, yes . . . I've made a decision. I'm not going to run the risk of having *The Times*, or someone else outside, breaking the story and blowing it up out of proportion. I'm going to have a release drawn up for the press, saying that there have been some minor—not serious—threats made, a few small *unrelated* fires—with no harm done—we are, of course, having them investigated—et cetera—your name will be prominently mentioned—"

I started to protest.

"—*and* the firm of Maloney, O'Neil and Sasser. Okay?"

"Fine."

"But, Sasser—?"

"Yes—?"

"I'm also seriously considering getting an additional investigating team."

"Fine," I said. "I don't blame you."

He nodded grimly.

Big Bill Braddock and Terry were just arriving as I closed Whitehead's door.

"Do you know what this is all about?" Braddock boomed.

"I imagine it's something to do with Billy Bob Johnson," I said. I glanced at Terry. "Give me a minute before you go in. Okay?"

He looked at me quizzically. "Sure—"

We moved away from Whitehead's secretary. "Why didn't you mention your affair with Toni Hastings?"

"Ah, Jim—"

"It was none of my business, I know. But, my God, there I was going on about her, and you never . . ." I tried my best to grin. "I feel stupid, Corporal Jones."

"Ah, gee, Jim—you were so excited. And it's the first time since—well, you know—that I've seen you really excited that way about anybody."

"I'm embarrassing you. I'm sorry."

"Hey, come on, buddy. I embarrassed *you*. Besides, it was all over, and"—Terry made a funny face—"it was only a little bit of an affair."

We both laughed, grateful for the laughter.

"If it ever happens again—" Terry was very solemn—"and I doubt that it ever will—but just know—if it does—" he grinned—"I'll do the same thing."

"Fuck you, Corporal Jones—"

"Fuck you, Sergeant Sasser—"

Terry ducked into Whitehead's office.

I passed Billy Bob Johnson in the hallway, dressed as usual like someone who was on his way to a rehearsal of *Grand Ole Opry*.

I said: "I hear you've got what could be a big story?"

His eyes narrowed. "Who told you?"

"Mr. M. Seabury Whitehead—"

"Oh. Well, it's big all right. *Drugs*."

"No kidding. You mean there really are such people as drug dealers—?"

"Ha—Ha—" Billy Bob sneered. "Stick to your frickin' investigation."

I bowed.

"This drug story's gonna be big. Frickin' big."

I started down the hallway again, headed for my rendezvous with Sam Bigelow.

"Hey, Jim—*Jim*."

I recognized the voice immediately. It was Kate Morgan, one of the best and brightest correspondents at RBS. "Come on in—let me take a look at you—"

We embraced. It had been a few years. "Don't run away. I've got to get this"—she waved a script—"over to P.J. Then I want to talk." She broke into a smile. "God, but it's good to see you."

"It's great to see you. And I'll be right here."

"Good—"

"May I use your phone?"

"Sure. Use anything—"

I called the office. Libby answered. Nothing new. Both Maureen and Joe were out interviewing people.

I said: "Take down a name for me."

"Have you forgotten how to say, please?"

"Please—"

"Say it as if you mean it."

"Libby, would you *please* take down a name for me?"

"Of course, Peaches, anytime."

"Buzz Berman." I spelled it. "Ask Joe if there's *anything*— and let him know that I stressed anything—at all yet on Buzz Berman. He was head of RBS News before Northern came in."

Kate came back in as I hung up. We sat and talked for a good ten minutes. Near the end, it came out that she had been making a point of seeing Dick Ainsley every day since he'd been sacked. It was typical of Kate.

"You know—just to give him someone to talk to."

I nodded.

"At least, he doesn't drink so much while I'm there." She smiled sadly. "I slow him down a little bit anyway."

"I'm sure you do."

I looked at her admiringly. "My God, Kate, how long have we known each other?"

"Who knows. A long time, Jim."

"Why the hell don't I ever attract a woman like you—?"

She smiled. "You mean black?"

"You know—"

She nodded.

I gave her a hug and a kiss—"How're the kids?"

"Fine—"

"Roy—?"

"Just made full professor."

"Do you think you two will ever—?"

"No." Kate said. "We're destined to stay . . . just friends."

I looked at Kate Morgan and thought of the contrast to Mona and Susan Mazur. "Maybe I'm just thought of as a sex object, Kate. Maybe that's the problem."

"Not by me, Jim." She covered her mouth. "*Whoops*—"

We both laughed.

"Good to see you, Kate—"

"Good to see *you*, Jim—"

I headed down the hallway toward Sam Bigelow's office refreshed.

Kate Morgan was that kind of woman.

Chapter 15

At fifty-one, Sam Bigelow was still the same weight as he had been in college. He was an ardent skier, a six-handicap golfer, a superb doubles player, excellent at chess, a winner at poker—and you still liked him.

He bounded around from behind his desk as I walked in.

"Hey, Jim"—we shook hands—"you're looking great." He grinned. "As I said on the phone, I was beginning to wonder if you were going to give me a call."

"Saved the best for last—oh, oh—I think I said that before."

"An original line like that can stand repeating."

"Saved the best for—"

"*Once*."

He offered coffee. I declined. He insisted that I try his new tobacco mixture, and, as we puffed away on our pipes, we caught up on our lives for a pleasant half hour.

When it came to Northern Industries/RBS, the conversation turned sour. Sam's story was no different from any of the others.

"They came in and cut off my balls, Jim. It was, 'Welcome aboard Northern—and here are a lot of pink slips for you to sign. Now sit down and get to work.' "

I said: "I ran into Charlie Bohanan the other day. We had breakfast at Ed's Place."

Sam Bigelow scowled sorrowfully. "Christ—there's an example. Charlie Bohanan and I worked together for *twenty-six* years, Jim."

"I know. He doesn't blame *you*, Sam."

"Christ—"

"Not a one of them blames you."

Sam looked at me hard. "You know what I feel like, Jim?"

"Knowing you, I can imagine."

"It's like—like—hell, I don't know." Sam slammed his fist on his desk. "It's like being first mate on a sinking ship, and telling your crew, sorry fellas, there's no room in the lifeboat for you—but the Captain *ordered* me to get in this one all by myself."

We sat in silence.

Finally, Sam said: "It seemed that all I did for weeks was sign those Goddamn pink slips." He leaned toward me. "You know, I even had a nightmare about pink slips. I never have nightmares, but . . ."

"They all know that Northern picked the individuals to be fired."

Sam scowled. "Talk about being a coward. You know, after the first bit of anger wore off—I was sort of glad that *they* chose the people to cut, and that I didn't have to make those decisions."

"It's not cowardly," I said. "It's human."

Sam was looking out the window. His voice grew thick. "But I handed out those slips to every man and woman myself—one at a time—in person. I owed them that, by God."

"That's you, Sam—"

"Yeah . . . at least I did that. . . ."

We smoked on our pipes.

After a few minutes of silence, I said: "You mentioned something on the phone about an early drink."

"Yeah, I did, didn't I? Sometimes, I make some sense." Sam glanced at his watch. "Well, it's early—but someplace in the world the sun has crossed the yardarm." He gave a small chuckle. "Charlie Bohanan . . . always . . . says that. . . ."

As he turned away from the window, there were sudden tears in the corners of his eyes.

I picked a hotel, with a good bar, on the Upper East Side, on the other side of the park from RBS and ABC. Sam Bigelow needed a drink with a friend at a quiet spot. He didn't need to run into any broadcast types for an hour or two.

As we raised our glasses, I asked, "How's your golf game?"

"Shot a seventy-five at Winged Foot on Sunday."

"If you weren't such a nice guy, I could hate you for that," I said.

We talked golf for several minutes. Sam Bigelow ordered a second drink and began to relax a bit.

"You know, Jim, the pleasant thought just passed through my mind that I might get just a little high tonight."

"As your physician, I'm prescribing it."

"Good"—he clinked my glass—"thank you, doctor."

"How about some dinner, too."

"You get better every minute."

"Italian—?"

"Great."

"Capriccio? . . . Or Nicola Paone? Terry took me to lunch there—"

Sam shook his head. "Isn't that something? Terry and I work in the same company, the same building. And we never seem to see each other anymore. Since they moved him out of the sports department. It's"—his scowl returned—"it's this Goddamn Northern—that's what it is. Oh—" he fished in his briefcase and pulled out a thick manila envelope—"here's the stuff you wanted from the sports department. How's your investigation coming?"

"We're getting there—"

I steered the conversation back to golf, and things were pleasant again. Sam had a third drink, while I nursed a beer.

He leaned back on the bar stool, crossed his legs, and let out a long, relaxed sigh.

"There—that's better," he said. "You're just what the doctor ordered tonight, Jim."

He noticed the direction of my gaze and grinned. "Ever since that terrorist threat we had at the Pan Am Games. The company insisted on it."

It was a holstered pistol strapped on the inside of his left ankle.

"And you still wear it?"

Sam shrugged. "These days . . . who knows? It's comforting."

An officious young man, probably an assistant manager, approached us. "Is either of you gentlemen Mr. Sam Bigelow?"

"That's me."

"You're wanted on the phone, sir."

"Thank you."

Sam smiled slightly as he put down his drink. "Why did I have to tell Agnes where I'd be? Maybe the Goddamn building is burning down."

"Shall I order you another one?"

He grinned. "Hell, yes."

When Sam was out of earshot, the bartender asked, "Is that Sam Bigelow of RBS Sports?"

"That's Sam, all right."

"I thought I recognized him. Seems like a real okay guy."

"You hit it right on the head. He's the best."

Sam was frowning when he returned. "Forget this round. I've got to get back. No debauchery tonight."

"Something bad?"

He nodded. "As usual." He pulled some bills from his pocket. "Give me a rain check, will you?"

"You've got it." I pushed his proffered bills aside. "Go ahead, Sam. I'm going to finish my beer."

"Okay—" Sam looked at me for a long moment. "Hey, Jim, it was so damn good to see you." He shook my hand. "Thanks for letting me talk so much."

He waved and turned toward the door.

I called, "Good night, Sam—"

He didn't turn. "Good night, Jim. Thanks." For the first time since I'd known him, Sam Bigelow was slightly stooped as he walked.

It was ten minutes after ten in the morning, but I was still yawning. Libby handed me a mug of tea.

"It'll help you wake up, Peaches." She grinned satanically. "And here it is, the beginning of another day and"—she pointedly drew a large X over the previous day on her calendar—"one more day has gone by in our—*sentence*."

"You're subtle," I said.

"Very."

"Any calls?"

"One. A Miss Susan Mazur. So far—nothing from your friend Mona." She pretended to snicker.

I gave Libby a quick kiss on the cheek. "Libby . . . I'm going to ask you a serious question. Why do you think women like Mona call me all the time?"

"Mona is a wo*man*. Not a wo*men*."

"She's only one of several—"

Libby eyed me.

"Well . . . a few others. One or two."

"That's better."

"But you know what I mean—why someone like Mona?"

"You mean, why women with a few loose screws call you?"

"If you want to get technical."

"I have no idea." Libby's lips curved slightly in a smile. "What's all this about?"

"Aw, I don't know. Maybe . . . well, I ran into Kate Morgan yesterday, and she's so . . . ."

"Oh, oh—hoist the Mayday flag—"

"No, no . . . it's just that . . . one of these days, I'd like to get a phone call from some woman who wasn't contemplating suicide, or a woman who didn't discuss her newly acquired wealth while wearing frighteningly clinging leather pants—"

"Don't tell me all the dreadful details, but you've obviously had a couple of rough days."

"Ah, yes, indeed. I have."

Joe Maloney came into the office. After he had poured himself a mug of tea, he brought Libby and me up-to-date on what he and Maureen had been doing.

I told him about my own adventures, and half an hour later, we left the office together, ready to do battle for another day.

Mr. Beauregard Jolay was back on duty. He was lurking under the marquee of the movie house on the other side of Fifty-Seventh Street.

I waved to him.

His expression indicated that he obviously felt that my wave was a betrayal of good manners due his profession. One should never wave at someone who was supposed to be secretly shadowing him.

Joe said: "At least his nose job wasn't ruined."

"And he's done away with the cape and the top hat."

"Yeah," Joe grunted, "but that big bandage on his nose does sort of make him stand out in a crowd. Just a bit, anyway."

I waved again.

Mr. Beauregard Jolay turned his back on us in disgust.

Joe shook my hand. "Okay, Jimmy, here we go again. We're both in for one long day of hearing everybody tell us how much they hate Northern, how things used to be, or what a son of a bitch Billy Bob Johnson is."

"Maybe one of them will say—*And that's why I want to confess.*"

"Only in the movies—" Joe started to walk away—"How about dinner tonight? I'll be seeing Maureen later. Why don't you give Libby a call?"

"You're on. See you about seven."

Actually, it was at precisely seven o'clock when Joe and I met again. Along with Maureen. But it wasn't at Maloney, O'Neil and Sasser. It was in R. Randolph Fulton's office at RBS.

Randy's place was a scene of pandemonium. One of Randy's obligatory female friends was there—someone who, undoubtedly had been waiting patiently, along with Randy, for a property worthy of her obviously enormous talents, but in this instance, the young protégée was screaming hysterically.

Randy Fulton was there, his usual sartorial perfection terribly askew, one sleeve nearly ripped off his jacket, bloodstains on his torn shirt, his nose bloodied, and a deep scratch in one cheek.

Also there was Richard Ainsley.

Joe was holding Ainsley in a double hammerlock and cursing at him to calm down.

The police arrived moments later.

We were lucky. Joe knew the lieutenant, and Maureen knew one of the sergeants from her days on the force. When the police cleared the room, they were allowed to stay.

And when, a few seconds later, both the lieutenant and the sergeant, came running back out of Terry's office and headed down the hallway, both Maureen and Joe were with them.

The explanation for everything was awful to look at.

Billy Bob Johnson lay back over his desk chair, his arms dangling on either side, his eyes bulging blankly, his tongue protruding slightly from one corner of his mouth.

A white silk scarf was wrapped around his neck.

Billy Bob Johnson, formerly Vice President of News for the Republic Broadcasting System, was very, very dead.

Chapter 16

If Groucho Marx had done it, it would have been hilarious. Jackie Gleason would probably have done it differently, but with equally amusing results. If the closet door had opened, and George Burns had been there smoking a cigar, he would only have had to say, "Hello," and everyone would have fallen to the floor with laughter.

But when the closet door of Billy Bob Johnson's office opened, and Dr. Antonia Hastings emerged, the effect was decidedly lacking in jocularity.

Her eyes, as always, emitted a blueness of almost laser intensity; but her face was strangely expressionless, almost as if she were in a trance.

No one spoke for what seemed like a very long time.

Finally: "Well, I'll be a son of a bitch," the lieutenant said.

She looked at him, but still said nothing.

"You playing hide and seek? Or is that just your way of relaxin' in the afternoon?"

She looked around the room, at the police officers and the rest of us. "Where's Billy . . . where's . . . Mr. Johnson?"

The lieutenant only stared at her.

Her face, for the first time, showed some expression. "What's happened? . . . Something's happened?"

"Something very serious," the lieutenant said.

Her gaze fixed on the disheveled desk. "Oh . . ." Her voice was almost inaudible. "Oh . . . my God. . . ."

She slumped to the floor.

Joe Maloney sat on the edge of his desk and announced, apologetically, as he lit his cigar, "On a day like this, I'm allowed one or two extras."

"Sure—" I didn't protest.

It was about eight-thirty and both Libby and Maureen had just left to have dinner together. Joe and I had decided to stay at the office awhile longer.

Joe puffed appreciatively on his cigar for a moment or two. "I'm glad Charlie's on this one. He'll be a big help."

Charlie was Lieutenant Charles MacBain. We had met him as we were leaving the RBS Broadcast Center.

Joe had introduced me as his partner, and the two of them had spoken together for a few seconds. Charlie had agreed to call Joe later in the evening.

"While we're waiting, let's draw up a list of suspects," Joe said. He chuckled. "Which, I guess, includes just about everybody *but* Billy Bob Johnson."

He pulled in an enormous blackboard from his storage room.

The first name he wrote on the board was Richard Ainsley. The second was Dr. Antonia Hastings. He was writing on a blackboard with white chalk, and yet, as I looked at her name, the chalk took on the blue hue of her eyes.

"You still with me?" Joe asked.

"Yeah . . . sure. . . ."

Joe wrote Randy Fulton's name on the board.

"Joe—he was the one we found holding Dick Ainsley."

"Until we know what the hell that was all about, we put down his name, Jimmy."

"Okay."

"Now give me the names of all the technicians, the news correspondents, et cetera, you've talked to who've been fired."

"Charlie Bohanan . . . Frank Carpenter . . . Pete D'Amico. . . ."

We went on like that for an hour. Joe had to pull out a second blackboard. He stood before it for a moment, appraising. "We almost forgot," he said. He wrote down Terry Jones's name.

"Aw, come on, Joe."

"Look, Jimmy, we're gonna take off the gloves now and play hardball. I know, I know. . . . I mixed a metaphor. But now it's hardball."

"Joe—"

"I know you've got some feelings for our dear Doctor Hastings . . . but when, for some Goddamned reason, she comes out of a closet in Billy Bob Johnson's office . . . after sleeping with Big Bill Braddock—now I know you don't like to hear this—then moving on to Terry Jones . . . then leaving Jones for the cowboy from New Jersey . . . and when"—he looked hard at me—"when the cowboy from New Jersey is found dead . . . Terry Jones's name goes on the board. *Okay?*"

"Okay," I said.

Around midnight, Lieutenant MacBain called. Joe talked to him for several minutes, occasionally making a note or two on his pad.

As he hung up, Joe said, "Well, Jimmy . . . it looks as if you and I jumped to a mighty big conclusion."

"How's that?"

"Well, so far"—he stressed the two words—"*so far*—we don't have a murder on our hands."

"He's still alive—?"

"Yep." Joe shook his head in amazement. "Those emergency guys are something. He's unconscious, but he's alive."

"I'll be damned—"

"Yep. They just let everybody go."

"What did Toni . . . Dr. Hastings have to say?"

"Well"—Joe rolled his eyes to the ceiling—"she *says* she was in the office talking to Billy Bob. She *thinks* she remembers something hitting her on the head. From behind. The next thing she knew she came to—in the closet."

"Any marks on her head?"

"Very, very slight."

"And what was that whole scene between Randy Fulton and Dick Ainsley?"

"Another funny story. Fulton says he was in his office, door closed, *interviewing*—his word—the young woman with the big—"

"—enormous talents."

"Yeah." Joe smiled. "Anyway . . . it was late, and his secretary had gone home, so when he wanted the phone number of a certain restaurant, where he'd intended to continue his interview with the young lady with the . . . enormous talents, he went out to look it up in his secretary's rolodex—"

"Yeah—?"

"He found Ainsley out there, checking out the rolodex himself."

"And the blood—"

"When he accosted him, Ainsley went bananas. Came at Fulton like a madman."

"But that doesn't mean that Dick Ainsley had anything to do with Billy Bob Johnson."

"No, and that's why the police let him go. But Charlie tells me he's going to be under surveillance twenty-four hours a day. He's their prime suspect. They'd have locked him up by now, if it weren't for a phone call in the middle of the fight."

I said: "I'm not following—"

"The young lady with the enormous et cetera, says she reached for the phone on the secretary's desk with the intent of bashing Ainsley over the head with it. As she reached for it—it rang. Knee jerk reaction—she answered it. She thought the voice said it was Johnson calling Fulton."

"Then that means Johnson was still alive when—"

"It's truly amazing," Joe said in mock wonder, "how rapidly your mind works. And here's something else for you. Randy Fulton says he saw your buddy Terry Jones walking down the hallway toward Johnson's office. About ten minutes earlier."

I said, "Did he see Terry go *into* Johnson's office?"

"No, And, of course, the police aren't going to arrest a guy for walking toward an office. But it does mean that we have enough people involved to fill *three* blackboards."

"But not Dick Ainsley now."

"Him, too," Joe said. "Just because some young, hysterical actress under stress, in the middle of a bloody fight, *thinks* a Southern sounding voice on the other end had identified itself as a Mr. *Johnson*—doesn't mean that he's not a suspect. In short, everybody is a suspect."

"Except me and thee."

"Exactly."

In unison, we said, "*And I'm not too sure about . . .*"

Joe looked at the blackboard. "Disheartening, isn't it?"

"Yeah."

Joe sighed. "What d'you say we call it a night?"

We left ten minutes later.

When I got to my apartment, there was a message on my answering machine to call Kate Morgan. "—Call up to midnight, Jim. Otherwise, give me a ring at the newsroom. I'll be in early, around eight." Kate's voice sounded very somber, very serious.

It was one-thirty. I made a note to call Kate in the morning.

The phone rang. It was Joe. He said: "Charlie MacBain just called. Johnson's dead."

"Then it's murder—"

"There you go again"—Joe's voice was chiding—"mind like a steel trap."

"Joe—?"

"Yeah?"

"I can't think of anything clever. Good night."

"Good night, Jimmy."

Chapter 17

I said to Libby, "You make the best scrambled eggs in the world. I don't know how anyone could make eggs taste this good."

Libby doffed her Red Sox cap. "It's all in the wrist," she said. "But everybody starts with the same thing—an egg."

"The wrist—that's what makes the difference."

The phone rang.

"I'll get it," Libby said. "You finish your toast and eggs."

I read all of William Safire's column while Libby chatted away in my study. When she returned to the kitchen, she said, "It's Joe on the phone."

I went into the study and picked up the phone. "Yeah, Joe—"

"I just heard from MacBain. He says that last night, in combing over Billy Bob Johnson's office, his guys got the strong suspicion that someone in a hurry had gone through the files. Now this morning, the RBS Personnel Department reports a break-in."

"Does MacBain have any ideas?"

"None. You?"

"None."

"And Jimmy—here's what Maureen and I think. To hell with the murder, that's for the police. Let's stick to figuring out who's making the threats. That's what we've been hired to do. Agree?"

"Absolutely."

"Good."

"I'll be in around noon. And so will Libby. She got me to promise that if she came over and made me scrambled eggs, the two of us would list reference stuff she can be reading for the book."

From the kitchen, came Libby's voice, "I'll resort to bribery—anything."

"Okay, see you then, Jimmy."

"Wait—"

"Yeah?"

"Anything yet on Buzz Berman?"

Joe sighed wearily. "As I have said many, *many* times, Jimmy—the second there is, I'll let you know. Okay?"

"Okay, Joe. Sorry."

"Don't be sorry—" Joe tried to sound jolly—"just try to stay off my back about Berman."

"I'll try," I said.

"Jimmy—?"

"Yeah?"

"You're not going to cry now, are you?"

"Just until I fall asleep."

"Oh, good," Joe said. "See ya'."

"See you, Joe."

At twelve-thirty, I remembered to call Kate Morgan.

"What's up?"

"I'd like to see you" was all she said.

"I'll be right over."

She lowered her voice. "No—not the newsroom. How about the deli on the corner of West End Avenue?"

"Murray's?"

"That's it."

"I'll be there in ten minutes."

"Perfect."

I ordered a corned beef on rye with mustard, and Kate had the same.

When the food came, Kate sipped at her coffee for a moment. "Jim, I'll just tell you straight out, and then we can talk about it. I'm pretty sure—"

She stopped talking, her eyes on the door behind me. I turned. It was Sam Bigelow.

I said, "Hi, Sam. Do you know Kate Morgan?"

"By reputation, certainly."

Kate said: "Jim and I used to work together when he was still at RBS."

"Kate was eleven at the time," I said.

Sam laughed.

Murry said: "Here you go, Mr. Bigelow." He placed a bag on the counter.

Sam accepted his change. "Thanks, Murray. Nice to meet you, Ms. Morgan."

Kate nodded and smiled.

"And, Jim—thanks again for the other night."

"Too short, Sam. Use your rain check soon—"

"I will—" He gave a wave and went out the door.

Kate waited only a moment before she put down her cup and said very briskly, "Here it is Jim. I'm pretty sure that the person making these threats is Dick Ainsley."

I said nothing.

"I didn't know of any other way to put it. Just straight out—I know how much you care about him."

I finally said: "You're sure . . . ?"

"Well . . ."

"You're positive?"

"No—"

"Well, then—"

"Jim, I've been over there virtually every day since he was fired. I've noticed things. The more he drank, the more obvious things became. I can't pinpoint anything exact, but . . ."

She looked at me beseechingly. "I want to be wrong—"

"I know," I said. "I'll go over and confront the old bastard."

"I'm sorry, Jim."

"I know, Kate. I know."

When he appeared at the door, Dick Ainsley looked the worst I'd seen him since it all began.

He was unshaven, the bags under his eyes were bigger than

usual and his robe was a dirty napkin. His voice betrayed his state of mind more than anything else. It was a distant voice, weak and exhausted sounding. And, of course, he was coughing.

He tried to smile. "Oh . . . Jim. Good morning."

I said: "Hello, Dick."

"Come in, come in—"

As Kate had warned, his apartment was a mess.

"I just got out of bed a few minutes ago," he said.

"If you're having breakfast, let me come back in half an hour."

"No, no. You're not spoiling my breakfast. It's too early for breakfast—let's have a drink."

I must have looked at him blankly.

Dick said: "Nick Charles—"

I shook my head.

"*The Thin Man*."

"Oh—" I nodded.

"I always loved that line. Someone asks Nick Charles if he'd like some breakfast, and Dashiell Hammett has him say, "No, it's too early for breakfast—let's have a drink.""

Dick laughed weakly, and I did my best to join him.

"Have one with me?" He had been pouring himself a glass of bourbon.

"Sure—why not?" Why not, indeed, I thought, with what I was about to do.

Ainsley poured a second glass of Jack Daniels. "Water?"

"Please."

"Can't give you any ice. Afraid I ran out." He snorted a laugh. "About a week ago."

He slumped down into an old wingback chair, obviously the place where he spent most of his time; newspapers and magazines, filled ashtrays and dirty glasses were strewn around it.

"Sit down, sit down, Jim . . . please."

I sat, still trying to figure out how to begin.

Dick Ainsley took a long swallow of his drink and smacked his lips the way bad actors in a movie will do. "Ah . . . now that's the ticket. First one today. Now I'm waking up. Had a late night last night."

I said: "I know."

He straightened slightly. "You know about last night?"

"Yes."

"All of it?"

"Yes."

"My fight with Randy Fulton?"

"Dick—I was there. I saw the end of it."

He rubbed his face with one hand. "Christ, I don't remember. I suppose I must've had quite a bit to drink when I got home . . . the police and all . . . it's no fun. . . ."

I decided right then, just as Kate Morgan had with me, that there was no nice way to put it, so I said: "It's you, isn't it, Dick? You're the one who's been making those threats."

He looked at me for a moment before he finished off his glass of bourbon. "What a funny thing to say, Jim."

"Nevertheless, it's you."

He was up and pouring another drink, his back toward me. "If I had been, Jim . . . would you blame me?"

"I don't know."

"*I don't know*—? Ah—it's so good to have steadfast friends." He coughed—once.

"Billy Bob Johnson is dead. He died six hours after they got him to the hospital."

"I had nothing to do with that."

"The receptionist . . . Mary Francis Fahey?"

A pained expression appeared on his face. "She was . . . a very special young woman."

"But you—?"

"Of course not." He sat in his chair again, but leaned out toward me. "What the hell is this, Jim. As I recall, we used to be pretty good friends. As I recall"—his voice was getting louder, more intense—"we were sitting in this very room, just a few days ago, chortling about old times together."

"Dick, I—"

"*As I recall*—I used to say to guys who talked to me like this—'*Go fuck yourself*'—"

"Dick, calm down just a bit—"

"Calm down. *Calm down.* I haven't been calm since the Northern takeover, when my friend—my *friend* "—he stared at me for a second to make his point—"told me that my name was on the axe list. That was a friend. And I'll tell you something else—he wouldn't come over here and accuse me of killing anybody. Certainly not . . ."

There were sudden tears in his eyes.

"Certainly not . . . that beautiful . . ."—his voice was growing thicker and softer—". . . that special young woman . . ." —it came out in one long sob—"*Mary Frances Fahey. . . .*"

He wept now, great spasms shaking his body.

After a very long while, he stopped. "I hurt . . ." he said. He stood. "I hurt . . ." he said again. "They kicked me out of the only thing I ever really loved. And as ignominiously as possible."

He furnished his drink with great care and poured himself another. "As ignominiously as possible," he said again. "Can you imagine . . . after thirty years . . . *thirty years* . . . being fired by some fool from Secaucus, New Jersey, who wears cowboy clothes and calls himself Billy Bob Johnson?"

"Dick . . . I'm sorry about . . . everything."

He looked at me now. "You see, Jim—when I found out that these bastards were going to wine me, and dine me in the beginning—because they needed to have me around for a few months—and then they planned—*up front*—to kick me out—I got sick. And there was rage in my heart. And I've carried that rage inside me for months."

He was silent. I waited.

"But . . . no . . . I didn't send those letters," he finally said. "What made you think that I had?"

"Does it matter?"

"No . . . I suppose not. . . ."

"But you didn't—?"

He turned his head sharply and met my eyes: "*No.* I told you . . . no."

He was silent.

"So," he sighed. "You've been going around investigating your friends. Your . . . *former* . . . friends."

We looked at each other. I stuck out my hand. "Please, Dick. I *am* your friend. Always have been."

His eyes met mine. A slight smile came to his lips, and he shook my hand. "That's good to hear, Jim," he said. "That's good to hear."

We both relaxed a bit.

I waited a long time to get nerve enough to say it: "Dick, you've been under a horrible strain—how about going for some help? Some therapy?"

"Me? See a psychiatrist?"

"Think about it."

"For friendship's sake?"

"Yeah. For friendship's sake."

He gave his half smile again. "Okay. I'll think."

"Good."

"But Johnson's murder—?"

"Your word is good enough for me, Dick. But I can't speak. . . ." I stopped myself.

"What—?"

"Well . . . the police."

He suddenly looked very uncomfortable.

"Would you like me to leave, Dick?"

"Yes . . . I think so. I'd just like to be alone now."

"I understand."

At the door, he said, "D'you see this glass?" He drained it. "If this is my last drink of the day, I'll call you tomorrow. At any rate, I'll call the next time I'm sober. I'd like to tell you something." His face clouded. "As one ex-newsman to another."

"You're on."

He smiled again. "Because in my current condition, you wouldn't put much faith in what I'd have to say, even if I told you your name is James Sasser."

"Prove it."

We both laughed.

"See you, Dick."

"Take care, Jim."

We shook hands and I left.

I called the office to ask Libby to tell everyone that I wasn't feeling well and wouldn't be in. Then I went to a bar . . . where nobody knew me . . . and I spent the rest of the day talking about baseball, football, golf . . . anything but television, radio and *ex-newsmen*.

Chapter 18

Joe Maloney was standing forlornly behind Maureen, gently kneading the back of her neck.

The two of them were staring glumly at one of the huge blackboards in Joe's office.

Finally Maureen said, "*Shit*."

Joe sighed. "I hate that word."

There was a long silence. Joe kept rubbing the back of her neck. I sipped my tea.

Maureen put down her mug, still staring at the blackboard.

"I still say, *shit*," she said.

Joe sighed again, "Yeah . . . you're right."

There were just five names listed on the blackboard. At the top of the list was the name—*Richard Ainsley*.

Joe stopped rubbing Maureen's back. "After all that work, we thought things were just beginning to pay off. Ainsley was our number one suspect."

"*Shit*," Maureen said again.

Joe frowned. "Maureen, once, under the circumstances, is okay. Twice, that's okay, too. Three times—*Enough*. Please."

Maureen nodded, her eyes never leaving the blackboard.

Joe looked at me, a pained expression on his face. "Are you sure, Jimmy? How d'you know Ainsley's not . . . well . . . not telling the truth?"

"I know—"

"Yeah, but he's not a saint. Nobody is. He can lie, can't he?"

"Sure, but he's not, Joe. Not this time."

Joe tapped his chest over his heart. "It's here that hurts."

I nodded sympathetically.

Joe lit a cigar. "But one thing's not gonna wash, Jimmy. The police are gonna be questioning Ainsley. Everybody—Kate Morgan, too. And who knows what she'll tell them." Joe sighed. "And, Jimmy—there've been *two* murders now."

"I believe him there, too, Joe. He didn't kill anybody."

"Hey—he's your friend. What the hell."

"What's that supposed to mean?"

"Nothing, Jimmy." Joe sighed again. "Well . . . let's hope that Charlie MacBain and his Merry Men solve the murder of Billy Bob Johnson—your friend isn't the man, of course"—Joe carefully averted his eyes as he said that—"and we find out—*for sure*—that someone else is making trouble at the network."

"Let's hope so," I said.

I was walking up along the park to clear my head when the limousine pulled up beside me.

It was threatening at first, until the back window came down and Susan Mazur's head poked out. "How about a ride?"

"Sure, I'd love a ride."

"Hop in."

I got in beside her and started to give the driver my address. "Uh-uh," she said. "We're going up to my place. You've *still* never been there—have you?"

"No—"

She smiled and sat back in the seat. "*My* place—not his, driver."

There was something indescribable about her apartment that made it seem to ooze eroticism from every corner.

Susan was dressed accordingly. She was wearing one of those silky blouses she seemed to favor, and the usual groin-crushing and mind-boggling leather slacks.

She read my mind. Hell, anyone could have. She smiled. "Sometimes staring isn't being rude at all."

"I'm sorry . . . I'm . . . well . . ."

She struck a maddeningly provocative pose. "Go ahead—" I thought . . . Oh, God, what I thought.

"What're you thinking?"

"It's hard to say."

"Oh, that's no good."

She opened wine and we drank as we listened to some music.

"Being rich is so much fun, isn't it?" she said.

"Yes. I suppose it must be."

"What do you mean, you suppose?" She smiled. "You're rich, aren't you?"

"No, I'm . . . well-off."

"It's so easy to get used to, isn't it? Being rich, I mean. I mean . . . it only took me about two hours."

I had to smile. "It took me just a little longer," I said.

"To get used to being . . . *well-off?*"

"Yes."

"Well, whatever you say—everyone says you're rich. *And—* everyone says you're the same guy you were in the old days. Nothing went to your head, they say."

"That's always good to hear."

She did her best to sound casual. "Since you've been back around RBS, have you had a chance to meet many friends from the old days?"

"Oh, a few."

"People like Randy Fulton and Terry Jones?"

"That's right."

"Anybody else?"

"As I said—a few."

"Uh. . . ." She tried to laugh. "Any *women* from the old days?"

"A few."

Her mouth compressed slightly in tension.

"I didn't know that Dr. Hastings had been here that long."

"She hasn't. How did you know that I'd seen her?"

"I saw you together at Des Artistes. Remember?"

"Oh yes."

"And that beautiful black woman. The correspondent."

"Kate Morgan."

"Yes, I saw you with her, too. Has it helped you any?"

"Helped with what?"

All the muscles in her face were tense now. "Well . . . your . . . investigation."

"What makes you think I'm doing an investigation?"

"Well . . . it's a rumor going around."

"Just like the rumor that I'm rich?"

"Well . . . that's no rumor, is it?"

"And seeing old friends—is no investigation. Is it?"

She looked at me.

I wondered why she was so interested in the people I'd been seeing.

Chapter 19

I got the phone call at four in the morning. It was Dick Ainsley.

"Sorry, Jim," he said. "I waited as long as I could. I was going to try to make it till six, but. . . ." He let the word hang.

"Are you okay, Dick?"

He chuckled. "No." Another rueful chuckle. "Because I haven't had a drink in . . . thirty-nine hours. That means . . . I'm *not* okay."

I rubbed at my face, trying to wake up.

"You still there, Jim?"

"Right here."

"I don't think I'm going to last much longer, Jim. I'm trying. But I don't think I can make it."

"I'll be right over."

"Jim—?"

"Yeah."

"I'm sorry."

"Hell, Dick. Cut it out. I'm coming over."

He greeted me at the door, a weak smile on his face, and an attempt at a joke. "Thirty-nine and a *half* hours," he said. Then quickly, "I'm sorry, Jim."

"*Dick*"—I held him by both shoulders—"Now, what can I do? Do you want me to call *A.A.* I've got a good friend. A physician."

Ainsley shook his head and smiled weakly again. "No, Jim. No, I was just trying to stay sober long enough to talk to you *while* I'm sober. Now I can have a drink."

He moved to a table where he had a bottle of bourbon and a pitcher of water. "Had 'em all ready," he said. "Don't have to waste a minute."

"Dick, are you sure? You've gone this long."

He smiled and glanced at his watch. "Thirty-nine hours . . . and thirty minutes . . . and *thirty-three seconds.*" He looked at me. "Would you agree that I'm stone-cold sober."

"Yes. That's why I think you ought to let me—"

He cut me off. "Good. So here goes."

He raised his glass. "Cheers—*Chaio—Chin-Chin—A votre santé—Nostrovya—Prosit*—and God Save the Queen." He drank. "*Ah—*"

He looked at me quizzically, his head cocked to one side. "Still sober?"

"Yes."

"Good. Then here goes. Something is rotten in the State of the Republic Broadcasting System."

I waited. Finally, I said, "What?"

Ainsley began to laugh. "I don't know," he said.

I had the awful feeling that Dick Ainsley had fallen over the edge.

He got himself somewhat under control. "How's that for the big scene, huh?"

"Dick—"

"No, wait—*wait*." He took another swallow, poured more bourbon into his glass, and began to pace the room. "I'm jumpy . . . I'm nervous . . . I'm scared."

"Well, sure you are. And why not? After what you've been through. Why don't you let me call—"

"No, no, *no*. Not about the drinking, God *damn* it. Can we just forget about that for a *minute*."

There was perspiration on his forehead. He wiped at it with a trembling hand. "I'm frightened because I think someone might be out to kill me."

I waited.

He drank again.

"I didn't write the letters. I told you that. Right?"

I nodded.

"Did you believe me?"

"Of course."

"Even though—I think you'll agree—I had every reason to threaten those bastards—after what they did to me—"

"Dick—"

"—And I could even have *blackmailed* a few of them, and they knew it. If I'd threatened anyone—*If* I had—I could've made it stick. It wouldn't've been just some silly threat from someone who'd been hurt, and was being lied to, and was about to be *thrown out on his ass like a common*—"

I got him by the shoulders again.

"*Dick*."

He threw his drink into my face.

And then, suddenly, he was calm again.

"Oh, my God, Jim. Forgive me."

"It's okay, Dick." I wiped at my face with a handkerchief.

"Oh, my God—"

I could hear his breathing. His eyes were bright. But his voice was low again. "But I *really—really—had* proof for blackmail."

He laughed. It was almost a cackle.

He fixed another drink for himself; his breathing was very loud now.

He raised his glass in my direction and took a deep swallow.

"Two of us were working on it. Buzz Berman assigned us to it. He was still head of news. Before the late cowboy from Secaucus.

"It was our . . . extra job. Sort of our newsroom hobby. Then we got a few lucky breaks and got hot. At that point, Buzz put the whole project undercover. It was a secret, even to the rest of the newsroom."

Ainsley growled, "Then the Great God, Northern Industries, came in, Buzz was out in two days—Billy Bob Johnson was the new V.P. of News—and I was off the project."

I waited a minute or two. "Who was the other correspondent?"

He said nothing.

"You won't tell?"

"Of course not. *I'm* in danger now. But I don't have to drag someone else in with me. Anyway—they know who was working with me."

"Who's *they?* RBS?"

He was suddenly like a little boy. "Won't you, please, have a drink with me. I feel so . . . I don't know."

"Sure. Sure I will."

Dick kept talking as I fixed myself a weak drink. "I told you I didn't write the letters. I didn't. But what if those few people believe I did. And they also think that I have the power to blackmail them . . . my God. . . ."

He was frightened to death.

"Who was the other correspondent you were working with, Dick? I could find out right away if—"

Ainsley shook his head. "It's too dangerous."

"But you're scared out of your mind. Why not tell me?"

He was dogged. "Too dangerous . . . for me, too."

I tried another tack. "What was it . . . the smoke, I mean . . . a romance? Embezzlement?"

He shook his head.

"What then?"

"Drugs."

That stopped me. "Drugs?"

He nodded. "Oh, Christ, now I *have* talked too much." His chin began to tremble.

"Who did you think it might be?"

Dick said: "I stress . . . *might* be."

"Who?"

"And I stress *if.* We were only suspicious."

"Who?"

"We had no proof."

"For God's sake, Dick, cut it out. You get me out of bed at four in the morning, I come over here to try to help—and you play games."

"I'm sorry—"

"Don't be *sorry,* Goddamn it. Just tell me."

"With the first one, we were pretty certain. But with the second one, we had no proof. We were only suspicious."

"*Dick*—in plain English—who at RBS did you suspect of having something to do with a drug operation?"

"No . . . I can't tell you who we were pretty certain of. I'd be killed for sure. Oh, Christ, why didn't I keep my mouth shut—"

In frustration, I said almost jokingly, "All right—how about someone you're *not* certain of? How about *anyone*?"

He looked at me. "Dr. Antonia Hastings," he said.

I stood there looking at Dick Ainsley. Finally, I put my glass down. "But you had no proof," I said. "You were only suspicious."

"That's right, Jim. Only suspicious."

Chapter 20

Libby adjusted her Boston Red Sox cap and sighed. "You're mad, Jim. You're terribly, terribly mad."

"I beg your pardon."

"I said you're terribly, terribly mad."

"What happened to *Loco?*"

She frowned.

"Last week you were calling me *Loco*. What happened?"

"Oh," she smiled. "I finished that Louie L'Amour book. Now I'm rereading some Evelyn Waugh."

"Ah—that explains it."

She persisted. "But why are you wearing your silly deer-stalker hat, pacing the office and looking so agitated?"

I told her about Dick Ainsley.

"Four a.m.? No wonder you look so tired," Libby said accusingly.

I blew her a kiss.

"You two sound like Mutt and Jeff," Joe said.

Libby pulled her Red Sox cap tighter on her head and went to get herself some coffee.

Maureen O'Neil came into the office fast, her eyes snapping with excitement. "The police have just picked up Richard Ainsley," she announced.

"Arrested him?" Joe asked.

"No, just for questioning."

"Goddamn it." Joe Maloney slammed down his coffee mug. "MacBain never even gave me a call."

The phone rang. Joe grabbed it.

"Hello? . . . Hello, Mac . . . what's happening?" He listened for a full minute. "Thanks, Mac. I really appreciate it." He hung up.

The three of us were waiting expectantly.

Joe said: "They've picked up Ainsley, all right. Also R. Randolph Fulton, Dr. Antonia Hastings and the brunette with the"—he grinned at me—"the—enormous—talents—who was with Fulton."

"Routine?" I asked.

Joe eyed me. "Jimmy—nothin' is ever routine. Nothin'."

The four of us sat around Joe's office, discussing Dick Ainsley.

Joe shook his head. "Jimmy, this isn't easy to say, because he was a friend of yours, and I know how loyal you are. But . . . he's pretty screwed up right now."

"I know."

"So, when he says he was onto a drug story, *possibly* involving RBS—he could be right . . . *Maybe*."

"If we could only find out who he was working with."

Joe sighed. "See what I mean, Jimmy. Ainsley wouldn't tell you. Maybe because there *wasn't* anybody else."

Libby said, "You know, sometimes it seems that—Maureen, what the hell are you doing?"

Maureen rose suddenly, and without a word, slammed the full weight of her body against the door.

"Oh, my God—" came an anguished cry from the other side.

Maureen pushed the door open, revealing the outer office. On the floor, on all fours, was Mr. Beauregard Jolay.

"You've done it again," he moaned. "My God you've done it again. I can't believe it."

He was delicately touching the tip of his nose.

Maureen moved towards him.

Beau's anguish quickly changed to fear as he leaped up. "Keep away from me. *Please*."

Joe growled. "What the hell are you doing sneaking around my office?"

"I wasn't sneaking." Beauregard Jolay's eyes never left Maureen.

"The hell you weren't."

Maureen moved only a step closer to him, but Beau gave a screech of fright and clutched at his nose.

Joe pointed a finger at him. "I want an answer. Why?"

Beau gasped. "Please—is it broken again?" he asked plaintively.

"You're fine," Joe said.

"Is there a mirror—?"

"Hey, pal—*why*?"

Beau took a deep breath. "I came . . . to tell you something." He waited.

Joe said, "And—"

"I'm . . . I'm being followed."

"Well, my goodness gracious. You're being followed. And why, pray, do you want us to know that?"

"Well . . . since . . . I'm following you"—he glanced in my direction—"and since there's no reason for anyone to be following me, I thought . . . well, that someone else was *really* following *you*." He looked pleadingly at me. "Do I make sense?"

I nodded.

Joe grunted. "Who is it?"

Beau Jolay shook his head. "I don't know."

"Man or woman?"

"I'm not sure."

Joe snorted in disgust. "Okay, shall we start all over again? What were you doing sneaking around my office?"

"That's the reason. I *swear* it." Beau lowered himself further into the corner.

"It's a limousine," he said to Joe.

"What—?"

"I'm being followed by a limousine. If—" he finished lamely, "I'm being followed."

"Okay, Maureen," Joe shook his head, "take him into your office, and we'll ask him a few questions."

"Oh, no, please. *Please*." Beau's voice rose two octaves.

Maureen moved in and grabbed Beau's arm. "Let's go—"

As the door was closing, I heard Beau's voice, "Before we start, do you have a mirror?"

I called Terry Jones and asked him to have lunch with me.

"Great—where do we meet?" Terry asked.

"Let's have it in your office."

"You're serious?"

"Yep. A sandwich and black coffee for me."

"God, you *are* serious."

"I'll see you around twelve-thirty—"

Joe and Maureen returned with their captive. They had learned nothing more from Beauregard Jolay.

In the end, the three of us spent several sympathetic minutes discussing the state of Beau's proboscis, convincing him that his profile was as dramatic as ever.

He left with the agreement that he would lurk outside and resume his surveillance of me, while, for the rest of the day, at any rate, Maureen would follow Beau.

At around noon, I walked up to RBS. Ambling across Central Park South, I remembered the Beau-Maureen arrangement, and wondered if I were the only person in the city to be under observation by a follower, who was himself being followed, and, perhaps, both were being followed by someone else. I decided that, knowing New York, I was probably only one of several persons in such a situation.

I arrived to find Rafael Miguel, himself, replete with camera and crew, in front of the RBS Broadcast Center.

"Well, if it isn't my old colleague, James Sasser." He spread his legs wide in his man-of-destiny pose, a clenched fist on his hip, his head thrown back in a flashing smile. "Hey, man. This is your lucky day. You're just in time. I'm going to do a stand-up for a big story."

"I was *feeling* lucky today," I said.

His glistening smile widened. "You got it."

He introduced me to his crew. After the greetings, he got down to the business at hand with his cameraman: "Just start wide. When I walk into frame, push in a bit. I'm going to end up on one knee. Get me there on a medium close-up."

As the crew was setting up, I asked, "What's the story?"

Raffie shook his head. "Can't talk about it. Got to save myself for the camera."

"Something you've been working on?"

"No—it just broke. About ten minutes ago."

"Another scoop?"

He laughed. "Hey, they called *me*. Not the newsroom."

It's not easy to be casual and say, "Besides your series on prostitution—what's your other long-range stuff?" But I tried. "Anything on drugs?"

He threw back his head and laughed, legs automatically in place for a Burt Lancaster–like pose. "Hey, you know I keep all my things a secret until I break 'em."

"You told me about prostitution in"—I did a breathy imitation of his dramatic delivery—"*yes, even in the small towns of America.*"

He smiled. "Hey, man, that's good." He clapped me on the back. "Hey—that just slipped out about the prostitution. I hadn't seen you in so long. I guess—even I—felt like bragging a little."

"You—brag?"

Raffie grinned. "Hey—"

"But you're not working on a drug story?"

He gave me his best pose and his finest quality, Triple-A rated Rafael Miguel laugh. "Hey, would I tell you if I were?"

"All set," the cameraman called.

Raffie was immediately all business. "Okay, start out on the sidewalk, get the RBS logo, the whole schmear. Now, as they start toward the door, you two guys"—he spoke to two uniformed guards—"will open the door so they can enter—*hey,* you're gonna be on TV, how *about* that—and then get the hell out of the way and don't let anybody in." To a third guard, he shouted, "And nobody comes out of the elevators while we're shooting, right."

He accepted a microphone from the sound man. "When we start, I'll be off camera, but I'll walk into frame almost immediately, maybe three or four seconds after we roll. Okay, here we go—"

Raffie got himself in position, tested his mike, and shouted, "Ready—and roll 'em."

"Speed—" shouted the sound man.

"And action—" Raffie waited a split second and began. "It was on this sidewalk at the RBS Broadcast Center that—"

"Cut—" It was the sound man. "Sorry, Raffie. I'd better replace the battery." Raffie was amiable. "It's okay, man. Better safe than sorry." He took his battery pack out of his hip pocket and handed it to the sound man.

While the battery was being replaced, he told me his latest

story. It began with a Cuban, a Yugoslavian, and a Scotsman at a bar in Argentina.

"Here we go, Rafael—" The sound man was finished.

"Thanks, Jake." He stuffed the unit into his hip pocket, took off his jacket while the sound man reaffixed the aerial to his shirt with gaffer's tape, and put on his jacket again, all the while continuing the story, which ended with the Argentinian bartender saying, "That's right, gentlemen . . . but that's in Uruguay."

It was a very funny story, and we both laughed, Raffie clapping me on the back several times.

The sound man had waited dutifully for the end. "Can I have a level, Rafael?"

"Sure, man—"

In a minute, they were ready to go again and Raffie was in place. "Okay—roll 'em—"

"Speed—"

Raffie, poised to begin, turned to me, repeated the punch line, and laughed a second time. Seconds later, he shouted for action, and immediately the television persona of Rafael Miguel, investigative reporter, advocate for all, concerned citizen, defender of the downtrodden, and protector of the people, was ready for the camera.

"It was on this sidewalk at the RBS Broadcast Center that . . ."—he strode into camera range, his face stern and serious, his voice husky—". . . a young woman who had just been graduated from NYU after seven years of part-time study . . . her a fiance, too . . . she probably sat at this desk . . . anguished to see . . . we'll never know . . . on this spot . . ."—As promised, he was now on one knee: if Al Jolson had been a newsman, he would have ended like that—". . . And moments ago, *I* learned that . . ."

I watched in wonder. How did he get away with it?

". . . *I* knew her, *I* cared for her, we all did, and *I* . . ."

It was amazing how often Raffie could slip the pronoun *I* into a story; I sensed the climax coming up.

". . . that man who pretended to defend her, that man who worked side by side with me at RBS News, that man who came

143

that night and—in cold blood—killed her on this very spot—killed her with his ruthless hands—that man has just confessed to the crime to detectives of the New York City Police."

Raffie, his eyes wet with tears, raised his hands, as if in prayer—making sure that he didn't block his face—and delivered his ending. "That man was Richard Ainsley, formerly of RBS News. *Richard Ainsley* . . . may God have mercy . . . on your soul."

It was stunning.

Tears now gushed from Raffie's eyes. "Quick, move in and get me a real tight shot of my face," he shouted in his normal voice. "Still rolling?"

"Still rolling—"

Tears still streaming, Raffie gave it everything he had. In a barely audible voice he whispered, "This is Rafael Miguel"—a stifled sob—"RBS News."

He collapsed in bereavement.

It was one of his finest performances.

The cameraman was apologetic. "I'm afraid we'll have to go for another take, the—"

"*Shit*," Raffie said.

After several minutes of shouts, accusations and threats, they did it all a second time.

The second time, Raffie cried even more.

Chapter 21

"Ham and cheese on rye with mustard—coming up." Terry was at his office conference table.

"I'll just have a container of coffee," I said.

"Hey," Terry looked worried, "you gotta eat."

I had to smile. "Terry, I really doubt that I'll die of chronic malnutrition if I don't eat a sandwich for the next hour or so."

"Well . . . okay." Terry handed me a container of coffee. He unwrapped his own sandwich, took a bite, and leaned against his desk. "God—" he muttered. "You had to hear about it during one of Raffie Miguel's stand-ups."

"He even cried," I said.

"Doesn't he always?"

"But on both takes."

Terry shook his head and swore. The intercom buzzer sounded.

Terry answered. "It's for you." He handed me the phone. It was Joe Maloney.

He tried to be as gentle as possible. Coming from Joe, it was very touching. "I'm sorry to tell you something like this over the phone, Jimmy, but I'm afraid I've got some pretty bad news."

"I think I know already, Joe. You mean Dick Ainsley's confession."

Joe's voice sounded relieved that I knew. "How'd you find out? It only happened a few minutes ago."

I told him about Raffie's news piece.

"Did he have the irony angle, too?" Joe asked.

"What's that?"

"About what they actually pulled him in for?"

"I'm not following."

"They pulled in everybody connected with the Secaucus cowboy's murder. But Ainsley then up and confessed to the murder of Mary Frances Fahey. MacBain tells me that Ainsley even came to them. *Before* they went to pick him up."

"They didn't suspect him at all?"

"They *had* no real suspects. Oh, sure—they had Ainsley on the list, and Rafael Miguel, and Randy Fulton, some mailman in the Bronx, a high-school sweetheart, and, just for the hell of it, her fiance even—but they had no *real* suspect."

"And Dick just up and confessed."

"Yeah. They're askin' him all kinds of questions about Billy Bob Johnson, and he just keeps shakin' his head and mumbling 'no, no, no,' and Mac says, all of a sudden, Ainsley just went kinda crazy and started ravin' about RBS and how he hated them, and how the one thing he'd had was this beautiful, young woman, and then she'd fallen in love with someone else and then—Mac says he just stopped and got all calm and everything and says, *'Yes, Officer, I killed Mary Frances Fahey.'* "

"Poor Dick Ainsley."

Joe Maloney clucked his tongue. "*Poor* Dick Ainsley killed that girl, Jimmy."

"Yeah."

"Jimmy—?"

"What, Joe?"

"Jimmy—I don't think I'm usually the kinda guy who makes a habit of hitting guys when they're down, but—in this case—I think I'd be doing you a favor by going for the knockout while you're reeling a bit."

I knew what was coming.

"Jimmy"—Joe continued doggedly forward—"Jimmy, he was a close friend. You worked with him. You respected him. You care about him. Okay. But he's also a guy who—now listen to me, Jimmy—a guy who has just confessed to the cold-blooded murder of a young woman of twenty-four who was about to be married."

"Yeah, Joe—"

"Jimmy—*fuck* poor Dick Ainsley."

"Okay, Joe—"

"It's over, Jimmy. You can feel bad for him all you want. But it's over." He gave me one more rabbit punch for good measure. "Except for whatever else he might confess to. Who knows."

"Thanks, Joe."

"Okay. Be pissed. But somebody had to spell it out for you."

"I wasn't being sarcastic."

"Okay. See you soon?"

"Yeah."

"Take care of yourself, Jimmy."

"I will, Joe."

I took a ham and cheese then. And had a beer instead of the coffee. I recited Joe's conversation to Terry.

"He's right," Terry said. He lit a fresh cigarette. "Who knows what Dick Ainsley will say next—now that he's talking."

We finished our sandwiches, and I got ready to leave.

"Where're you going now?" Terry asked.

"Back to Joe's office. I'm preparing myself for another stern lecture from Joe. And Libby. Probably even Maureen."

"Stiff upper lip and all that," Terry said.

"God knows I'll need it." I stopped at the door and snapped my fingers.

"What—?"

"I just remembered why I came. Dick Ainsley's confession put everything out of my mind . . . And, ironically, what I'm about to tell you was told to me . . . by Dick Ainsley. . . ."

I repeated what Ainsley had said. I didn't mention Dr. Antonia Hastings.

"A drug operation? Here at RBS?"

Terry started for the door. "Dick Ainsley has a screw loose—but let's go down and see Sam."

Sam Bigelow was stunned. "My God—drugs—"

"But let me stress, it was all the speculations of a man who was almost completely unhinged."

"I know, but"—Sam rubbed at his face with both hands—"Drugs. My God."

I left quickly, leaving both of them looking pretty glum.

"Uh, Jim . . ."

"I know, Sam. I don't really feel like dinner, either."

He smiled weakly. "Thanks, Jim."

I closed the office door and took a deep breath. It is always a relief to leave a wake.

I took a cab back to Joe's office. He was the only one there, sitting with his feet up on his desk, smoking his pipe.

I heard myself sigh. "It's been some day. . . ."

"Yeah . . ."

I concentrated on filling my own pipe and lighting up.

Joe cleared his throat several times. When he finally spoke he said, "I'm sorry about what I said on the phone about Ainsley."

"Forget it—"

"I'm not taking anything back—I'm just sorry I had to say it."

"It's okay, Joe."

Joe nodded.

"It's been some day. . . ." I said again.

"Yeah . . . some day."

Joe reached out and held my forearm. "Jimmy"—he was looking straight into my eyes—"you can't change anything with Dick Ainsley."

"I know, but—"

"*Anything*. He did what he did. There's no way anybody could've changed things."

We sat there for a very long time. Just smoking our pipes.

After a while, Joe got up. "Men's room," he mumbled.

When he came back, he had the message pad. He ripped off the top sheet and handed it to me.

"Forgot to tell you. This came in about ten minutes before you did. Mona. She said it's an emergency."

"The minute she wakes up in the morning—it's an emergency."

Joe grinned. "What is it with you and women?"

"I don't know. It's awful, isn't it." I was serious.

"Hey, I was just making idle chitchat. I wasn't readying myself for an analysis of your psyche."

"Ah, Joe . . . why can't a real woman get interested in me?"

"What's wrong with Susan Mazur? She's pretty real."

"No, she's not. Besides—she wants something. I don't know what it is, but that's why she's playing up to me."

"Okay—the good Doctor Antonia Hastings, then? Not bad."

"Yeah . . . I wish I could figure her out. She's a stranger one, even, than Ms. Mazur. No, I'm talking about a *real* woman, Joe. You know what I mean."

"Yeah, Jimmy . . . I do."

Joe knew I was thinking about Nancy . . . seven years now . . . and I still missed her as much as before.

We looked at each other for a moment. "You're okay, Joe," I said.

"So are you, Jimmy. So are you. . . ."

Joe opened two bottles of ginger ale and handed me one. "Charlie MacBain's gonna call me when they allow Ainsley to see people." He turned with a sheepish smile on his face. "I . . . thought . . . you'd probably want to."

"Thanks, Joe."

"Here's mud in your eye."

"Cheers."

We talked sports for half an hour. It was a relief. The phone didn't ring.

Maureen came in while I was opening our second round of ginger ale. She gave me a kiss on the cheek and relieved me of one of the bottles.

"How was the day with you and Twinkletoes?" Joe asked.

Maureen smiled a Killarney smile. "You know, he's actually a pretty nice guy. I had a chance to talk to him before I came up. He's okay."

Joe winked in my direction. "Do you usually have long conversations with people you're following?"

"You know I don't. But Beau is so . . . I don't know, childlike. Besides he did something pretty clever. And sweet."

"Oh—*Beau* now, is it?" Joe winked again.

"Yes, Beau. And stop winking at someone else when I'm talking to you. You think that's stupid in other people. And you're right." Maureen had definitely scored. "Somehow Beau managed to get ahead of me and pop out of the phone booth in the lobby as I was coming back to the office. That was clever. Then he was so sweet—"

"—he's *sweet,* all right."

Maureen shook her head in mock sadness. "And you actually think you're being clever. You poor thing. I pity you."

"Joe nothing–Maureen two," I announced.

Joe said, "Thanks." Then to Maureen, "How is he so—*sweet?*"

"Yes, I pity you," Maureen repeated. "He said he just had to compliment me. That, even though he knew I was following him, he hadn't been able to spot me once. Wasn't that—extremely—*nice* of him to say?"

"Very. But then how was he able to leap out of the phone booth and confront you?"

"He'd followed Jimmy back here. So he figured I'd be right behind somewhere. Clever, huh?"

"Yeah," Joe said. "Very. And sweet, too."

I jumped in to break it up. "What d'ya' think? Am I being followed?"

"Maybe, yes. Maybe, no. There're limousines with tinted windows all over Manhattan. I can't tell one from another." She shrugged her shoulders. "I don't know—"

Joe snorted.

"Yes—?" Maureen asked prettily.

"The answer is probably, no, he's not being followed." Joe said. "Twinkletoes my be—extremely—*nice,* but he's not playing with a full deck."

"He's a good guy," Maureen replied defensively. "He's always wanted to play Richard the Third."

It came so quickly out of left field that Joe and I had to laugh.

Maureen grew more defensive. "We just got to . . . talking about things. He says he won't give up trying to break into the theater. I like that. Guts. And he says your friend Terry Jones,"—she turned to me—"is the only person who really believes in him. Jones encourages him."

"That's the way Terry is."

"He adores Terry Jones. On top of everything else, Jones saved his life in Viet Nam."

"That makes two of us."

Maureen looked at me quizzically.

"Uh—Terry sort of did me the same favor once," I said. Inside my head and my stomach there were suddenly a million memories.

That more or less stopped the conversation.

"How about another ginger ale," I finally said.

Joe and I split one. Maureen passed, deciding on her apartment and a warm bath.

"And come in late tomorrow," Joe said as she was leaving.

"Aw, Joe." She came back to give him a bear hug and a kiss. "Good night, all," she called over her shoulder.

At the door, a devilish grin on her face, Maureen said, "Joe—"

"Yeah?"

She deliberately screwed up her face and gave *me* an exaggerated wink as she said, "Joe—you're *sweet*."

She left.

"Joe—nothing. Maureen—"

"Three," Joe said.

About ten minutes after Maureen left, the phone rang. It was Charlie MacBain, NYPD.

Joe took the call and, except for a few mumbled "Yeahs" and "uh huhs," he listened.

"Okay, Mac. Thanks. We'll talk tomorrow."

He hung up. "Ainsley's got a lawyer. A good one. Partner in a Park Avenue firm. And you can see Ainsley tomorrow if you like."

A picture of a haggard Dick Ainsley, holding a half-filled glass of bourbon in his hand, and pouring in even more, came to mind and wouldn't go away.

Joe broke the silence. "I've got a great idea, Jimmy."

"Yeah—"

"Jimmy, me boyo, let's hie ourselves over to P. J. Clark's, and have a couple of those absolutely perfect burgers, and a lot of beers, and piss in those beautiful big urinals, and talk with some of the lads, and plan to sleep late in the morning. And forget all about this—shit."

Chapter 22

I was busy replacing a light bulb when Libby came in the door all smiles.

"Ah, James, there's absolutely nothing in the world that quite matches a lovely morning in October."

I stood quickly and embraced Libby Nolan.

When I let her go, she said, "While I certainly appreciate your show of affection, I feel forced to ask—what the hell was that all about?"

I tried to sound actorish. "I shall explain myself at once."

She tipped her Red Sox cap and grinned. "Not bad. Sort of—Mick Jagger at the Old Vic."

"It was a perfect Peter O'Toole and you know it."

"As you were saying—"

"Yes, as I was saying, while I can't *stand* to be referred to as *James*—from you, it is music, indeed."

She was momentarily embarrassed. "Well . . . thank you . . . James."

"Aw, Libby—" We embraced again.

A moment later, she asked: "Are you going to see him today?" She didn't look up from the package she was unwrapping.

I thought for a moment. "I don't think so."

She glanced up, surprised.

"I've seen him four times," I said. "And he still hasn't really spoken to me."

"I thought *twice* was enough," Libby said.

I sighed. "I just thought I should keep trying."

"Why?"

"I don't know. Guilt."

"You know something, James," Libby looked up again, "sometimes you're as nutty as a fruitcake. Joe's right."

"What does Joe say?"

"The same as I do." Her smile was warm. "Look—Richard Ainsley killed a young woman. So why do *you* have to feel guilty?"

"I don't know." I shook my head. "I feel that I somehow—betrayed him."

"Betrayed him?" She snorted deprecatingly. "How?"

I looked at her, trying to frame an answer.

"How?" she asked again.

"I don't know."

"See what I mean?" She snorted a second time. "Sometimes you're as nutty as a fruitcake."

We finished our separate tasks in comfortable silence. It's good to have friends who can tell you that sometimes you're as nutty as a fruitcake.

Five minutes later, the phone rang. It was Terry Jones.

His first words were: "They've started again."

"What?"

"The letters—to everyone."

"I'm a little slow this morning, Terry."

"The threats. They've started again."

I didn't answer.

"You still there?" Terry asked.

"Yeah . . . I'm just thinking . . . then that means he didn't do it."

"What—?"

"Dick Ainsley didn't do it. He's in jail."

"Huh?"

"Just a minute." I called to Libby and caught her just as she was heading out the door. "They've started again," I said triumphantly.

She looked at me quizzically.

"The letters—the threats. And Dick's in jail. He couldn't have done it."

She didn't answer for a moment. "That's nice."

"That's *nice?*"

"He killed somebody," she answered laconically. She closed the door and left.

Back on the phone, I said to Terry, "That's great news."

Terry's voice had much more than a touch of asperity in it. "Jim—as Vice President of The Republic Broadcasting System, I'm just slightly more concerned that people in my company have received—*once again*—letters that threaten them—than I am pleased that Richard Ainsley, a confessed murderer is in jail, and, therefore, couldn't have written those letters."

I didn't answer.

"You still there?"

"Still here, Terry."

"Well, for God's sake, *say* something once in a while, will you?" Then quickly: "I'm sorry, Jim. I'm on edge."

"No need to apologize."

"Well . . . anyway, there we are. Whitehead would like to see you right away. I'm sorry about the suddeness of this. I'll owe you one."

"You won't owe me anything. When?"

"Half an hour?"

"You've got it. Where?"

"Meet me in my office. We'll go in together."

"I'll be there," I said. I started to hang up.

"*Hey*—" Terry yelled into the phone.

"Yeah?"

"Thanks, Sergeant Sasser."

"You're more than welcome, Corporal Jones."

"You look like a man who could use a cup of coffee."

It was Kate Morgan, looking as splendid as ever as she crossed the Broadcast Center lobby towards me.

"If it's with you—yes." I glanced at my watch. I had fifteen minutes before my meeting with Terry.

Kate noticed my gesture. "D'you have time?"

"Absolutely."

I followed her down the stairs to the commissary, where we got our coffee and found a table in one corner.

"I don't have to ask you, why the long face," Kate said.

"It seems to get longer every day. I've gone to see him four times. Not a peep. Has he spoken to you?"

She sighed. "He's said 'thanks' a couple of times. I take him a few things. That's all." She sighed again. "My God. Dick Ainsley—a murderer."

"Yeah . . ." I sighed myself

We were silent for a while.

Kate shook her head and smiled sadly. "I still can't believe it. I worked in the same newsroom with the man for nearly fifteen years."

"Did you ever work on a story together?"

"Sure. Dick was always willing to give a hand on anything."

"No, I mean were you ever assigned to something together?"

She thought for a moment. "No . . . never even once. Too bad. . . ."

"Yeah. Too bad . . ." I said.

Everybody was at the meeting. And every face bore a dour expression that said: *The threats have started again*.

Near the end, Big Bill Braddock tried to pick up spirits by being loud.

"Just remember, Jimbo"—Big Bill got me with a whack to the back for the third time in ten minutes—"I'm here if you need me. I'm"—I had wondered how he was going to get in his favorite phrase—"*Always—shoulder—to shoulder—with—you*."

"Thanks."

"And Jimbo—"

"Yes?"

"Ah . . . well, that's it. Count on it."

"Thanks."

Everyone moved to shake my hand, and Big Bill felt moved to slap me on the back one last time.

Apparently touched by such a show of emotion-charged unity, Whitehead rose himself to shake my hand. "We've got to end this blasted thing," he said.

"I'll do my best," I said.

"I know you will. I know." He shook his head and sighed. But as he was about to leave the room, he turned back with an obviously important afterthought: "My wife loved the book, by the way. Your first one. She'd never read it."

"Hardly anyone has. It only sold a few thousand copies."

"She had a suggestion, though. Why not—now I haven't read it, so I hope I get this right—why not have the hero be an electronics wizard, instead of an architect. I forget why. My wife can tell you."

"It's a bit late, I'm afraid," I said. "The book came out over seven years ago."

"Yes . . . yes, I suppose it is. Well, I told Edna I'd tell you, and I did."

He turned to the door again and, then, suddenly brightened. "But if you ever run into the problem again—"

"I'll remember the suggestion," I said.

"Good, *good*. I'll tell Edna."

"And tell her thanks."

"Yes—" His smile suddenly faded. "We've got to end this blasted thing," he said again.

Everyone in the room agreed.

M. Seabury Whitehead made his exit.

Chapter 23

In my dream, I was sailing somewhere off Martha's Vineyard and a telephone was ringing in the cutty cabin. When I finally woke up and turned on my reading light, the alarm clock showed five minutes past seven.

I turned it off. But it kept on ringing.

I finally got the idea and picked up the phone. "Yes—?"

"Hello, Jim?"

"Who's this?"

"It's Joe."

"Hello, Joe—what d'ya' know?"

"You're not gonna like this, Jim."

"Good. Then call me later and tell me all about it."

I hung up.

The phone rang again, immediately.

"Okay, you've got me. What?"

"I'm afraid I've got some bad news, Jim. Very bad."

I pulled myself into a sitting position. "My kids—?"

"No, no, sorry. I should've said that first. Sorry. No, it's Richard Ainsley."

"What happened?"

"He's dead, Jim."

"Oh, my God." I knew instantly what had happened. "He hanged himself."

"No—it looks as if someone killed him. Poison."

"When—?" Not that it mattered.

"They found him about an hour ago."

"Poisoned—?"

"Yeah. First guess is arsenic. They'll know for sure later this morning."

"Who did it?"

"No idea, Jim."

"Any clues?" I didn't quite know what I meant, but I asked it anyway.

"Other than the list of his visitors—there's only one. It makes no sense, and it might have nothing to do with Ainsley's death, but at this point they're not discounting anything."

"What's the clue?"

"*If* it's a clue."

"Right."

"Well, they found something sort of scratched out on a five-by-seven card in Ainsley's cell. MacBain says—by the way, I haven't seen it—in fact—"

"Right, Joe. *What—is—it?*"

"Well, apparently from the way the handwriting looks, Ainsley must have tried to write it just moments before he died."

"What did he write, Joe?"

"Oh—" Joe half chuckled. "It's probably so screwy that it's nothing—"

"*What*—did it say, Joe?"

"Well—it only said, *Penn-Columbia*. That's all."

We were both silent for a moment. I could see what Joe had meant.

Joe finally said, "Kinda sounds like an Ivy League game, doesn't it?"

"Yeah. And you were right. It's not much."

"And there was something else. Not much either, though. In the same kind of scribbled handwriting, there were three letters: *ELN*."

"Did that mean anything to anybody?"

"Nope? To you, Jim?"

"I'm afraid not."

"Well, that's it. That's all there is so far. Of course, they're combing the cell. No autopsy results yet."

"When will they have those?"

"Don't know. Wanna have some breakfast, Jimmy?"

"Good idea."

"I'm buying. Least I can do after getting you up."

"I'm grumpy as hell in the morning, Joe. Sorry."

A relieved Joe said, "McGurk's in an hour then?"

"McGurk's in an hour."

McGurk's is open twenty-four hours a day, and the atmosphere is always dynamic. At eight-fifteen in the morning nearly all of the tables and booths on the left were filled with people eating breakfast. And even at eight-fifteen in the morning, the long bar on the right was filled with mostly serious drinkers. Almost everyone in the place worked at RBS or ABC, those on the left getting ready to work, and those on the right, at the bar, news crews, reporters and editors, just finishing up an overnight shift.

Joe and I found one of the rare empty booths and ordered.

"Jim—how about a drink?"

It was Charlie Bohanen. I hadn't seen him since the day in Ed's Place, when he had just been laid off.

"Hey, Charlie, meet Joe Maloney."

Joe and Charlie shook hands.

"How about a drink," Charlie suggested a second time. He had a well-filled brandy snifter in his hand.

Joe shook his head, and I said, "It's a bit early in the day for me. Haven't even had breakfast yet."

Charlie feigned disgust. "Boy, oh boy, you guys are a lot of fun. Well—" He downed his brandy in one swallow. "I'll drink alone then. Good to see you, Jim. Nice meeting you," he said to Joe, and with a wave he turned back to the bar.

Joe and I had just finished our ham and eggs, and were on a second cup of coffee, when he was back again, a little the worse for the drinking.

"I . . . didn't want to mention it before, in case you hadn't heard. But I noticed Ruth came by your table. So I guess you know by now."

"Yes," I said. I didn't elaborate.

"Goddamn it," Charlie said. "Things sure went to hell in a hurry for old Dick Ainsley, didn't they?" He sat down with us.

We talked about Dick for a little while. Several others drifted over from the bar and joined the conversation. While we talked, Charlie Bohanen returned to the bar twice for a refill of his brandy snifter.

By the time Joe and I were ready to leave, he was drunk. "Have just one with me, Jim. How 'bout it?"

"No, thanks. We've got to run."

"Aw, come on, just one. I been up all night . . . I walk in here . . . Ruth comes in, just back from doin' a stand-up on Dick's death for the local news . . . screw breakfast, we all have a drink . . . damn. . . ."

There were tears in his eyes. Joe and I got coffee refills and moved to the bar with Charlie.

"Up all night," he said again.

"How come?" I asked.

He bridled. "Why not? Just because I'm not directing sports anymore, doesn't mean . . ."

"I didn't mean that, Charlie."

"Aw, hell . . . I know you didn't. Sorry. . . ." He finished off his brandy. "Toothache . . . killing me. I was on my way to a dentist . . . now I don't even feel it. . . ."

He ordered another double brandy and drank deeply. "I . . . didn't think it had to be. . . ."

"What had to be?" I ventured.

He looked at me questioningly, his eyes dull. "What had to? . . . Nothin'. Nothin' at all." He took a deep breath and exhaled very loudly. "Oh, boy, I think I'm drunk. . . ."

With the help of some others, I got him into a cab. Just before it drove away, he rolled down the window and peered out. "Poor Dick. Huh . . . ?"

"Yeah," I said. "Poor Dick."

Chapter 24

We walked all the way back to Joe's office on Fifty-Seventh
Street. Joe said nothing the whole way, until he closed the office
door. He had a frown on his face. "Okay, Jimmy. Just a few
questions. And I'm serious. So think it over and give me serious
answers."

I nodded.

"*One*—Do you *seriously* want to pursue the solution of who's
writing those letters? *Two*—Do you *seriously* want to investigate
Dick Ainsley's murder? Personally, I think the police are just a
little bit better equipped for that than we are. And *three* . . .
answer *one and two*—and then I'll ask three."

Joe was peering at me very intently.

"Fair enough, Joe. Number one—yes, I'd like to pursue it
about the letters. Those letters have caused a helluva lot of harm.
They might be one of the reasons that Dick Ainsley fell apart. He
ended up saying he killed the girl. Did he? I don't know. And why
did someone kill *him?* Of *course,* I don't expect to do a better job
than the police—but I *damn well* want to find out who's sending
those letters."

"That's vehement enough, all right."

"Dick Ainsley was my friend—and as his friend—no matter
what he says—*said*—until I find out more, I'm going to assume
that he *didn't* kill that girl."

"But Jimmy, he admitted it."

I took a deep breath. "I owe it to Terry *and* to him—and I
damn well owe it to myself, my own self-respect—to try to clear
his name if I can."

Joe looked at me. "Okay, Jimmy. Whatever you say. But

there's still my third question"—he grinned—"Do you have any idea where to start?"

I waited. It was hard to admit. "No—"

Joe laughed. "At least you're honest."

"But it might help if you'd locate Buzz Berman."

"We've been *trying* to find Berman, we'll *continue* to try to find Berman, and I'm sure that we probably *will* find Berman. Then what?"

"Well . . . it might help."

"Sure, Jimmy."

"*Find* him—Goddamn it."

Joe looked at me. "Sure, Jimmy."

There was suddenly a cloud of embarrassment hanging over the office. Joe eyed me quizzically. "You okay, Jimmy?"

"I'm fine," I said.

Joe stood. "What is it?"

I shook my head. "I don't know. I'm way over my head. I feel I've screwed up somehow."

Joe put both hands on my shoulders. "No, Jimmy. Not true. You've been disappointed by a friend. You're frustrated. You're sad. But you didn't screw up."

"I don't know. . . ."

The phone rang. Joe answered. It was MacBain.

"Hello, Mac . . . anything new?"

He listened for a moment or two.

"Thanks, Mac." As he replaced the receiver, he said, "It was poison, as they suspected. Arsenic. And something else."

"God—"

"He tells me—with arsenic, you can give it to a person slowly. So it affects him slowly. No sudden convulsions. Nothing. They just get weaker and weaker over a period of time. Nobody notices any dramatic changes. So no guard will say, 'Yeah, I noticed something really wrong right after so-and-so left.' "

Joe's face was grim. "And with Ainsley—well, it fit right in. For those nine days when he didn't talk to visitors, when he looked askance—no one was surprised. But whoever was doing it realized they didn't have all day. So, at the very end, they hit him with something else. Probably Veronal—the police lab is still working on it."

"What do they think about the note?"

"Mac says it was Ainsley's writing all right. And his fingerprints were on the paper *and* the pen they found. They think that maybe—*big* maybe—in his last minutes, he might have figured out what was happening and realized who did it."

"Do the police have any ideas about what the note means?"

"Nothing. Their guess was just like ours: *Penn-Columbia* sounds like an Ivy League contest of some sort. And *ELN* means nothing at all."

I had another thought. "Do you still have that unabridged dictionary I gave you."

"Sure." Joe grinned. "I keep it on a stand in the reception area to impress visitors. Why?"

"I just had an idea. ELN might be a *word*. You know: an *eln*."

"Yeah. Sounds like a unit of electricity or something."

"That's where we've been going wrong." I was suddenly very excited. "We all thought that *ELN* was a set of initials—or an acronym—and it's really a word."

My excitement lasted just long enough for me to discover that no such word exists in the English language, at least not in the one as defined by Merriam Webster and friends.

"Hey"—now Joe was excited—"Maybe it's *elm*. That's a word. It's worth a phone call to Mac—" Joe started to dial.

"And I'll call Libby. Maybe it's a word in another language."

When Libby answered, she said: "I've already heard about Ainsley. I'm sorry, James."

"Thanks."

I told her about the note.

"*Penn-Columbia* and the initials *ELN?*"

"That's what we were told. Initials. I just had the thought that it might be a word. But it's not in the unabridged."

"I'll look it up in my crossword dictionaries," Libby said. "If *Eln* isn't a word, it should be. It sounds like one of those puzzle definitions. You know—*A measuring instrument used by surveyors.*"

"And I just had another thought. Maybe its German—or Scandinavian."

"That's an idea. Let me see what I can find out."

"Thanks, Libby."

Joe was hanging up the other phone as I turned to him. "Is it a word?" he asked.

"Libby's going to work on it. What about you?"

"No dice. Mac says it's definitely E L *N*."

"It could be in anything. Finnish, maybe. Hungarian."

"Jimmy, there's one thing, though."

"What—?"

"Was your friend Ainsley given to speaking Finnish or Hungarian? In fact, did he speak anything else but English?"

"A little French, I think. You know, restaurant French."

"Well—" Joe looked doubtful.

"It's possible to know a word or two in a lot of languages without being able to speak them."

"Yeah, I guess you're right."

The phone rang.

Joe answered. "Maloney, O'Neil and Sasser . . . yes . . . let me put you on *hold* for just a minute. I'm here all alone. . . ."

To me, he said, "It's that nut case of yours—Mona."

I grabbed my cap and made for the door.

"I'm not here—I'll let you know if I have any luck."

"Luck at what—?"

"At finding any *ELN*s or at learning what Penn-Columbia game I should be buying some tickets for."

Joe waved.

"Take care, Jimmy—"

As I was closing the door, I heard Joe saying, "Sorry to keep you waiting . . . oh, yes . . . I'm sorry, he's not in just now . . . no, he's out doing research for his new book, *The Five Little Elns and How They Grew.*"

Chapter 25

At RBS personnel, I confirmed my memory: Richard Ainsley had, indeed, been graduated from Columbia University.

He had never attended the University of Pennsylvania, nor had he ever matriculated at Penn State.

I had no idea what to do with these bits of information, but as I dutifully recorded them in my notebook, it, at least, gave me the feeling of some accomplishment.

Next, I dropped by McGurk's. I was lucky; Ralph Bates was standing at the bar.

Ralph said: "After that lunch at Le Biarritz, I thought we'd be seeing a lot of you. Where've you been?"

"Odds and ends," I said. It took only a minute or two of chatter to maneuver the conversation around to Billy Bob Johnson's murder.

Ralph looked grim. "I'll even admit that when Billy Bob got it, my first thought was—good—now maybe they'll talk contract with me. No such luck."

And, inevitably, we discussed Dick Ainsley's death.

I wasn't subtle. "Did he ever talk to you about Penn or Columbia?"

Ralph laughed. "Now there's a question out of left field. But—yeah. Quite a lot. It surprised me."

"Why surprised?"

"Well . . . to tell the truth, I never saw Dick Ainsley as a guy who'd care anything at all about sports."

Ralph's face wrinkled into a sad smile. "He was crazy about fencing. Dick was on the team when he went to Columbia."

"Did he ever mention *Eln*?"

Ralph's grin widened. "Sounds like a beautiful blue-eyed

Scandinavian—like the lovely—he exaggerated a Swedish accent—*Ingrid Roberg.*"

He proceeded to give a complete description, rich in anatomical detail, of his most recent liaison, a mouth-watering young woman from the great state of Minnesota, who seemed to possess all things physical in enormous abundance.

I listened, until Ralph got to her elbows. "Elbows turn me off," I told him.

"You a prude?"

"Just about descriptions of elbows."

"If I had slides to go with my talk, you'd be interested."

"I'm sure I would. . . ."

We talked for a while longer, and I eventually made my exit.

No luck. I had learned absolutely nothing. Some private investigator.

I looked up Pete D'Amico in the phone book. We met at Ed's Place for coffee.

"I'm off the sauce for a while," he told me. "That's why it seemed wiser to meet here."

He was still without a job. He had even tried out of town. No luck.

We talked for a while. No help on Penn-Columbia. No help on *ELN*.

And I was no help to Pete.

Frank Carpenter, still troubled about being the ex-London Bureau Chief and his half-pay status, thought an *Eln* was a molecule of *DNA*. In fact, he was positive. He remembered it vividly from a biology test at Cornell.

He even went so far as to look it up in every dictionary he had, and to call the New York Public Library, before admitting defeat.

And so it went.

I spent three days, talking to everyone I knew in and out of RBS—friends at CBS, ABC, NBC, CNN, Fox—and I came up with nothing for *ELN* and a gallimaufry of Ivy League explanations for Penn-Columbia.

At the end of that third day, I called Joe Maloney.

I said: "I suppose you still haven't found the whereabouts of Buzz Berman."

"You sound surly," Joe said.

"Maybe. Have you?"

"You *are* surly. Ask me, on the other hand, if I've heard anything *about* Buzz Berman."

"I'm trying to smile, Joe," I said.

"Good—"

I pitched my voice, to a syrupy, saccharin timbre. "Why're you doing this to me, Joe?"

"You need a few laughs, Jimmy. You've been too serious lately."

I gave out a gay, light-hearted chuckle, somewhat like an operatic tenor, totally spurious. "How's that?" I asked.

"Much better."

"*Now*—have you heard anything ABOUT Buzz Berman?"

"Yeah."

"Wonderful—" And then it hit me. He really had. "How—?"

"His son Frank—"

"We should have gone there right away."

"Where the hell d'you think I went right away, Jimmy? I called Frank the afternoon you asked me to find Buzz Berman. No soap. He said he had no idea how to reach his Mom and Dad—and, at the time, he didn't. But I've been asking ever since."

"Joe, my hat's off to you—where is he?"

"The Florida Keys. Frank himself just heard from him this morning. And he called back and told his Dad you wanted to talk to him. Berman was just on his way out for some fishing—he'll call you the minute he comes back in."

I let out a long, happy sigh. "Great work, Joe."

"Persistent work, anyway. Come on over—maybe Buzz Berman will call."

"Wild horses couldn't keep me away."

"Hey, Jimmy—?"

"Yeah."

"You're the writer. I've always wondered what that means."

"What *what* means?"

"You know, wild horses, et cetera."

I smiled. "I have no idea."

"Oh . . ."

"But, I'll tell you what it means *today,* Joe."

"What?"

"It means: You're wonderful."

"Thanks, Jimmy."

We'd been in the office over an hour and the phone still hadn't rung, when Maureen entered, a triumphant smile on her face.

"I've solved one of life's minor mysteries" were her first words.

"And what might that be, pray tell?"

Her smile widened. She leaned back out into the hallway. "Beau, baby. Come on."

Beau, baby—also known as Mr. Beauregard Jolay, distinguished actor and security guard—entered the office looking extremely trepidant.

Maureen observed him proudly. "Go ahead. Tell 'em, Beau."

Beauregard composed himself, poised to speak, opened his mouth, and we heard a high, halting squeak.

"It's okay, Beau, baby." Maureen gave our Mr. Jolay a comforting pat on the back. "You can do it."

This time, Beau made it. "I think . . . I think . . . Richard Ainsley must have . . . written the threatening letters."

Maureen smiled approvingly. "Tell 'em why, Beau."

"Well . . . because they . . . stopped . . . when Mr. Ainsley was put in jail."

Joe snorted. "But they've started again."

Beau looked fearfully at Joe. "Yes, but . . . until the last . . . day he was in jail . . . there . . . were . . . *no* letters. Right?"

Joe scowled. "Yes—but now there *are.* They've *started* again."

Beau took a deep breath, moved behind Maureen, and groaned out, "That's because . . . because . . . *I've* been sending . . . this last batch."

Maureen quickly reiterated his point. "Just the *last* batch of letters. This *latest* round."

"Why?" I asked, looking at him.

Maureen answered. "This is the really embarrassing part." As if to prove that it was, Beauregard Jolay blushed.

"Why?" I asked again.

"Well . . . Beau is really . . . in his heart, I mean . . . an actor. If he can't act all the time, then something like this . . . surveillance . . . is, well, sort of the next best thing. I mean, it's not acting, but it's kind of like acting."

Joe and I were silent.

Maureen nudged Beau. Reluctantly, he spoke again.

"So when the letters stopped—after Mr. Ainsley went to jail—my surveillance job at RBS was over . . . all that I could see for myself was . . . back to being a security guard. So I . . . started to write some . . . threatening letters myself. That way"—Beau was miserable—"that way . . . well, you know . . ."

Joe and I looked at each other.

Beau whispered something into Maureen's ear.

"He says he's very sorry," Maureen said.

"That's real sweet of him," Joe said.

Maureen looked at me. "What're you going to do?"

"Tell him to stop," I said.

"He already has."

"For good."

"He has. For good."

I looked at Maureen. "You like him?"

"Beau's a nice guy," she said.

I sighed. "I'm going to give the story to Raffie Miguel."

Maureen frowned. "Aw, Jim, you can't."

I shook my head. "No—I want M. Seabury Whitehead and all the boys at Northern Industries/RBS to know that it's over."

"But, Jim—Rafael Miguel is the last person to give the story to. By the time he gets through, they'll have Beau in chains on a galley ship, somewhere in the South Seas."

"I agree," Joe said. "You want to let RBS know it's over—fine. But Rafael Miguel is bad news. He'll just *exacer-* . . ."

"*-bate*."

"Yeah—"

I smiled. "I know my man. Raffie is the *only* reporter—or as Raffie would say—the only *broadcast journalist*—I could give it to, without supplying any names, not supplying a single source, or a single detail, and still get the story out. A story that will satisfy old M. Seabury."

"How?"

"Watch. Observe. I am now going to place a phone call to Rafael Miguel, RBS News. And I shall play him like my very own violin."

I knew my man, indeed. When I got him on the phone, I had an inspiration: I purposely spoke in a whisper. A very dramatic whisper.

"Raffie, it's Jim Sasser."

"Yeah, Jim. What is it?" Without missing a beat, Raffie's voice was a whisper, too, and, of course, much more dramatic than my own.

"I've got a scoop—so naturally I called you."

"Naturally," he whispered.

Chapter 26

The stage was set.

The offices of Maloney, O'Neil and Sasser were dimly lighted. Music of a mysterious nature was playing on the tape deck.

Everyone whispered.

Joe was seated in Maureen's office, his back dramatically facing out into the reception area. Beau had staged the setting and lighting in a most dramatic way.

"I still think you're crazy," whispered an extremely reluctant Joe.

"Of course I am," I answered. "You've known that for years."

"*Shhhh*—"

He whispered again: "It's not necessary to leak the story. Just sit on it."

"It *is* necessary. We've got to plant a story that tells the world that the problem's been solved. The case is closed. Now, there's only one reporter in the world so lacking in scruples that he would do a story without sources, without background, and without facts, and—"

There was a guarded knock on the office door.

"—and, even as I speak, that man approaches. Maureen, close the door to your office. Beau—just remember to look heroic and to keep your mouth closed."

Beau nodded nervously.

I moved to the door, reached for the door handle, and had a last-second, brilliantly inventive idea.

"Maureen—Beau—put on your gloves. Hurry."

Maureen screwed up her face. "Jim, you're getting crazier and crazier."

I smiled. "This is just the sort of thing that will appeal to Raffie. He'll love it. It adds just the right extra touch of drama."

"But, what does it mean? Wearing gloves."

"How the hell do I know. But, believe me, it's perfect."

By the time there had been two more guarded knocks—I had told Raffie on the phone that he should be as quiet as possible—we were ready.

I opened the door a crack.

"Is there anyone with you?" I whispered.

His whisper was hoarse with anticipation. "Just my crew—"

I interrupted him with a gloved finger to my lips. "Have you told them why you're here?"

"No—"

"Anyone?"

"Of course not."

"Good. Thank God, I can trust you."

Raffie's face did its best to look Lincolnesque. "If you can trust anyone, you can trust *Rafael Miguel*." His voice rang with heroic sincerity.

"*Shhhh*—!"

"Sorry—" A whisper again.

"That's why I called you," I said. And I anticipated his first question. "You and nobody else. I would never even *consider* giving the story to anyone but you."

Raffie did his best to suppress his smile of pleasure.

"Put on your gloves," I commanded.

His expression was one of puzzlement. "Why?"

My whisper became so low as to be barely a whisper of a whisper. "This—must—be—kept—a—secret—"

I must say that I did that so well that it actually seemed to make sense.

"I don't think I *have* any gloves," Rafael Miguel looked worried.

"It's late October," I commented, scorn in my voice.

"I just don't happen to have any with me."

"How about your crew?"

"I'll ask."

As he turned away to consult with his film crew, I closed the door again, forcing him to repeat a guarded knock, and allowing myself the pleasure of censuring him yet again for employing too loud a whisper.

So far, it was fun.

He had gloves now. Much too large. But once he donned them, I allowed him to enter the office.

As I closed the door, he said, "What about my crew?"

I shook my head. "Not on your life."

"Aw, but, Jim—"

"There's no way. Just you. You're the only one to see this man—"

"But how am I going to shoot a story?"

"Raffie, you can do it. I have faith in you. I've seen you produce some great stories before with a lot less to go on." And my antic mood made me add, "In fact, with almost *nothing* to go on."

He nodded. "Yeah. Let me learn what's what. I'll figure out a way to shoot it."

"That's the spirit."

Raffie's chin rose several millimeters.

I became suddenly brisk. "Well, let's get on with it." I introduced him to Maureen—and to Mr. Beauregard Jolay. "He's one of the heroes of the solution," I said. "Of course, his actual role can never be revealed. But, just for a spot of color, Raffie, he's an RBS employee." What the hell, I thought, Beau could use a little positive publicity.

The whispered introductions took only a few seconds. Still brisk, I said: "Okay, Maureen, open the door." And to Raffie, "He's in a straight jacket—don't worry."

Maureen opened the door, very slowly, revealing her dramatically lit office, the chair, the back, the figure apparently trussed and tied, wearing a huge, wide-brimmed fedora, actually Beau's own, and looking for all the world like a larger-than-life reincarnation of some long forgotten Gothic menace.

"There's your man, Raffie." For dramatic effect, I added, "The poor devil."

"What do I say?" Raffie asked, for the first time since I had known him, *nearly* at a loss for words.

"Just tell him that you're here. That it's really you. It'll make him happy. Soothe him, *poor devil*—he only turned himself in to Mr. Jolay, here, once he knew that you'd visit him. And that you'd be the one to tell the world that he's no longer a menace."

Raffie stood a bit taller and thrust out his chin. His whisper was stentorian and strong—for a whisper. "Whoever you are—*I* am here. Your story will be told—by Rafael Miguel. Have no fear. *Rafael—Miguel*—is with you."

Raffie relaxed and looked at me. He lowered his whisper. "How was that?"

"Beautiful. Inspiring."

He preened. "You really think so?"

"Of course."

He braced himself a second time. "Maybe I should give him another shot."

"I think that that was fine—"

But Raffie had already let fly with a second salvo. "Your secret is safe with *me*. *Rafael Miguel* will never reveal who you are." Raffie had momentarily forgotten that he had never known the name of the figure in the first place.

At that point, Joe almost ruined everything by letting out a long, low moan worthy of Hamlet's father's ghost.

But Raffie responded in kind. "And I salute you, too, brave man. *Rafael Miguel* salutes you." He stepped back and whispered into my ear, "My God, talk about great communicators, I can even interface with loonies in straight jackets."

I nodded in apparent admiration. "Remarkable," I said, gently backing him out of the room and motioning to Maureen to close the door.

"Now do you want the full story?" I asked.

"You bet. Shoot." Raffie pulled out his notebook. "Uh—Jim—?"

"Yeah—?"

"Can I take off my gloves to write? It's pretty difficult with gloves."

"One glove," I said, in another burst of creative genius.

Raffie complied, an expression of gratitude on his face.

I waited until he had sat at the reception desk, pencil poised, before I began. "He's from a wealthy—and *nameless*—family. He has never done anything like this before. Then came the breakdown. The family, now that it knows of his problem, will see that he's well taken care of and benevolently incarcerated for the rest of his life. But thank God for you, Raffie—"

Raffie nodded—like a dog wagging his tail—at the mention of his name.

"—if he hadn't admired you so much, he might never have revealed himself. Now as to the background of how Beauregard Jolay, a *loyal* RBS employee . . . ."

It took only three or four minutes to give Raffie the rest of the so-called story. As he slipped his notebook back into his pocket, I immediately ordered him to put on both gloves again.

He was unctuously appreciative. "Thanks, Jim, I'll never forget this. Never. And anytime, buddy—I don't have to tell you—*anytime*—you can count on me."

We shook hands manfully.

"Now can I use your phone for one call?"

"As many as you like."

He called the Empire Hotel and booked a room—all in an excited whisper.

After he had slipped back out to the hallway, still whispering, still wearing gloves, Maureen asked, "Why the hotel room?"

"I know Raffie. I have a pretty good idea," I said. "We'll watch the news tonight to see if I'm right."

Anchorman Lance Murdoch was on camera, just finishing his lead-in to the story. "—And for that report, here's correspondent Rafael Miguel—"

The scene was a darkened hotel room, draperies drawn, the camera angle, from just above floor level, showing a crouched and whispering Raffie Miguel surrounded by a high barricade of chairs, a desk, pillows, the edge of a bed, an armoir, apparently every stick of furniture the room could muster.

For no reason whatsoever—unless one knew Raffie—the sound effect of surging, rushing water, a flood, sounded beneath his hoarsely whispered impassioned commentary.

". . . and if I had anything to do with this poor creature's turning himself in—and I did . . . haunted man . . . imagine . . . me, Rafael Miguel, the only broadcast journalist he could trust . . . a wealthy, *nameless* family . . . your nation's *crying* need for better mental health programs . . ."

Raffie's appropriate reaction was to cry, too.

"Better mental health programs . . . in the name of *God* . . ."

Someone whose name he frequently invoked.

". . . yes, tonight I plead for the right of the public—in the name of common sense and decency—sometimes *not* to know . . ."

For no reason, except of course, to enhance the scene, Raffie raised himself and cast a furtive glance over his barrier of furniture at God knows what, and finished with:

". . . and so I pledge to you, all of you, my friends, my admirers, those who love me—and even my—*enemies*—"— Raffie's expression was one of disdain for that *handful* of misguided fools who did not adore him—"I pledge to all of you, no matter what, the threat of prison walls or iron bars, I shall never—*never*—reveal this poor, simple, haunted creature's name. . . ."

He leaned back against his barrier, exhausted, but brave. "In the name of decency and better mental health—*never* . . ."

The sound of rushing waters increased, and reached a crescendo, as a dam burst, a dike collapsed, and all was swept before it.

". . . *Rafael Miguel . . . RBS NEWS, reporting.*"

Anchorman Lance Murdoch looked just slightly cross-eyed as he reappeared on camera.

Chapter 27

The flight to Miami was most pleasant. I sat next to a man named Bashline, one of my favorite outdoor writers, and a man I had never previously met, except on the printed page. He proved to be a delightful fellow. We talked about bone fishing, politics, Armangnac, the delicate art of minnow filleting, and beers of the world.

As a result, the flight seemed to last about twenty minutes.

We parted at the Miami airport; I headed for Hertz and a rental car, while he waited to be picked up by Ted Williams. If I hadn't been in a hurry, I'd have dawdled a bit, hoping to shake hands with the one man for whom I had once gladly traded four dozen baseball cards.

The drive down to the Keys was uneventful, and, once I got past Homestead Air Force Base, beautiful.

At Windley Key, I stopped for some coffee, knowing I was getting close. Buzz and his wife were staying on Lower Montecumba Key, just south of Islamorada.

Forty-five minutes later, I was there.

"Good to see you," Buzz said. We were standing on a spit of land that stuck out into the ocean. He raised his mug of beer. "And your mustache."

"Same here. What d'you think of it?"

He appraised my upper lip. "Not *too* bad . . ."

We drank and looked out at the Gulf Stream.

"You certainly picked the perfect spot to hole up," I said.

"Yeah, great, isn't it?" Buzz grinned. "Molly picked it."

"How'd she know about it?"

Buzz grinned again. "She didn't. Once I got the axe, we hopped in the car and headed south. Kept going until we were headed down the Keys. Stopped here, spent one night—dropped anchor."

Buzz's directions had said, the first motel on the left after the causeway from Upper to Lower Montecumba Key.

I had almost not turned in because the place hadn't looked like a motel. No neon lights, no huge signs, none of the garish glitz.

But when I did, I could see why Buzz and Molly had stayed. It was a big, solid building. Huge rooms. Clean. Simple. Quiet.

After I had showered, Buzz and I had taken our beers and simply walked around the area for several minutes, chatting, enjoying the constant, cool breeze, enjoying the closing of the day over the Gulf Stream.

We finished our beers at the same time.

"Time for dinner," Buzz said. "Let's go back and try again. Maybe she'll change her mind."

But Molly was adamant. "You two want to talk." We protested. "Besides, I've got a good book." Another protest.

"And—if we're going to get up at five a.m. for fishing, I need my rest," she said to Buzz. To me she said, "He's a year younger than I am, you know."

We had dinner at a place called the Green Turtle in Islamorada. It was a first-class spot, typical of such a place on the Keys. Crowded, vibrant, vital, lots of laughter, conversation, and great food.

And the sign on the screen door said: *Gentlemen will please wear shoes and shirts.*

We had fresh yellowtail, stone crabs, and, of course, began it all with conch chowder laced with sherry.

Buzz and I talked about a lot of things—sports, politics, life in general, and naturally, life at RBS. The old days first, then the Northern Industries takeover.

He told me how they had let him go. It had been brutal. But typical of Buzz Berman, he made a funny story out of it.

Near the end of what had been a superb meal, he screwed up his face in that off-center grin of his and said, "So that's it, Jim. It was awfully nice of you to come all the way down here to see me."

I looked at him for a moment and heard myself laugh. "Well, there's a little bit more to it than that."

"I kinda thought there was."

"Is there some place a little quieter than this?"

"Well, you've always been pretty much of a barfly, so I think I know the spot."

We drove a few miles north to a place called the Cheeca Lodge. It was a fairly grand place, with a nine-hole golf course, swimming pools, elaborate cottages, and a main building of considerable grandeur.

"All of a sudden, you're not in the Keys when you come here," Buzz commented. "But for a time like this, it's okay."

We walked through an impressive lobby, a large comfortable bar, and sat on a terrace, where we had our drinks.

After a few minutes of enjoying the breeze and the soft evening light, Buzz said, "Well—?"

"I'm glad you asked."

He chuckled.

I had worked with Buzz for years before I left RBS. We knew each other well. So, without hesitation or careful choosing of words, I told him of my latest involvement, what had transpired, what had gone right, and what had gone wrong. Right up to the moment before I had flown down to see him—ending with Ainsley's cryptic *ELN* note.

Buzz's grin grew wider and more off-center than usual, and he allowed himself to chuckle with pleasure.

"You've been a busy little bee, haven't you?"

"Yes, but that's not why you're gloating."

"I'm not gloating."

"What, then?"

"I'm remembering. Reminiscing."

"About what?"

"Oh . . . ELN . . ."

"It means something to you—?"

He nodded. "Yeah. It sure does. I'd forgotten all about it, imagine."

"You're deliberately tantalizing me—trying to drive me crazy—"

He held up his hands. "Okay—" A gurgling chuckle erupted a second time. "Remember about eight, nine years ago—when Randy Fulton was still in the news department—before he moved into programming and became R. Randolph Fulton. Remember that redhead?"

I shook my head.

"Sure, you do, she was always following him around. I finally banned her from the newsroom, and she took to meeting him every night at McGurk's."

I shook my head again.

Buzz's voice rose with frustration. "The redhead like—*this*." He created her figure with explicit gestures. "The first *Ten*— before we knew the term. Ah—" Buzz grew more animated— "I've got it. She was the first one—*ever*—for whom Randy Fulton began his perpetual task of trying to—*find something worthy of her obviously enormous talents*."

I stood. "You mean . . . what was her name? . . . Carlotta?"

Buzz slapped the arm of his chair. "That's it. *Carlotta.* The Redhead. The Ten. The *this*—" Again his hands were most descriptive.

"And she's the key to ELN?"

"No—"

"Then what—?"

"She started it."

"I'm not following."

"And Kate Morgan?"

"Kate *Morgan?*"

"Yeah." Buzz chuckled again. "I still can't believe it. After all these years. I'd forgotten all about it."

"Buzz, you've said that three times. Counsel is prepared to stipulate that you'd forgotten all about it. *"But*—what had you forgotten?"

Buzz smiled amiably, remembering. "It's what Kate did. She and Dick Ainsley and I were over at McGurk's one night, having a burger and a few beers, and Randy Fulton was with the redhead—Carlotta. She's standing at the other end of the bar wearing—they used to be called—hip huggers. You know, low-cut jeans. Only Carlotta was wearing a bare midriff with her hip huggers, and her hip huggers weren't exactly hugging her hips. They were way below her navel. And Dick and I are making serious observations about her physiognomy, as scholars often do when confronted with such an unusual and highly orgasmic specimen." Buzz guffawed again, "But Kate didn't see the lovely Carlotta that way at all. Kate thought that she was crude, cheap, and an embarrassment. Dick and I chose to disagree with her. The three of us carried on a highly civilized and scholarly debate about Carlotta's character for some time. Oh—that was fun. Yep, that was some evening."

Buzz sipped at his brandy and settled back in his chair, the smile never leaving his face.

I waited. Nothing. Finally, I said, "That's it? That's the end of the story?"

"Randy broke up with Carlotta right after that."

"But *ELN*—?"

"Oh, yeah, that's right." Buzz leaned forward. "Well, the next day, Ainsley and I were in my office together when Kate came strolling in, wearing somebody's raincoat. She turns, drops the raincoat, turns back to us—and she's wearing hip huggers that are just like Carlotta's of the night before. And she's chewing a wad of gum with her mouth open—just as the lovely Carlotta did. And wearing lots of—I had to admit—rather cheap and gaudy-looking jewelry. Much like Carlotta's. Then, in an awful Brooklyn accent—quite similar to the lovely Carlotta's—she says, *Hi, guys, what's doin'?*"

Buzz slipped to his knees on the floor of the terrace and began to salaam. "Dick and I got down like this, laughing like hell, and we surrendered."

I waited. "And that was it?"

He got back into his chair, still chortling. Yep. Kate had made her point, all right."

"And ELN?"

"Oh, yeah. Dick was the one who noticed."

"Noticed what?" I had lost all pretext of being patient.

Buzz grinned, his mind still back on the scene from years before. "Dick said, 'Where's your belly button?'"

"Where's your *belly button*?"

"Yeah. That's how it started."

"How *what* started?"

"ELN—"

"How—?"

"Dick said, 'Where's your belly button?'"

"I know Dick said, *Where's your belly button?* I heard it the first time. But what about *ELN* and Kate?"

"That's it," Buzz said. "From then on, that was our nickname for her. When Dick said—"

"*Please*. I know what he said."

"Well, when Dick said that, I took a ʟook myself. Sure enough. Those hip huggers were cut so low that there wasn't much more torso left to go—but there wasn't a belly button in sight."

I had never, of course, gone through the looking glass with Alice, but I knew now exactly how she must have felt during much of her stay in Wonderland.

"Not a belly button in sight. . . ." I murmured, taking deep breaths.

"Right. So I look at Dick, and Dick looks at me, and we both start to laugh all over again. Kate starts to laugh, too, and she says, 'Some people are *inners* and some are *outers*. Now I'm an *outer*—but I'm—*low*.' With that she pulls down her jeans, just a touch—as I said, she had *very* little space to work with—and we see her belly button. Get it—?"

I didn't get it.

Buzz said, "The ELN came later that same day, right after the evening news. Kate joined Dick and me at the bar at McGurk's, and Dick said, 'Well, if it isn't old *E-L-N*.' After that, *E-L-N* was the word. Just for the three of us, of course. We were great buddies in those days. Three Musketeers."

"Dick—I still don't understand *E-L-N*."

"Oh? I thought you'd catch on. *E-L-N*—*Extremely Low Navel*." Buzz chuckled again. "Yeah. That's what we used to call her. Just among the three of us. Old *E-L-N*."

The waiter brought our drinks. We touched glasses and drank.

Buzz reached over and clapped me on the back. "Good to see you again."

"Same here, Buzz—"

Then I remembered why I had wanted to find out what *ELN* meant. It meant *E-L-N*.

And *E-L-N* meant Kate Morgan.

"Let's go inside," I said. "I'm cold, all of a sudden. And there's one thing I forgot to tell you."

Inside, at the bar, I told Buzz about the *Penn-Columbia* part of the note.

"E-L-N *and* Penn-Columbia. Well it's a pretty good guess that Dick meant Kate when he wrote ELN. Although, why he didn't just write Kate is beyond me. As for Penn-Columbia, I'm afraid I can't help you." Buzz searched my eyes. "Anything else you *didn't* want to tell me?"

I smiled. "Mr. Berman, you have an extremely suspicious nature."

"Too many years in the news business." Buzz scratched at his cheek. "But give me a few years down here and I'll probably be handing over my wallet to the first guy with long sideburns who wants to sell me banking stock in Bimini."

I didn't laugh with him. Instead, I heard myself sigh. "Damn. It would have to be Kate Morgan."

"Hey, give her a break, will ya'. So it's Kate. What's that prove?"

"Maybe you're right, but it does bring to mind a few more questions—"

"Shoot—"

"Kate and Dick Ainsley never worked together, did they?"

Buzz looked puzzled. "Jim, they were in the same newsroom together for years."

"I know. But they never actually worked on the same story. As a team, I mean. Right?"

Buzz Berman took a while to answer. He sipped at his brandy. Finally, he smiled. "You know, what I'm about to tell you was a secret for so long, that my knee-jerk reaction, even now, is for denial and more secrecy. Habit."

Nevertheless, he noticeably lowered his voice. "During one nine- or ten-month period, helter-skelter, Kate and Ainsley did a bunch of drug-related stories. Along with everything else they did. Both developed a feel for the streets, made good contacts out there, and they both developed a damn good rapport with the NYPD Narco Squad. So—"

A man and a woman entered the bar room and sat on stools near ours. They were having an argument.

"So"—Buzz stood and led the way back out to the terrace again—"it didn't take a genius to figure out that it might be a good idea to put 'em together as a team."

"And nobody else in the newsroom knew about the arrangement?"

"No one else at RBS, even."

"But they didn't work exclusively on drug stories."

"Nope. I just made it clear that I wanted them to work as a team on the drug stuff."

"And why the secrecy?"

"Just a feeling. No real reason. As a matter of fact, I was about to call off the cloak and dagger part when Kate came to me and told me that she and Dick suspected a drug connection that reached right into RBS itself."

"And what did they eventually come up with?"

"Nothing."

"They'd been wrong?"

"I don't know."

"Why not?"

"Right after that—less than a week—Northern Industries arrived, bugles blowing." Buzz raised his hands, palms upward. "They called me in, introduced themselves, said, we love what you've been doing—good-bye."

I remembered our dinner conversation.

Buzz read my thoughts. "I didn't get into all the really ugly details at dinner because I had you laughing. But when I walked in the next morning, I found all my stuff in boxes in the hallway, and Billy Bob Johnson, wearing a cowboy hat, sitting behind what had been my desk the day before."

"All in good taste—"

"Oh sure—he called me buckaroo and asked me ten dozen questions about the news department in about ten minutes—then he said it was all a *frickin'* shame, as he walked me back out of my office and had his secretary call a porter to get my things out of the building."

Buzz sighed, not unhappily. "What the hell—it's over. Molly and I are going to get on just fine."

I heard myself saying, "Then by the time you left—Dick and Kate had found nothing further on the possible RBS-drug connection."

"No—"

"And you'll please excuse that thoughtless, insensate question just now—"

"No need to apologize, Jim." He smiled to put me at ease.

"You always were a tenacious reporter when you got on a story."

"Never tasteless, though. Sorry, Buzz."

"Aw, forget it. No"—he answered my question—"at the time of my fast exit from RBS, they'd found nothing further. But I *do* know that Billy Bob Buckeroo had planned to keep the arrangement with Dick and Kate just as it had been originally set up."

"But that's all. Dick or Kate never talked to you about it after you left RBS."

"Don't forget, Molly and I cleared out as fast as we could. I hardly saw anybody."

"And here you are. . . ." My eyes were on the moonlight on the ocean.

"Yep. Not bad, huh? Let's get back to the motel. Have a nightcap. Maybe Molly will join us."

But Molly was fast asleep when we got back. There was a hand-lettered sign from her, written on a shirt cardboard: *Don't forget. Five a.m. Fishing. Sleep well, Toots.*

"Toots—?"

Buzz's blush was noticeable even in the moonlight. "For thirty-five years."

"Not bad," I said.

We took our drinks and walked out to the spit of land. We didn't talk for a long while.

Finally, Buzz said, "It's awful about Dick Ainsley, isn't it?"

"Terrible."

"And what was the girl's name?"

"Mary Frances Fahey."

I heard Buzz sigh. "My God. Just about to be married. What the hell got into Dick—?"

The wind came up, warm and sweet. The sound of the Gulf Stream was low, rumbling, and calming.

We finished our drinks.

"Ah, well—" Buzz said again. We started back to the motel.

"Say hello to everybody for me, will you, Jim?"

"Of course."

"Tell 'em—Molly and I are having a fine time."

"You bet."

Buzz shook my hand. "We'll be back from fishing by around nine-thirty. Breakfast with us before you leave?"

"You're on—"

"Good. G'night, Jim."

"G'night, Buzz."

When I got to my room, I called New York and got Joe Maloney out of bed.

"Put a tail on Kate Morgan," I said.

"Why?"

"I'll explain when I get back. But do it tonight. As soon as you can."

"You've got it, Jim. See you tomorrow?"

"Late afternoon." I hung up the phone, undressed, and went to bed. I had not a single pleasant dream.

Chapter 28

Susan Mazur was at the Miami Airport. I wasn't surprised.

I see her here,
I see here there,
I seem to see her everywhere.

"What a wonderful coincidence," she said. And then immediately, "Let's have a drink."

"What are you doing in Miami?"

"Waiting for you."

"Very thoughtful."

"Are you catching a plane back to New York?"

"Yes—"

"What airline?"

When I told her, she followed me to the counter, and, while I checked in, she bought herself a first-class ticket on the same flight.

As we headed for the lounge, I said, "Is this one of your

hobbies—standing in airports, waiting for a friendly face, and then flying with whomever it might be?"

She smiled. "No. Only you."

"That sounds vaguely ominous."

She pretended to pout. "It was supposed to sound mysterious. I'm trying to change my image. I've been told recently that I'm much too forward."

"You? Never—"

In the lounge, Susan did the ordering. Naturally, it was champagne. After the first sip, she stood to take off her raincoat, and—what I now knew to be her standard maneuver—to stretch.

At the end of that brief—no more than a minute in time—moment, every male eye in the place was upon her.

"Well done," I said as I raised my glass to her.

"What do you mean?"

"Ah, ah, *ah*—don't feign innocence with the old professor here."

She smiled. "It *is* wonderful to have it. I mean, it doesn't make me a better person or anything, and God knows I did nothing to deserve it—it's just there—but it's—well—comforting to have."

By *it*, I assumed that she meant her body, but I didn't bother to pursue the thought. It was much more enjoyable, and certainly more worthwhile, to simply appreciate its magnificence.

She was wearing a T-shirt that had the words *Miami Dolphins* stretched tautly across the front, a silk scarf at her neck and a short skirt.

She noticed my approving appraisal of her legs. "I didn't even get a little tan, did I? How pale."

With legs like that, one could stand being overly self-critical.

"Well, what do you expect, standing around in airports all day?"

She smiled. "Actually, I was here to do a survey for *Three W-S*. We're going to do a segment on Bone Fishing with Ted Williams."

Three W-S stood for *Wonderful World of Weekend Sports*, one of Sam Bigelow's creations, and an RBS Television staple for nearly twenty years.

"All by yourself?"

"Yep. The Sports Department finally trusts me to do a survey on my own."

"Where do you plan to shoot it?"

"Islamorada. It's the best place on the Keys for Bone Fishing." She smiled proudly. "And I found this out all by myself."

I looked at her over my glass. "How long were you in Islamorada?"

"Since yesterday."

"Where did you stay?"

"The Cheeca Lodge. Very spiffy."

It's a wonder we didn't run into each other," I said.

"Why—were you there, too?"

"Not at the Cheeca. But in Islamorada."

"Well, well. Small world," she said.

We drank more champagne. And Susan stretched again as we got up to board our flight.

There was a message from Terry Jones on my machine, inviting me to either lunch or dinner the next day. I called his secretary and agreed to lunch.

Next, I called Joe.

"I'm back," I said. "Anything happening?"

"Not much, Jimmy. I put a tail on Kate Morgan right after you called. It's gonna cost. I put on a good one. A square of four guys. I figured you'd want it done right."

"Good man, Joe."

"But so far—zilch."

"Okay. Let's wait and see for a while."

"You're the doctor. See you in the morning?"

"I've got a luncheon meeting with Terry Jones. I'll see you after that."

"Take care, Jimmy."

"You, too, Joe."

I brewed a pot of tea and made myself a cold turkey sandwich, with lettuce and mustard and mayonnaise on white toast.

I watched the news on CNN while I was eating. But I didn't hear that much. I kept thinking of the flight up from Miami.

Susan Mazur had certainly gone all around the mountain trying to find out what I'd been doing on the Keys. She had used every play in the book.

Except a direct question.

We lunched at Des Artistes, at a back table by the bar, overlooking the main room.

Terry was in an ebullient mood.

He lit a cigarette. "It's a perfect day, isn't it? A drink?"

"I'll pass."

"One martini, up, please. And my God"—he smiled broadly at the young waitress—"I love your new hairstyle, Carol."

"Thank you, Mr. Jones." She returned his smile as she turned toward the bar.

I grinned appreciatively. "You're in a fine mood."

"Yeah, one of those days. And you're looking pretty fine yourself. Picked up some sun on the Keys."

"My God, but you're omnipotent, Corporal Jones. How'd you know I was down on the Keys?"

He chuckled. "The good executive knows everything. Actually, I was in Sam Bigelow's office trying to beat down his sports budget when that magnificent one came in. You know who I mean—"

"Susan Mazur."

"That's it. She had a survey for Sam. Said that you and she had just happened to run into each other on the plane." He looked at me with mock seriousness. "Holding out on old Uncle Terry, are we?"

"We just happened to meet at the airport."

"Oh, sure . . . thanks, Carol." And as Terry lifted his glass, he sighed. "Well, if that's your story—cheers."

"Cheers."

We ordered, and I had to smile to myself, when, as early as the asparagus vinaigrette, Terry got right down to business, and I knew, immediately, why he had invited me to lunch.

"Well, looks as if you have everything all wrapped up, Jim. Nice going."

"And Raffie Miguel got another heart-pounding story."

"You saw it—?"

"Sure—"

"Well, it wasn't *that* bad—" Terry paused and looked at me critically. "Say—you didn't have anything to do with that, did you?"

"What do you think?"

"What do *I* think?" Terry smiled. "I think that I don't like the sound of your—*What do you think?*"

"I'm surprised," I said, "deeply wounded, and hurt."

"Oh, sure you are. My apologies. At any rate, it's all over now. And all is calm at RBS. Something we haven't known for months, and for that we thank you."

I sipped at my beer. "But there're still a few loose ends to tie up."

"Such as—?"

"Well—Dick Ainsley's death for one thing."

Terry looked embarrassed. "Jim—I don't know quite how to put this—but . . . well . . . the threats, the sabotage—that's over. And that *was* the main thing, and"—his voice got just a bit too hearty—"you *certainly* did one *hell* of a job in straightening that mess out—"

I smiled out of appreciation for what he was trying to do. "Thanks, Terry—it's hard to tell a friend that maybe he isn't *quite* a private detective after all, isn't it?"

He was completely flustered. "I mean, Dick Ainsley and the girl and all that . . . that's more or less for the police, don't you think?" He looked at me, and I felt a great sweep of affection for

Terry. All of a sudden he was a young and earnest twenty-year-old back in Vietnam again.

I put a hint of the Shakespearean bravura actor into my voice and made a joke of it. "I'm sorry I lost my head about my abilities as a sleuth, old boy."

"Aw, Jim—"

"No, you're right, Terry, I *did* lose my head. Of course it's a job for the police."

I decided, then and there, not to tell Terry that I was going to continue for a while. It was too embarrassing for him.

Terry looked relieved. "I did feel as if I were in one of those movies where the second lead has to tell the champ that someone else is going to be the starting quarterback."

We laughed and drank some white wine and got onto football with that. Just as I was reliving a great Bucknell victory over Colgate, R. Randolph Fulton, wearing a garish new bow tie, arrived with a young woman who obviously possessed, in the eyes of R. Randolph Fulton, at least, great artistic powers and incredible creative talents, and who was someone for whom he was trying to find a project which was *worthy of her obviously enormous talents.*

"Jim—Terry—how are you?"

We waved in friendly greeting.

"Having lunch?"

"Yes—care to join us?"

"No, thanks. We had a burger at McGurk's. We're just going to have a refreshing libation at the bar."

Randy always talked like that when he was swept up in one of his creative throes.

"You haven't introduced us," I said, rising from the table, as did Terry.

"Oh. Sorry. Gentlemen, may I have the great pleasure of introducing you to someone who is going to stand the television world on its ear. Astrid—this is Mr. Terence Jones, vice-president of the entire RBS Television Network"—Astrid made appropriate cooing sounds—"and this is the *distinguished* American author, Mr. James Sasser, who is—" Terry snapped his finger excitedly—

"I've got it. Who is going to write us a pilot for something which is—" here it came again—"worthy of your *obviously—enormous* talents."

Like one of the old theatrical managers who played the same roles and read the same lines night after night, Terry, by now, could wring every last drop of emotion from every syllable of his favorite phrase. Astrid was, obviously, overcome.

Randy continued on: "And gentlemen, it is my great pleasure to present Ms. Astrid Anderson."

Terry and I made awkward half bows while Astrid Anderson smiled at us. She was indeed, lovely.

Randy chortled. "Can you imagine. This morning, Human Resources sent her to our *legal* department. *Imagine*. But I took one look at her and thought that I saw something"—Terry and I bit our lips and managed not to laugh—"something that I call *talent*. I grabbed one of the advance scripts of *Five On a Bed* and asked her to read for me. Gentlemen—" Randy appeared to be about to swoon—"Gentlemen, I can only tell you that I have *never* heard anything like it in my *life*."

Astrid's smile grew broader, brighter and even more lovely.

"She's got *it*. Do you agree, gentlemen?" Randy asked.

Terry and I said that, of course, we did, and, out of politeness, tried to sound as excited as Randy. But it was extremely difficult. Randy was on a very high plain.

As they were about to leave, Astrid leaned towards Terry and kissed him on the cheek. Terry blushed. Next, she did the same with me. I'm sure that I blushed even more.

Randy looked annoyed, but gamely smiled at us and led Astrid to the bar.

Terry and I sat down again. We looked at each other. And we both began to laugh.

"She didn't say a word," Terry finally said.

"She doesn't have to."

"Amen."

"Astrid Anderson," I sighed. "My God, she's absolutely stunning."

"Nobody," said Terry, "will ever accuse R. Randolph Fulton of not recognizing beauty when he sees it."

We gazed over at the bar. Randy was in heaven.

We finished our lunch in high spirits, discussing everything from Astrid Anderson to Zero Mostel.

As Terry was signing the check, he said, "Now that your sleuthing days are over, champ, would you mind dropping by and saying sayonara to old M. Seabury Whitehead? He'd appreciate it. And—indirectly—" Terry smiled—"so would I."

"Sure. When?"

"Why not now?"

"Fine."

Terry looked relieved.

R. Randolph Fulton came running over to us as we got up from the table. Behind him, Astrid Anderson was smiling at us from the bar.

"She wants it all in writing," he blurted out.

"What—?" I put my hands on his shoulders to settle him down.

"Astrid."

"What about her?"

"She wants it all in writing. All the hogwash I've been shoveling. *Imagine*."

"She does—?" I started to smile.

"Yeah." Randy's face was a landscape of anguish and agony. "Imagine—in writing."

"Yes. Imagine."

"Jim—she's a Goddamned *lawyer*."

It made the day.

Chapter 29

Back at the offices of Maloney, O'Neil and Sasser, I brewed myself a pot of tea, washed my face, and called Kate Morgan.

"*Jim*—" I could hear the smile in her voice. "I was just thinking about you."

"I was thinking of you too. So I called."

Laughter joined the smile in her voice. "So you did."

"How about dinner?"

"Tonight?"

"Yes. There's a new French place on First Avenue in the Seventies."

"Oh, Jim, I'm sorry. I just can't make it tonight." Her voice sounded suddenly troubled.

"Roy—?"

She was hesitant. "Well . . . yes. We *were* married once, you know."

I tried to be light. "You two can never really stay apart for long, can you?"

"Uh . . . no, it seems that way."

"Well, okay, but you've got to give me a rain check."

"I was just about to ask for one."

"Good. Tomorrow night?"

She laughed. "Tomorrow night would be just fine."

"Great—I'll call you tomorrow And say hello to Roy for me."

"Oh . . . yes, I'll say hello."

We each mumbled a good-bye and hung up.

I sat looking at the phone for a moment or two.

"Well, she didn't exactly stand you up, Jimmy."

It was Maureen's voice from behind me. I turned. "I didn't realize you were here."

She smiled. "For a very good reason. I just came in."

I looked at her quizzically. "And why do you feel that you need to soothe me. Do my feathers look ruffled?"

"No, but your voice sounds a little thin. It always does when something upsets you."

"I didn't realize—"

"Yep. It always does."

I felt Maureen's cool fingers on the back of my neck. She began to massage my shoulder muscles. "Two minutes and then you do me—right?"

"You're on," I said.

Joe Maloney called at eight the next morning. "Wake you up?"

"Would it matter?"

"Well—no. But it seemed like the decent thing to say."

"Very decent. The answer is, no. I just got out of the shower."

"Oh, good."

"You sound disappointed."

"Hey, Jimmy—go back to the shower. You're a pain in the neck this morning."

"Sorry."

"How long will it take you to get down to the Parker-Meridian?"

"Twenty minutes."

"Good. I have some news about Kate Morgan. She finally did something besides work and go back to her apartment."

"I know," I said.

There was a pause. "Boy, you're no fun at all this morning," Joe said.

"I know. Breakfast will fix me up."

Joe was already seated, having some coffee, when I arrived at the Parker-Meridian. As always, the place was filled—French, British, Europeans in general.

The buffet was opulent, replete with everything imaginable for an orgy of breakfast dining, except, possibly, some peacock feathers and a vomitorium.

We talked about nothing in particular while we ate.

Finally, over fresh coffee, Joe said. "You're looking a lot better."

"I'm feeling better."

"Now, do you want to hear anything I have to report about Kate Morgan, or do you know it all anyway?"

"I'm afraid I know most of it," I said. "Last night she had dinner with ex-husband and nice guy, Roy."

"Amazing," Joe said. "How do you find out things like this?"

"I talked to her last night."

"Remarkable," Joe said.

"Elementary, my dear fellow."

"So you talked to her before she went out?" Joe said.

"Yep."

"With some guy on Sutton Place. *Not* Roy."

"What—?"

"But of course you already knew that."

"She was out with some guy on Sutton Place?"

"See—I'm sure you probably knew that before I did."

"Joe—I surrender. Where was Kate Morgan last night?"

He grinned. "Okay, are you gonna sit up straight now, put your feet firmly on the floor, and listen?"

Involuntarily, I sat up straighter.

Joe was enjoying himself immensely. "Two of my guys were with her last night. Here's their report." He consulted a notebook.

"Left RBS building at 7:14 p.m., walked to her apartment building at Lincoln Towers on West End Avenue. Entered building. Left at 7:43 p.m. Took a cab to Jim McMullin's Restaurant on Third Avenue and Seventy-Third Street. Sat at the bar and had a wine spritzer. At 8:14 on the dot, a limousine pulled up outside. She had paid for her drink when she got it, so the moment the limo pulled up, she left the bar and got into it. It drove her to—can't read the address, I'll get it later—anyway, to an apartment house on Sutton Place. She got out of the limo, went to the apartment building and took an elevator. One of my men, pretending to be the limousine driver who had just let her out, told the doorman that she had left one of her gloves in his limo—it's an old trick—and during all of this he found out that—very possibly—Kate Morgan had gone up to the apartment of a Mr. Francisco Guzman."

"Francisco who—?"

"*Guzman*. She stayed there, or at least in the building, until 9:45 p.m. when another limousine appeared and took her straight back to West End and Seventy-Second. From there, she walked back to her apartment."

Joe closed the notebook and slipped it back inside his jacket. "In case the name Francisco Guzman doesn't ring a bell—he is *reputed* to be one of the kingpins who is trying to make peace between the Medellin Group and the Cali Group. And in case their names don't mean anything—they're both cocaine cartels—from Colombia. As in Penn-*Columbia*?"

Joe stood up, triumphant. "And since I'm only human, I can't resist saying, just once more—but, of *course*, to you it was already elementary, I'm sure."

I sat there wondering what it all meant. What bothered me most was that I had a vague idea that I just might *know* what it all meant. And I didn't want to be right.

I sipped at my coffee, vaguely aware that Joe was watching me intently.

"What're you brooding about, Jimmy?"

"I'm thinking that the first thing I have to do is see Kate and confront her."

"*Confront* her. Hey, Jimmy. *Confront?* Remember that Fred Allen joke you told me once? About the broadcasting executive whose job it was to come to his office every morning and find a molehill on his desk, and then he had until the end of the day to turn that molehill into a mountain?" Joe guffawed. "Aren't you maybe kinda making a mountain out of a little molehill? So you ask her to dinner and she turns you down. So she says she's gonna have dinner with her ex-husband. And she doesn't. So what? A molehill, Jimmy."

"If that were all, Joe."

"Yeah—" He shrugged. "I know—"

"Joe . . . We've had a lot of screwy things happen here. Not just this incident with Kate. And we've had three people killed. Why?"

"I don't know, Jimmy."

"And I don't know either. But we both think you've found at least part of the answer. You found Colombia."

"Maybe—"

"So I'm going to see Kate Morgan and talk to her about last night."

"Okay, Jimmy."

Joe looked worried.

Chapter 30

It was just noon as I entered the RBS Broadcast Center and made my way to the network news area.

As is normal in a newsroom, everyone was scurrying, always just about thirty-seven seconds behind schedule.

I found Kate in her cubicle, marking up the transcript of an interview.

"Jim—"

"Impulse," I said. "I was doing some research at the Lincoln Center Library"—a lie—"felt the need for some sustenance, and thought I'd drop by to see if you'd have a sandwich with me."

Kate smiled. "I thought we were going to have dinner tonight."

"Now *I* have to beg off. Sorry. But how about now?"

"Well, I don't know—I'm just going over this transcript—"

"And—you've just marked the last page. When do you start editing?"

"Two o'clock."

"Who'll you be working with?"

"Paul Fogerty."

"Well, there you are. You'll be in perfect hands. Come on—let me enjoy the pleasure of your company for a good deli lunch."

It bothered me only a little bit that I was surprisingly good as a dissembler.

I wasted no time at Murray's Deli. As we were stirring milk into our coffee, I said: "How's Roy doing?"

"Oh, just fine."

"Was he in good spirits last night?"

"Very."

"Good." I pretended to joke. "The full professorship hasn't gone to his head, has it?"

"No—" Kate smiled. "But he's very proud of it."

"He should be."

Murray served us our corned beef sandwiches, and we busied ourselves with applying the mustard.

"Where'd you have dinner last night?" I asked her. "Anyplace new that I should know about?"

"Ah, no—not really. We were somewhere down in Soho. It was pleasant enough, but nothing to write home about."

"Remember the name?"

"Uh—no. Actually, I'm afraid I don't." Kate smiled. "As I said, it wasn't anything to write home about."

"What did Roy think?"

"He seemed to like it. Naturally, I didn't say anything."

"Naturally—"

I took a sip of coffee, took a deep breath, decided that now was as good as any other time, and let her have it.

"Why are you lying to me, Kate?" Two deep frown lines immediately appeared between her eyes. "You didn't see Roy last night."

She looked at me, the frown lines growing even deeper.

I said it again: "Why are you lying?"

"I don't know what you mean," she finally said.

"Of course—"

"And I'm puzzled—taken back, actually, Jim. You're just about the last person I could think of who would invite me to lunch in order to call me a liar."

"Well, I—"

"And—now that I think about it—it was obviously premeditated. My God"—her voice rose—"you actually came in to see me, all love and kisses and smiles, and planned to come over here and call me a liar."

"Now, Kate, I wouldn't call it that—"

"No—" She laughed. A harsh snort. "Well, what *would* you call it, Jim?" She looked hard at me. "What did you do—have me followed?" And when I didn't answer, she said, "My God, you *did*." She looked away.

My attack had suddenly turned into a retreat, a rout, in fact.

"The fact is, you didn't have dinner with Roy," I said. Somehow, that seemed to be a most inadequate response.

She didn't bother to look at me. "Followed," she repeated. "You *actually* had me *followed*."

We sat there silently. Not eating, not talking. Murray cast us a wary and worried glance.

Finally, Kate said, "Why, Jim?"

"Well, Kate . . ." I didn't finish.

"It couldn't be—you're not jealous, are you? No—of course not." She let out a long, sad sigh. "My God—you actually had me *followed*."

That was it for my initial attack. It had sputtered and failed. I needed time.

"I'm finished with lunch," I said. "Are you?"

"Yes. Thank you for lunch." There was a rasp of asperity in her voice.

I paid the bill and we headed back to RBS.

Just as we got near the Broadcast Center, I said, "You're in this drug stuff up to your neck, aren't you, Kate?"

I heard her inhale sharply. She didn't reply.

"Aren't you?" I said again.

Again, no response.

"Let's take a little walk in the park and we can talk about it," I said.

She offered no resistance. We kept on walking to Central Park West and entered the park at Seventy-Second Street.

A couple of joggers loped past us, their faces grim. "Do you want to tell me about it?" I asked.

"Suppose you tell *me*."

"I'd much rather have it the other way around."

"You'd much rather have it—" Kate stopped walking. Her hands were on her hips and she was scowling. "Jim, I'm totally confused by your behavior. Surprised, perplexed, confused—and *angry*."

"I have the feeling that—"

"*Let—me—finish*." She took a deep breath. "You had me followed last night. Today, you've called me a liar. And now, out of the blue—*out of the blue*—you accuse me of being—and may I quote—*in this drug stuff up to your neck*. Now—do you mind telling *me* what this is all about."

"Don't you know, Kate?"

"Oh, Jim. Only questions. No answers." Her expression was suddenly one of pleading. "Tell me this is some kind of joke, Jim. Tell me this is all pretend. Because I don't know what's going on."

"Oh, come on now, *E-L-N*, I'm sure you do."

"No, really, of all people to suddenly begin some kind of attack on me—"

She stopped talking.

I waited.

"What—?" she finally said.

"Nothing."

"No . . . you said . . ."

"I said: come on now, I'm sure you do. Meaning that I'm sure that you do know—"

"*Stop it*—" Her eyes had narrowed.

"Okay—*E-L-N*."

She pulled a pack of cigarettes from her pocket and quickly lit one. I had only seen her smoke once or twice before in all the time

I had known her. She inhaled deeply and blew out the smoke very slowly.

She tried to smile. "Where did you hear that?"

"Dick Ainsley."

"Dick Ainsley is dead."

"I know. But I heard it from him."

"Oh—" She visibly relaxed. "It used to be an old joke"—she tried to laugh—"Do you have any idea what it means?"

"As I understand it, *E-L-N* stands for *Extremely Low Navel*. As you say—a joke."

"Yes"—the smile was frozen and nearly grotesque—"so then that's what this whole thing was—a joke. My God, you had me going for a minute there." She touched my cheek. Her hands were very cold. "Jim, don't do this again. It's really not very funny." And as an afterthought, she said, "And not like you at all."

"No—you're right, it's not."

She took another drag on the cigarette and tried to loosen the smile on her face.

"Actually, I heard it from Buzz Berman," I said. "A couple of days ago."

"But you said—"

"I know. I just wanted to see if you knew about the note." Her eyes widened. "What note?"

"A note—"

She tried to lash out—"Jim, I'm warning you not to start up this silly nonsense again. It's not funny, it's not amusing, and, quite frankly, I'm getting pretty damned sick of this whole crazy conversation." But her voice was lacking in force and conviction.

I said: "I saw Buzz two days ago. We had a long talk."

"How is he? Doing well, I hope."

"Yes, he is, I'm happy to report. He asked about you."

"I'm sure he did. Did he ask about anything besides my navel?"

"He hopes you're doing well. I told him that you are."

She nodded.

I said: "Naturally, we talked about the old times. So, of

course, your name came up quite a lot—as well as Dick Ainsley's. Buzz told me about the covert drug team he set up with you and Dick."

She eyed me. Her voice was noncommittal. "Yes . . ."

"You told me that you never actually worked on a specific story with Dick Ainsley."

"Did I?"

"Yes. And obviously, you did. You lied to me."

She frowned. "So we're back to that, are we? Kate the liar."

I said: "On the other hand, maybe the lie was a knee-jerk reaction to protect a covert investigative team. That's what happened with Buzz, too. At first, he denied it—out of habit."

Too quickly, she said: "Yes, that's it. Habit. Dick and I were undercover from the first day on." She smiled slightly. "That was Buzz's reaction, too, huh? Interesting."

"But apparently you never really came up with much of anything."

"No, not really. But don't forget this was always a kind of part-time job."

"That's what Buzz said. Please—he wasn't criticizing. He considered you and Dick his two best reporters."

She smiled. "That's good to hear."

I got close to her, got her eyes focused right into mine, and said: "Now what had you found out—about two weeks before the Northern Industries take-over—when you came running into Buzz's office."

"Why . . . I don't remember."

"Aw, come on now. You don't remember. You told him that you and Dick had found a drug connection that might go right into the heart of RBS."

"Yes . . . maybe . . . I'd have to look at my notebooks."

"Have to look at your notebooks—*please*. You remember. What *had* you found?"

She was wooden.

"Okay," I said. "What happened between the time of your report to Buzz Berman and the Northern take-over?" Her eyes were glazing over. "What happened *after* the take-over? I know that Billy Bob Johnson kept you and Dick Ainsley on as his covert investigative drug team."

She didn't answer. I waited.

"I'd . . . have to look at my notebooks," she finally said again.

"Ah, yes—so you said."

"Privileged information."

"Yes. Of course."

I waited for a covey of joggers to pass, before I said: "You asked about the note before. Would you still like to know?"

She looked at me without speaking. Finally, she nodded her head.

I made her wait for the answer. And when I spoke, I made myself speak very slowly. "After he was murdered, the police found a note in Dick Ainsley's cell."

She only nodded her head.

I said: "Of course, the note isn't their only clue, but it's a big one."

I stopped and waited and forced her to ask the question.

She took a deep drag on her cigarette. She looked at me. She took another drag and dropped her cigarette to the ground. She finally said: "What was in the note?"

I was deliberately evasive. "Oh, not much. It was pretty short."

"But can you tell me what it said?"

"Oh . . . of course."

I smiled. And waited. The frown lines between her eyes deepened. "Are you having fun?" she asked.

"The note said: *Penn-Columbia.*"

She waited. "That's all? Just Penn-Columbia. What do they think it means?"

"That's something I can't tell you."

"Privileged information again?" She smiled.

"Sort of."

"It all sounds very mysterious."

"Actually, it's pretty straightforward, once you know what Penn-Columbia means."

"And do the police? Know, I mean."

"No—"

"And do you?"

"Yes. Well, I had to have it explained to me by my partner. But, yes."

She tried to smile. "Remarkable. Just two words. And you can deduct a meaning from them. I'd have thought it was some sort of Ivy League shenanigans."

"Well"—I watched her closely—"actually, there was a bit more to the note. One more indecipherable word—or that's what the police thought. But I found out differently."

"I'm afraid I'm not following. Another word? With no meaning?"

"Well, that's just it—if it were a word, it would have no meaning. But it's not a word. It's initials, actually."

Her eyes jumped, almost imperceptibly, but it was obvious that she had guessed. Nevertheless, she played it out to her last card. "Initials?"

"Yes," I said. "*E-L-N.*"

She didn't speak for a very long while. We started to saunter slowly along the path. After several dozen yards, Kate said: "So you know all about it then?"

I didn't know if she was capitulating or testing me, so I said, "No, of course not. Not everything."

"But enough."

"Enough to involve you."

"Then you're in danger, Jim." She wasn't looking at me now, and she was speaking rapidly. "No more jokes from you, Jim. Not now. This is serious. You mustn't be seen with me. Where's that sublet of yours?"

I told her.

"Meet me there in twenty minutes—" And with that she turned on her heel and retraced our steps, walking as rapidly as possible.

I had been waiting for her for nearly an hour when the bell sounded. I pressed the buzzer to the street and went out to meet her at the elevator.

She glanced furtively around the hall as I led her to the apartment. Once inside, she said, "I remembered that you'd mentioned that there's no doorman for your building."

"Is that important?"

"Very. I was serious when I said that you and I shouldn't be seen together. Now how much do you know?"

I had to say something.

"Well—obviously, I've got a line about the RBS connection to this drug running. . . ." I waited, hoping for a reaction from her, but there was none. "And I'm certain of your involvement, Kate. . . ." This time she frowned, just slightly, but I had obviously scored, so I took a chance: "Dick Ainsley, of course. . . ." Her mouth twitched. Still on target. "And . . ."

Yes, indeed. And what else.

She was watching me intently. "And—?" she said.

"Well, and all the rest. Columbia is, quite obviously, *Colombia,* the country. It hardly takes a genius to figure that out—and so forth. Of course, I'm just getting started. There are lots of things I don't know, but give me time. Once things begin to unravel, it all usually falls apart pretty fast and—"

Falling victim to the sound of my own voice, feeling, for a moment, like some brilliant detective on *Masterpiece Theatre,* I had taken my eyes off Kate Morgan; but when she said, much too softly, *"Jim—"* animal instinct made me look at her, quickly, without question.

She had a pistol in her hand. It was aimed at my chest.

"Aw, Kate . . ."

"I'm sorry, Jim. I told you this was serious."

"Kate . . ."

"Sit in that chair and put your hands on your knees," she said.

I did as commanded, and we faced each other.

"My, my, you certainly sound professional," I said, pleased that my voice didn't betray the awful fright that was starting up in my stomach.

She shook her head. "You can't quite understand that you've involved yourself in something that's terribly, *terribly* serious, can you, Jim?"

"Oh, I've figured that out all right," I said. "As far as I can remember, this is just about the first time I've ever sat in a chair and had an old friend point a pistol at me. Tell me, are you going to shoot me? What exactly do you plan to do?"

Her mouth was so pinched with either tension or rage that, when she spoke, whatever she said was unintelligible.

"I beg your pardon," I said, trying desperately to sound breezy.

"I said . . . I don't know." Her voice was very low, almost a whisper.

"Excuse me?"

"I don't know—" Her voice was shaking now.

"May I suggest—"

Kate dropped the gun to the floor and her voice was a keening wail, "Oh—I—don't—know—*what to do*—"

I held her in my arms while she cried.

After a long time, she said, "I never wanted this, Jim. Never. You don't know how many times I've literally prayed to God that it would all go away."

"How deeply are you involved, Kate?"

"All the way, I'm afraid." She lifted her face from my shoulder and looked up at me. "I only did it for Roy and the children, Jim."

I could only sigh.

"It's true."

"Just for Roy and the children? All this drug money—just for them? Please, Kate."

"It's not the money—"

"Come on—"

"No. It's not the money. Don't you understand. We stumbled onto this thing—Dick and I. We thought we had the beginnings of a great story. We were naive enough to forget about the consequences. There were threats. Anonymous, of course. They threatened Roy through me. Then the children. Jim, I've been scared to death for months now."

"Did they threaten Dick Ainsley, too?"

"Both of us. That's one of the reasons Dick started to drink so much."

I poured us each a generous dollop of Armagnac. "How long since you've called in sick?"

She frowned quizzically. "I don't know—"

"How long? A week? A month? Six months?"

"Years, I suppose. I can't remember when."

"That's what I thought. You're not on the air tonight, so call Tom Fogarty, tell him where your transcript notes are, and let him get started with the editing—you've got the flu."

She hesitated.

"Do it. You and I are going to talk. Because you need to talk to someone, Kate."

Tears rolled down her cheeks. "Oh, Jim—I do, I do."

She had been so tense for so long that the brandy took effect almost immediately. The story poured out of her.

The first break for the Kate Morgan–Richard Ainsley covert drug team had occurred when Dick had got onto a new angle of a story about intra-Mafia killings. Everyone had been reporting the deaths as part of an internecine war among the various families. But in following up what was a minor drug-related story, Dick had rooted out what seemed, at the time, a possible, but very unlikely, connection between the Mafia deaths and a move by a Colombian drug cartel, the Medellin Group, to establish its territorial rights over the so-called Cali Group for the distribution of drugs in the New York area.

Kate and Dick had worked on this angle for several weeks. Then came their second break: a small, twin-engine plane had crashed in the Florida Everglades. The plane was loaded with cocaine worth several million dollars on the street.

One passenger could not be identified. He died in the ambulance on the way to the hospital. He spoke only Spanish.

The pilot was dead on impact. The pilot's name was Giraldo Diaz. When alive, he was bilingual. When alive, he worked for RBS Sports.

That news hadn't seemed so important to Kate and Ainsley until, more from old habits as reporters than any great perspicacious sensitivity, they had routinely checked out the source of the plane.

"The plane belonged—may I have another brandy, Jim?"—I was already pouring it for her—"the plane belonged to a small commuter airline called *Air Penn*. Have you ever heard of it?"

"I'm afraid not."

"They have a most interesting itinerary. Want to hear it?"

"Of course."

"Okay—here's the Air Penn itinerary. Pittsburgh, Pennsylvania—to Erie, Pennsylvania—to Bradford, Pennsylvania—to Williamsport, Pennsylvania—to Harrisburg, Pennsylvania—to Altoona, Pennsylvania—to"—she took a deep breath—"*Bogota, Colombia.*"

It took a second to sink in. "*Bogota, Colombia?*"

Kate smiled, or tried to. "Not literally—no. But *Air Penn* also leases out planes. Giraldo Diaz had leased the plane from *Air Penn. Air Penn* officials swore that they had no idea that he had used it for the transportation of drugs—"

The snifter slipped out of Kate's hands and fell to the rug. She looked at it for a second. "I think I'm drunk," she said.

I waited for her to talk some more, but she was silent.

"Anything else—?" I ventured.

She looked up at me, her eyes large and frightened. "I've talked too much already. No more. For your sake, Jim."

"Does Roy know?"

She shook her head. "Only you . . . and Dick . . . and Billy Bob"—she smiled ruefully—"see what I mean? They knew . . . and they're dead. And now you know. Just don't know *too much*, Jim."

"I won't. Where were you last night?"

She frowned. "I *wasn't* with Roy. Okay?"

"Okay, Kate—"

She smiled. "But thanks for the talk, Jim. I've been carrying it all in here"—she pointed first to her head and then to her stomach—"all alone for too long. But, Jim—stay out of it. Go away. That's my best advice. Heed it."

She picked up the pistol from the floor and put it back in her raincoat pocket. "Sorry, about the melodrama." She grinned with embarrassment.

"It's okay," I said.

At the door she turned. "You're . . . not going to"—she tried to make a joke of the words—"*turn me in* . . . or anything, are you?"

"Wouldn't think of it, Kate."

"Thanks." Before she closed the door, she said very seriously, "Stay out of it, Jim. And for both our sakes—*stay away from me.*"

After she left, I poured myself another brandy and stood looking out the window at the park. It had started to rain.

I turned on the radio. Something by Schubert was playing. A symphony. I listened to the whole thing, trying to will myself to relax.

Just as it ended, the phone rang. I picked up the receiver. "Hello—?" Silence at the other end. "Hello—?" Silence. And then, whoever had called me, hung up.

I stood for a moment, looking at the phone. The FM announcer was saying, ". . . so if your life is becoming just a bit too tense, a bit too hectic, why not consider this. . . ."

I turned off the radio.

Chapter 31

The flight left right on time, took just under an hour, and the sun was shining when we landed at the Greater Pittsburgh Airport.

Rusty Carpenter was waiting for me at the gate. I didn't spot him at first, because, by now, Rusty was pretty gray.

We shook hands and headed out to the parking lot for his car. As he started it, Rusty said. "Just to ease your mind, everything's jake. I shot film for two hours. The guy must think you're going to do a network documentary on Air Penn—and he's already seeing himself promoted from flack man to vice president."

"You're sure he doesn't suspect anything?"

"Suspect?—Forget it. He's so cooperative—he'd probably do your shirts for you if you asked him."

"And he believes that I'm back at RBS News—?"

"Well . . ."—Rusty guffawed—"I don't know how to break this to you, Jim, but he never even knew you left because—well, he's not too sure who you are in the first place."

I laughed with him. "How about you?"

"Oh, I'm fine. He knows me from KDKA. He was even at my retirement party last year. I just told him that I got tired of retirement, and I'm doing a little free-lance for the RBS network."

"Did he ask why our Pittsburgh affiliate wasn't shooting the story?"

"Yeah, he did."

"And—?"

"I just gave him a look of disdain and said, please, this was a *network* job."

We both laughed.

As we came out of the tunnel and saw Pittsburgh below us, golden and sparkling, Rusty said, "I came this way so you could get a good glimpse of the city. I'll take the ramp off, and we'll drive along the Monongahela up to Mount Washington. There's a great restaurant called *Maud's Place*—overlooks everything. Beautiful. Great food, too. The best."

"Sounds perfect. I'm assuming that he's going to meet us there."

"Right. His name is Randall Furman."

"Does he expect me to do an on-camera interview?"

"Don't worry. I shot a million feet of Mr. Furman—at his desk, racing into the building, catching a cab—you name it. I told him you're going to voice-over everything." Rusty pulled into a small parking lot. "Here—" He handed me a notebook. "Just pretend to take notes."

"And what about the names?"

"He'll have them. I gave him a wink and let him know it was a quid pro quo arrangement. No names—no *quo*."

"Did he ask for a reason for my wanting the names?"

"Sort of. I was vague. Something about a demographic mailing list for the RBS sales department."

"It almost sounds real," I said.

"Yeah. Damned if it doesn't."

As he opened the car door, Rusty asked, "How long've you had the mustache?"

"A while now. What d'you think?"

Rusty pondered his answer. "Well . . . the word *gigolo* comes to mind . . . or maybe—"

"Thanks," I said.

We got out of the car and went into the restaurant, an old house, renovated and refurbished into a delightfully cozy spot that overlooked the entire Golden Triangle of Pittsburgh.

I whistled my admiration.

"Yeah," Rusty said. "It's something, isn't it? I knew you'd love it." Rusty lowered his voice. "I also picked it because, like many a P.R.–flack-man type, our man likes a superior free lunch as often as he can promote one."

A young woman greeted us. It was obvious that Rusty was a fairly regular customer. "Hello, Mr. Carpenter," she said, "Maud had to dash out for a bit, but she gave you your favorite table and suggested the Dover Sole."

"Thanks, Mary." To me, Rusty said: "Wait'll you see Maud. She's beautiful."

"Oh, and your guest is already here, Mr. Carpenter."

She took our coats, checked them, and led us in to our table. A very short and very rotund man stood as we approached.

Sotto voce, Rusty murmured, "Randall—Randall Furman." In a normal voice, he said, "Randall—say hello to Jim Sasser."

We got through the greetings, got through ordering drinks, and got through the obligatory two jokes that most public relations men seem to consider absolutely vital to the beginning of any business luncheon. One of the jokes was actually funny.

As the laughter died down at the table, I said: "Do you have the list of names?"

Jones looked surprised.

"Do you—?"

He hesitated. I glanced in Rusty's direction. "Go out to the car, open the trunk, and destroy that tape."

Randall Furman turned red-faced. "Hey, wait a minute—ah—Jim, it's right here in my pocket."

I feigned anger. "Then what was the big surprise act?"

"No . . . surprise," he held up his hands in a gesture of mollification, "I was just—taken back, that's all." He tried to chuckle. "Yes, sir, you're certainly fast. 'Course down here in Pittsburgh everything's slower than up where you come from. Here you go—"

He held out a long and thick manila envelope. I took it from him and opened it. "This is complete—for the past three years?"

"Complete. *Absolutely.*" Randall Furman's face got even redder as he tried to look as honorable as George Washington, unfortunately, in his case, an impossibility.

"Every person for the past three years who has leased an Air Penn plane?"

"Every name. And," he added proudly, "after each name, the number of times they leased and the dates."

"Well done—"

Randall Furman beamed.

"But if it's not what you say"—I tried to sound casually threatening, as if I were the sort who could quite easily say, *off with his head*—"if it's not, this piece we're doing will never see the light of day."

"*Trust me,*" Randall Furman said.

"Fine."

I stuffed the thick envelope into my jacket, pulled out the notebook supplied by Rusty, and picked up my menu: I segued quickly from fairly unpleasant to briskly pleasant and smiling: "What do you say we order and then get started with the interview."

Randall Furman smiled and visibly relaxed. "I heard the— uh—hostess suggest the Dover Sole to you—"

I managed to get through, what seemed to Mr. Furman, at least, a complete and thorough interview over the appetizer alone by bombarding him with a series of staccato questions, never letting the pace lag—and by asking him such leading questions as could never fail to melt the heart of any public relations man, questions designed to invoke answers that covered everything from how Air Penn thought always of passengers before profits, to their special considerations for children, the elderly, the lame, and the lonely.

I ended with a real doozy. "And what is your last thought at night, Mr. Furman—"

"Randall—call me, Randall, please—" There was a hint of tears in his eyes, so much had he come to believe his own baloney.

"Randall . . . your last thought as you lie on your pillow, ready for sleep?"

"Well . . . uh, Jim . . . I guess I think of Air Penn—"

"Of course—I *knew* it."

"Yes, of course . . . uh, as you say . . . but I think of Air Penn—*and* Mr. Fishbein, Bill Fishbein—"

"The president of Air Penn—"

"Yes—"

"Your boss."

"Well, I never think of Bill Fishbein as my boss—more like—an uncle—or a brother."

"Of course. So you think of him?"

"Yes—"

"*Every* night—?"

"Yes—"

"Is there some sort of unsavory overtone to this that I'm missing?"

"*Jimmy.*" It was Rusty, giving me a decidedly dirty look.

I shrugged an apology to Rusty, and tried to save myself from my own silly sense of humor, by sounding even more deadly serious with Mr. Randall Furman.

"I tried to joke with you, Randall, admittedly a joke in bad taste—and one I know you don't take seriously for a minute— because you were getting pretty emotional—too emotional for your own good, I thought. But I can see that that's simply the way you are about your job." Again, another golden leading question: "Your life—from your first thoughts in the morning to your last thoughts at night—your life is *Air Penn,* isn't it?"

"Yes . . . yes it is." Randall's voice was thick and hushed, awash in his own hogwash.

"And"—I risked it one more time—"how you can help good, old Bill Fishbein make Air Penn an even better company—the best."

"Yes, that's true, Jim—"

"And, of course, how you can, in your own way, ease the myriad burdens on Bill Fishbein's shoulders."

"Yes—oh, *yes—*"

"Randall"—I reached across the table, clapped him on the back, and in my own hushed voice said—"you're quite a man."

"*Thanks* . . . Jim. *Thanks.*"

Randall Furman, Vice President, Public Relations, Air Penn, blew his nose and wiped the inchoate tears from his eyes.

As I sat once again in the office of the Vice President of Human Resources for Northern Industries/RBS, I silently wondered if he and Randall Furman were distant relatives. Probably. Now, at least, I knew why that feeling of déjà vu had overwhelmed me earlier in the day when I had met Randall Furman in Pittsburgh.

". . . highly unlikely, in any case, and completely against our normal modus operandi. . . ." I pretended to listen as best I could.

". . . and that's about it, I'm afraid, Mr. Sasser." He had finally concluded his peroration, and he was very pleased with himself: He had said *no*. Moreover, he had taken seven and a half minutes to say *no*. It had made for a most satisfactory ending to the day for my blinking friend.

I tried to sound extremely calm, but, somehow, menacing. "May I suggest that you pick up the phone and call"—for the first time, I remembered the initials, just when I needed them— "M.S.W."

"Who?"

I played my ace. "Mr. M. Seabury Whitehead, of course."

"Really—"

"Or I'll call," I continued, my voice still calm and, I profoundly hoped, menacing.

That got him. His expression changed. He was uncertain.

I smiled in what I hoped was a warm, calming, *menacing* way. "Sir, why don't you make it easy on yourself and simply let me look through the personnel files. That's really all I'm asking. You let me do it a few weeks ago. There was no problem then—"

"Yes, but now I—"

"Now—why, I don't know"—again a warm, yet menacing smile—"you're being uncooperative. I have no desire to report any of this to Mr. Whitehead, but if you don't grant my simple request—"

"All right—" He was petulant, peevish—"go ahead and look. But don't take anything with you. And be neat."

"Of course—"

"I must insist on that."

"Indeed." I was determined not to let him have the last shot. "By the way," I said, in as pleasant, charming and ingratiating a manner as I could muster, "It's nice to see that your position hasn't been *terminated* or that *early retirement* hasn't been thrust upon you—"

His eyes twitched even more, and he dabbed at the sweat on his forehead with a handkerchief.

"—yes," I smiled, "It's nice to see that you're still with us. For now, at least."

A job that I had assumed would take an hour or two at the most was taking nearly the entire night. My main problem was myself. I have a kind of cluttered mind, not particularly logical, and utterly incapable of performing any task that requires simple organization.

After only an hour, I knew that I should have brought Libby Nolan with me. She can do more research in one morning than I can in a month.

"Ah, Libby, just ten more to go and it's *only* four in the morning." During the last hour or so, I had taken to talking to myself every once in a while, so talking to a Libby who wasn't present, seemed somehow a perfectly sane thing to do as well.

My problem would have been immediately obvious to anyone else. I had assumed that only one or two people from RBS would have leased a plane from Air Penn. Fine. But, obviously—to anyone else—a man or woman leasing a plane for a nefarious drug scheme could hardly be expected to sign the lease, *John Doe, Drug Dealer and Employee of the Republic Broadcasting System*.

So I had to take every name on the list supplied by Mr. Randall Furman and clear it with the list of every employee at Northern Industries/RBS.

"It would have been a hell of a lot easier if I could even be doing this the old fashioned way," I murmured to myself— "manually going through filing cases. But—no—now everything has to be on a bloody *computer*."

I fought back my desire to strike out physically at the evil device.

At a quarter to five in the morning, I finally checked out the name *Wellington Zweig,* who had leased an Air Penn freight plane two years before, found that he was not, and had never been, an employee of RBS, and my job was finished.

I had ended up with three names. All three had leased an Air Penn plane, two of them more than once, and all three worked for RBS.

"Who's there?" I tried to ask it very calmly.

There was someone standing behind me. *I knew it.* There was not a doubt in my mind.

No answer.

"Yes—?" I turned, the hair on the back of my neck suddenly electric, the electricity that always comes with fear. If I had been a dog, I would probably have growled.

"Well, well, it's Jim. What're you doing, Jim?"

"Just going through some personnel—excuse me—*human resources* files—"

"Why—?"

It was Sam Bigelow. He was smiling.

"Oh . . . just finishing up things."

"Well, you're certainly diligent, I'll give you that. It's going on five in the morning." Sam's smile broadened and he looked around the room. "Are you . . . all alone?"

"Yeah," I said. "All alone."

As he glanced away. I shoved the list into my inside jacket pocket.

"Finishing up, huh," Sam said. "I thought you already had. Finished, I mean."

"Oh . . . I had."

"I thought so. M.S.W. is singing your praises and"—Sam Bigelow chuckled—"Big Bill is echoing the praises and taking full credit for hiring you."

"I'm glad everybody is happy," I said.

"Well . . . then what are you doing here, burning the midnight oil?" Sam's smile was indulgent.

"It's just my compulsive nature. And—your Vice President of Human Resources is a pain in the neck. He's given me a hard time from day one—including today. He said he hoped that I'd been neat with his files. I didn't want to give him the satisfaction. Of course, he won in the end . . . I've been up for most of the night. . . ."

It made no sense at all, but I hoped that, taken as a whole, it would satisfy Sam. It seemed to.

"Yeah—he's an unpleasant little son of a bitch, isn't he?"

"Very." I stood, noting that Sam Bigelow had remained between the door and my position. "What are *you* doing here, Sam? Up all night, too?"

He shook his head. "Just in early. RBS Sports is going to cover the tournament down at the Garden. I'm giving a new producer his head on it. I want to make sure he gets started off on the right foot."

"How are things at good old RBS Sports these days?"

Sam laughed. "Frugal, Jim, frugal. Like everything else at RBS."

I moved toward the door, wondering if he were going to try to stop me. He merely followed.

As I turned off the lights and locked the door, I said: "In your opinion, did I leave the place looking neat?"

"Very," Sam said.

"I may need your testimony—"

Sam chuckled. "You'll get it."

As we walked back out through the main part of the personnel department, Sam said, "It's awful isn't it? You and I've still not really gotten together for a good long dinner."

"You've got the rain check," I said.

Sam nodded. "And I'll be calling in the next few days—"

Out in the lobby, I said: "It was good to see you, Sam. Even at four forty-five a.m. in the Human Resources Department."

Sam chuckled. "A bar would've been better." He shook my hand. "Take it easy, Jim. See you soon."

He started for the main bank of elevators.

"Say, Sam—?"

He turned, still smiling.

"Sam . . . how come you . . . just . . . showed up in the file room just now?"

He thought for a moment. "You know . . . I don't know."
He shrugged. "I didn't even think about it . . . just kind of went
there . . . thought somebody might be in there . . . and there
you were. . . ."

Sam Bigelow laughed. "Funny, isn't it? Weird. Those mys-
tics may have something after all. Well . . . see you, Jim."

He started for the elevators for a second time.

"Say, Sam?—ever hear of Air Penn—?"

Either he didn't hear me or didn't want to. An elevator door
was opening; Sam waved to me, without turning around, as he got
in.

"Take care, Jim—"

Chapter 32

It was nearly one in the afternoon when I woke up, but I was
refreshed.

I showered, dressed, and called the offices of Maloney,
O'Neil and Sasser.

Maureen answered.

Joe was lunching with a potential client, Libby was lunching
with my agent, and Maureen announced that she would be
agreeable to having lunch with me.

"I'd love to," I said. "But I just got up, so I'll call my
lunch-breakfast."

"Well aren't you the slugabed—"

"I was up all night."

"My, my."

"*Working*—"

"Oh. My apologies."

"At lunch, I'll show you the results of my nocturnal labors."

"You talk funny when you just wake up," Maureen said.

"What about Wolf's? You can get some eggs and I can have a sandwich."

"You're on."

Maureen was already seated back in a corner by the window when I arrived. When she saw me, she waved.

"I've just ordered a bottle of Beck's—make it two?"

I made a face. "Last thing in the world I want when I just get up."

"There's hope for you, then. Very little, of course, but hope."

"Thanks." I ordered tea from the waitress, along with ham and toast. Maureen ordered a hot pastrami on rye.

As we ate I filled her in about my trip to see Buzz Berman, the solution of the *ELN* puzzle, the covert drug team of Dick Ainsley and Kate Morgan, Kate's admission to being involved in the drug situation, my trip to Pittsburgh, the Air Penn list, my search through the files—and the strange appearance of Sam Bigelow.

Maureen let out her breath in a low whistle. "My God, but you've been a busy little bee, haven't you? How much of all this does Joe know? Anything at all?"

"Everything but last night."

Maureen let out her breath again. "So what are you going to do?"

"Well . . . I was sort of hoping . . . that I could give you the three names from RBS personnel that checked out with the Air Penn list of lessees. I was sort of hoping that you could track them down for me."

Maureen looked at me, an expression of amusement in her eyes. "You were *sort of* hoping that, huh?"

"Well . . . sort of."

She laughed.

"Okay, Jimmy—let's see the list. I'll *sort of* see what I can do."

"Thanks, Maureen." I pulled the list out of my breast pocket. "You're great."

"Sort of—"

The three names on the list were all men. They all worked at RBS, of course, but more important, more coincidental, more *fascinating,* they all worked in the RBS *Sports* Department.

Maureen dramatically announced that she had all three names tracked down before our food even arrived.

I took it as a joke. "No, really—how long do you think it will take? And don't get too annoyed with me, I know it won't be easy. I'm well aware that one guy on the list is even named Smith."

Maureen smiled. "Good. Then you actually *looked* at the list."

"Of course. My God, I've been up all night looking at that thing."

"And you didn't notice?" She held the list in front of my face.

"Notice what?"

"Under their names—"

"*What*—under their names?"

"Their addresses"—Maureen's smile broadened—"*And* their phone numbers."

I was silent.

Maureen tried to stifle her laughter, but she failed.

"Now you see how difficult this sort of thing is for me," I said defensively.

"Not difficult, Jimmy—*impossible.*"

"—Heads up." The waitress brought our food.

During the meal, I filled in Maureen with a more detailed accounting of my exploits, particularly the conversation with Buzz Berman and the episode with Kate Morgan.

"Sounds as if she's scared stiff," Maureen said.

"That's an understatement. And she's afraid she talked too much to me. Afraid she's putting herself in even more jeopardy."

"And you, Jimmy—?"

"Naw—"

"Stop being silly." Maureen's eyes blazed. "What if she tells . . . whoever she can tell—that she let you know about Air Penn."

"She won't. Not Kate."

"*Not Kate*. A week ago you'd have said the same thing about her and drugs."

"Maybe—"

"Of course you would. If she talks, you're in trouble. And you've got to look at it as a possibility that she'll talk. So watch yourself."

I held her hand. "Okay, Maureen. I will."

"Good. Now—" she drew her hands away and picked up the Air Penn list—"let's decide how to go about this."

Maureen decided.

She called each man's home and identified herself as a Miss Blodgett in Northern Industries' Human Resources Department, which was about to incorporate into its own computer pool, the information from the RBS computer printouts. She wanted to check, addresses and phone numbers.

It was such a simple plan that it worked. Two men were still at work at RBS, and the one who was off for the day, Smith, we luckily caught at home. The whole thing took ten minutes.

As Maureen hung up the phone, she said morosely, "There's only one problem, Jimmy, fairly major."

"What—?"

"So—*what*. What do we have now? The answer: nothing. So they all live where they say they live—so what?"

"You've got a point," I agreed glumly.

We sat for a good five minutes without saying a word.

"Jimmy—?"

"Yes?"

"I just had a thought. I said: 'So they all live where they say they live.' Well, look—" Maureen held up the list. "Bracken lives on Staten Island, Pebbles lives in Brooklyn—and Smith lives in New Jersey. On a road. No town."

I frowned. "You'll have to explain it to me."

Maureen was smiling. "I'll explain it on the way. If I'm right, you'll buy me dinner."

She went to the phone.

"Who're you going to call?"

"Hertz."

"Hertz—?"

"I'm going to rent a car. We're going to drive out to take a look at where Mr. Smith lives."

It took just over an hour and a half, driving almost due west from the George Washington Bridge, to get to Campton Road, slightly about Route 80, in northwestern New Jersey.

It was suddenly almost rural. There were even letter boxes on poles along the road.

After a dozen or so letter boxes, we spied one with *Smith* painted on the side.

"Just keep moving," Maureen said. "I want to see something."

After only an eighth of a mile, she grunted in disappointment.

"What's the matter?"

"Looks as if I buy *you* dinner," she said.

"I'm confused."

"That's my fault, not yours." She sighed. "When you see a place where we can turn around, let's go back to Route 80—and the city."

It took another mile before I spotted an intersection and a place to turn.

"Son of a *bitch*—" Maureen let out a war whoop. "Turn around down there—"

"I'm going to—"

"And come back this way—"

"Of course—"

"You saw it, too, then?"

"I don't know what you're talking about," I said.

"You will—"

After turning around, coming back up the road, I spotted it. Another mailbox with *Smith* on it. "Hey, Maureen, did you see this one—? And I'll bet it's the right Smith."

Maureen was smiling. "What makes you think so?"

"It says *A. Smith*. The other one just said *Smith*. Our guy's name was Albert Smith. Get it? A. Smith. It probably stands for Albert."

Maureen's laughter came in a burst. "Oh, Jimmy—"

I was petulant. "I must be pretty funny," I said.

More laughter.

"Go ahead. Enjoy yourself."

"I'm sorry—"

"Sure."

"I couldn't control myself—"

"You certainly seem to be having a dandy time," I said.

"I am—but don't you see why? Sure, this Smith is our Smith. But what's even better is that this Smith—our Smith—is in the *right place*."

She smiled at me, waiting.

"I still don't get it."

"You don't?"

"I didn't even understand why we came out here in the first place."

She was smiling gleefully. "Drive down for another quarter of a mile. Stop the car. We'll both get out and look under the hood."

I did as I was told, feeling pretty dimwitted.

Standing at one side of the raised hood, Maureen said, "Take a look back at the home of our A. Smith. What do you see?"

I peered at the house with great concentration. "A house, a yard, a vegetable garden, a barn, a—" I shook my head. "What—?"

Maureen's face was flushed. "What's different between this Smith's house and the other Smith's house?"

I shook my head. "I don't know. Just *tell* me, Maureen. No more quiz show."

"This Smith's house is in the *right place*," she said again.

"What the hell"—my voice rose in frustration—"is the *right place* supposed to mean."

She grabbed my arms with both her hands and looked me squarely in the face, her eyes dancing excitedly. "*This* Smith-has-a-*great-big-level-field* behind his house."

"Do you know, you have the most beautiful eyes, Maureen—"

She pursed her lips in annoyance. "Do you have *any* idea of what I'm driving at?"

I thought for a second. "To tell you the truth . . . no."

"Okay . . ." She spoke as if to a child. "This Smith . . . has a field . . . which is probably . . . extremely suitable . . . for the landing of small planes."

I looked at her. "Oh—"

"Yes," she said, "Oh—"

"Well, I'll be a son of a bitch."

"I believe I already said that."

"Yes, I believe you did."

I called Rusty Carpenter in Pittsburgh the minute Maureen and I got back to Manhattan. He immediately agreed to help. I knew he would.

"I just might know somebody," Rusty drawled.

"Hell, you know everybody in Greater Pittsburgh, don't you?"

He chuckled. "Almost, I guess. And I think I've got just the person . . . yeah, she's perfect."

"*She*. I might have known."

Rusty chuckled again. "I'll see her first thing tomorrow. The minute we come up with something, I'll give you a call."

"Thanks, Rusty. And tell *her*—thanks, too."

Rusty laughed.

The next week was busy and fun. I wrote out the first draft of an interview with an up-and-coming real estate tycoon, did the second draft of another chapter, and interviewed a brash and rich off-Broadway producer from Texas who said at the end: "I'd give anything to have this interview come out good and positive, you know what ah mean?"

He did everything but wink at me.

"I'll see what I can do," I said.

"Good, boy. Good, boy—"

I was a good ten years older than he.

I spent an entire afternoon at The Players, either in the library or shooting pool; I spent another afternoon with Libby Nolan in the New York Public Library; I called Dr. Antonia Hastings and found out, according to her taped voice on the answering machine, that she was in Los Angeles for the week; I had lunch once with an old friend; I had drinks twice with Joe; and three times I caught glimpses of Susan Mazur. Always at a distance. Once in the Metropolitan Museum, once as I crossed Madison Avenue, and once while buying theater tickets on Forty-Fourth Street.

The fourth time wasn't at a distance. I literally walked into her, coming out of the paperback section in the back of Double-day's on Fifth and Fifty-Fifth.

"*Well*—" The collision caused her bag to slip from her shoulder. She quickly stooped to pick it up.

I tried to come to her aid, and we bumped heads.

"Well," she said again, "what a surprise to see you."

"Why?"

"Well, I mean . . . it's been a while since we've seen each other."

"But I've seen you at least three times in the last week alone."

"Well . . ."—she smiled playfully—"I haven't seen you."

It all ended up with the two of us having lunch at Capriccio. I got an appreciative nod of the head from Ray as he greeted us and led us to a table: I was obviously becoming a successful boule-vardier.

Over the first sip of our kirs, I said, "I've begun to wonder if you're following me."

She smiled.

I said: "I suppose I was just flattering myself."

Susan Mazur said, not unpleasantly, "if I'd wanted to see you, I'd have simply called you up." She smiled again. The captain brought a phone to the table and plugged it in. "It's for you, Mr. Sasser."

It was Maureen.

"How did you know I was here?"

"You called me and told me where you were going to be.

Remember? That was only half an hour ago. What're you drinking over there—British naval rum?"

"Your wit is a thing to behold," I said. "Only my enormous self-control keeps me from collapsing with laughter. What's up?"

"Rusty Carpenter is on the other line. He says he's got something. If you want, I can conference the two of you together."

"Good."

"Don't hang up now"—a series of clicks—"Hello, Mr. Carpenter?" Rusty's voice: "Hello—?"

"Go ahead," Maureen said.

"Hi, Rusty, it's Jim."

"Howdy, Jim, how are you?"

"Fine. What've you got?"

"My contact at Air Penn has just transacted an interesting bit of business. A plane lease to one of our three friends."

"Which one?"

"Albert Smith."

"Did he do it"—I glanced at Susan—"in the name of . . . ah . . . the company he works for?"

"You with somebody?"

"Yes."

"Nope. He signed his own name."

"How long is . . . the agreement?"

"A week. Starting tomorrow."

"Thanks, Rusty. Thanks a lot. I'll get back to you when I can."

"Boy, oh, boy, but you're brief today." Rusty chuckled. "Can't wait to get off the phone with me."

I glanced at Susan. "I'm with a beautiful woman. Is that a good enough reason to be brief?"

"Anytime—" Rusty's voice got serious. "What's this Air Penn stuff all about, Jim? A guy can't help but be curious."

"I'll let you know when it's all over, Rusty. In the meantime, I thank you from the bottom of my heart."

"Okay." Rusty's voice was very serious. "But keep your head down, Jim."

"Always, Rusty. Always."

Susan was pretending to scan the menu. "Anything important?"

"Not really."

"It sounded important."

I smiled. "Right now it's very important that we have a good lunch and enjoy ourselves."

She smiled. The captain approached to tell us about the specials of the day.

I thanked him for the telephone. He nodded and motioned to a busboy to take it away.

I wondered if Susan Mazur really had been following me for the past week. Or the past God-knows-what?

We decided on *carpaccio* with fresh figs, pasta, and a veal chop.

And *I* decided—once again—that I wasn't too sure about Susan Mazur.

Chapter 33

The next day was Tuesday. We counted Tuesday as Day Number One.

Certainly no one could fly to God knows where, pick up a load of drugs and fly back, if indeed, that was what anyone would be doing, in one day. So we didn't drive out to the small farm of Mr. A. Smith on Tuesday evening.

On Wednesday—Day Two—we waited as well.

On Thursday, Maureen got worried, and Joe and I agreed with her. We drove out to the area, rented motel rooms, and, under cover of the early evening darkness, drove to a spot that gave us a good view of the farm.

We took turns watching and dozing. But by dawn, nothing had happened.

Joe yawned. "Anybody feel like breakfast?"

We all did. After breakfast, it was back to our rooms for a shower and some sleep.

"Don't call me, I'll call you," Joe said. "I'll see you for dinner at six. And let's take some sandwiches tonight—"

After my shower, I tossed and turned for a full two or three seconds before I fell off to sleep.

Loud and prolonged banging on my door woke me up. "Let me in—it's time to go. *Wake up*." It was Maureen.

I fought to wake up, and would have lost the battle if Maureen hadn't continued her harangue at the door.

As I opened it, she said, "Are you awake?"

"What do I look like?"

"I'm not sure—"

"I'm awake," I said. "And I feel awful. Absolutely awful."

"I hope you showered before you went to bed."

"Well, as a matter of fact—"

"Good. Then shave and get dressed. I'll wake up Joe now. And hurry." She looked at me accusingly. "We're late."

A few minutes later, as we assembled in front of the car, Joe said to me, "You look awful."

"I wouldn't have mentioned it, but so do you," I said. "I feel as if I hardly slept at all."

"Same here."

Maureen had taken care of getting what passed for breakfast while Joe and I dressed. "I have coffee and doughnuts—that's good enough," she told us. "I'll drive. You can eat on the way out to the farm."

"And *sandwiches*—" Joe was grief stricken.

"I have those, too."

"Oh?" A more relieved tone of voice from Joe.

We drove for a while in silence. I was in the front seat next to Maureen, and Joe was in the back. Suddenly, directly behind me, I heard Joe's hushed, yet emotional voice. "The sun—"

I waited for more. Nothing was forthcoming until—"The Goddamned *sun*—"

"What about it?" I asked.

"The *sun*—"

"What about—?"

"Look at your watch. Look at your *watch*."

I did. My watch said *eleven*.

"Maureen—what time is it?"

She kept her eyes on the road. "About eleven I'd guess. What's your watch say?"

"Eleven."

"Well, there you are."

"Eleven in the *morning*—?"

"Of *course*, it's eleven in the morning," came Joe's voice from the back. "If it were eleven at night, it'd be dark, for God's sake."

"What's the idea?" I sounded petulant, but I didn't care.

Maureen didn't look at me, but continued to watch the road, driving quickly and furiously. "It occurred to me that we'd made one mighty big assumption. We assumed that any plane running drugs would land at night. Why?"

"Well . . . I don't know. They just do, don't they? Rum runners, drug runners—they always do."

"How do we know that?"

"Well—movies, television—it just makes sense. It's more secret. Less noticeable."

"Ah, *ha*. Less noticeable? Here in fairly densely populated northern New Jersey, I'm not so sure. Maybe a plane landing during the *day* would be less noticeable. More routine. Less given to speculation by neighbors than the sound of planes landing at night with—I don't know—torches, attention-drawing emergency landing lights, that sort of thing."

"Well—maybe," I said grudgingly.

"At any rate—" Maureen barely negotiated a curve.

"Hey—"

"At any rate, this is Day Number Four. If we were to come back tonight, stay up all night, and see nothing—then this would've been one wasted wild-goose chase. And we'd never know."

"And this way," Joe groused from the rear, "we'll get no sleep at all and know that you've had a bum theory."

"But if I'm right?"

"We'll see."

"My idea makes sense." Maureen said doggedly. "It's a possibility. More than a possibility. It would be less attention getting for a small plane to land during the daytime than to—"

"You said that before." Joe was in a vile mood.

"Don't you agree, Jimmy?" Maureen glanced over at me.

"Well . . ." I said decisively, "*Maybe*—"

"Thanks a lot," Maureen said.

"Some theory." Joe's voice was filled with scorn.

Maureen scowled at him. It was three in the afternoon and no plane had been spotted. In fact, there hadn't been any kind of life at all around the farmhouse.

Another hour droned by.

"Any more sandwiches?" Joe asked.

"You had the last one," Maureen said.

"I'm thirsty," Joe said.

Maureen looked at him. "You sound like a baby."

"But I'm thirsty."

"*But I'm thirsty*—" Maureen mimicked him.

I said, "As a matter of fact, I'm kind of thirsty myself—"

"*What?*" Maureen looked at me sternly.

"Nothing."

No one said anything for the next twenty minutes or so. A miasma of anger hung over the three of us like a cloud.

I was wondering how we were going to get through the night with the sorry combination of our exhaustion from lack of sleep and our foul moods—when I heard the buzzing.

Maureen heard it, too.

We exchanged glances and listened. It got closer. The sound changed from a buzzing to a drone.

Then we saw it as it popped out of a cloud. The plane circled and came down lower and lower.

"It's too big to land in that field," Joe said.

I silently agreed.

"But that's what he's going to do," Maureen said.

"*Try* to do—"

The pilot came in with landing gear extended and full flaps, reversing engines the split second he touched down. He made it with about fifty feet to spare.

"Oh, my God—*that's* a pilot." Joe's voice was filled with admiration.

"He made it then—?" Maureen had closed her eyes when it looked as if the plane would roll into the woods and crash.

"He made it," I said, "with almost nothing to spare."

"A twin-engine Cessna," Joe announced.

He could have been right. I had no idea what the plane was; I knew only one thing—that it was awfully big to land in that field.

A minute or so went by. Five minutes went by. Ten minutes went by. Nothing happened. No one got out of the plane. No one approached the plane.

"What the hell—?" Joe murmured.

"Beats me—"

Finally, a figure emerged from the house and sauntered casually toward the craft.

"The glasses—" Maureen commanded. She tapped me on the shoulder.

"What—?"

"Hand me the glasses."

"What glasses?"

"*What* glasses—the field glasses."

"I don't have any field glasses."

Maureen's lips were tight and she looked at me with disdain. "You—don't—have—any—field—glasses?"

"Of course I don't. Why would I?"

"Well—" She gestured toward the farmhouse—"if you did, we just might be able to see what the hell is going on down there instead of watching"—someone had just emerged from the plane and was proceeding to meander, just as casually, toward the figure sauntering out from the farmhouse—"instead of watching a couple of *match sticks*."

I had nothing to say.

"Hey, look—" Joe was pointing toward the barn. A small tractor, one of the kind that suburban husbands enjoy riding while gardening, came rolling out of the building. Besides the person driving it, two other figures emerged from the barn as well, all moving with the same elaborate slowness.

"Not such a silly way of doing business after all, is it?" Maureen was still tight-lipped.

"Not at all," I agreed.

"Everything relaxed, no hurry, no alarming movements or sounds—just easygoing and simple." Maureen's voice got a slight edge to it. "Nothing that will cause suspicion or concern among the neighbors—not the way scurrying about or *landing at night* would."

Simultaneously, Joe and I gave her a rub on the back and said, "You were right, Maureen."

"I'm sorry I was such a grouchy kid." Joe's face asked for forgiveness.

"Me, too," I said.

Maureen tried not to smile, but she did. "You're forgiven. But you're both on indefinite probation. Now"—Maureen was all business again—"Jimmy—hand me the bazooka."

"Maureen . . . I didn't bring a bazooka . . . in fact, it never even occurred to me that we might—"

Maureen laughed. Really laughed. Fully and loudly.

"Aw, Jimmy—I'm only kidding."

"Oh—"

"But it's nice to see how contrite you are."

Joe and I laughed with her. Everything was all right again. The miasma of anger had completely disappeared.

It took all of half an hour for the match sticks—there were six of them, including the pilot and the copilot—to maneuver the plane into the barn.

As the sliding doors were being pulled shut, Joe said: "Now what?"

It was a rhetorical question: he expected no answer: all three of us were wondering—"*Now what?*"

The sliding doors were never opened again. No one emerged from the barn. No one went in or came out of the farmhouse.

The days were getting much shorter, and it got dark early. As the first bit of gloaming descended over the area, a light went on in the downstairs of the house, followed by a light in the upstairs as well. There was no illumination at all around the barn.

"It's almost dark," I said. "I'm going to wait a few more minutes and then sneak in for a closer look."

"I'm coming with you," Joe said.

As I started to protest, Joe said, "*Jimmy*—I'm coming with you."

"Okay. Maureen, you'll stay—"

She smiled an almost dainty smile and said with deliberate coyness, "Should I bake some blueberry muffins while you're gone? I'm coming."

"Maureen, this is no time for nonsense. Someone should get in closer to take a look. That will be Joe and me. Someone has to stay here to protect the car. That will be you."

She nodded. "Okay, Jimmy. But if you get into any trouble— give a holler. I'll be there"—she patted the hood of our car— "with the cavalry."

The barn was very much larger than it appeared to be from the road.

"I'm going to check out the house," Joe whispered.

"Good idea—"

"Don't get into any trouble while I'm gone—" He slipped away into the tall grass and the darkness.

I moved in closer to the barn. It wasn't until I got right up to the side facing the road that I realized why it had appeared, from our vantage point, that only the farmhouse itself was lit: the few barn windows that existed had all been painted out. A faint scratch of light here and there was all that slithered through.

As planned, I waited at the wall for Joe. Nearly five minutes went by before he came back.

"What'd you find?"

"Nothing. So far as I can tell, there's nobody in the house."

"What about the lights?"

"Obviously, somebody turned them on. But there's nobody there now."

"Probably everybody's in here." I told him about the opaqued windows. "Let's make our way around to the front."

We found the miniature tractor at one corner. And, beside it, a door that was cracked open by a quarter of an inch. I started to ease open the door.

Joe's hand gripped me at the wrist. "Hey, Jimmy—"

"What?"

"Why the hell are you and I doing this?"

"Well . . . just for the love of the hunt, that's why."

"You sound like George Plimpton," Joe said.

"Thanks . . . I think."

The sudden sound of singing came from the road up near the farmhouse. Young men's voices. A car horn blew. Nothing. It blew a second time, longer and more persistently.

There was scurrying, and muffled voices from inside the barn. We heard what must have been one of the sliding doors being pushed open.

A moment later, a heavyset man ran past us, only ten or fifteen feet away, and headed for the farmhouse.

At the house, what looked like half a dozen young men, still singing, were now weaving their way up to the front porch.

The heavyset figure that had raced past us stopped and shouted in an agitated voice, "For God's sake, Al, hurry up. They're headin' for the house now."

"Keep your shirt on—" A second figure ran past us—no doubt Al.

Together, they raced up to the house to meet the gang of choristers.

"We'd better get the hell out of here," Joe said.

"Not now, Joe. It's just the sort of diversion we need."

"Okay, Jimmy. Now I know I must be nuts. Listening to you—that's the litmus test."

We crouched down beside the tractor. And like an echo it came back to me. That voice: *"For God's sake, Al, hurry up. They're headin' for the house now."*

That voice was familiar.

Up at the farmhouse, the happy band of nocturnal visitors had now broken into "Far above Cayuga's waters . . ." except that they weren't singing that, really; only the melody—with the wrong words. Obviously, they were boys from Syracuse.

"Joe, did you recognize that voice? The first one that—"

"Get down, Jimmy—"

The happy band of boys had begun to run, laughing, shouting, one or two still singing, down the short distance from the farmhouse to the barn.

"Hey—come back here—what the hell do you think you're doin'—?"

That voice again.

"Hey, you bastards"—the other voice, no doubt the voice of Albert Smith—"stay the hell away from my barn."

They still came pell-mell down the hill.

In the moonlight, the first man—*the voice*—stopped in his tracks and pulled something from his pocket. The screech of a referee's whistle filled the night air. From inside the barn, another whistle blasted back. The sound of the sliding doors slamming open sounded like the rumble of heavy artillery, followed by the sounds of several engines being started at once.

I crept out past the tractor to get a better look.

At least two, perhaps three, paneled trucks came hurtling out of the barn and headed out for the road.

It was so sudden, and so shocking in a funny way, sort of like the beginning of a Keystone Kops chase scene, that the boys momentarily stopped their running and broke into laughter.

And as they started for the barn again, a shot rang out. Then two more shots, followed by a blast from a shotgun.

* * *

Everyone was shouting: the high whine of the paneled trucks as they raced to the road in second and third gears added to the din—another shot and another shotgun blast—the weapon, in sudden silhouette, pointed up into the air.

Joe and I took advantage of it all and sprinted around to the sliding doors. But they slammed shut as we rounded the corner of the barn, and we heard the hasp being slapped into place and padlocked as we got close.

"What the hell—"

The man who had locked the door turned on us. He was big, and he had a revolver that shone in the moonlight.

"Run, Joe—"

Our retreat was fast, furious, and frightened.

Rounding the corner, I ran into someone: "Hey—Al—what the hell's goin' on—"

It was *the voice*. I scrambled to my feet and ran again.

"Hey, *you*—"

I kept running.

"This way, Jimmy—" It was Joe.

I ran toward him, and together we made for the road at a right angle from the farmhouse, separating ourselves from the boys from Syracuse, hoping that they would be the diversion we needed.

Climbing the steep bank to the road, we heard Maureen's voice, a low tentative, "Jimmy—? Joe—?"

"Here we come—"

Relief. "Oh, thank God. . . . Hop in."

With Maureen at the wheel, we started down the road toward Route 80.

"Look out—"

We were rounding a bend, and another car was coming at us, mostly in our lane.

"Hold on—"

Maureen headed for the shoulder. The cars hit, but because of Maureen's fast maneuvering, we sort of slid along each other's

238

side until we ground to a halt in the field, about fifty feet off the road.

"Everybody okay?" I could see that Maureen was, and when I turned to the back, Joe raised a thumb in salute.

I quickly clambered out of the car and started for our assailant. "What the hell was that all about, you stupid son of a bitch?"

A frightened face stared back at me. It was Susan Mazur.

"Susan—"

The car started to pull away.

"Susan—"

She headed for the road.

I ran back to our own car.

"Can we move, Maureen?"

"You bet."

"Then—I've always wanted to say this—*follow that car*. It's Susan Mazur."

Up ahead, the other car turned.

"She's heading back to Route 80," Maureen said. "I wonder if she was going out to the farmhouse?"

"So do I. And the answer is probably . . . *probably*."

After five minutes, she'd lost us, somehow, and we gave up the chase.

There wasn't much conversation on the drive back to New York.

At one point, I asked Maureen, "Would you like me to drive?"

"No, thanks."

"Are you sleepy?"

"Not a bit. I'm so tired I'm wide awake."

"Me, too," Joe said.

We drove some more in silence.

After a while, Joe said, "It must've been a drug drop, all right."

"Um."

Joe snorted. "A Penn-Columbia drug drop."

"Yup."

I glanced at Maureen. She seemed to be alert. I closed my eyes to think.

I realized now, of course, why Susan Mazur had announced that she had come into a huge inheritance. Susan had wanted a reason for having, suddenly, excessive amounts of money to spend. So she had invented a reason. An ersatz uncle.

And *The Voice* . . . who did it sound like? . . . someone I knew . . . but who . . . ?

"And all three of these guys who rent these planes work for RBS Sports," Joe said.

. . . sports . . . *The Voice* . . . of course . . . Yes, that was the guy all right.

The Voice . . . belonged to Charlie Bohanen, former ace director for RBS Sports.

"Jimmy . . .?"

"Yeah?"

It was Maureen. She was smiling, her eyes still on the road. "Are you okay? You're sort of groaning."

"Was I? Didn't realize it. I was thinking. That guy I thought I recognized, Joe—he worked for RBS Sports until a few weeks ago. He was one of the ones laid off. His name is Charlie Bohanen."

"Is he the one I met in McGurk's one morning? Half in the bag?"

"That's the one."

"You're sure about his voice?"

"I'm sure."

Joe made a clucking sound with his tongue. "I'll be damned. . . ."

We drove on in silence. I couldn't help myself: The picture of the head of RBS Sports came into my mind.

Sam Bigelow.

Sam Bigelow . . . standing silently behind me . . . at five a.m. in the morning . . . in the records room.

I closed my eyes again.

Chapter 34

I slept late the next morning, took my time over the morning papers, glanced at three or four magazines and, in general, dawdled over breakfast.

I called Sam Bigelow at twelve thirty-five.

"I'm just about to go out to lunch with Toni Hastings," he said. "Care to join us?"

"Thanks, I'm pretty tied up. But actually, I was calling you about dinner tonight. I thought it's about time for you to retrieve your rain check."

"What a helluva good idea. But no rain check. Dinner's on me. And no arguments."

I said nothing.

"Jim? You still there?"

"You said—no arguments."

He laughed. "Good man. Let's say—about eight?"

"Perfect."

"D'you mind meeting me here? I've got to hang around for some conference calls from Los Angeles."

"Not a bit. What time?"

"Let's say around seven-thirty. I'll lay on my most luxurious limo."

"Seven-thirty it is."

I made a point of arriving at the RBS Broadcast Center at six forty-five.

The Sports Department wing was buzzing almost as nervously as a newsroom. People were scurrying everywhere. But as I expected, Sam's secretary had gone for the day. Her desk was empty.

Sam's office door was closed. Without hesitation, I knocked twice and quickly thrust open the door.

"Hey, what the hell—oh, it's you, Jim."

Sam Bigelow looked very surprised. So did the person sitting next to him.

The person sitting next to him was Susan Mazur.

"Sorry to burst in like this," I said. "I'm usually not so rude. But then, I'm usually not this late."

Sam glanced at his watch. "It's only six-fifty."

"Yeah," I said, "and I'm only twenty minutes late."

Sam frowned. "No you're not. We said seven-thirty."

"Oh, *seven*. I thought it was six-thirty."

Sam tried to smile. "Seven . . . thirty."

"Well"—I laughed at myself—"in that case I'm early."

"Very. So your record of punctuality is still intact."

"Good." I looked straight at Susan Mazur and smiled. "And how are you . . . *this* evening?"

Her eyes didn't waver from mine. "I'm just fine," she said.

At that point, the door opened and Kate Morgan hurriedly entered the office.

Our eyes met instantly and hers widened. "Well . . . Jim. How are you?"

"I'm just fine," I said. "And"—I glanced at Susan Mazur—"she's just fine, too."

Kate frowned and glanced at Sam, a questioning expression on her face. "Should I . . ."

Sam was in charge again. His voice was brisk. "Jim, I'm afraid this might be a little dull—"

"I can't imagine anything in your department being dull, Sam."

"Well—" he gave his hearty laugh—"we're not all that exciting all the time—"

"Yes, but with the sports department hooking up with the news—" I glanced at Kate Morgan, who averted her eyes—"it must be something pretty good. What're you cooking up, Sam?"

Sam looked at me. I smiled.

"Well . . ." Sam smiled back, "it's . . . it's just a trifle premature just now—"

"Oh, come on, Sam. I'm not going to sell it to ABC."

Sam guffawed. "Who says they'd want to buy it if you did?"

"*It*—?" (My God, but I was being boorish.)

"Yeah"—Sam smiled—"*it*. And that's all you're going to get from me."

"Okay," I said. "I'll make my exit and let you begin your secret cabal."

On my way out, I gave Kate Morgan a pat on the shoulder. There was a light mist of perspiration on her forehead.

Sam Bigelow took me to my favorite French restaurant in all of New York, La Caravelle. The food is always sublime, the service is always superb, and, of course, everyone is treated like a king.

In fact, as he led us from the bar, where we had had a drink and chatted with the dependably warm and friendly Albert, Monsieur Claude spread his arms and indicated our table with a flourish: "Gentlemen—the table of—*kings*."

We accepted that and settled in for a fine meal.

The only thing missing was Sam. Or rather, a completely congenial Sam.

Sam is usually a wonderful dinner companion, lively conversationalist, witty, amusing, and informed, no matter what the topic might be.

But this evening he stuck to one thing: sports. *Sports*. That was it. That was all. And when I asked him a question about anything else, he always chose to find some way to answer it with a comment about sports—or else he would answer it with a question right back to me.

At one point, I said, "Remember when the exasperated Englishman says to the Irishman, 'Do you realize that you chaps always answer a question with another question? And the Irishman says, '*Do* we now?' "

Sam looked at me. "What—?"

"It was a joke, Sam."

"Uh . . . oh, sure. Who told you that? Sean Dillon?"

"Himself."

Sam nodded. "I thought so." He really smiled for the first time. "It's good. Very good."

He lightened up just a bit after that, enough, at least, to get us through coffee and port.

As always, departure from La Caravelle was as wonderful as everything else. I was treated as if I were a combination of José Ferrer, Maurice Chevalier, Charles de Gaulle, and the recipient of the *Légion d'Honneur*.

"*Au'vois, monsieur, et merci.*"

"Au revoir, and thank you."

Even Sam's somber mood of most of the evening was overwhelmed by the warmth. Out on the sidewalk, he said, "Whenever I go there, I always silently thank you for introducing me to the place."

"And I thank you, Sam. It was a wonderful meal."

Sam's limousine was waiting for us on Fifty-Fifth Street. "How about riding back up to the Broadcast Center with me? I'd like to show you our new set for *Wonderful Weekend of Sports*. Get your opinion."

"What if I don't like it?"

"We'll tear it down." Sam guffawed.

As the driver was opening the door for us, Sam said, "I'd have Eddie take you home from there, but I promised him I wouldn't keep him too late tonight." He looked apologetic. "We can call a radio cab."

"No need. I'll walk home from the Broadcast Center. I could use the air."

"Ah, good—" Sam settled himself into the backseat of the limousine. "And now, with the Northern takeover—we even pay for the limos ourselves, you know."

Sam sighed. "*Pinched Pennies Produce Profits.* . . ."

He sighed a second time.

TV-22 is the designation for the newest studio at RBS. It is enormous and sparkling, with all kinds of stuff that people love to refer to as *state of the art*. By day, it is a dynamic and exciting spot.

But by night, with only a few work lights turned on, it seemed eerie, almost haunted, and there was that chilling silence that exists in a huge darkened space, a silence that seems vaguely dangerous, a silence that seems almost to have sound.

"Anybody here—?"

After Sam called, I almost expected an answer: *"Only me—the darkness."*

"Fred—? You here—?"

No answer.

"He's probably sacked out in the control room," Sam grumbled. "Come on in. We can see the set pretty well with just the work lights."

We made our way cautiously across the studio floor.

"*Damn it*—" came from Sam up ahead. "Watch yourself. I ran right into a monitor."

We got across the rest of the studio without any problems.

"My eyes are getting used to the dark," Sam said. "How about you?"

"Yes. It's a lot better. I can almost see."

Sam guffawed. "Well—here it is," he said. "Home Base. The new set for *Three-W-S*." Sam sighed. "God—seems a long time ago that this show went on the air. Remember?"

"Sure. And they didn't call the *Wonderful World of Weekend Sports* Three-W-S then. It was more chic to say, I'll give it three weeks."

Sam sighed again. "Well, we made it."

"*You* made it, Sam."

"We all did."

Sam began to clamber around the set, explaining it to me, an air of almost reverence in his voice.

"This is where Jack'll sit . . . when he's not out on a

remote . . . Roger over here . . . Ann right here . . . the
R.P. here . . . come on up. . . ."

I climbed up on the set with Sam, just to please him.

"Have you been on the air with it yet?" I asked for something
to say.

"Just dummy runs. But it really works. It's gorgeous—
and—it's practical."

"You're in love—"

Sam laughed, "Yep. A little. We're going to do a dry run at
the West Virginia–Rutgers game at Giants Stadium. Then we'll go
on the air with it for the Penn State game."

"Penn State–Alabama or Penn State–Pitt?"

"Penn State–Pitt. Joe Paterno doesn't know it, but my plan is
for Penn State to beat the hell out of Alabama. That'll make the
Penn State–Pitt game the biggest game of the year."

"And if they don't—?"

"They will," Sam said. "I've already scheduled the Blimp to
be down there. Full coverage. Fourteen cameras, the Blimp,
eighty-six thousand plus fans, the biggest collegiate football game
of the season, and—the new set—*with* the new Blimp."

I tried to suppress a laugh as I peered into the gloom. "I wish
I could see it."

"By my guest," Sam said. "Come on down with me and the
crew. Courtesy of RBS Sports."

"I mean the set," I said.

"What—?"

"Sam—it's so dark in here. . . . *You* see the set because
you've seen it. Me—I'm not seeing too much."

"Oh . . ."

"I can hardly even see your face."

"Well . . ." Sam sounded deflated—"Anyway . . . I
wanted you to take a look at it." The two of us climbed off the
platform. "What d'you think? I mean—of what you can make out
of it."

"It's great. Just great."

We stood there for a moment in the eerie darkness. When he
spoke again, Sam's voice had lost all of the excitement of a

moment before. His voice became flat again, the way it had sounded all through dinner.

"You've been keeping pretty busy, haven't you, Jim?"

"Yes, I have. I'm back on the book and really working hard."

"I wasn't talking about your book just now. I meant"—he moved in the darkness—"well . . . things in general. I meant—in general—you've been keeping pretty busy."

"Oh . . . yeah . . . I have."

He was behind me now. I forced myself not to turn my head to try to see him.

"Sort of burning the candle at both ends."

"What do you mean?"

"Oh . . . you know. The RBS investigation and all. It must have taken a lot of time from your writing."

"Well, yes—there were some long days."

"And . . . nights."

It seemed that he was directly behind me.

"What're you driving at?" I asked.

"Driving at? Oh, nothing."

I tried to appear to be casual. I took a couple of steps forward. As I stopped, I heard Sam move. And once again he had positioned himself directly behind me.

"I mean, if I *did* mean anything—and I didn't—I might have meant Susan Mazur." Sam chuckled. "Rumor around RBS was that you spent *quite a few* nights with our Ms. Mazur."

I turned. When I did, I found him so close that our noses nearly touched. "Yes . . . I did."

"Charming, isn't she?"

"Yes."

"Recently—?"

"What?"

"Any nights with her—recently?"

"No . . . not really."

"No?"

"No."

"Oh . . . I'm disappointed. For your sake I mean. I've only admired her from afar." He guffawed again. Sam never did that.

He might laugh, chuckle, chortle, or even on rare occasions, giggle—but, until tonight, I had never heard him *guffaw* like some silly rube. "What's she like?"

"Very nice. And—well, you've seen her."

"Oh, yes, indeed I have. But you haven't?"

"Haven't what? I'm not following."

"Haven't seen her . . . recently, I mean."

"No?"

"Certainly not in the past few nights."

I thought of the crash and Susan Mazur at the wheel of the other car. "No," I said, "certainly not in the past few nights."

We stood there for a moment, face-to-face in the near darkness, the sound of a kind of sinister stillness permeating the silence of the studio.

"Hey—I've got an idea. Wait here." I could see Sam moving away from me. "I'm going to go up to the control room. Even if Fred's not sacking out up there, maybe I can at least throw on some scoops so you can see the set a *little* better, anyway."

I waited in the center of TV-22 while Sam made his way to the control room. He seemed to be running into nearly everything in his path. It was easy to follow his progress, which was marked by a series of bumps, followed by angry oaths, culminating in one final crash and a frustrated cry of "*Another Goddamned Monitor.*"

"You okay?"

"Barked my skin, that's all, but I'm almost at the control room door so—"

That's when the lights went out. Everything. It was totally, absolutely, completely dark.

"Sam—?"

I was suddenly frightened. I felt like a child in the dark, and found myself turning defensively in all directions, afraid that whichever way my back was turned was the direction from which something fearful and frightening might attack.

"Jim, did you hit a switch or something?"

"No, did you?"

"I don't think so."

"Let's get out of here, Sam—"

"Yeah. Keep talking so I can find you. Then I'll lead us out."

"Okay. I'm here . . . right here . . . I'm here."

There was a crash. "These *Goddamned* monitors—"

"Sam–?"

"Yeah—keep talking—"

"I'm here . . . right here . . . one . . . two . . . three . . . I'm here . . . four . . . five—"

It was a shot. No doubt about it. I hit the studio floor fast and heard it ricochet around the equipment.

Sam's voice: "You okay, Jim?"

"Yeah. And you?"

A second shot. This one hit a camera just above my head.

"Keep talking, Jim—"

"I don't think—"

Another shot. This one even closer.

No more talking. I started to crawl in what I guessed was the general direction of the exit.

There were two more shots. And twice more Sam called out to me. But my shouting to Sam had ended for the night.

Too many minutes later, soaked in sweat, and hands trembling, I had found the exit door. As I pushed it open, light streamed in from the hallway, and a final shot rang out and hit the wall above my head. I leaped into the hall and pushed the door shut behind me.

Several production assistants' desks were lined up along the opposite wall, replete with telephones, filing cases, and typewriters. Without the slightest concern for Sam Bigelow, even if he were required to spend the rest of the night in TV-22, I pushed desks and filing cabinets up against the door.

It was ten minutes past midnight by the time I got back to the sublet. I immediately got out of my clothes and donned pajamas, slippers, and a robe.

The phone rang. It was twelve-twenty a.m.

Joe's voice said: "Hello, Jimmy—I won't apologize for calling so late, because I know you must've just got home."

"Hello, Joe. How'd you know that?"

"I've been calling every ten or fifteen minutes since about eleven."

"Something up?"

"Yeah. I've got some news you ought to know. And sit down, Jimmy. Otherwise this might just knock you down."

"What is it?"

Joe's voice got even more excited. "I think Terry Jones might know Francisco Guzman."

"Who the hell is Francisco Guzman?"

"The Sutton Place apartment."

"Joe—I'm not following too well."

"Jimmy—that apartment on Sutton Place—where we think Kate Morgan might have gone the other night—"

"Oh, yeah—"

"Well, she probably did. Because our guys have spotted Terry in that building twice now."

"But *in* the *building* doesn't mean in the *apartment*."

"It's too close, Jimmy. Walk away. Walk away from it right now. Announce to the world—friends and enemies—that you're through with it. Mean it. And go back to your book."

"I can't, Joe. I just can't."

"Why not?"

"I . . . well . . ." I smiled at Joe through the phone. "It's a new feeling for me—the love of the hunt. I guess there's a little more George Plimpton in me than I realized."

"Some answer," Joe grumbled.

We talked for a few minutes more. I didn't tell him anything about the shooting incident in TV-22. That could wait until morning. Joe was entitled to a decent night's sleep.

As we were hanging up, I thought: When I tell him about the shooting, Joe will want to go to the police. Hell, he'll be right.

"I'll see you in the morning then."

"Right. Sleep well, Jimmy—"

"You, too."

I opened a bottle of St. Pauli Girl and turned on WNCN. More Mozart.

The phone rang.

"Oh, thank God it's you. . . ." It was Sam Bigelow. "Are you all right?"

"I'm fine Sam? How're you?"

"Still scared to death. Those were real bullets, you know."

"I know."

"I've called the police. Have you?"

"I thought I'd do it in the morning."

Sam clicked his tongue. "Aren't you the cool one though. Not me. My hands are *still* shaking. How'd you get out?"

"The way we came in."

"I tried that, too, but whoever the son of a bitch was blocked it up."

"Then how—?"

"Fred came back. Swears he'd only gone to the men's room. Swears he didn't hear any shots either. Came back in through the control-room exit door—saw the work lights were out—threw 'em back on. Nobody there. Just me out in the studio. The bastard got away." Sam took a deep breath. "But you're okay. . . ."

"Fine, Sam."

"Thank God. Well . . . get some sleep. We'll talk in the morning. Thank God," he murmured again as we hung up.

Well, well . . . I sat on the couch and poured some beer into my glass. I took a long swallow. Then I turned up the volume on the Mozart just a bit more.

I took another swallow of beer. Well, well . . . As Alice was wont to say in *Wonderland . . . things are getting curiouser . . . and curiouser.*

Chapter 35

I woke up very early and couldn't get back to sleep; so I lay in bed and ruminated about what had happened during the past few days.

The death of Dick Ainsley—the revelations of Buzz Berman—the Dick Ainsley–Kate Morgan connection—Kate's clandestine meeting, probably with Terry Jones in an apartment rented under the name of Francisco Guzman—Kate's confession or, rather, quasi-confession—Air Penn—the connection of Air Penn leases with RBS Sports—*Sam Bigelow*— (My God, but that was a tough one to swallow)—the New Jersey airstrip—Susan Mazur—TV-22 with Sam last night . . .

Last night . . . those shots were real, all right. And Sam's call to me afterward . . . an alibi? . . . to look innocent? . . . Possibly. . . .

Yes. *Curiouser and curiouser.*

The phone rang. It was Maureen.

"Did I wake you, champ?"

"No. What's up?"

"Nothing much. Joe just called. He won't be in until around twelve. How about some breakfast?"

"You're on. Give me forty-five minutes and I'll meet you at the Parker-Meridian."

"I'm starving—"

"Half an hour—"

"That's more like it."

I showered quickly, shaved, and was dressing when the phone rang again. It was Mona.

"Hello . . ." Her voice was weaker even than Camille, a second or two before death.

"Mona—?"

"Oh . . . is that you, Jimmy?"

"Yes—"

"Everything is so . . . dark."

Ah—something new. Now everything was so dark.

"I think I'm going, Jimmy . . . fading. I haven't . . . I haven't eaten . . . since . . . yesterday."

"When yesterday?"

"Breakfast. And even then, I only had one egg, and *one* slice of toast."

"My God—"

"Without any jam—"

"Mona—"

"Yes . . . yes, I'm fading."

Then and there I decided to counterattack. Enough is enough.

"I wish I could help, Mona."

"*Wish you could help?*" She had temporarily forgotten her weakened condition. But she quickly regained the death rattle in her voice. "Wish . . . you could . . . help? You mean . . . you're just going to . . . abandon me?"

"There's nothing I can do, Mona."

"Oh, there are . . . lots of things. I thought that you . . . might come over and . . . feed me grapes or something. You know . . . one at a time. To help me regain my strength."

"No, Mona—"

"You *keep saying* . . . you . . . keep . . . saying that."

I glanced at my watch. If I didn't hurry, I'd be having brunch—not breakfast with Maureen.

"I've got to run now, Mona. Eat a grape or something. One at a time."

As I replaced the receiver, I was Marshall Foch. From now on, I would always counterattack: *Ils ne passeront pas.* (The spirited sounds of the "Marseillais" caroled through my mind.)

I glanced at my watch again. Oh, my God—I hastily finished dressing and headed for the Parker-Meridian Hotel.

Joe came in as we were having a second cup of coffee. He said: "That new answering service is great. Not only did he tell me where you were—but he even said you sounded hungry." He gave Maureen a quick kiss on the cheek. I had never seen him do that before, and for some reason it was unsettling to me.

"No kiss for me," I said. I never talk like that.

Joe eyed me. "*Well* . . . ?"

"Well, what?"

"My *well* refers to the strongly worded recommendation I made to you last night regarding the book you're working on."

"I don't recall—"

"My suggestion was that you announce an end to all of these sleuthing activities and return to the green and peaceful fields of writing."

I shook my head.

"Why, Jimmy?"

"I don't know."

Joe was frowning. "You always say that."

"Well . . . you mentioned the book. This whole thing I got the three of us mixed up in . . . it's a lot like a book, I suppose. To paraphrase Samuel Johnson: It's bad enough to *start* writing something. But then you have to finish the damn thing."

"So—?" Joe's frown deepened.

"So I want to finish, that's all. If that's an answer."

Joe sighed. "Okay."

"Thanks, Joe."

As he pulled out his notebook, he said to Maureen: "We're all set on the Curtiss deal. No quibbling—they just signed. That's why I'm back early."

Maureen smiled. "Take some credit. It's because you set up everything so well."

"Okay." Joe leaned over and kissed Maureen again. This time on the lips. "There—credit taken. Thanks."

I bit my tongue and didn't make a second silly remark.

Joe flipped through a few pages of his notebook until he found what he wanted. "This is Stone's last report," he said.

"Who's Stone?"

"He's one of the guys I hired to follow Kate Morgan." Joe smiled. "Sounds like a book title, doesn't it? *Stone's Last Report*. Let's see . . . oh, yeah. That apartment on Sutton Place—the one with Francisco Guzman's name on it. As I told you—Terry Jones has been spotted in the building. Twice."

"Joe, I still say—"

"Wait. This morning our man Stone saw Terry Jones enter the building again."

"Well—"

"Just let me talk, Jimmy—for *once*. And I'm talking about drugs." Joe peered at me. "I'll start *my* list with Kate Morgan."

"But she told me—"

"*Exactly*. She *told* you."

"But Terry's not mixed up in this. There's got to be some explanation."

"Okay. *Maybe* we find an explanation. For now—Terry Jones goes on the list. Agreed?"

I sighed. "Agreed."

"Good. Kate Morgan, Terry Jones. Who else?"

"Susan Mazur," Maureen said.

Joe nodded "Kate Morgan—Terry Jones—Susan Mazur. Who else?"

I said: "Charlie Bohanen. I'm dead certain that that was his voice I heard out in New Jersey."

"That's better."

"And there's more," I said. "*Worse*."

I told the two of them about the incident of the night before in TV-22.

Joe whistled. "Holy Mother of God."

Maureen said: "And he actually called you up afterward and asked if you were all right?"

I said: "Well, there's always the possibility that—"

Joe said: "Jimmy—stop trying to be Billy Budd. *He* was the one shooting at you."

"Now tell him about the incident in the records room," Maureen urged.

Sheepishly, I did.

"And it was five o'clock in the morning?" Joe repeated.

"A little before five—"

Joe groaned. "And what was his explanation as to *why* he was there at five in the morning. Did you ask him?"

"Yeah."

"What'd he say?"

"Well—he thought for a moment, and then he said he wasn't sure. He'd just come into the building—and just gone there. No reason."

"*Wonderful,*" Joe said.

"Joe, you can cut out all the cleverness. It's not needed. I already suspect Sam Bigelow."

"My God—there's hope," Joe said.

Maureen said: "So now we have Kate Morgan, Susan Mazur, Charlie Bohanen, *Sam Bigelow*—" She shook her head in disbelief. "Do we throw in Dr. Antonia Hastings?"

"Throw her in," Joe said. "What the hell."

"How about R. Randolph Fulton?" Maureen asked.

"Why not everybody who works at Northern Industries/RBS?" I said.

At that point, someone hit me hard, directly in the middle of my back.

"*Jimbo*—" It was Big Bill Braddock himself. "Thought that was you."

I said: "What if it hadn't been?"

He laughed. "You know Doctor Hastings, don't you? Jim Sasser—Dr. Antonia Hastings."

"How do you do, Dr. Hastings?" I shook her hand.

"How do you do, Mr. Sasser?" She smiled. The eyes grew even bluer with the smile.

I said to Braddock, "We've met a few times."

"Oh, hey—that's right." He snorted and gave me an enormous wink.

Maureen and Joe said hello.

Braddock apologized for his rudeness and introduced them as well. "Looks like everybody's here today."

I said: "Well, at least the important people."

Braddock laughed so loudly that, for a moment, I thought I'd actually said something funny.

"Won't you join us?" Joe asked. He didn't mean it.

"No, thanks," Big Bill said, "Toni has . . . Dr. Hastings . . . ah . . . has some figures to give me so that I can spew them out to the board today and sound halfway intelligent. Excuse us, won't you—" A quick snort of laughter as he pointed a finger at me and repeated "—*at least, the important people*—take care, Jimbo—"

They went to a table in the far corner of the restaurant.

"My *God*," Joe said.

"Well, he's not called Big Bill Braddock for nothing."

Joe faked hearty laughter. "There you go again," he said, in a pretty fair imitation of Braddock's voice.

"Give me a break," I said.

"*Another* one—" Joe laughed even louder.

On our way out, we went to the news store to get a newspaper for Maureen.

As we left the store, and crossed the hotel lobby, Maureen said, "Well, well . . ."

"What's that mean?" I asked.

She directed my gaze back into the restaurant.

Kate Morgan was just joining Big Bill Braddock and Dr. Antonia Hastings.

Chapter 36

Back in the offices of Maloney, O'Neil and Sasser, we found a lot of messages on the answering machine. Only one was for me; Sam Bigelow's secretary asked if I would call.

When I did, Sam said, "How're you feeling this morning?"

"Fine. How about you?"

"Still a little shaky," Sam said. "I don't like people turning out lights in one of our studios, and then firing a few shots at me and my guests."

"Your guest didn't think too damn much of it himself."

Sam cleared his throat. "I've written memos to everyone who should know about it within the company—Whitehead, Braddock, Terry, et cetera—security, of course— and those memos are going out now. And I've called the police. In fact, they should be here any minute. Where're you?"

"Fifty-Seventh Street—"

"Can you come up?" His voice was actually saying, you'll come up, of course.

"Sure," I said. "Give me ten minutes."

"Good. Meet us in TV-22."

"Ten minutes," I said again.

There were two plain-clothes men, both in their late thirties, both looking very competent. Sam, with his usual attention to public relations, had laid on a fairly opulent buffet. There were rolls, pastries, bagels, and toast—replete with smoked Irish salmon, with chopped onions, egg whites, and capers.

The two detectives had only coffee, and divided a small sweet roll.

They were chatting with Sam as I entered the studio. Sam introduced me. Their names were Black and Grey: it was no joke they told me before I could react. They were used to smiles when they were introduced; they obviously were tired of them.

They waited until I got myself a cup of coffee before they asked Sam and me to describe what had happened the night before. They asked us to walk through it.

We did, describing as best we could, what we were talking about at the time.

When we got to the point where I had remained standing in front of the sports set, while Sam had gone to try to turn on some more lights, the detective named Grey asked his first question.

"And you went all the way into the control room—like that?"

"Well . . . no . . . no," Sam said, "not like this . . . no. Actually, I was"—he quickly retreated to the bottom of the stairs, which led up to the control room door—"actually, I was right about here."

"We asked you to try to describe, if possible, *exactly* where you were last night."

"Oh . . . yes. Yes, you did. Sorry. Well, if I were to describe *exactly* where I was, it was right here."

"When the shooting started."

"Yes."

"And not inside the control room?"

"No. Outside, here."

"And where were you when the lights went out?"

Sam smiled. "I never thought anyone ever *really* asked that question."

Grey sighed wearily. "Nevertheless, when the lights went out—where were you?"

Sam said: "I'm afraid I don't follow."

Grey said: "The lights went out before the shooting started. Where were you?"

"Oh, yes. Of course." Sam guffawed. "I'd make a poor witness, wouldn't I? It happened only last night, and already I've forgotten the sequence of events. Did you, too, Jim?"

I said: "No, I remembered."

"Well, you're a better man than I am then." To Grey, he said: "I was right here. At the foot of the stairs."

"And not inside the control room."

"No, not at all. I never made it. Right here. Then the lights went out."

"And when the shooting started—?"

"Right here, too. It was almost immediately after the lights went out. Wasn't it, Jim?"

"No," I said. "First you tried to get back to where I was standing. You asked me to keep talking so you could find me."

"Oh, that's right. That's right—I did."

"And did you?" the detective named Grey asked me. "Keep talking, I mean."

"Yes, I did," I said. "I counted out loud—things like that."

"And where were *you* then? When the lights went out—and Mr. Bigelow asked you to keep talking, so he could find you?"

"Right about here. Right where I'm standing now. In front of the sports set."

"What happened then?" Grey asked.

"Well . . . I started to talk, then Sam . . . I suppose . . . started toward me."

"That's it—that's it. I remember now," Sam said. "I started towards you—and I ran into a monitor—probably this baby right here." He moved to a large floor monitor and slapped its top.

"And then—?" Grey asked.

"And then the shots started."

"Not quite," I said. "You asked me—a second time—to keep talking."

"Uh . . . *yeah* . . . right . . . I did."

"And I started to talk again."

"Right—"

"And *then*—the shots started," I said.

"Right."

Grey waited for us to continue.

"And that's it," Sam said.

"No . . ." I said, "you called to me again. I answered—and there was a second shot. You shouted for me to keep talking—I started to say that I didn't think I should—and there were two more shots."

"Uh . . . yeah, I remember now," Sam said.

"At about that time," I said to Detective Grey, "I decided on no more talking. And I started to crawl toward the exit."

"Any more shots?"

"Two more," I said. "And Sam called to me two more times."

"But you didn't answer."

"No—"

Grey turned to Sam. "True—?"

Sam shrugged. "Well . . . if that's the way Jim remembers it . . . it's probably true. I just don't . . . remember."

260

Grey looked at me. "Then what—?"

I told him how I had crept across the floor and out the door. How bullets hit the wall above it. He noted what could have been bullet holes. I took him to the hallway and pointed out the desks that I had shoved against the studio door.

We went back inside TV-22, and Grey asked Sam to explain his own escape. He told of making his own way to the door, and finding that he couldn't push it open.

"I thought the son of a bitch firing at us had done it. And here it was Jim here."

"What then?" Grey asked.

"Well . . . I was in a quandry. I was trying to figure out just what the hell I *could* do when—whammo. The lights went on again. Fred Myers—he's one of our technicians—had thrown 'em back on."

"I see—" Grey looked at Sam Bigelow, reflectively for a moment. "Did you see this door"—he pointed to the door I had used for my escape—"open and close when Mr. Sasser got out?"

"Yes—"

"Did you see Mr. Sasser?"

"Not exactly. I saw someone run out."

"And who did you think it was?"

"Mr. Sasser. I mean—Jim."

"Did you hear shots as he ran out?"

"Yes—"

"How many?"

"Just as Jim said. There were two shots. Two shots in rapid succession."

"Were there any after that?"

Sam thought for a moment. "I think those were the last."

"Um hum." Grey turned to his partner and they mumbled in low tones for a moment or two. He eventually turned back to Sam. "Excuse me," he said. "And when the lights came on again, you—?"

"The lights came on again—I saw Fred Myers in the control room—I asked him where the hell he'd been—he said the men's room—he said he hadn't seen anybody or heard anything. That's it."

"When can we see Mr. Myers?" Grey asked.

Sam said: "Let me call scheduling to see—"

Three men came into the studio. Sam called to one of them. "Billy—is Fred Myers going to be with you guys today?"

"I think so, Sam. Would you like me to call scheduling?"

"Thanks. Would you?"

"Sure, Sam."

"And dig into the food. There's plenty for everybody." To the two detectives he said, "Is that all you guys are gonna have?"

Detective Black said. "Thanks. Maybe some more coffee."

"Please—" Sam said.

While the stagehands helped themselves to the buffet, Detectives Grey and Black prowled around the studio and the control room.

The stagehand named Billy called from the wall phone, "Fred'll be in at four today, Sam."

"Here? TV-22?"

"Right."

"Thanks, Billy." Sam introduced the two detectives to the stagehands, explaining the detectives' presence as he did.

After the introductions, Grey turned to Sam and me. "That's all for now. We're going to look around a bit more."

Grey said: "And we'll need someone to introduce us when we meet Mr. Myers."

"Call my office," Sam said. "I'll come down myself."

"Thanks," Black said. He extended his hand, as did Grey. "We'll be talking soon."

"Thanks for coming."

Out in the hallway, Sam said, "I hope you have a few hours free."

"For lunch? Afraid I'm not set up for lunch, Sam. I just finished a late breakfast."

"Oh, no—" Sam said. "I'm not talking about lunch. You and I are gonna take a little drive."

I looked at him.

"Have I got a surprise for *you*," Sam said.

He seemed to be smiling.

Chapter 37

We all make mistakes. And I'd just made a doozy.

We were in New Jersey. Sam had asked his driver to put in a cassette—"Something by Mozart . . . and turn it up"—so we hadn't spoken the whole way.

Several times Sam had glanced at me and smiled. It was all just a bit unnerving.

We crossed the Hudson by way of the George Washington Bridge, went out a few miles on Route 80, then turned down either the Garden State Parkway or the New Jersey Turnpike, I'm never sure which is which. During the trip, I knew that I'd been an idiot to agree to the ride. But, on the other hand, I had to find out what it was Sam wanted. Otherwise, everything so far would have been in vain.

After several minutes of driving south, we got off the turnpike, or the parkway, and headed west. The music ended right on cue, just as the driver pulled up into a parking lot and came around to open my door.

"Where are we?" I asked Sam.

"Oh—" his eyes crinkled "—somewhere in New Jersey."

"I know that. But where?"

"You'll see," Sam said.

The driver stayed with the limousine. I reluctantly followed Sam toward a large building, feeling rather foolish because I was so passively allowing myself to be led to potential slaughter.

We rounded a corner of the building. "There it is," Sam said, gesturing out to a field.

And there it was, indeed. The Goodyear Blimp, in all its glory, tethered to a mooring mast mounted on a huge tractor-trailer rig.

"Four years of pestering them, followed by four months of negotiations—and now we've got it." Sam was beaming. "I've coveted this thing for RBS since the first time I saw it on ABC. And now all four of them will be seen *exclusively* on"—he punched out the words—"the *Republic Broadcasting System*."

I said, "Congratulations."

"Thanks." Sam shook my hand. "Thanks."

We walked around the blimp, appraising its lines, with Sam describing it, and talking about it, as if he were some helpless stripling who had just fallen in love.

"We're going to try it out this coming Saturday—the West Virginia–Rutgers game in the Meadowlands. A dry run. Then off she goes to Beaver Stadium for her first time on the air for us at the Penn State–Pitt game the following week."

A Captain Nestor appeared. Sam introduced me to him. The Captain explained, in great detail, all of the technical and logistical facts surrounding the ship. He gave us a tour of the crew bus and the van used as a kind of command car. He, too, seemed to love it almost as much as Sam did.

Several of the crew appeared, including a radio technician named Peterson who seemed quite nervous. It wasn't until Peterson clambered into the ship, and Captain Nestor started to help Sam in, that I realized that we were supposed to actually go up in the thing.

"I . . . don't think so, Sam. Not today, anyway." I knew it was already too late.

"Aw, come on—just a short ride. It'll be fun."

"I have acrophobia."

Sam guffawed. "You? You were pretty high the other night at La Caravelle, and you seemed happy enough to me."

"That was from wine—not a blimp."

"It's the same kind of high. Only with this one—you don't get headaches."

It was a lost cause. Captain Nestor was already helping me up the aluminum ladder.

Sam was grinning. "We'll fly right over Giants Stadium.

We'll have a real bird's-eye view—just the way the crew will during Saturday's game."

Captain Nestor made sure that we were seated comfortably and assured us there was no need for nervousness—speaking mostly to me during that part—explained where and how the cameraman would be positioned during Saturday's game (there was a great gaping door at one side of the gondola) and explained the relatively few controls that he had to deal with—"after all, it's a blimp and not a Seven Forty-Seven"—the engine was started (a shattering noise at first) and we . . . floated off. We didn't *take off*. We simply began to *float*; it was a very, very strange feeling.

All the way to the Meadowlands, and for much of the time that we floated over Giants Stadium, the good captain did most of the talking, mostly in order to answer the questions fired at him by an eager Sam.

After a short while, I got used to the engine noise, but I never got used to the idea that I was up in a blimp with Sam Bigelow at my side, several thousand feet above the earth—with a huge door on one side that was wide open.

And I had good reason. As we were turning to head back, Sam eyed, first, the great opening and then me. "It's kind of scary, isn't it?" He nodded toward the opening.

"Very."

"It's a long way down from here."

"It certainly is."

He was quiet for a moment; then he said, "Kate Morgan tells me that you've been pestering her."

"Pestering? Is that the word she used?"

"Yeah—pestering. Of course, she says it with a smile."

"Did she tell you what I've been pestering her about?"

"No."

"I was asking her about some of the drug stories that she and Dick Ainsley worked on."

"Oh, that's right. Yeah. She might have mentioned drugs at that."

I said nothing.

Sam's eyes were on the nearly floor-to-ceiling opening of the gondola when he spoke again. "Just how much do you know about her . . . drug investigations, Jim?"

I looked at the open door myself. "Oh . . . a bit, Sam. Just a bit."

"You know, Jim—it's a different world now—from what it was when you were working the news—"

"I know," I said. "Now—nobody's a newsman. Everybody calls himself a *journalist*."

"I wasn't talking about the cosmetic changes, Jim. I was talking about the world outside. It's a very *dangerous* world outside now, Jim. Very . . . dangerous."

"I know that," I said.

"Do you? I hope so."

We were silent again. Both of us were still looking at the opening.

After a moment, Sam said, "You've wrapped up your little job at RBS, haven't you, Jim?"

"Yep. It's all . . . wrapped up."

"That's good," Sam said. "That's good to hear."

A moment later, he said, looking directly at me, "*Completely* wrapped up? *Finito—finis—alles?*"

"*Alles,*" I said.

"Very good," he said again. "You did a fine job. Very fine."

"Thanks," I said.

Captain Nestor turned to look back at us. "Everything okay back there?"

"We're just fine," Sam said. He smiled at me.

"Good. We're comin' back into port."

Sam continued to smile at me.

We were standing beside the now-tethered blimp, finishing off our thank-yous to Captain Nestor and his crew.

"Glad you enjoyed yourselves," he said.

"Oh, we loved it," Sam said, still smiling at me. It seemed that he hadn't taken his smiling eyes off my face for the past ten minutes.

"We wanted to rename her the *Seabury*," Sam said.

"What—?"

"The blimp. We wanted to rechristen it the *Seabury*, after M.S.W. Actually, our first idea was to call it the *Whitehead*, but he's too modest for that. So we took his middle name. Would've made a nice touch, don't you think?"

"Oh, very—"

Sam sighed. "But Goodyear said, no. Couldn't budge 'em during negotiations. It's traditional for them to name them after America's Cup winners." Sam sighed again. "It's a pity. *Seabury* would've been perfect."

We waved to the captain and started for the limousine, where the driver was waiting with both back doors flung open for us.

Sam was still smiling as we got in. "I was glad to hear up there that you're all finished with your job. But I *am* sad to know that I won't be seeing you around the Broadcast Center anymore. I'll miss that."

"Oh, you'll see me around."

"But I thought—"

"There're still a few . . . odds and ends to clean up."

"Oh—"

"I just didn't feel too comfortable mentioning that up there."

"Oh, why not?"

"Well"—I smiled myself—"I just had the strangest feeling that if I had—mentioned it, I mean—you might've tried to kill me."

Sam laughed. "Really? And how would I do that?"

"That open door. You might've pushed me out."

"In front of two witnesses—?" Sam laughed again. "Don't be silly."

"At the time, it didn't seem too silly—"

"If I were seriously considering something like that, I think *now* would be a much better time. Immediately *after* a somewhat harrowing ride. Just when you're safe on the ground once more—just when you're relaxing, not on your guard—"

We were pulling out of the parking lot, beginning to pick up speed, and Sam was reaching under his seat for something. I pushed the door open and rolled out, wondering if it would work, since I had never tried anything so completely lacking in caution in my life. I hit grass rather than pavement, and began to run like hell.

Chapter 38

The man at the motel counter was very wary and most reluctant to show me where his pay phone was. For one thing, I had not arrived at his motel in an automobile; I had arrived on foot—something that was not just unusual, it was something that had never occurred in his twenty-odd years of motel ownership.

Fortunately, I had plenty of cash. After I asked him about the phone, I gave him a twenty. That assuaged him somewhat. He pointed to an alcove on his right, never speaking, and never taking his eyes off me.

I called Maureen and Joe.

Joe answered. The moment he heard my voice, he said, "Where are you? Where've you been?"

"Somewhere in New Jersey."

I heard Joe exhale. "And you're okay?"

"I'm fine."

"Thank God. Now I'm going to go to the police and tell them everything we know. I don't know why in hell I didn't do it days ago."

"Joe—you can't. We haven't had time—"

"*Jimmy*. We haven't had *time*? Time to what? I'm not Ellery Queen—and you're not Sam Spade. It's wrong. Wrong as hell."

"Maybe you've got a point, but—"

Joe whooped. "Maybe I've got a *point*? Jimmy—look what happened to you last night in that studio—"

And today, I thought. My blimp ride.

Joe said, "You're sure you're okay?"

"Fine."

"Then I'm going to go to the police. I'm not asking you—I'm telling you."

He waited for my response. "You still there, Jimmy—?"

"Yeah—I'm still here."

"Well—?"

"You're right, Joe."

"Good—"

"But, Joe—"

"Now, come on, Goddamn it. No backing out—"

"I'm not. But I need transportation." I raised my voice for the benefit of the motel owner. "Would you send a car for me. I have no way of getting back to the city."

"What happened?"

"Thanks," I said.

"What's wrong with you—?"

"A limousine would be fine—just fine."

The motel owner had the beginnings of a smile on his face.

"Would you be so kind as to tell me where I am exactly?" I asked him.

More relaxed now, he gave exact directions from Manhattan to his motel. I passed the information on to Joe.

"A limousine out to *there?* How'd you get out there?"

"Well," I said, "a stretch seems a bit ostentatious—but they're so comfortable—why not?"

"Oh, sure," Joe said, "why not?"

"I'll be waiting," I said.

"Well . . . it's gonna take a while. I'll call now—but it's gonna take a while."

"Fine," I said. "I'll be right here at the good old"—I glanced at the name on the desk—*Dew Drop Inn*."

The owner smiled at me again, benevolently this time.

We played hearts—his favorite card game. At the point where he had won an even twenty dollars from me, he made us cold chicken sandwiches. Very good, too.

At thirty-one dollars and fifty cents, the limousine arrived.

By now, we were old card-playing comrades, and, as we

shook hands in farewell, I thanked him, and he thanked me, and we parted the best of friends.

My sublet was on West Sixty-Ninth Street, about halfway into the block, but it was one-way against us, so I had the driver drop me at the corner of Columbus and Sixty-Ninth. As I was handing him his tip, I noticed a vaguely familiar figure standing on the corner.

It took only a moment to place him. It was Mr. Beauregard Jolay.

As I got out of the limousine, I said, "Hello, Beau. I haven't seen you in a while."

He looked embarrassed. "Hello Mr. Sasser."

"How's your nose?"

"I . . . beg your pardon?"

"The last time I saw you—I regret to say—there was a great deal of concern that your proboscis had been, perhaps, dented slightly out of shape."

"Oh . . . no. It's fine." He touched it, as if to reassure himself.

"Well—"I didn't really know how to end our slumping conversation—"that's fine. That's just fine. Take care of yourself now."

"I will," Beau said. "Ah . . . you, too."

He smiled an embarrassed smile.

I walked on up the sidewalk toward my apartment. As I got closer to it, the outline of the man standing on the far corner, on Central Park West, came more and more into focus. It, too, was familiar.

As I got to the entrance of my building, I couldn't say to myself with certainty, but it was . . . probably . . . Charlie Bohanen.

In the lobby, the doorman was talking on the intercom, but he nodded, and mouthed a greeting.

From the other side, someone else said, "Hello, Jim—I've been waiting for you."

I turned. It was Susan Mazur.

I was slowly getting the idea.

Susan smiled at me.

I had started to back toward the door when I first saw her; now, without subtlety, I turned and ran. Outside, I glanced left. Charlie Bohanen—there was no doubt now—was sauntering toward me. To the right, Beau was doing the same.

The direction of my charge was obvious—Beau.

From fifty feet away, I could see his eyes widen. "Your *nose*—" I hollered.

"Oh, *no*—" He put his hands up to his face and fell to his knees on the sidewalk.

I ran past him, made a right at the corner, and headed up Columbus at full tilt. My only thought was to keep running. It wasn't a very good plan. Two blocks later, I was at the RBS Broadcast Center, and exhausted. In desperation, I ran into the reception area.

Agnes Sevinsky was sitting behind the reception desk.

"Mr. Sasser—are you all right?"

"No—"

She tried to smile.

"*Really*, no," I said. There was no time to explain. "Look, Mrs. Sevinsky—Agnes—if anyone asks—*anyone*—you haven't seen me. I'll explain later. Please?"

She looked confused.

"*Please*—"

She nodded.

I wedged myself in behind the huge RBS logo that stood near the rear of the lobby.

Seconds later, I heard the voice of Charlie Bohanen. "Have you seen Jim Sasser?"

"Why . . . no, Mr. Bohanen."

"No—?" His voice rose. "Come on, Aggie—I can see it in your face."

"Well, really—"

"Come on, Aggie."

"Well . . . the elevator—"

"Thanks—"

I heard his footsteps as he moved towards the elevator bank. Someone else entered the reception area.

"Over here—" Bohanen called.

"Right—" It was Susan Mazur.

A few seconds went by before Bohanen called to a newly arrived third party, "Will you *hurry up?*"

Footsteps scampered across the lobby toward the elevators. "Don't hit my nose," Beau whined.

"Who the hell would want to hit *that?*"

"Just what do you mean with that remark?"

"Will you get *in,* for God's sake."

There was the sound of elevator doors closing. I exhaled and stared to crawl out from behind the logo.

"Oh, hello, Dr. Hastings. How are you this lovely evening?"

"Why, hello—"

I froze.

"Oh—Dr. Hastings—are you all right?"

"Just twisted my ankle. Very slightly. I'll just sit here for a moment. I'll be fine."

I should have known. They were all in it together. Every *Goddamned* one of them. And here I'd been, a carefully watched pigeon, as I went about my job of finding out who was sending those letters—letters that threatened to upset their wonderful, Colombian apple cart.

What an idiot I'd been.

And now, Dr. Antonia Hastings was sitting there, controlling my escape route, just as she had begun to control my heart with those damned eyes. I thought of the laughs they must have had, as she and Susan Mazur compared notes about my breathless advances, and how the others had all laughed, too, as they had *all* compared notes.

Mrs. Sevinsky said: "Good evening, Mr. Bigelow."

I heard Sam's voice. "Good evening, Mrs. Sevinsky."

"And Mrs. Morgan—good evening. My, I'm busier this evening than I've been in months."

"Busy, Mrs. Sevinsky?"—Sam's voice was a trifle too loud—"That's the way to *be—busy*."

Mrs. Sevinsky said nothing.

"Sorry, Mrs. Sevinsky . . . too many cups of coffee."

"Well, well, Mrs. S.—how are you this fine evening?"

It was R. Randolph Fulton.

Hail, hail, the gang's all here, I thought.

There was not one whit of doubt in my mind that I might be even remotely paranoid about the situation. It seemed abundantly clear that damn near *everyone* was out to get me.

The others dispersed—even the temporarily crippled Dr. Hastings—but Randy Fulton remained.

Of course. Randy was much more equipped to guard my escape route than anyone else there.

Well, R. Randolph Fulton, you *might* be friend, but I rather suspect that you are foe. And if you were stationed at the door to guard against my exit, then you have to go.

I slipped out from behind the logo, determined to get out those doors.

He heard me and turned in my direction, standing between me and the lobby doors. "Jim—of all people—"

I hit him.

But one thing immediately went wrong with my plan. He didn't fall down.

He staggered back, put a hand up to his jaw, scowled—and started for me.

I ran back through the two banks of elevators, down the hallway, made a left, and ran down another hall, headed for the stairway at the end. My plan was to cut through TV-12 into TV-14 and then down the stairs to the editing rooms, and out that way to the loading dock and the street on the opposite side of the block. As I started up the stairs, I heard Randy Fulton close behind me.

The door to TV-12 was just opening as I got to it. It was Susan Mazur who was coming out. I bolted past her.

TV-12 is RBS's largest studio. Only work lights were on, but as I dashed through, I could make out Bohanen and Beau Jolay at the far end.

"*Hey—*"

I ignored the shout and made it to the control room, where I knocked off the work lights, leaving Bohanen and Beau in darkness.

The control rooms to TV-12 and TV-14 are back to back and connected. I ran through TV-14 to the door that led to the hallway, and the stairs down to the editing room.

As I entered the hall, someone shouted, "*Jim—*"

It was Sam Bigelow. He was with Dr. Antonia Hastings.

I ran down the stairs.

The editing room was filled, running at full tilt, as it always is.

I made my way through as quickly as possible, without drawing attention to myself.

But at the loading dock, I was thwarted again. Kate Morgan was at the door, talking to two very large, goon-like looking guys.

As they turned, I leaped—thanking God, as I did, that it was there—into the side door of one of the huge semitrailers used by the RBS remote units.

No one had seen me do it.

I waited. Moments turned to minutes.. Minutes stretched out to ten . . . fifteen . . . twenty.

I heard men's voices, and then there was the closing sound of the huge sliding door through which I had entered the trailer—and then there was darkness.

Nothing happened. I sat in the darkness without even the small stabilizing comfort of knowing how slowly or how rapidly time was passing.

I cursed myself for being so conservative in dress, particularly when it came to wrist watches: why in hell *didn't* I wear one of those enormous and complicated watches, which looked as if one could, just with the aid of the watch, navigate the QE2 across the North Atlantic?

I stared venomously at the spot on my own wrist where my plain and useless watch must have been—not even a half-hearted blink from the damned thing.

Another hour or so went by. (I would never know how long; my watch again.)

Voices. The dull sound of another truck door slamming. The engine started, and we began to move.

Chapter 39

After what I guessed to be about an hour, I began to experience my first feelings of misgiving.

What if we were on our way to . . . say, Pittsburgh? All the way to Chicago, even? Los Angeles?

Wonderful.

I would starve to death. No. I would die of thirst before I would starve to death.

Really wonderful.

I was on the verge of throwing in the sponge and hollering like hell for help when we, quite noticeably, slowed down.

I held my breath. We slowed down even more. Then we stopped, only to start up again. A stop light? We were moving very slowly after the stop—and winding. About ten minutes went by. Another stop. Some maneuvering now. Backing up. Pulling forward. Backing up again. There were several minutes of this sort of thing.

Finally, a complete stop that stayed a complete stop. Again, I waited.

There was the sudden sound of steel striking steel as the heavy door latch was unlocked. Next came the welcome sound of the huge door being slid open.

I was about to shout with joy, and happily reveal myself,

when a man's voice asked cheerfully, "Is that you driving tonight, Bucky?"

I knew that voice.

"It's me, all right, Sam. Looks like you're stuck with me."

A rolling laugh greeted that announcement, and Sam Bigelow said: "Hey, Bucky—I'm in luck. Best damn driver in RBS Sports."

"Aw—you say that to all us teamsters, Sam."

"Sure—but every time I say it—I mean it."

Both men laughed.

I had the feeling that I must have accidentally applied some honey-flavored deodorant after my morning shower—I seemed to be attracting everybody.

"Hey, Sam—"

I *certainly* was.

"Sam—I'd like you to meet someone—"

It was good, old R. Randolph Fulton, Vice President of Programming for Northern Industries/RBS.

How the hell had he gotten out here—wherever *here* was—so fast? It was easy, I decided. His Alfa Romeo could beat a heavy tractor trailer any day of the week, even after giving away a head start.

Sam said: "What the hell are you doing out here?"

So—Sam wasn't expecting him. Maybe Randy was okay.

"Oh, you know—big game tomorrow. Big night tonight."

Or was this an attempt to appear casual in front of the teamsters?

"Sam," Randy said, "I'd like you to meet Ms. Solveig Bjornsen. I'm thinking of signing Ms. Bjornsen to a developmental contract . . . just as soon as I can find a property that's—"

But Sam Bigelow was curt. "Randy, I'm sorry. But not just now. We're way late on this West Virginia–Rutgers setup—and tomorrow's our first time out with the Blimp. Okay?"

Randy was somewhat petulant. "Well . . . sure. I didn't realize—"

Sam said: "I'm not usually this brusque, Ms. Bjornsen. But I'm sure you understand. Nerves."

Ms. Bjornsen said something that was unintelligible, but sounded somewhat as if she were saying that, indeed, yes, she understood.

"I'll just show Ms. Bjornsen around now. She's never seen a sports remote before. We'll be certain that we don't get in anyone's way," said Randy, in a voice that made sure that it sounded miffed.

Sam said: "Fine. Oh—Ms. Bjornsen, will you be at the game tomorrow?"

Ms. Bjornsen said something that sounded as if she didn't quite know if she would be there or not.

R. Randolph Fulton said that they would both be there, and added peevishly, "And we'll try our best not to get in your way tomorrow, too."

Sam had a sugar-coated smile in his voice as he said, "Well, that's wonderful, Ms. Bjornsen. RBS Sports will be having a little cocktail party right after the game—in the Stadium Club. Drop by. Please. And we can have a little chat."

Ms. Bjornsen said something that sounded as if she would be delighted to attend the party.

Completely mollified, Randy thanked Sam profusely for the invitation, and went off, his gusto totally restored, explaining to Ms. Bjornsen that this was how things were begun at RBS, talking to everyone, picking everyone's brain, until they finally found that property that would be worthy of her obviously *enormous* talents.

I never saw Ms. Bjornsen, but I knew exactly what she looked like.

Also, from the conversation, I knew that we were outside Giants Stadium.

The unloading began. I stayed back in my corner of the trailer and waited for either the moment when I would have a chance to get out undetected or the moment when I would be caught.

Other trucks pulled up beside us. The rest of the crew began to arrive. They were, indeed, very late in setting up for a game.

I wondered if Sam Bigelow had been lulled into lateness by the closeness of Giants Stadium to RBS headquarters. I decided that Sam was too much of the experienced professional to have allowed that to happen. It had to have been something else.

Me?

They had momentarily stopped unloading the trailer I was in. I waited to be sure before I crept to the edge of the door and peered out. Mobile floodlights had been set up to assist in the unloading.

I slipped out the door, lowered myself, and stayed close to the truck.

We were, as I expected, very close in to the stadium. There was shadow there; if I could make it into the shadow, I could ease myself around to the area opposite the RBS setup and make my escape.

It was my second time in the swamplands of New Jersey in one day.

I was up by the cab of the truck now. So far, so good. I saw Sam Bigelow a good hundred feet away, talking with Dr. Antonia Hastings. Randy Fulton joined them. He was no longer with Ms. Bjornsen; he was alone.

If I could make it through about twenty-five feet of open space, I would be in the back of another tractor trailer, and from there, I could step into the shadowy safety of the stadium.

I started out, trying to walk casually, not too slowly, not too fast.

"Hey—"

I stopped dead. I shouldn't have. I was out there naked in the light.

"It's Sasser—" It was the voice of Charlie Bohanen.

I saw Sam Bigelow and his group look in my direction. They saw me.

I started to run toward the stadium. It was the only place to go. Everything else was exposed and open in the parking lot.

"*There*—" Someone else's voice.

I was clawing at the fencing material of the gate, clambering up it as best I could.

"*Gate Eleven—there he is—*"

I made it over, dropped to the ground on the other side, and started to run down the corridor in a lateral direction.

I ran as hard as I could for over a minute. I had to stop. My chest burned. My legs felt weak. I was near one of the runways leading up into the stadium proper. I cursed myself for my weakness in stopping and ran up into the stadium.

It was pitch dark inside.

I started up an aisle. Perfect. I could lie down behind a row of seats. I would be like a needle in a haystack to find. They could never . . . *Ahhh.* . . .

. . . I actually saw little red dots like stars when it hit me. . . .

Then blackness.

Chapter 40

I had no idea how long I had been lying there. I did know that I had one awful headache.

The whole inside of the stadium was lighted, a dull, half light, like very early morning. There were just enough lights turned on to allow the RBS crew to work, not the full complement of game lights.

I tried to raise my head farther. I could. I felt enormous relief. When I had first opened my eyes, it had felt as if I were paralyzed.

I saw what had hit me. In the darkness, I had quite brilliantly run right smack into a metal railing.

I heard a few shouts and some laughter from down along the sidelines. I looked in that direction. No sign of anyone I knew—and didn't want to see—and didn't want to see me.

I sighed. My eyes felt heavy. I tried to blink. I fell back into sleep or unconsciousness.

When I opened my eyes again, it was morning, and there were people there.

Sam Bigelow was one of the people.

I tried to sit up.

"Easy . . ." Sam smiled at me.

I struggled some more.

"Easy, champ—easy."

"I'm . . . okay."

"Sure—sure. But easy does it."

His smile widened.

Someone. A woman. A nurse? She was dressed in white—put an ammonia ampule under my nose, and it made me sneeze, but it cleared my head very quickly. She put something cold on my forehead.

"He'll need an X ray," she said.

Sam clucked his tongue and continued to smile at me.

Two men appeared with a stretcher. Apparently, they knew me.

One of them said, "Hey, Jim, what made you think you were a night runner?" His laugh was hearty, but forced.

The other one said, "Yeah, Jim—" and forced himself to laugh, too.

They were very gentle as they rolled me onto the stretcher.

The first one said, "Almost like that time in Baltimore when you broke your leg, huh?"

I remembered him then. "Oh, hi, Sweeney. How goes it?"

"Not bad," he said.

The second one said, "I think you looked better when you didn't have that mustache."

"Thanks," I said.

As if inspired, he said, "Some people just don't look right with a mustache."

I couldn't top that one, so I said nothing.

They were very slow and careful in getting me down the aisle. I could see Sam's face the whole while, and he never took his eyes off mine. At the bottom, Randy Fulton and Dr. Antonia Hastings were waiting. Also Beau Jolay and Susan Mazur.

"Where're you taking me?" I started to rise up.

"Hey, champ—" Sam's hand on my chest was forceful.

"Someplace where you'll be safe"—he chuckled—"from your-self."

As soon as I can, I thought. Just as soon as I can—

We were under the stadium now. I readied myself. I would roll off the stretcher and call to Sweeney and his pal to help me as I rolled. I'd tell them Sam was out to get me, that he was . . . What the hell was I thinking . . . he was *Sam* . . . their beloved boss for years . . . they'd think I'd flipped my—

"*Jimmy*—are you okay?"

It was Joe's voice. Good, old Joe Maloney—"*Joe—cover me*—"

I rolled off the stretcher.

"This way, Jimmy—*this* way—"

Joe was behind me. I turned quickly—God, my head . . . there was Joe . . . out of focus . . . Joe . . . back in focus . . .

"*Jimmy—here*—"

I ran to him on funny-feeling legs like rubber springs.

Joe's gun was drawn. "Back, you sons of bitches—" When in doubt, Joe always bellowed.

Sam Bigelow tended to *roar* when confronted with an unexpected and baffling situation. He roared now: "Just what the hell do you think you're doing?"

Joe bellowed back: "I'm a friend of Jimmy Sasser's, and I'm getting him out of here—*and* I've got a gun on you—okay?"

"By God, nobody pulls a gun on me—" Sam roared—"and I can warn you right . . ."

Joe lowered his voice to me while Sam Bigelow roared on, "Enemies, Jimmy?"

"Enemies," I said.

"How badly are you hurt?"

"I'm okay. Just a little shaky."

To Sam and his cohorts, Joe bellowed, "After we disappear, count to a hundred—and even *then,* I might be just around the corner."

We started to back away from them.

"I don't think I can make the climb over a gate," I said.

"The one behind us is open," Joe said. "I just came in that way."

We continued to move away from the group. As we backed around a corner to the gate, I saw Sam reach down to his left ankle. I remembered that he carried that pistol there.

"Joe," I said, "he's got a gun."

"Then let's get out of here. Can you run?" Joe looked doubtful.

"Sort of . . . yeah, I think so."

"My car is back behind the RBS trailers. Pretty close in. We can use the trailers for cover."

"Then lead on. I'm right behind you."

Joe shouted back around the corner, "I hope you're still counting—" To me, he said, "Let's go." He started off at a fast lope, glanced back over his shoulder after about fifty feet, saw that my attempt at running was a wobbly, walking jog, and came back to get me.

"Here we go, Jimmy—" He pulled one of my arms over his shoulders and helped me out through the parking lot. By the time we got to the temporary village of RBS Sports vans, I was barely moving my legs, sadly aware that virtually all of my weight was on Joe.

"Sorry, Joe—"

"It's okay, Jimmy, me boyo, it's okay."

We were within the colony of vans. Safe for a moment. Joe was breathing heavily, and he slowed down to a near stop to catch his breath.

That was when the first shot was fired.

It hit the tractor-trailer wall just over our heads.

"Christ Almighty—" Joe had his pistol at the ready again.

I got a glimpse of Charlie Bohanen and Beau Jolay, some fifty feet away, scampering between two trailers. Someone, probably Susan Mazur, was with him.

"We'd better get to my car fast—" Joe, his pistol cocked, started to drag me again.

There was another shot. It seemed to come from yet another direction.

"Bastards," Joe grunted.

I tried to help him by moving my legs more, supporting myself more; I didn't contribute very much.

Another shot.

Joe groaned.

He crumpled down to the ground, and I went with him.

"Bastards." Joe groaned through clenched teeth.

"How bad, Joe?" His eyes were squeezed shut, his teeth making grinding sounds.

"Don't know . . . Jimmy. Don't know . . ."

He groaned again.

I tried to roll him off me, and finally succeeded after three attempts. I got up on my hands and knees and started to examine him. It was his side. He'd been hit in the right side, just below the shoulder.

"I'll get someone," I said.

"Get your ass out of here—"

"No. Your gun—" I said.

"*Jim. Jim—over here.*" It was a harsh, urgent whisper.

"What—?"

"*Here—*"

It was Terry Jones. He was peering around the corner of the next equipment trailer.

He was in focus—he was out of focus—my head ached—Joe groaned again—I was confused.

"Jim—over *here.*"

"I can't. They hit Joe."

"Come with me—"

"I *can't.*"

"Yes, you can."

"I can't . . . they hit Joe. . . ."

Terry came across the open area between the two trailers fast, in a low crouch.

"Yes, you *can.* And *they* didn't hit him."

"What—?"

Terry's gun was nearly in my face.

"*They* didn't hit him. *I* hit him. That's why you *can* come with me."

He waved the muzzle of his gun back and forth. His eyes were brighter than usual, the pupils large and dilated. "Let's go—"

I reached up in front of my face and pushed the pistol aside. "Christ, Terry—"

"Don't start that—"

My voice almost failed me. All of a sudden there was no breath in my lungs. All I could see was the gun pointed at me, held in Terry's hand. *Terry's* hand, for Christ's sake.

"Terry . . . aw, Terry . . ."

His voice was harsh. He gestured with the gun: "*Move it—*"

He made me drive. He sat in the backseat, exactly behind me with the gun pointed at my neck.

He made me drive very slowly, which was just about all I could manage anyway.

After his initial directions, Terry remained virtually silent. *Virtually,* because the constant grinding of his teeth was louder than the sound of the car's engine.

He was frighteningly nervous and impatient when we reached the spot where the blimp was tethered.

He had used a minimum of words to explain to the ground crew that Captain Nestor, the pilot, would be the only one going up with us in the blimp, and that if they attempted anything at all out of the ordinary while freeing us from the mooring mast and getting us airborne, he would most certainly blow off Captain Nestor's head.

Nestor's expression was one of extraordinary calm throughout all of this harangue.

Terry, on the other hand, was drenched in perspiration, his face pale, his hair matted and wet, his eyes blinking quickly, nervously. He smoked one cigarette after another.

Inside the gondola, Nestor, as pilot, was at the controls in the front, on the left side of the car. Terry had me sit on the floor behind Nestor, but facing the rear of the cabin. He, himself, sat facing me.

"One bullet kills all," he said, his voice pitched high, his speech staccato and fast. "Very efficient. Okay, Captain—"

Nestor's orders were crisp, displaying no emotions whatsoever. The crew worked in absolute silence. It was all very eerie.

We were airborne.

"Giants Stadium, please, Nestor." Terry gave out a little laugh.

Nestor was resolutely silent.

"Nestor will get us there in good time," he said to me.

Terry had requested a clipboard and stationery before we took off and had gotten dangerously nervous when it hadn't been immediately forthcoming.

"Don't . . . really . . . just *don't*," he said to me, moving the muzzle of the pistol slightly from side to side. "I have the most amazing peripheral vision—oh, that's right, you know that, don't you?"

He began to write with great intensity, glancing up quickly and nervously every few seconds.

Once, my hand slipped, and I fell back just slightly; he was on his feet in a cat-like crouch, the pistol shoved out in front of his body—his eyes wide.

For a split second, I expected to be shot. But after a long, tense moment, his body began to relax.

"Slipped," I said.

He smiled, just slightly.

"Okay," he said.

He wrote some more, feverishly, a man on the edge of the edge.

Finally, he was finished. He looked up at me, a kind of smile on his face, but his eyes weren't really focused.

"Well, well . . ." he said. His eyes seemed slowly to focus.

"Well, well, *well* . . ." he said again. He capped the pen, held it up as if it were a dart, and flipped it out the gaping door on the side of the cabin.

"That's done," he said.

He frowned. As an afterthought, he said, "I hope that doesn't hit somebody."

A moment later, Nestor said: "We're just about over the stadium."

"Good. Just fly around it for a while—just the way you do for a game. Okay?"

"Yes, sir," Nestor said.

"Good. Because"—Terry smiled at me—"I want to talk to my good buddy here."

I waited.

Terry glanced at the open side door. "Did you know that we pay double time to the crew when they're up in this thing?"

I shook my head.

"Have to. It's in the union contract. But we didn't fight it in negotiations. Seemed only fair. But still you couldn't get *some* guys to work a game in this thing if you gave 'em a year's salary."

He glanced at the door again. "Can't blame 'em. It's a helluva long way down from here."

I wanted my mind to be racing, to be filling my brain with idea after idea of what to do, of how to escape, but instead I felt almost lethargic from the tension, almost, of all things, sleepy.

Terry's handkerchief was sopping wet as he wiped his face. He noted the wetness and, therefore, the uselessness of the handkerchief and threw it out the side door as well.

"Well, buddy . . ." He contemplated me for a moment or two, and then said: "It's all a question of greed, you see." He thought for a moment. "Yeah . . . it's really all a question of greed."

I made no reply.

"And weakness, too. Yeah . . . yeah, that's more . . . accurate. Greed *and* weakness."

He looked at me, his brow deeply furrowed. "It's really all a question of greed *and* weakness. Or"—he half smiled—"weakness and greed. No—no, wait a minute—let's get this right—" he pounded a fist on his knee—"It's really a question of—in this order—*Greed*—and—*weakness*—yeah, in . . . that . . . order."

The sweat was running down his cheeks. He made no effort to wipe it away.

He took a deep breath and exhaled slowly. He took another deep breath, seemed to try to hold it in order to calm himself, and then exhaled slowly for a second time.

"Ah, Jim—" he finally said. "Nam, and Company E, and the 360th Engineers seem a long way away, don't they?"

I nodded.

"And then—sometimes—it feels like just two or three days ago. Right?"

"Yes," I said, thinking of this moment.

Terry's eyes grew wistful. "Sometimes, after I got back, I'd think that I'd give anything to be the boy . . . young man, I was before Nam. Just out of college and all. You know what I mean."

"Sure. I've had thoughts like that myself."

"You have?"

"Sure. My guess is that everybody does."

"Yeah . . . probably so. Everybody."

Terry smiled, started to chuckle and ended in a strangled cough.

"You okay?"

"Yeah . . . *No* . . . who is, anyway. Right?"

"Maybe."

"I was just thinking—as it turns out, it was my old college roommate who got me started in this whole thing. See the irony?" Terry's eyes were dangerously bright. "See the irony in the *whole thing*. Here I am, yearning to be as I was before Nam—just a callow college graduate—and what do you know—I run into my old college roommate—rah, rah—boola, boola—and here I am all *fouled up* in this mess."

He wiped an arm at the sweat on his forehead.

"But it still gets down to—" he took another deep breath and exhaled slowly and sadly—"to greed. Yep. Greed and— weakness."

He was silent for almost a minute, just looking at me sadly.

"All fouled up," he said again. "That's me—all fouled up. Agreed?"

He waited. I finally said: "I don't know, Terry."

He laughed softly—sadly. "Oh, you know," he said, "you know."

He wiped an arm again at the sweat on his forehead. "He O.D.'d. My dear, old college roommate O.D.'d. You see in this business, you're supposed to stay clean. Always. *Clean*. Let the customers get hooked."

He laughed sorrowfully. "Now I'm not talking about the business of banking, or manufacturing, or farming—and *certainly* not about the business of broadcasting. No—certainly not about that. No—I'm talking about the business of drug trafficking."

He waited for a reaction from me. I said nothing.

"Are you surprised?"

I nodded. "Yes."

"So am I. Now that I say it . . . to you . . . out loud . . . so am I."

The engines droned on.

"How—?" I finally said.

He shook his head. "I don't know. Honest to God, I don't know."

We looked at each other for a very long time.

Finally Terry said: "No . . . I know. Of course, I know. Greed. Not money. It was greed. And there must've been something—must *be* something else . . . all fouled up inside me."

"Terry, I can remember—"

"—That I wasn't such a bad sort when you met me. Good. Keep that thought. Right to the end."

He stood suddenly. "I thought my dear, old college roommate was an idiot to get hooked on the stuff. I was right. And so am I—an idiot. Because I'm hooked, too. And I don't like myself very much at all."

He moved the muzzle of the pistol back and forth across my face. "Sorry about all this, Jim. I'm sorry."

To Nestor, he said, "Would you take us right over the middle of the stadium, Captain. The very middle."

Nestor said nothing.

"*Would* you, Captain—"

"Yes, sir."

"Good."

Terry motioned me up with his pistol. "I guess you'd better stand now, Jim." He glanced out the big door. "Give you a better view."

I stood.

"Are we right over the stadium now, Captain?"

"Yes—"

Terry nodded. He said to me: "The question I had to ask myself was—did you know too much, Jim. And *did they know about you.*"

He squinted at me. "But you don't, I'm pleased to say. And even more pleased to say—*they don't know ANYTHING about you. Anything.*"

He dropped what he'd been writing to the floor of the cabin. "Here's your insurance policy."

I started to stoop to pick it up.

"No—better stand, Jim."

"Okay, Terry."

"That's better, Jim."

"Okay."

His eyes were just about the saddest eyes I've ever seen. "Jim . . . we were . . . well, you and I know . . . anyone who was in Nam knows . . . and I just wanted to tell you . . ." He sighed. "Aw—you know. Don't you, Jim?"

"I think so, Terry."

"Good."

He straightened himself to his full height and stood almost at attention. "Jim—here's a last favor. Last one. I swear."

"Sure—"

"Say—'Hello, Corporal Jones'—to me."

I frowned. My throat was thick.

"Say it, Jim. Please. I want to hear it. For old time's sake. Please."

I looked at him. Grotesquely at attention. His pale face awash with sweat. His eyes bright.

"Say it, Jim. *Say it*—"

I tried to swallow. I couldn't. Finally, I said: "Hello . . . Corporal Jones."

Terry smiled strangely and saluted. "Just wanted someone I liked to say good-bye to."

We stood looking at each other.

"One more . . . Jim."

I shook my head.

"Please . . ."

I swallowed again.

"Please . . ."

"Hello . . . Corporal Jones."

The smile widened and saddened. He saluted again. Very slowly.

"Good-bye . . . Sergeant Sasser."

He jumped. And he was gone.

Chapter 41

Of course, it was raining. It had to be raining. I had met Terry Jones in the rain, and now I would say good-bye to Terry Jones in the rain. It was only fitting.

It was a cemetery in Maryland, just north of Baltimore.

There were a lot of people present; Terry had always had many friends.

And his family was large, too. So there were a lot of big, black umbrellas all around. It reminded me of the scene in *Our Town.*

"Ashes to ashes and dust to . . ."

That's all there were—ashes. That's all that was left of Terry Jones, the boy, who, a long time ago, had saved my life.

My tears mingled with the rain.

And the fool of a minister—he had no idea at all who Terry Jones had been, what he was like, how brave he once was, how sad he had become.

". . . Yes, to you, Lord, we give the soul of Terence Jones, Junior. . . ."

My God, nobody called Terry, Terence Jones, *Junior*."

Afterward, I spoke with Terry's father and his mother. His sisters were quiet and pale, their husbands looking so terribly sad. His brother kept gulping and couldn't talk.

Back at the Jones's house, where we all had coffee, I made a point of talking to Terry's wife, even though I didn't want to. I talked briefly, too, with Terry's daughter, Carolyn.

Butch and I—Terry's son—had never met, but we had talked on the phone so many times that it seemed that we had: we had a slow walk together around a couple of nearby blocks.

We talked about a lot of things, baseball and boating, and, of course, about Terry. I promised to call Butch often, and he asked if he could call me, and I said, oh, yes.

I didn't once tell him that he was the head of the family now, and to take good care of his mother.

Afterward, Maureen and Libby Nolan and Joe Maloney and I—along with Sam Bigelow and Toni Hastings and Randy Fulton—called cabs for the station.

Waiting for them out on the front porch, Sam said, "There's a really good bar on the way. Gorsuch House—the RBS crews always go out there whenever we're in town for a game."

"Is it a good place to drink?" Randy asked.

"The best," Sam said.

"We could miss a train—"

"Or two," Sam said.

Randy nodded grimly. "I'm game."

Two cabs pulled up.

"I think it's on Charles Street. Gorsuch House," Sam said. "The drivers will know—"

It started to rain hard again as we ran for the taxis.

It was pouring by the time we got there. But Sam was right. It was a perfect spot.

Predictably, Randy Fulton said: "*Some watering hole—*"

After the first round, I put my raincoat back on and started for the door.

"Where're you going?" Libby asked.

"I need to get something."

"It's coming down cats and dogs out there."

"I'll be right back—"

I'd spotted a drug store a block away as we were driving up. It wasn't that far, but I was soaked by the time I'd walked there, bought what I wanted, and headed back.

Libby looked perturbed at my appearance. "You look like a wet washcloth," she said.

I went directly to the men's room, did what I had to do, and reappeared.

At first there was dead silence as I came out. Then a few gasps. Then applause. Then laughter. And then a host of funny comments.

The mustache—was *GONE*.

We had oysters and crab cakes and plenty of beer. Sam and Randy drank bourbon.

And we told stories, some funny, some sad, and most about Terry, of course.

And we got pleasantly, sadly sloshed.

Even the completely-in-control-at-all-times Dr. Antonia Hastings let herself go a bit.

"How did you know it was Terry?" She asked me as she finished a schooner of draught.

"I didn't—"

"No, really. How did you?"

"I really didn't. Near the end, I suspected. But I wasn't sure until the *very* end. And then, only because Terry told me."

"But up until then?"

I surveyed the three of them: Sam Bigelow and R. Randolph Fulton and Dr. Antonia Hastings.

"Well, actually, you're all part of it," I said.

There was quick babble of hasty denials.

"Oh, I don't mean the drugs," I said quickly. "I mean all of the little ancillary schemes that were being hatched. Wittingly or unwittingly, you were all part of those."

"You know something, Jim?" Sam's face was very flushed

and smiling. "That's the biggest bit of balderdash, baloney, hogwash, folderol and nonsense I've ever heard."

"I beg your pardon—?"

"In other words, pure—"

"Don't say it, I hate the word—"

"—*persiflage.*"

"Oh—"

"You talked—but you didn't say anything."

I stood up, drink in hand, and bowed stiffly.

"Very well," I said, "I rise to your challenge."

I took Randy Fulton's hat from the coatrack, bent the hat so that it assumed the shape of a vintage Basil Rathbone chapeau and, thus armed, I faced them: if I were going to play the role of The Thin Man summing up, I needed all the props I could get.

I leaped lightly up onto a chair and snapped out my words à la William Powell.

"Why don't I start at the beginning," I said, and smiled to myself.

It was *exactly* the way William Powell would have started off. "*In the beginning,* it seemed mighty strange to me that Big Bill Braddock was wearing red suspenders that first night when I met him. Then Buzz Berman was missing, while Dr. Antonia Hastings liked to frequent the Café des Artistes—a place where you, Randy, took me to lunch—*then*—it all started to fall into place when Dick Ainsley *and* Rafael Miguel were both wearing red suspenders as well—"

I paused dramatically: "It became obvious at this point. Suspenders—red or otherwise—are called *braces* by the British. That could only mean one thing. Toledo is in the state of Ohio—but *Detroit*—is—in—the—state—of—*Michigan.*

"*That* could only mean one *other* thing—the Maltese Falcon must have been taken by—"

I stopped. They were all looking strangely at me, all faces filled with embarrassment: For me.

I wondered why I was doing this, turning an awful afternoon into a clownish charade.

"I'm sorry," I said.

No one spoke.

"I was . . . trying to joke a little."

Sam coughed.

"I'm sorry." I said again. "I guess I'm a little crazy."

"Hell, we've known that for a long time," Sam said. He tried to smile.

"It's just . . . well, Terry and . . . everything that's happened . . ."

"Try again," Joe Maloney said.

"It's okay, Jimmy—we understand. Just try again."

"Well . . . everyone was pretty shaken by the Northern Industries takeover of RBS. . . ." I stopped. "I'm being serious now," I said.

"We know," Joe said.

"Well . . . immediately after the takeover, there were large-scale firings. Hundreds of people were let go en masse.

"But not Dick Ainsley—

"*But*—Ainsley found out that he was a marked man, too, though, unlike the others, he wouldn't be fired immediately. Northern planned to keep Dick on the job for about three months—let him feel secure—get what they wanted from him—*then* let him go.

"When Dick found out about their plans for him, he went off the deep end. He'd had half a nervous breakdown already, of course, and this pushed him over the edge.

"So, for three months before he was actually sacked—he wrote those threatening letters. He *knew* that news of the threats would leak out. And he wanted to bring down Northern/RBS any way he could—and to hell with the consequences. One of the consequences, of course, was the possible exposure of Terry's drug operation. Even though—by then—Dick was a part of that operation—he didn't care. He was in a blind rage against Northern and RBS. He wanted to rip them apart and to hell with anything else. So he wrote his letters—and told *no one*—"

"We've known for days now that Ainsley wrote the letters," Sam said. "But what happened after that?"

"It's pretty simple," I said, "—*if* you know the answers."

Sam guffawed. "Well, tell me what we know—because I'm kind of missing something here."

"Okay. Going back earlier—there was the drug operation. We now know that Terry ran it—Charlie Bohanen was his lieutenant—and the RBS Sports Department was the unknowing facility that was used for cover."

I took a drink. "Everything was fine until Dick Ainsley and Kate Morgan—working on one of their drug stories for Buzz Berman—got an inkling that one of their leads might go right into RBS itself. They suspected Sports.

"When Terry heard about their suspicions from Buzz, he made sure that Kate and Dick were quickly absorbed into his little project. And it didn't take much proselytizing on Terry's part to convert them. Money's the lure. Kate does it—she tells herself—for the kids and Roy—and for Terry. You see—Kate Morgan was in love with Terry. Dick tells himself it's all for Mary Frances Fahey. But, in reality, it was all really—in Terry's word—*Greed*.

"And now we're back to the Northern Industries takeover. Buzz Berman is fired. But the man who takes his place—Billy Bob Johnson—without telling Ainsley or Kate Morgan—puts Rafael Miguel on the story. And Raffie works *alone*.

"Now once they became a part of Terry's drug operation, Kate and Dick reported next to nothing about drugs—and *exactly* nothing about any *RBS* drug connection—to anybody.

"And after Ainsley is fired, Kate keeps it that way. So far—so good. Things settle down for a while, and Terry thinks he's weathered the storm.

"But then the letters start. At first, they're just an annoyance. But they won't go away. They become more frequent, more threatening. Word starts to leak out—rumors begin to abound in the industry. Old M. Seabury Whitehead is fit to be tied and wants to bring in someone to do an investigation.

"Terry panics. It's the last thing he wants. A good investigative team, looking for the source of the threatening letters, *could* accidentally uncover his whole drug operation. That, quite obviously, would be disastrous for Terry, since he was, by now, in cahoots with a minor spur of the Medellin Cartel, which, as we all know, along with their rival, the Cali Group, controls the Colombian cocaine traffic in New York.

"But old M. Seabury is adamant—he wants an investigation. So Terry came up with an idea, which he finally sold to you, Sam: Hire me—Jim Sasser—as the investigator, for all the reasons we both know."

Sam smiled. "I hope your feelings aren't hurt—but it took a helluva lot of selling on Terry's part before I agreed."

"Not hurt a bit, Sam."

"Good—"

"Because you were right. I *wasn't* the man for the job. And *Terry* knew it. That's why he *wanted* me. Nevertheless, when you finally gave in to Terry—and the two of you convinced Big Bill Braddock—and then the *three* of you went in to Whitehead with the idea—it wasn't so difficult to convince *him*, was it?"

Sam shook his head. "United front and all. His three top men. Hell, by the time Terry was explaining it to old M. Seabury, it sort of made sense to me, too."

I had to laugh. "So everyone is convinced—reluctantly or otherwise—that I'm just the man for the job. I'll walk around, wearing my old RBS school tie, find out who the letter writer is—and keep it all within the hallowed halls of dear old RBS."

"That's about it," Sam said.

"And Terry even convinces himself that maybe I *can* pull it off. But, no matter what happens, he thinks, I'll keep the Old Man happy for a while. And most important, because of my inadequacies as an investigator, there's no way in hell that I'll inadvertently uncover the drug operation with the Colombian cartel.

"But right off the bat, things went wrong. You—" I pointed to Toni Hastings—"were so nervous about losing your job after the take-over, that you overreacted and pulled a second-rate Mata Hari act—not to mention, a gun—to get me to see Big Bill that first night."

Toni started to say something, but stopped herself.

I looked at her. Her blue eyes looked back at me, always apparently beckoning, but always saying . . . "ummm? . . . no . . . not really."

"You were—" I tried to find the words—"you were so . . . *peripatetic* . . . that you raised some questions around the campus. From being Big Bill Braddock's mistress to—"

"That word is so . . . inappropriate . . . so old-fashioned," she said. "Really—"

"Yes. Quite right. Old fashioned . . . yes. At any rate, your *peripatetic* journey from Big Bill Braddock—to Terry—to Billy Bob Johnson was a bit—unusual, wouldn't you say?"

She walked towards me, shaking her head.

"You *are* wicked, aren't you?" she said. She smiled.

She smiled again, just before she slapped my face.

She said: "You know, I don't have to say anything."

"Yes."

"But I will. I have never been anyone's . . . mistress, as you put it so delicately."

She sipped her drink. "However, I am aware that I'm—in addition to being extremely intelligent—a rather attractive woman—"

R. Randolph Fulton sighed.

"—But I was, as you have suggested—" she took another sip and swallowed slowly—"very timorous . . . and very . . . concerned about my position with RBS once Northern took over."

"So you were just covering all the bases."

"No," she said. "Not *covering*. Just *touching* all the bases."

Sam Bigelow coughed and grinned at me. "As you were saying, Jim . . ."

"Yes—*as I was saying:* Terry and Charlie Bohanen had only time enough to heave one brief sigh of relief at M. Seabury's agreeing to have me as the one person to investigate the letters—*if* I accepted—when lo and behold, Mary Frances Fahey was murdered.

"And, by the way, Mary Frances Fahey wasn't quite the angel that we all thought. Of course, neither was she the devil. As we know, Dick Ainsley was completely smitten by her. At first, she treated him pleasantly enough—then she took favors from him—and then she took money—a little, at first. Then a lot. But at precisely Ainsley's lowest moment—as he was suffering the torment of having been booted by Northern/RBS—Mary Frances told Dick to take a walk.

"Dick flipped. He begged her. He implored her. He offered money. Big money. And to prove that he could back up his money offer—he made a fatal blunder—he told her how he got it. At that moment, Terry was entering the Broadcast Center, just as Mary Frances—sickened by what Dick was admitting to—turned back into an angel and threatened to expose everything. Dick Ainsley was outraged—and Terry was cold-blooded. They killed her.

"The next day, Dick Ainsley was drunker than usual, while Terry couldn't meet me for lunch—a *wrenched back*—remember Randy?"

"Sure—he was out for a few days."

"Wrenched *nervous system* was probably more like it."

"And you suspected Terry that early on?" Sam said. "Amazing."

I laughed. "I didn't suspect *anybody*. But thanks for the compliment."

"But you *did* suspect me for quite a while," Sam said, a little sadly.

"Yeah, I did, Sam. I *certainly* did up in that blimp. And I was *justifiably* suspicious of you. After all, that was the day after I thought you'd killed the lights in TV-22 and tried to kill me, as well."

"Who did fire those shots?"

"Terry again. By then, he was sorry he'd ever campaigned to have me hired. I was getting close, however accidentally, and he wanted me to quit. But you're right, Sam—there was a while there when I didn't trust you any further than I could spit."

"Hey, can you help it if I look sinister to you?"

I pulled Randy's trilby to an even more rakish angle on my head. "What I seem to have in frighteningly large amounts, my dear Watson—is tremendous *hindsight*. With that—I can explain anything—once I've been told . . . *exactly* . . . *what* . . . *happened*. And Terry's letter . . ."

I thought of Terry: Good Terry, brave Terry, sweet Terry . . .

(What the hell went wrong . . . ?)

. . . My eyes came into focus again. I realized that I'd been staring.

I tried to smile. "*Anyway*—Terry's letter explained a lot of it—and, after that, it was easy to piece the rest together. Without it—well . . .

"Probably the biggest turning point was the revelation that Dick Ainsley was the one who was writing the threatening letters. *Before* that, it seemed prudent for Terry and the others to overlook his drinking. But once it came out that he was the creator of those letters—it made him a loose cannon on deck. So, when Kate found out it was Ainsley—they told her to tell me. They thought that if I exposed Ainsley, the letters would, of course, stop—and, more important, so would the investigation.

"And he might have made it through," I said, "if only Billy Bob Johnson hadn't scampered into Whitehead's office with the news that just *perhaps* the Drug Mob had a tentacle right into RBS."

"Was Terry in Whitehead's office at the time?"

"He was. He heard it all. Now he trusted Kate Morgan—and he had good reason—she was madly in love with him—so he knew that she hadn't supplied any new information. Kate had been finding *nothing* for Billy Bob.

"But the minute Billy Bob ran into Whitehead's office, Terry knew that there was another reporter—in addition to Kate—who was working on the story. They didn't know that Rafael Miguel had been secretly assigned by Billy Bob—so they immediately suspected *Dick Ainsley*."

"But he was already out of RBS," Maureen said. "He'd been fired."

"Sure," I said, "but the Medellin Cartel plays by some pretty dirty rules. Naturally, they assume that everyone else does, too. When Terry reported all that, it was *immediately* suspected that Dick Ainsley's firing was a ruse, a hoax—and that he was still working for RBS News and secretly selling out the drug operation.

"They let him know what they were thinking and asked for an explanation. By now, Dick was a twisted mass of loose nerve ends, and he shorted a central-nervous-system circuit. When the police called him in for questioning, he ran to them and confessed—solely—to the murder of Mary Frances Fahey, in hopes that that would put him in a more favorable light with Terry.

"It didn't help him at all, of course. By now, the drug boys were afraid that he was so unhinged and talking so much—he'd continue to talk. They decided to shut him up."

"Who killed him?" Maureen asked abruptly. "Dick Ainsley, I mean—who killed him?"

"Kate."

"Not Charlie Bohanen?"

"No. Kate Morgan. That's something that I should have suspected long before I got Terry's letter. Back when I was still with RBS, Kate did her first series on science. It was even her major in college—chemistry. Kate was taking small gifts of food to Ainsley while he was in jail. Foods laced with arsenic. And, on that last day, Veronal. By the time Dick caught on, it was too late. The minute I heard that Dick Ainsley was killed with a poison, I should have suspected Kate. But, as I said before, I never did claim that I was Sherlock Holmes."

"And a good thing, too," Libby said.

"I thank you. No—Kate Morgan did it. She and Dick Ainsley had worked together for a lot of years. She was afraid of what the drug mob would do to him."

Randy Fulton guffawed. "What could they do worse than what Kate did? She killed him."

"They could do a lot worse."

"Oh—"

"Even before Ainsley was dead, Terry and his troops had rifled Billy Bob's files, RBS personnel files—everything. When they turned up no record of any other reporter on the Special Drug Unit besides Kate—they figured that, with both Billy Bob and Dick Ainsley out of the way, they'd squelched their problem."

"Jimmy—" It was Joe Maloney looking at me with a grin on his face—"may I ask you a question?"

"Sure—"

"I hope I don't hurt your feelings."

"You won't."

"Well—speaking only for myself—but with the thought that—even though I have one arm in a sling and a crutch under the other—I might be expressing the feelings of at least a majority of those present—would you shut up for about five minutes, so the rest of us can enjoy a few more crab cakes and beer?"

I grinned, and—when the laughter, and then the applause, broke out from the others—I laughed along with them.

About ten minutes of eating and drinking later—after three great Sean Dillon stories in a row from Joe—the last, and best, ending with: "Well, Sweeney says, 'I think I'll risk *one* eye' "—a *thoughtful* R. Randolph Fulton had a *thought*.

"I was just thinking," Randy said, "you've been talking about the Cali and a Medellin Cartel—?"

"Right—"

"—and how organized they are . . . well . . . I mean— aren't we all just possibly in a little trouble?"

"I don't think so," I said.

"Don't *think* so isn't quite good enough," Randy said, trying his best to sound flippant.

"No—Terry's exact words were—they don't know *anything* about you. So they don't know *us,* and we don't know *them.* Besides, they've got more than enough fights to fight: whole governments, drug control agencies, *each other* even."

"But"—Maureen's brow was furrowed—"What about Beau—and Kate *in* prison or out—and—all the others, for that matter?"

"Terry was the lone liaison between his operation and the Colombians. They operate that way for obvious reasons—the fewer people who deal directly with them, the fewer they have to worry about."

"And there's another thing I don't understand," Maureen said.

"What?" I asked.

"People."

"What about them?"

"Why were so many people out to get you, Jimmy?"

Sam Bigelow stood up. "*I* wasn't. *Remember?*"

301

"Yes," I said, "you weren't, Sam. In fact, *nobody* here was. You—" I looked at Dr. Antonia Hastings—"I still haven't figured you out. But you had nothing to do with Terry Jones's operation. I know that now.

"As for Susan Mazur . . . I finally understood why she came on to me so strongly. At first, I thought she did because I was Terry's friend and could possibly help her keep her job. Then she started to brag about all her money—so the protection angle didn't make sense. Now I know: Terry had assigned her to keep an eye on me when he couldn't or Beau couldn't. Her big windfall was drug money, of course—and she talked too much for her own good.

"Then there was Charlie Bohanen—I mentioned Beau—and a few others. But that was all."

I turned. "I'm sorry about that right to the jaw, Randy. I should've known that you had nothing to do with any of it. You couldn't harm a flea if you tried."

"Well, now, Jim," R. Randolph Fulton tried to assume a more formidable stance, "I can be rather daunting at times, you know."

"Oh, yes, Randy. I know."

"Yes—*very* daunting, indeed."

"*Indeed.*"

I turned to all of them. "What I'm trying to say is this . . . I apologize. To all of you. At one point, I mistrusted just about everyone here. As it turned out, it was only my buddy Terry and his gang—trying to get to me so they could put the lid back on their operation."

"Yeah—" Joe Maloney made a face—"It was only your *buddy.*"

"Yeah," Sam Bigelow scowled.

Dr. Antonia Hastings did something very uncharacteristic. She was standing behind me, and she put both hands on my shoulders and gave me a sympathetic squeeze.

"The way Terry . . . well . . . it must hurt a lot," she said.

"Oh, it hurts all right. But in a way different from what you think."

"What do you mean?"

"It hurts that Terry's gone. It hurts that what happened to Terry happened. It hurts that Terry got involved in the whole *damn thing*. That hurts a lot."

"But he was hunting you down."

"Yes, but—"

"He tired to kill you—"

"Not in the end. And that's what counts."

"Only the end counts?"

"It has to. *Now*. Terry's gone. So I'll remember just the end."

"I sure as hell don't understand you," Sam Bigelow said.

I looked at Sam. "Sure you do, Sam. In all that time—when we were closing in on his operation—when he knew that I was getting nearer to the truth—he never called on the mob for help. He never turned me in."

"Yeah, but, Jim, he was *after* you. I mean—"

"Sure, he was. He was desperate—he was on drugs himself—"

"He tried to kill you."

"Maybe—"

"Don't tell me he took you up in that blimp for the fun of it. It was to kill you."

"Sure, it was. Sure. But in the end . . . he couldn't. So in the end . . . Terry saved my life . . . again."

"But—"

"—In the end . . . he couldn't do it. And that was Terry's last gift to me."

Chapter 42

I called all four of my kids in chronological order.

"How about a couple of weeks in Paris—L'Hotel Royale?" was the question.

After a pleasant and amiable conference call, it was agreed that we would spend a week in Paris, a week in London, and return on the Concorde, just to see what it was like.

With a smile on my face, I called my travel agent.

Next, it was a call to Libby Nolan.

"Good mornin', me darlin' Libby Nolan. And how is Columbia's favorite Professor Emeritus of History?"

"James—?"

"*C'est moi.*"

She sighed. "You shouldn't be drinking at ten in the morning."

"I haven't been drinking."

Silence.

"I haven't."

"Then why all the shouting and the revelrous syntax?"

"I'm in a revelrous mood."

"I gathered that."

"Because I'm all set to start hard work, steady work, disciplined work again on the book. Are you game?"

"My place or yours?" Libby said. "In half an hour."

"Not quite so fast."

"All right—an hour then."

"How about three weeks?"

Silence again.

"Libby—?"

A long, tortured sigh, "Yes—?"

"I want to take three full weeks off. I'll come back fresh and rarin' to go."

A grudging—"Where are you planning to go to freshen up?"

"Paris and London."

A sarcastic—"Oh, *sure*—"

"With the kids. The whole of the Sasser Tribe."

"All four?"

"All four."

"How'd you manage to get everybody together at once?"

"Luck. It just worked out for once."

"Just what you need. It'll do you a world of good. All of you. When will you be leaving?"

"Friday."

"Wonderful."

"Want to join us?"

"No, thanks."

"For a few days—"

"You go and have a great time. I might spend a week or two in Martha's Vineyard. We'll *both* come back rarin' to go."

We talked a bit about the book, and I hung up with Libby's blessings and best wishes for a good vacation.

The next couple of hours were happily spent at my travel agent's office planning what was going to be a perfect time.

After that, I called Maloney, O'Neil and Sasser to see if Joe or Maureen, or both, would have lunch with me.

"I can't and Maureen is out," Joe said. "Sorry."

"I'm lonely," I said.

"How lonely?"

"What do you mean?"

"Your friend Mona called. And that R. Randolph What's-His-Name called. Maybe there's a lunch there."

"It's never lunch with Mona. She's probably on top of a telephone pole somewhere. I'll try Randy Fulton."

"And try *me* tomorrow, I'm buying—"

"It's a deal."

Randy was very excited. He'd actually been poised to call me when I'd dialed him. He wanted to take me to lunch at the Des

Artistes. He wanted me to meet someone. The *Someone* was what had him excited.

"A woman?" I ventured.

"You guessed right."

"Remarkable."

"It *all* is—"

"I'd love to have lunch with you," I said.

"*GREAT*." I'd never heard Randy so ebullient. "I've already made a reservation. Twenty minutes?"

"Fine."

Randy and I walked into Des Artistes at almost exactly the same time.

"Oh, boy, oh, boy, oh, *boy*—" were his first words.

"This must be some woman."

"Oh, she is. Oh, my God, she *is*—"

We were shown to our table.

"She'll be right along," Randy said. "She's always punctual."

"Another commendable trait."

"Everything *about* her is commendable—Is extraordinary—Is fantastic. Oh, my God what a woman. And wait'll you hear about my plans—"

"Oh, I've guessed those, too."

"You have?" Randy looked pleased.

"Sure."

"Amazing," Randy said. "It must show."

"Sure—her name is Ingrid, or Erika, or Kristin, or Astrid—she has blonde hair, blue eyes, has the body of a young Nordic Goddess—and *you*—you're looking for a property that will be worthy of her obviously *enormous* talents and—"

Randy was shaking his head. "Hey, time—*time*—" He made an official's time-out signal with his hands. "You've got it all wrong, Jim. Really. All wrong—*completely* wrong. I don't know how you got an idea like that. No, I—"

"—Mr. Fulton? Your guest has arrived."

"Oh—" Randy literally sprang up from the table. "—excuse me, Jim."

In a second, he was over at the entrance, enveloping his guest with puppy-like affection.

His guest was a complete surprise.

She was lovely. But in a way different from what I'd expected. Randy's guest wore almost no makeup; her chestnut hair was pulled back from her face in a simple style; her clothes were tasteful, and her manner was most pleasant and even somewhat shy.

She was nothing at all like a Nordic Goddess, but she was the loveliest of young women, one who ingratiates herself instantly, without effort, without even speaking. In short, I liked her immediately.

"Jim—this is the angel I was talking about." Terry's smile seemed as broad as the room.

"How do you do," I said, and, unconsciously, I bowed.

She smiled. "How do you do—" Her voice was low and utterly charming.

"Jim—" Randy almost sang it out—"this all happened in just about forty-eight hours. This is my *fiancée*." He chortled boyishly. "This is—*Mary*."

Lunch with Mary—and with the new, and much improved Randy—was delightful.

Randy eventually calmed down sufficiently to speak in almost a normal manner, and Mary, in her quiet way, was a perfect luncheon companion. They touched each other a lot as we talked, and when Mary spoke or Randy spoke, each silently consulted the other with adoring eyes.

They were, obviously, very much in love.

As they were leaving, I said, "Randy, this has been, by far, the best lunch I've ever had with you."

"Oh, the same here, Jim. By *far*—I mean . . ."

I laughed. "It's okay. Usually, we tell silly jokes and talk foolishness. Today—well, Mary was here. So it was the best lunch we've ever had."

Randy beamed. "The best. Because Mary was here."

Randy and I shook hands, and Mary allowed me to kiss her on the cheek.

They left holding hands, each seeing nothing but the other.

Only then did I spot Dr. Antonia Hastings. With the exception of a couple at the opposite end, she was the only one at the bar. I went over.

"Mind if I join you?"

"Oh . . . hello . . ."

The first time I'd seen her even remotely out of control had been at Terry's post-funeral wake. She was that way again—not drunk, but not in icy control either.

"Hello—" I sat next to her.

She looked at me, a slight smile on her face, those eyes, bluer than ever.

"What're you drinking?" I asked.

"Gin and tonic."

"Two, please, Romeo," I said to the bartender.

"Romeo—?"

"That's his name."

Romeo nodded and smiled. "Romeo DeMarco," he said.

"Oh . . . hello, Romeo," she smiled at him. "Nice to meet you."

He nodded again.

We didn't speak until Romeo brought our drinks.

"Cheers."

"Cheers—"

"Been here long?"

"Since about noon."

"Any lunch?"

She shook her head.

"That's not the best—"

"I know," she said. "And no lectures—please."

"Sorry."

"It's . . . okay."

She looked at me as she raised the glass to her lips, and she kept her eyes on mine as she drank.

"No one seems to like me," she said. "I've assessed my situation and discovered—to my surprise—that no one likes me."

"Well—that's a bit exaggerated, I'd say."

"Oh, possibly one or two people do. Perhaps Romeo, does—"

"Excuse me—?" Romeo had been talking with the couple at the opposite end. He turned now and smiled tentatively at her.

"Sorry," she said. "I was just saying how nice it is to know you."

"Same here—" He paused expectantly for a moment or two before turning back to the couple.

She smiled at me. The blueness deepened. She touched my hand.

"It's all my fault," she said. "I should have warned you. I should have warned you in the very beginning—"

"Warned me of what?"

She smiled. "I'm in love."

"You are?"

"Very. Couldn't you guess?"

"No . . ."

"Very much in love. Intensely."

She looked at me, her eyes painfully blue, that strange smile on her face.

"I've told you all along. I've never slept around. Haven't I told you that?"

I nodded.

"I've only loved one person—ever."

"Yes—?"

"Myself," she said.

I looked at her for a very long time, letting it all sink in, and then I started to laugh. She laughed with me, and the two of us laughed so fully and completely that Romeo DeMarco and the couple at the other end joined us, just because the laughter was so hearty.

As it was all dying down, she paid the check. To Romeo, she said: "Thank you very much, Romeo." And to me, she said: "You really shouldn't go around calling women mistresses, you know."

"I know," I said.

"Bad form. *Very* bad form."

"I know."

"Well—good afternoon."

"Good afternoon."

She started to leave, stopped, and turned back. "Oh—and have a *wonderful*—rest of your life."

She blew me a kiss as she continued out.

"Some woman," Romeo said.

"Oh, yes—*some* woman." I let the laughter roll out again. "Once I work it up a little, I can dine out for months on this story."

Romeo smiled. "Another drink?"

"Please. Just a club soda this time."

Pete Johnson came in right after that, and we started to talk about golf, something we both do better than play it.

"Phone for you, Jim—" Romeo handed the receiver to me over the bar.

"Thanks, Romeo."

It was Mona. "Your friend Joe told me where you were," she said.

"Mona—sorry about the other day. How are you?"

"It doesn't matter to you, so why do you ask?"

"It *does* matter, Mona—"

"I could have died."

"Don't *say* that, Mona—" (My God, how many times had we gone through this same dialogue.)

Then she threw in a curve: "But *fortunately,* I realized that I can't really depend on you. I've leaned on you much too much."

I was completely baffled. If this were some new ploy on Mona's part, it was working.

"So I called—*Roland.* He's been waiting in the wings for so long. *He* came right over. He's here now. We're alone."

"You are—?"

"Oh, my sweet, sweet Jimmy, it's all so painful for Mona to say. But . . . well . . . Roland and I—oh, I can't say it to you, Jimmy. It would hurt you too, too much."

"Say it, Mona, I can take it. *Say it—please.*"

"Oh, Jimmy—"

I choked up my voice for her. "You were always so thoughtful, Mona."

"And you will always have first place . . . well, second—an *important* and *significant* second place—in my heart, Jimmy."

"Good-bye, Mona—"

"Good-bye, Jimmy—"

I hung up the phone, handed it back to Romeo DeMarco, and said, "Drinks for everybody, Romeo—you're looking at the luckiest man in the world and a candidate for entry into the *Guinness Book of World Records*: I've just been jilted by two of the most maddeningly attractive women in the world, in the brief time span of four minutes and thirty-seven seconds. And now I'm a *free man*."

"Congratulations?" Romeo asked questioningly.

"Yes."

"Then—congratulations."

"I thank you."

The bar telephone rang again.

Romeo answered. "Another one for you, Jim."

It was Joe. "I think I'd better warn you, Jimmy—I did something dumb. I told that Mona where you are."

"Don't apologize, Joe. Believe it or not, Mona just gave me the brush."

"Hey, great. And you sound pretty great yourself."

"I am. All the pressure is off. It's playtime."

"You deserve it," Joe said.

"Thanks."

"Give yourself some impetuous reward for hard work well done."

"Hey, Joe, I'm beginning to like you more and more."

"Good."

"In fact—here's an impetuous reward—is Ms. Maureen O'Neil in?"

"Due here in about fifteen minutes."

"Ask her if she'd like to have dinner with me."

"Sure . . .(?)"

"You said *sure* with a question mark."

"Did I? Well—anyway—that's impetuous all right."

"That's what freedom and rewards are for, Joe—impetuosity. Ask her."

"Sure, Jimmy—"

"I'll call back later—I'm in the midst of buying another round."

We had a wonderful two hours or more at dinner.

I poured the last of the wine into Maureen's glass.

She nodded a thanks. "Well . . . it's all over." She sighed. "It's over."

"Yep. It's a sort of let down. But it's over."

"What're you going to do now?"

"Vacation. With my kids. I can't wait."

"How many do you have?"

"Four."

She smiled. "D'you know—I've never met them."

"Not even one?"

"Nope."

"Well, we'll have to fix that. First thing. Right after we get back."

She smiled again. "Then it's back to writing for you?"

"Right."

We looked at each other for a while.

"And I've been thinking . . ." I rubbed at my chin. "I might just try to grow a beard while I'm on vacation."

She examined my face. "With a mustache?"

"Yeah, I suppose so."

"Well . . . it might not look *quite* so silly . . . if there's a beard around it."

"Thanks."

"You're welcome."

I kissed her.

And I meant it.